Rewriting Marguerite

REWRITING
Marguerite

JacLynn Herron

OHANA
PUBLICATIONS

Copyright © 2021 by JacLynn Herron
All rights reserved.
Printed in the United States of America.
ISBN: 978-0-578-94873-7

Book design by Judy Gilats
Cover images:
Ferns © Judy Gilats
Palm tree © pngtree

Logo design by David Welty

Ohana Publications, Saint Paul, Minnesota

for Thomas Jess Herron

1

*C*ontemplating my future as an author, I hovered over the Keurig and waited for a cup of house blend to trickle into my favorite coffee mug. For the last eleven months, writing had become tortuous, a foreign and frightening experience for a semisuccessful author of Minnesota-based mysteries. Since my husband Harry's death, my inner critic had flourished. It relentlessly chided, "Who would want to read this drivel? Stay in bed! You know you want to . . ." The powerful cerebral voice ruled, and eventually I caved in like an undercooked loaf of bread. First, I stopped my writing exercises. Then I avoided the simple act of powering up my MacBook Pro.

Now, out of sync and detached from my writer's soul, I feared that my creative spark, the essence that I joyfully had kindled and stoked in my previous life, was about to be snuffed out—not ceremoniously—but quietly. Left behind would be a dusty mound of ash, susceptible to the slightest breeze. Then one puff would finish the job, and just like Harry and the doomed characters in my murder mysteries, I would disappear, right here in New Brighton, Minnesota.

Granted, the sentences had not disappeared. My brain was still able to robotically string together subjects and verbs. But faded imagery and flat characters emerged. And the plot, the essential seed for any mystery, was so deeply mired in gray matter that it had failed to germinate.

In addition, on this morning, I was confronting the latest of a lifelong string of defining moments, turning eighty, alone. Today was my first birthday in decades without Harry. No mugs of hot coffee and warm caramel rolls arrived by tray to the bedroom. No jovial company broke the silence. No handwritten card with a silly haiku hid under a cloth napkin. The absences stung.

I had anticipated a tough morning. In preparation the night before, I had pulled out a pristine notebook and, with a favorite pen, neatly printed "MP" on the cover. Then I positioned both on the bedside table for the first morning of my new decade, an appropriate day, I thought, to reinstate the writing of morning pages. The writing exercise was a brain cleanse, a mental housekeeping that had served me well over the years.

The process, gleaned from Julia Cameron's book *The Artist's Way*, was simple and required nothing more than a blank notebook, a pen, and my willingness to fill three pages with whatever spilled out of my head immediately upon waking. The goal was to record what the brain was thinking as fast as the pen would allow with no pausing and no concern for punctuation, grammar, sentence structure, or content. During the process, subconscious thoughts were given a voice and a new residence on the page. Once written down, their departure uncluttered the right hemisphere of the brain, home to a creative source which now had room to thrive. When my right brain was enjoying its freedom, mystery novels flourished. At least, that was how things used to work before grief, depression, and my inner critic ganged up on my creative spirit.

My early morning writing had been sidelined after

Harry's death, just like other aspects of life that had been upended by his sudden departure. Some days, the realities of living without Harry rooted me to the bed; before I was able to place both feet on the hardwood floor, I needed to muster every ounce of energy and motivation. On other mornings, I awoke feeling empty, untethered, and fearful of floating away without his support. Neither of those extremes nourished my creative soul. I was yearning for some middle ground.

Also, I was learning that I must proceed cautiously because widow territory was rugged terrain, dotted with landmines of grief that exploded without warning. Sensory images reduced me to tears; memories, even happy ones, sapped strength and provoked mental retreats. My despondency, I acknowledged, needed processing, a valid reason for restarting the daily ritual of draining my brain into morning pages. My attempt was fitful:

APRIL 30, 2015—
I'm a writer, so write. Three pages, no stopping, MJ, or whoever you are. Who are you, anyway? I was christened Marguerite Jonella but have answered to MJ for as long as I can remember. Then I married Harry Burdick and became MJB. "Just like the coffee," according to Harry. Coffee. True Minnesotan that I am, I crave coffee. No frills. No milk, sugar, horrid artificial flavorings, toppings. Just strong, black, first thing in the morning. My reward for getting up. Then Harry left me. Now, not even coffee can lure me out of bed. But I should be congratulating myself. I've survived tricky adversaries. Winter! Bone-chilling, below-zero wind chills! Black ice! Hazardous sidewalks tried to take me out more than once. But I discovered the best defense—stay put, rarely leave the house. That's been my life since December. Wouldn't you think I could have completed the rough draft by now? Snowpack

*has finally dissolved into salty slop, and spring is showing
early signs. Yesterday, a pair of mallards waddled through the
yard seeking out a nesting place. Poor Mama—all that effort
just to have your eggs, or worse, your babies, devoured by
the predators that arrive in the dark. The first anniversary is
approaching—less than three weeks now. The first year is the
worst—isn't that what the other widows say? I don't believe
them, unless something miraculous is about to happen in the
next seventeen days. I was numb for the first eleven months, so
maybe they don't count. It doesn't help that Georgia is growing impatient. She wants my final chapters, if not on her desk,
at least in my computer. How can I tell her that my creativity
has dried up just like the umbrella tree in the living room?
All I know is that I'm tired, bone-tired, and the barnacles of
life weigh heavy on my chest. Happy 80th birthday, MJ!!!!!
Oh dear, I still have a page to go. But this notebook is college
ruled not wide ruled, so, can I be done?*

I abruptly tossed aside the notebook. It landed on the
foot of what had been Harry's side of the bed. Even though
I had reasoned that my birthday would be a good day to
restart a once-loved writing ritual, my attempt from a
semireclined position had been halfhearted at best. I slid
my legs over the side of the bed, paused a moment to let
blood reach my head, then stood up slowly and pulled the
bedcovers into place. Without Harry, the fitful sleeper who
always created a tangle of sheets and blankets, making
the bed was now a simple, five-second task. Just one more
reminder that he was gone.

No jostling for the first shower either. I had the bathroom to myself, and I stood under the showerhead until
the water ran cold. Carefully, I stepped out. Avoiding the
mirror, I grabbed a towel and wrapped it around my bony
frame. Then, like a pesky mosquito, the question that

had plagued me every morning for almost a year began to incessantly buzz. If I had been unable to get out of bed today or had fallen on the way to the bathroom, who would know? I was alone, and growing old without Harry was my new reality. I lowered myself onto the covered toilet seat and, with head in hands, surrendered once again to mind-numbing grief.

Although tempted to return to bed, I forced myself to dress and, with stiff fingers, halfheartedly styled the damp, unruly strands of salt-and-pepper curls that were springing to life upon my head. I grabbed the notebook off the bed and headed to my office, a room off the kitchen that used to be my favorite writing space. Settling into the wingback near the window, I reopened the notebook and read the scrawls that constituted the morning's entry. Oddly, I had begun my morning pages with an introduction of myself. What followed was a mishmash of stilted, random thoughts, not unusual for morning pages. But I had stopped prematurely before tapping any inner channel. I picked up a pen and gave it another go:

Like wayward children with minds of their own, defining moments demand attention. Much like the Volvo's GPS, each one screams, "Recalculating . . . ," a disconcerting announcement for an aged writer with a bone-deep lonesomeness that only widows understand. Defining moment: May 16, 2014. Harry did not return from his bike ride and, in an instant, everything changed. Wasn't losing a life partner enough? Now grief and despair have pushed me onto a frigid path that leads toward—Oh God! The ordinary! Is it too late to backtrack, or has my creative spirit become permanently embedded in a berg of ice? Forgoing morning pages was probably my biggest mistake. If I had dedicated the first thirty minutes of each day to purging my brain onto paper, perhaps I would have recognized my unhealthy trajectory before immobilization set in. Did I fear the animus I might tap each morning if I spewed my stream of consciousness onto the page? By default, I gave sorrow and depression long-term residency in my head where they teamed up with my inner critic and silently attacked my passion for writing. For too long I have been numb to the icy formation. What now? Is reigniting my creative spirit even possible? If I'm not a writer, then who am I? Another question. Perhaps THE question. Always there are more questions than answers in these confounded pages. To still be able to ask them offers a small ray of hope. Latch on, MJ. Warm up the brain. On this your 80th birthday, recommit to writing— starting with morning pages. Let this be the birthday gift you give to yourself.

2

*H*oping that the rest of my birthday would be less emotional than the first two hours, I paused when the phone rang. Checking the caller ID on the landline, I contemplated letting the answering machine kick in. Instead, I dropped into my office chair and picked up the receiver on the fourth ring.

"Hi, Georgia," I said as jauntily as I could muster. "How're things in the book business?"

I pictured my editor Georgia dressed chicly and sitting on a leather chair in her Chicago office. More than likely she was fidgeting with the pearl drop that hung from a gold chain around her neck. Over the years, I had become accustomed to this mannerism, which indicated anything from extreme concentration to unspoken annoyance with unmet deadlines. It was the one gesture that detracted from the otherwise strong, controlled demeanor of this young professional.

"I hope I'm tearing you away from your manuscript," said Georgia, ignoring the rhetorical question from her oldest author.

"Right enough," I replied with no remorse for the lie.

"Glad to hear it. Although, I half expected you to be

taking the day off. Happy birthday! Any special plans for the day?"

Her question prompted a reminder. "Yes, I'll be going out later with friends."

"Great. I was beginning to worry. You've been ignoring my emails." Niceties over, Georgia finally got to the point of her call. "When will I see the manuscript?"

"Sorry I'm so tardy," I answered.

"Listen, don't worry about final edits. I can handle them here. But I need to get the pages, MJ."

"I know you do, but the truth is, I don't have them yet." After a long pause I added, "I guess the story's trapped between the plaques and tangles of my withering brain."

I waited for a response and imagined the pearl being dragged back and forth along the chain. Finally Georgia spoke. "MJ, you've had a rough year. Losing Harry—well, I can't imagine. Just give yourself a break and forgo perfection. Finish. Even if it's rough, send it off. Let your editor do her job. That's what I'm here for."

This time it was my turn to pause before responding. "I'm nowhere near done. I've lost the suspense. It's all so cliché." After another long pause, I added, "I think the muse died alongside Harry."

I had verbalized my fear and had shared it with the one person who least wanted to hear about it.

"MJ, you of all people should know better," responded Georgia, minimizing my message. "You are your own worst critic."

Georgia was not hearing me. I detected thinly disguised impatience and judgment. Feeling like a disobedient child, I fought the urge to swear and rage. Georgia deserved better. For eight years, we had partnered successfully. Her editing skills, expertise in the publishing market, and consistent cheerleading had been crucial. Because of her, I had been able to launch seven mysteries in as many years. Now, I was poorly explaining the reality. Number eight had been born weak and was withering to death.

"You've been dormant too long," said Georgia after an uncomfortable pause. "You deserve to move forward."

There it was again, the unspoken message, from a thirty-eight-year-old no less. I should find a suitable shelf to store my grief and transition back to life, productivity, enjoyment.

"You're right." My terse agreement chilled the conversation.

After another pause Georgia continued. "I miss the verbal banter and jousting that used to accompany our conversations. Are you feeling okay? Have you seen a physician lately?" she asked, crossing the line between professional and personal.

"I'm not ill, if that's what you're asking," I shot back. "Or demented. The 'tangles and plaques' thing was my lame attempt at humor. I'm just old, tired, uninspired." I could almost picture Georgia breaking into a smile at my momentary feistiness.

"You can't do anything about your age, so get yourself moving. Get out! Get inspired!" she said. "I care about you."

"I know," I replied, deciding to ignore the lecture and embrace the compassion.

"I'll check back in a couple of days. And MJ—"

"Yes, my young, sweet, hard-nosed editor," I interrupted.

"—answer your emails!"

I hung up the phone and stared at the receiver.

"Well, that was a subtle butt kick," I said sarcastically to an empty office. In reality, I had been expecting the call. Georgia was a tireless, compassionate taskmaster. During our years of collaboration, we had grown close. After she heard about Harry's death, she had flown to Minneapolis before his memorial service to lend a hand. During the next eleven months, she had continued her support as best she could from a distance. Personally, she had stayed in touch. Professionally, she had given me much-needed space and had relaxed deadlines. Today's phone call, however, clearly indicated that she had grown impatient and would no longer enable my lack of productivity.

I swiveled the desk chair so I could gaze out the window. Overcast skies blanketed the Twin Cities of Minneapolis and Saint Paul. A gloomy Thursday was ushering in my new decade. Turning back to the desk, I booted up the computer. Retrieving reading glasses from atop my head, I opened my email and scanned the unread messages, a task I had been avoiding for over a week. Georgia's emails and birthday greetings from friends were interspersed between ads, electronic copies of the *Star Tribune,* and pleas for donations from a variety of nonprofits and political organizations. Rapidly deleting, I reduced the inbox to seventeen messages that needed attention and response. I began with Georgia's emails by firing off a short, general apology for another missed deadline. I offered no concrete commitment regarding the timing of completion.

Next, I moved on to personal messages from friends. One subject line grabbed my attention: Dad. Concerned, I opened the email from Peggy and read that her father, Ray Ingvold, had died eight days earlier in Phoenix.

Dad was hoping to return to Minnesota this summer for a visit. We thought there would be time, but his COPD got the best of him, and then he got pneumonia. It all ended so quickly. I'm so sorry I didn't call in time for you to talk to him one last time . . .

Guilt washed over me. Why hadn't I stayed in touch? I scanned the rest of the message.

We are following his wishes. He wanted no formal service. My brothers and I will be bringing his ashes back to Minnesota for burial next to Mother sometime in July. I'll let you know . . .

"Damn!" Tears blurred the text, and I slammed the cover of the computer shut.

In one continuous motion, I hoisted myself out of the chair and grabbed a tote that housed portable writing supplies. To the pens, pencils, and digital recorder, I added keys, wallet, a hard copy of my manuscript, and my process notebook. Then, after detouring to grab a rain jacket, I quickly exited through the side door that led to the attached garage, climbed into the gray Volvo, and backed out without any inkling where I was going. At the end of the driveway, I hesitated a moment before turning south. Even though a dull headache indicated the need for another cup of caffeine, I drove past both a Caribou Coffee and a Starbucks on Snelling Avenue as I headed deeper into Saint Paul.

Bread & Chocolate! The destination popped into my thoughts as I approached Grand Avenue. Taking an abrupt turn, I drove east to Victoria Street and pulled into a parking space behind the brick building that housed the bakery and coffee shop. Over ten miles from my house, it was not my usual haunt. But I had always loved its enticing name, and today was my birthday, after all.

I scanned the menu and ordered a breakfast panini with egg, provolone, and grilled onions and peppers on sourdough, a far cry from my usual piece of buttered toast with raspberry jam. While the sandwich was being prepared, I located an isolated table next to a window on the east end of the bustling eatery and sat down with a steaming cup of freshly brewed goodness. Savoring the first swigs of coffee, I scanned the establishment and observed the buzzing clientele. A group of middle-aged women, probably killing time until the shops opened, laughed and gabbed as they enjoyed chocolate croissants and other delicacies. A growing group of what looked like postsecondary students, judging from their T-shirts, backpacks, and open laptops, filled a long table. Others, a cross section of humanity, either sat down for a quick bite or grabbed to-go cups and flew out the door. Since there was always an empty table or two, I felt no remorse as I settled in for an extended stay.

I was not the only loner taking up table space. A gray-haired gentleman at a nearby table focused on the morning's edition of the *St. Paul Pioneer Press* and expressed an occasional "Humph!" to the universe. Alone but not, I opened my process notebook, the depository for all things related to my crippled literary child, *Seldom What It Seems.*

In short order, as if she knew that I did not want to delve into any difficult work, the young woman behind the counter loudly announced, "Marguerite!" and lifted up a basket containing a sandwich. Startled by the use of my given name (she must have retrieved it from my credit card), I approached the counter. She handed me a black, plastic, paper-lined basket with a nicely toasted and halved panini. Once back at the table, I quickly discovered that it tasted even better than it smelled.

Breaking through the dispersing clouds, the sun rose above the buildings on the east side of Victoria Street and bathed half of my table. Edging my chair into the sunny spot, I welcomed the rays as they warmed my chest. "Stay in the moment," I muttered with eyes closed as I slowly breathed in to the count of four, then out to the count of six, then in, out.

Bread & Chocolate bustled with the morning rush and then cleared out again. The chatty women left first. Confirming my supposition, they crossed the street and entered Pottery Barn. Later, the gentleman with the newspaper limped away, followed by a dispersion of backpack-laden young people. I had hoped that reviewing the jottings in my process notebook would reconnect me with the characters in *Seldom What It Seems.* Instead, even after two hours of reintroduction, they remained uninteresting strangers.

I stared out the window and focused on the steady traffic. When cars were forced to stop for the red light at the nearby intersection, many of the drivers reached for cell phones and began scrolling. After the light turned green, too many chose to proceed with steering wheel in one hand and cell phone in the other. "There needs to be a law," I said to no one and then chided myself for sounding like an old person. No, I said again, this time in my head, there does need to be a law! Then, continuing my procrastination, I counted drivers with phones in their hands.

Thankfully, Harry's death had given me an excuse to back away from intrusive and addictive social media. I rationalized that people who really wanted to contact me would call, the old-fashioned way. That thought served as a reminder that I had silenced my cell phone the night before. Digging through my tote, I retrieved my iPhone and found three texts from Claire.

Thinking of tomorrow and wondering if I can pick you up for your birthday lunch. It wouldn't be a bother. What say you?

Good morning and Happy Birthday!!!!! What about that ride? Noon?

Called your house. No answer. Are you out and about?

Chagrined, I called Claire.

"Morning, Claire," I said as quietly as possible to avoid being overheard in the cafe. After acknowledging birthday greetings, I apologized. "Sorry about being so hard to get ahold of—yes, I've been running a few errands—think it's better if I just meet you at the restaurant—thanks though—see you soon."

I had no desire to explain to Claire why I was sitting in Bread & Chocolate an hour before a birthday luncheon that had been planned in my honor. Clouding the day was an empty house with no pecan-studded caramel rolls, no haikus, and no Harry, but she didn't need to know.

In the remaining minutes before heading over to the birthday luncheon, I contemplated an important survival tactic that had gotten me through the last eleven months. The practice of driving to gatherings independently had become a defensive strategy spawned from an unsolicited warning delivered by a well-meaning widow shortly after Harry's death.

"Never turn down an invitation for a social gathering, no matter how unexcited you are to go. Mark my words," she prattled on with an edge of self-pity, "if you don't accept, they'll stop asking you."

At the time, I lacked the gumption to suggest that a widow's more desirable option might be to stay home with her own misery. For me, attending social gatherings without Harry by my side was excruciating. Creating and maintaining an artificial facade required stage presence of which I was in short supply, and every encounter further depleted my energy and sense of humor. After accepting an invitation, I, like the criminals in my novels, calculated in advance the means for a hasty getaway. Driving separately and parking down the street to avoid getting penned in accommodated quick departures. I became quite adept at arriving a bit late, checking in with partygoers, and slipping away when chitchat became insufferable. Often, my absence went unnoticed. If not, it was usually chalked up to MJ being "quirky" again, a return to my former self that friends found comforting.

The most uncomfortable gathering since Harry's death had been the annual retiree picnic of likeminded horticulturists and solar energy enthusiasts who had worked with Harry and his business partners in a thriving greenhouse business. They had known Harry well, and as a result, had respected and loved him. Although it had been thoughtful of them to include me in the July gathering, I knew from their pitying looks that I had made a mistake by attending so soon after placing Harry's ashes in the ground. I circulated, chatted with each person, accepted their sympathies, and thanked many for coming to his memorial service. With mounting anxiety, I skirted the buffet table, lavishly laid out with catered picnic fare, and navigated my retreat. Thankfully, no one followed. Perhaps they were somewhat relieved to have Debbie Downer disappear. After my departure, they probably resumed comfortable discussions involving travel plans, grandchildren, hip replacements, and home improvements, without dark thoughts of who among them might check out before the group's next gathering.

After the picnic, not wanting to return to an empty house, I sought solace in my car. I drove aimlessly, a practice that had become a stress-relieving habit during that first summer without Harry. I ended up at Lake Harriet, one of the picturesque bodies of water nestled in a residential area south of downtown Minneapolis. A parking spot close to the bandshell miraculously opened up as I approached, so

I pulled in. The smooth sounds of a jazz saxophone wafted through the open window.

Sitting alone in the car on that muggy July evening, I smiled through tears as I recalled Harry's pronouncement the summer before. "I would have married you sooner had I known what a cheap date you were going to be." He had punctuated his statement with a smile as he clandestinely poured sauvignon blanc into disposable plastic cups. As he passed one to me, I offered him a slice of Havarti sandwiched between his favorite rice crackers. We had stretched out on a beach blanket next to the bandshell's permanent seating and relaxed as the Minneapolis Pops Orchestra entertained visitors with a free concert. Just like the retirees at the picnic, we had assumed that our golden years would be numerous.

Alone with my memories, I sat in the car and attempted to make friends with a strange dichotomy, smiling and crying at the same time. They could coexist, I decided, without one diminishing the other. That evening, I took a tentative step in a healthy direction and vowed never to allow grief to overshadow the memories. But then winter arrived, and I lost my resolve. Instead, I followed the example of Minnesota wildlife who hunkered down for the cold, dark months. They did it to conserve energy and to survive. Maybe I did, too. I suppressed memories, even good ones, if they brought tears. Never realizing that my spirit was slowly freezing over, I witnessed the passage of cold, frozen months from an easy chair in my office. Fictitious excuses, such as contagious coughs, icy roads, or previous commitments, flew off my tongue in response to incoming invitations. The only indication that my previous self was fighting for preservation involved a concerted effort to monitor alcohol consumption. Fearing that I might disappear into a rabbit hole of my own making, I eliminated wine from my grocery delivery. Thankfully, months of questionable decision-making had not smothered all seeds of self-awareness.

Now, the snow and ice had melted, and I was venturing out of my hole. I considered my trek to Bread & Chocolate a minor coup. Perhaps it was another birthday gift, a subtle course correction prompted by Harry's absence, Georgia's call, and the confirmation of the not totally unexpected passing of Ray Ingvold, an old and dear friend.

3

I contemplated my birthday luncheon as I drove from Bread & Chocolate to Saint Anthony Park, a Saint Paul neighborhood about fifteen minutes away. Guests around the table would be my closest friends, the women in my writing group, the Write Women, as Harry had dubbed them. These women were the ones who held me for days after a police officer confirmed my fears when Harry's bike ride lasted too long. He had been hit by a speeding Dodge Durango driven by a young college student who had been momentarily blinded by the rising sun.

The officer had tried to be kind. "Would you like to call someone? How about a family member? A minister, perhaps?"

"Claire" was all I could say. He helped me dial the number, and I paced until she arrived. Within minutes, reinforcements, the women who would be at my birthday luncheon, tiptoed in. They supported their numb and aching friend through it all, the identification of the body, the return to an empty house, the planning and execution of a memorial service, and many of the other details that accompany the finality of losing a life partner. Over the summer months, they stayed close, plugged into my needs, and empathized as best they could. But eventually, I closed myself off. I gave in to envy as I witnessed their ability to return home to living spouses and/or well-manicured lives. I pushed them away. Now they wanted to help me celebrate my first birthday without Harry.

Claire had approached me weeks earlier with hints about the upcoming milestone birthday and a possible celebration. Undeterred by my lack of enthusiasm, she assertively clarified, "My dear friend, it is going to happen!"

To which I relented, "But I want no fuss—and definitely no surprises!"

"Can your closest friends at least take you out to lunch?" Claire asked, referring to the Write Women. "We are thinking Muffuletta. Twelve-thirty."

"That would be perfect," I said, choosing my words carefully to sound less like an ingrate, "with one condition. No presents! I'm downsizing and want and need nothing. NOTHING!"

"I'll make your wishes known."

I located a parking spot on Como Avenue in front of one of my favorite buildings, a historic Carnegie library built in 1917. Exiting the Volvo, I paused and inhaled an earthy scent, the product of the sun's rays on the moist ground. What had started out as a dismal, dreary morning was morphing, with the help of sunshine and a light breeze, into a pleasant day. After tossing my rain jacket into the back seat, I locked the car and glanced at my watch before crossing the street toward the restaurant. With time to spare, I detoured into a nearby gift shop. Finding beautiful and fitting sympathy cards for Peggy and her brothers, I proceeded to the cashier and, as an afterthought, grabbed a colorful, silk scarf from a nearby display and added it to my purchases.

"Happy birthday, MJ!" I muttered under my breath.

"Would you like a gift box?" asked the saleswoman motioning to the scarf.

"No need. But if you could remove the tags, I'll wear it."

The vibrant pinks and purples added a springtime touch to the black turtleneck and pants that I had chosen hours earlier when the weather and my outlook had been dreary. Chagrined, I realized I had left the house with no accessories, not even a bangle around my wrist. It had been customary for the previous Marguerite to stack bracelets on her left wrist before adding a ring or two, perhaps three. But that Marguerite had faded over the past year.

"Beautiful! Especially with your silver and black hair," said the saleswoman with a nod of approval at my new neck apparel. She tilted the mirror on the counter so I could take a look. Instinctively, I finger combed my hair in a vain attempt to tame the natural curls. After thanking her, I walked the short distance to the restaurant, a cozy bistro with a farm-to-table menu that changed with the seasons.

"Happy birthday, MJ!" said Claire as she met me at the door. As expected, she was dressed in her usual style, one that she laughingly defined as "casual elegance." Today, that meant a denim pair of trousers and a burnt orange cashmere tunic. From the neck down, her trim body could have passed for forty, but the facial wrinkles and the precisely cut, white bob added a decade or two. "We're got a nice private table over there in the corner."

I followed her to a round, linen-covered table with a small vase of daffodils in the center. Ginny and Pat bounced out of their chairs and greeted me with enthusiastic hugs and birthday wishes. Millie remained seated and tapped the vacant chair on her right.

"Sit by me, sweetie. I'm the only one here that can

commiserate. Turning eighty is a bitch. Like sticker shock. Unbelievable at first, but you'll get used to it. We have to, right?"

Millie was the oldest in the group and probably the most flamboyant. Full of spit and vinegar, my grandmother's description for edgy self-assuredness, Millie, eighty-two, continued to be as vibrant as any fifty-year-old. I had never met Owen, Millie's ex, but stories implied that Owen's love for Millie's money trumped his love for Millie. Their divorce had been finalized shortly after I had been introduced to her by our mutual friend, Claire.

Since then, Millie had thrived in her newfound independence. She retrieved her maiden name, became a travel agent, and ventured around the globe for vast stretches of time. Prodded by her friends to record some of her travel antics, she wrote side-splitting vignettes. When she had recorded a decent number, she paid to have them formatted and designed into self-published books that she never marketed. She simply handed out copies to her friends, shelved one for herself, and started fresh. Millie was the picture of contentment. Never fearful that her stream of wealth and privilege would run dry, she relished her rock-solid belief in the goodness of the world.

I pulled out the chair and sat down. On my other side, Ginny returned to her seat and began scanning the menu for options free of her latest diet restriction, gluten. Last year's no-no was carbs, and the year before that, all foods that originated from a four-legged creature. After moaning about the unwanted pounds she had gained since the last time the group had been together, she decided on a salad that highlighted asparagus, cherry tomatoes, gorgonzola, and basil.

"Good. That's done!" she exclaimed as she closed her menu with a slap, raised her eyeglasses off the bridge of her nose, and planted them on top of a head of black curls with half-inch gray roots. "So, MJ. How're you doin'?"

Leave it to Ginny to verbalize the question that others tiptoed around. The buzz at the table stopped, and all eyes turned to me.

"I'm getting along," I answered and then deflected the conversation with a question of my own. "How about all of you? I want an update from each of you. Anyone writing?"

Sensing my discomfort, Claire quickly assisted the pivot. "For a writers' group, we are a sorry excuse."

"Speak for yourself," said Pat, the youngest in the group and Ginny's sister-in-law.

"Yes, but you have to write for work," said Ginny. "You have a boss that demands it. I'm my own boss, and a very bad one as you know."

Ginny, inspired by her three sons and nine grandchildren, had successfully published several children's books. However, during the five years that had elapsed since her last book launch, writing had taken a back seat to family priorities. First, her husband Gary's failing health had prompted the two of them to list their home and half-acre lot, downsize their possessions, and relocate to a senior apartment. After that was accomplished, Ginny kept herself busy by helping her sons with flexible day care. "Now I get in the car each morning and ask myself, 'Which grandchild am I babysitting today?' Seems like one of 'em is missing school or day care all the time. But they're so darn cuddly when they're sick." She reached for her smartphone, scrolled to find the most recent picture of her "gang," and passed it around for all to view.

Instead of offering a compliment, Millie, being childless and not quite able to imagine how time with sick tots could be enjoyable, offered an unsolicited opinion. "Your boys are damn lucky to have an always-available babysitter."

"I just hope I live long enough to see grandchildren," added Pat. "I'm about ready to suggest that Pam skip the find-the-husband step and go right to artificial insemination. She will be thirty-three this summer."

"Still plenty of time," said Ginny with a smile highlighted by a huge dimple in each cheek.

"Maybe for her, but I want to have grandkids while I can still get up off the floor," said Pat.

"I can't believe I'm hearing that from the most fit among us," said Claire. "I wasn't a grandma until I was sixty-eight, and you're what? Sixty-one?"

"Sixty-three," corrected Pat.

"Sweet thing, I have blouses that are older than you," said Millie.

I welcomed Millie's comment and the chortles it created. If there was another topic besides widowhood that I did not want to discuss today, it was grandparenthood, another loss, since my only child had died at age seven. Emma's death had occurred decades before my friendships began with these women, and since I had never shared with them the pain of lost might-have-beens, they were oblivious.

"Looks like you ladies are enjoying the afternoon. May I take your order?" The waiter, young enough to still enjoy a miraculous memory, took our orders without the aid of a pad or pen.

Shortly, wine appeared, and conversation centered on others. I felt my body relax into the chair as I listened to the updates of women who thrived in each other's company.

The writing group, now eleven years old, had been spawned from an idea hatched between Claire and me. The two of us had met at the Loft Literary Center in Minneapolis during a class that was designed to energize creative writing. We paired up as writing partners for the daylong experience, and after responding to writing prompts, exchanged our creations and howled at each other's irreverence. A kinship began, and at the end of the day we scheduled another meeting, this time in a coffee shop. Eventually, we organized a writing group. Claire invited her friend Millie, a writer of humorous travel sagas, and I reached out to Ginny, an acquaintance who had successfully authored books for children. Eventually, we included Ginny's sister-in-law, Pat, a technical writer and artist by profession, who successfully combined both skills to create enormously popular graphic novels for young adults. In addition to adding zeal to our group, she happily designed book covers for all of us. Harry's moniker stuck, and together we became the Write Women.

We met loosely the first year. Then, at Claire's urging, the group established a more structured routine and convened at her home at 9 a.m. on the first and third Saturdays of each month. Inspired to write a cookbook with recipes she had collected from bed and breakfasts throughout Minnesota, Claire hosted a home-cooked breakfast. All of us eagerly tasted and evaluated each menu item. Once the table was cleared, manuscripts appeared, and the remainder of the time was devoted to readings and feedback.

On many occasions over the years, the structure was dispensed with and celebratory camaraderie and/or empathetic support monopolized the morning. Those times involved the sharing of a whole gamut of life events: births and engagements of children and grandchildren (Ginny, Claire), the coming out of a gay son (Claire called it Adam's "homecoming," to which we all cheered!), health scares and surgeries (Millie, Pat, Claire, and Ginny), treatment for a family member's alcoholism (Ginny), an unexpected death of a spouse (me), and, of course, birthday parties for all of us.

Even though Claire's extended stay with her daughter in California, Millie's twelve-week winter escape to her condo in Maui, and my withdrawal from anything that resembled a commitment had undermined the group's regularity during the last few months, our bond remained. Being in the company of these women, the people who knew me as well as I knew them, relaxed my tension.

"MJ, do you have a book that needs a cover?" asked Pat. "I'd be happy to start working on a design."

"Wouldn't I love to say I do, but no," I replied, surprised at my own truthfulness but still unwilling to go into any specifics about my hemorrhaging manuscript. "How about you?"

"Just finishing up the cover for *Unequal*. The launch is likely to happen early summer. I'll give you the date as soon as it's nailed down."

"It's one of your best, in my opinion," said Claire, who was the only one who had read the manuscript in its final form.

"Just in time for summer break, when all those teenagers will have too much time on their hands," added Millie.

"That's the plan," said Pat.

The rest of us followed with congratulations. One thing about the group, if one succeeded in getting a story between published pages, all celebrated and, like midwives, shared credit for the birth.

"Seems like Pat's the only one with something to show for the long, cold winter," said Ginny.

"No she isn't. I have something to share," said Millie, unbuttoning an ivory-colored satin blouse to show off a tan line right above her bra. "Got this in Maui. Right on the lanai."

"Button up before they throw us out of here," said Ginny as the rest of us snickered.

"When you're over eighty, you can do anything you want," she responded as she readjusted the blouse over her well-endowed bosom. "Remember that, MJ!"

"To MJ, on this most auspicious occasion. Happy eightieth birthday!" said Claire, raising her glass of Pinot Noir.

A chorus followed. "To MJ!"

"Happy birthday, MJ!"

Millie leaned over and whispered, "Just fake it 'til you make it, luv." Noticing my moistening eyes, she gave my knee a pat. She had no way of knowing that her endearment, "luv," was the culprit that had generated a wave of nostalgia and tears. I could almost hear Harry's voice, "You can do it, Luv."

I'm trying, Harry, I replied in my thoughts.

I looked around the table. All eyes were damp, and each pair searched for mine. Our little band had supported each other through too many hardships. I needed these women today, something they had known all along.

"Enough already," said Millie. "Pass that wine bottle. Do we need another?"

Artfully arranged salads and sandwiches arrived. As we ate and talked, the familiarity of the faces, voices, and laughter warmed my disposition, and in response my game face softened into a genuine smile. Exhausted by the lengthy luncheon, not to mention the glass of wine and overstuffed stomach (thanks to the Cobb salad and carrot cake so soon after the breakfast panini), I collapsed into the worn leather seat of the Volvo at 4 p.m.

The spur-of-the-moment breakfast had been crucial to my day's survival. Grounded and less anxious after an introspective morning at Bread & Chocolate, I had withstood, even appreciated, the onslaught of good cheer and best wishes from the Write Women. Not once had I looked at my watch or felt the need to pull a hasty departure.

Yet, one thought disgusted me. Had it not been for Claire's text messages, my birthday luncheon might have slipped off my radar altogether. I had mentioned the get-together to Georgia to avoid a pity-filled reaction to the possibility that I might be spending my birthday alone. But as quickly as I had grabbed my car keys and writing materials and headed out the door, all thoughts of the luncheon had disappeared. Maybe dementia was creeping up on me. Thankfully, I had checked my text messages in time.

As I maneuvered through midafternoon traffic, my mind drifted to the next milestone, May 16, the first anniversary of Harry's death. The lesson to be learned from my birthday, I decided, was that denial didn't work. Better to face May 16 head on.

Screeching brakes snapped me to attention as rush hour caused an abrupt slowdown in all three northbound lanes of Interstate 35W. To avoid the backup, I exited the freeway one mile before my usual route and wove through quiet, residential streets to my home in New Brighton. Finally, I turned into the driveway, hit the electric garage door button, and pulled the Volvo into its parking space in the attached garage. As the heavy, squeaky door unceremoniously lowered to close out the world, I inserted the house key into the deadbolt on the door that led directly into the back hallway. The lock gave no resistance when I turned the key, and as I tried to push the door open, I realized that what had been set was not the deadbolt but the lock in the doorknob.

"That's odd," I muttered to myself. I could not recall the last time I had used the turn button on the doorknob to lock the door. Years, for sure. Before the deadbolt had been installed, the flimsy lock on the doorknob was the only thing keeping unwanted intruders from breaking into the house from the garage. I hated how easily it could be sprung, and Harry hated how often he locked himself out without a key. Finally, he installed a deadbolt above the knob, and we both got in the habit of ignoring the lock in the doorknob altogether.

I placed the key in the doorknob, turned it, and heard the click of the lock moving in the chamber. Strange. It was during times like this that I needed Harry to say, "Just a senior moment, MJ. You were flustered. In a hurry this morning. No big deal." I entered the house, placed my writing materials on the desk, and searched through the cupboards until I found a dusty bottle of Chianti.

After giving myself a substantial pour, I turned around to read the clock: four-thirty. It was too early for pajamas. What I really needed was exercise, but instead, I sat down with my manuscript, turned to page one, and began to read. Seven hours later I turned the last page and, disgusted, pushed the manuscript aside. The plot was dead, just like Harry. Exhausted, I crawled into bed.

4

*M*orning pages and coffee occupied the first half hour of the day following my eightieth birthday. This time I sat at my desk as I wrote, taking my pen off the page only to skip from word to word or line to line. Recording three pages of random thoughts required surprisingly little effort, an improvement from the day before. After processing gut reactions related to my birthday, I wrote about the state of my manuscript, which was as flat and uninspired, I decided, as its author. The one-dimensional characters had become so boring and inauthentic that even I had been unable to develop any sort of sustainable relationship with them. Mentally, I pictured loyal readers throwing down copies of *Seldom What It Seems* in disgust. The plot, so embarrassingly dull and predictable, was exactly what it seemed. I knew Georgia was waiting for a bombshell, but all I had was a fizzle. I ranted in my morning pages. It felt good to blow off steam, and I hoped that the decompression would clear out some of the cobwebs.

Ping went my cell phone. I opened the text message from Claire and found a snapshot taken by a congenial waiter of five jovial women with wine glasses raised in a birthday toast. I tapped the picture, expanded it, and focused on the smiling faces of my friends. Then I zeroed in on my own. An unforced smile had remolded wrinkles into laugh lines, softening a face that was turning another decade older.

"Not so bad," I said.

I uploaded the photo to my Shutterfly account and ordered a print that soon would be available for pickup at a nearby Target. The snapshot was my one and only choice for "Marguerite's Birthday Book."

I walked into the living room and opened the glass doors of a cabinet that contained two of my oldest and most cherished possessions. The Campbell Family Bible, heavy and leather-covered, contained not only the King James Version but also the record of births and deaths of my mother Celeste's family dating back to 1852. I reached for the book next to it, "Marguerite's Birthday Book," a thick, eight-inch-square scrapbook with pages highlighting specially chosen photos, one taken each year on my birthday, starting when I was five years old. Back in the office, I opened the wooden cover and read the inscription in my mother's beautiful, calligraphic handwriting:

Marguerite's Birthday Book
for Marguerite Jonella
May you have many happy celebrations!
Love,
Mama and Papa
April 30, 1940

Threaded through reinforced holes, a stained, white, grosgrain ribbon bound the scrapbook pages between heavy, smoothly sanded pieces of black walnut. Each page was dedicated to one year, with the date at the top and a photo below. Short, handwritten captions, a few by Mama and the rest by me, described the photo and the birthday it represented. For me, the earliest photos conjured only foggy, incomplete memories of childhood. Mama's simple captions did not offer much detail.

When I turned twelve, Mama relinquished to me the job of keeping the scrapbook up to date. Offended, I wondered if she had tired of the whole thing. "I think you should decide what is important, what you want to remember," she had explained. With that in mind, I begrudgingly took on the yearly task and surprised myself with the satisfaction that accompanied the challenge of picking one photo as my favorite and concisely captioning it.

In many ways, Mama's subtle encouragement provided dry kindling for my creative spark. From the time I was old enough to compose a sentence, my observations, imaginations, and contemplations found homes in an endless supply of blank books. Thanks to Mama, every now and then, a new journal, tied with a decorative ribbon, found its way into my book bag or under my pillow. More than once, an especially coveted pen was dropped surreptitiously into the crock that served as a pencil holder on my desk. When I was needing an adult-sized bed, instead of a twin, Mama bought a daybed, filled it with pillows, and positioned it in front of a west-facing window so I would have the perfect place to curl up in the sun and write. I filled journal after journal with sketches, vocabulary, poems, and all types of stories. Thanks to Mama, I grew into adolescence never questioning my creative source. Now, I yearned to tap that source again.

I flipped to the end of the birthday book, which was as fat as it was wide. Mama, ever the optimist, had included at least one hundred pages. She had prepared for the possibility that I would live a long life. I turned to the last entry, entitled "April 30, 2014—Age 79." The photo was taken by Harry of the two of us. The caption read, "Celebrating at Cafe Marc—our favorite place, complete with baked Alaska!" No other words had been needed. Oblivious to what lay less than three weeks ahead, we were laughing at Harry's awkward attempt to position his cell phone for the selfie.

The photo, as expected, reduced me to tears. Each defining moment of my life had a before and an after, and this photo captured the carefree life before widowhood. I had expected the after to remain undocumented, with no birthday snapshot to mark my first birthday as Widow Burdick. But thanks to Claire, waiting for me at Target was a photo that would commemorate the first year of after.

5

A few words from my morning pages gnawed at me as I toasted a bagel. *Think I need to make peace with Silverwood. It meant so much to Harry*... Without forethought the words had flowed out of my pen, and in their wake, a ripple of discomfort continued.

The prospect of returning to Silverwood Park, a unique destination less than five miles from my house, challenged my equilibrium. Making peace with a place so integral to Harry's spiritual balance was especially challenging. I toyed with the idea for the rest of the morning. I could ease into it, I rationalized. Have a bite of lunch in the cafe, leave when I needed to. When midday hunger struck, instead of heading to the kitchen, I chose the garage, then gritted my teeth as I climbed into the Volvo and backed out of the driveway.

I drove down Silver Lake Road to a familiar turnoff. Once inside Silverwood Park, I proceeded down a paved road through stands of oak trees and budding birches. Near a large brick building, the road widened into a huge parking lot. As I exited the car, soft clanging of metal against metal beckoned me toward two flagpoles. State and country flags flapped in the stiff, chilly wind that penetrated my lightweight fleece jacket. I picked up speed, crossed the circle driveway, and entered a multipurpose building that housed a small cafe, an art display area, administrative offices, and a very large gathering space that I had rented for Harry's memorial service. Once inside, I walked directly up to the cafe's counter and ordered a favorite combination, a hot caprese sandwich and a cup of Mississippi Mud coffee.

"The sandwich'll take a couple of minutes. I'll bring it out to you. Need room for cream?" asked a lanky, young man sporting a name badge with his first name printed in uppercase letters.

"No, thanks, Dan. And no hurry with the sandwich." I handed him a ten-dollar bill. "You must be new—or not. I guess I haven't been here lately."

"I work here on and off," he said as he turned to pump my coffee from a nearby air pot. "During school breaks mostly. Once finals are over, I'll be full time."

"Good luck with those," I said, not wanting to probe any further. "I don't suppose you would know when Elle is working."

"She's on today," he said. "Just went on break because of the lull."

Dan gestured toward the empty tables in the seating area. The morning crowd had dispersed. Only two tables were occupied, one by a woman with a preschooler who had settled in near the children's book corner, and the other by a young man dressed in ragged jeans and sweatshirt hunched over a laptop.

With coffee in hand, I chose a small table by one of the huge windows that overlooked the lake. Pulling out the morning's edition of the *Star Tribune*, I contemplated the last time, other than this morning, I had bothered to do anything but transfer the daily paper from its position at the end of the driveway directly into the recycling bin. I had considered canceling my subscription but could not bring myself to follow through.

I could almost hear Harry's voice. "MJ, we need to support the print business."

"But we get it online," I would counter.

"So, we do both. I'm okay with that. How about you?"

Harry was right. The *Strib*, as he called it, was worthy of our support. Many of the smaller newspapers, like the community paper that had employed me decades earlier, had folded. Sadly, too many people were getting their news from social media.

I finished the national news and was about to begin the Minnesota section when Dan approached with the plated sandwich.

"Enjoy," he said. "I made sure it was nice and hot."

"Perfect! Thanks."

I stashed the paper and focused on the view outside the windows as I savored the sandwich. In the distance, the sun's reflection sparkled on the surface of Silver Lake. The short bridge that connected a small island to the shore provided the perfect spot for fishing. Today, three fishermen concentrated on bobbers as they warded off the chilling wind. On the paved hiking trail near the water's edge, walkers passed by as they circled the wooded park.

Inside, the atmosphere was warm and quiet except for an occasional giggle from the youngest patron, who was engrossed in a picture book. Adjacent to the cafe, a large, open space, periodically used for art displays, stood empty. The black leather couch and matching chairs that cozied up to an unlit, brick fireplace sat unoccupied. I relished the peace until a familiar voice broke the silence.

"Hey, MJ! Dan told me there was someone looking for me."

"Elle!" I rose and opened my arms for the hug I knew was coming. Her lean arms, surprisingly strong for such a petite person, wrapped around me tightly. Her black hair, cut asymmetrically around her thin, radiant face, was as straight as mine was curly. Several tattoos and piercings added to the mystique. In appearance, Elle could have passed for a high school sophomore. Actually, she was a college junior, street smart, and extremely intelligent. In the past, many conversations between her and Harry had led down interesting paths.

"She's a kid wise beyond her years, an old soul," Harry had said after a discussion involving their shared interests in horticulture and climate change.

"I've missed you, Elle," I said. "I was yearning for a caprese sandwich, and Dan toasted up a great one. Sit with me, if you have a minute. It's been a while."

I knew exactly when we had last seen each other, Valentine's Day. I had blundered that morning by thinking coffee at the park would be a nice diversion for the day is all about love, only to have a wave of nostalgia choke me the moment I caught Elle's attention. Diagnosing the onset of a panic attack, I turned and exited without even ordering coffee. I raced to my car and rummaged under the seat to find one of the bags stashed there for such an occasion. Hopefully, Elle had sized up my sudden departure as just one more example of my unpredictable behavior. Hopefully, she had not been alerted by other park visitors to the crazy lady in the Volvo who was hyperventilating into a paper bag.

"I guess I can stretch my break five more minutes," Elle said as she pulled out the chair directly across the small table from me and sat down. "I'm glad you came in. I've missed you. I've been meaning to call. Everything okay?"

"Fine, now that I have finally been reunited with my caprese sandwich. Just been crazy busy with my book."

"Too busy for a coffee break?" asked Elle.

"Well, when you are on a roll—." Slightly alarmed at my propensity to slip into an altered reality, I stopped midsentence. "So, tell me. What's going on in your life?"

"My roommate's giving me fits as usual, and I've been swamped with final papers and end-of-school stuff. All over soon. So, I've been thinking about your yard and gardens. I was wondering if we could work out an arrangement. Like last summer."

"You read my mind," I fibbed again. Yard work had not so much as blipped on my radar of concern, even at the outer edges. "I was hoping you could take care of things again. You'll have full control. What do you say?"

"Great," said Elle. "I can start soon. And the flower beds—can you spare some dollars for a few plants?"

"Maybe," I said, digging into my handbag.

"You really need color!" Elle added.

"I didn't know I looked that bad," I replied, this time feigning indignation.

"Your flower beds, MJ!"

I pulled out three twenties, my remaining bills, and handed them over. "For starters," I said.

"Thanks," Elle said as she rose from the table and pushed in her chair. "Gotta get back to work. I'll be over soon to check things out." She paused, locked her eyes on mine, and said, "So good to see you, MJ. Really!"

I replied truthfully this time before reaching up to accept another hug. "You, too—and good luck with finals." After she left, I retrieved the newspaper and turned to the weather prediction. Partly sunny with intermittent showers. Highs in the upper fifties. Yes, winter was over.

"No need for a paper bag this time," I muttered to myself twenty-five minutes later as I positioned myself behind the wheel of the Volvo. Raindrops, large and sloppy, had replaced the sunshine. I easily discarded my original plan to hike the trail. Instead, with a feeling of accomplishment, I turned the key, slowly backed out of the parking space, and headed home.

Seven minutes and four turns later I arrived at the gray, contemporary home that Harry had designed decades earlier. Instead of driving directly into the garage, which had become my custom, I parked the car in the driveway, climbed out, and scrutinized the front yard. It definitely showed signs of neglect. Neighbors on both sides had already raked lawns and uncovered plants. But in Harry's flower beds, daffodils, tulips, and hyacinths were fighting their way through mounds of decaying leaves. Some had already lost the battle. Thankfully, Elle had taken the initiative to suggest reinstating the preceding summer's gardening agreement. How many weeks would have passed before I would have acknowledged the need?

Along with her funkiness and spontaneous compassion, gumption was one of the qualities Harry and I loved about Elle. Shortly after she had been hired to work in the park's cafe, he had struck up a conversation with her and quickly discovered that she was a horticulture student at the University of Minnesota. Excited to find a kindred spirit who shared both his alma mater and his enthusiasm for digging in the dirt, Harry had peppered her with questions about her soil experiments. In the months that followed, more than once he had convinced her to pull up a chair at our table and join us during her break.

"I have been asked more than once," she had confided one morning, "if you are my grandparents." We laughed, but both Harry and I realized that such an assumption could easily be made. Our ages were about right, plus Elle's lankiness, dark eyes, and straight hair resembled Harry's.

"Grandparenting anyone would have been a trip, especially you," Harry had replied, putting concrete words around an unspoken yearning the two of us shared.

One cold January morning, an unusually large number of people had traipsed past the cafe to the banquet hall on the far end of the visitor's center. The hall was rentable for a variety of events, often weddings and large parties, but an occasion at eleven on a Wednesday morning struck both of us as odd. Harry sought out Elle, who was wiping off nearby tables, and asked what was going on.

"It's a memorial service," he reported back. "I guess the banquet hall has become a great place for not only weddings but also funerals. I can see why. The windows, the view, the peacefulness. We should talk about this, MJ."

"About what?"

"Our plans. Our funerals. What the other needs to know in case one of us dies," said Harry.

"Harry! You're spoiling a great morning."

"Okay, enough today. But we do need to talk about this," he said. "In the meantime just know that I want my service here."

"Really?" I asked, although I judged Harry's demeanor as a hundred percent serious. I was surprised. No service at all was what I wanted, and I imagined Harry's wishes would be similar.

"Of course. Look out those windows. Is there a better place?"

Four months later, he was dead, and our only discussion about funeral arrangements had been that two-minute exchange. In my numbness and grief, with the help of Claire and the other Write Women, I planned and executed a memorial service on a blissfully warm and sunny

May afternoon in a banquet hall overlooking shimmering Silver Lake and the flora that Harry so richly loved. People sat not in straight rows but around tables with beverages and cheesecake adorned with blueberries, strawberries, and raspberries. Many shared readings, songs, scriptures, and stories of a man who was healthy one minute and gone the next. Harry would have loved the gathering. But for me, the entire afternoon had been an out-of-body experience that eleven months later I had trouble conjuring up.

As a result, for months I avoided the park and the cafe. My only connection was Elle, who called shortly after Harry's death to offer condolences. She generously offered to mow the grass and spruce up the gardens in anticipation of the visitors who would arrive to pay their respects. Later, numb and grieving, I somehow found the wherewithal to ask if she would continue gardening throughout the summer. The arrangement worked well for both of us. Elle needed the money for school, and I needed someone other than me to tend Harry's beloved plants. That summer, Elle nurtured gorgeous flower beds, I was told. Truthfully, I hardly noticed. They could have turned into compost heaps and I would have been oblivious. Preoccupied, my scattered brain chased from one grief-laden detail to another: sending out death certificates to more places than I could imagine; contacting insurance companies, governmental agencies, and Harry's retirement account manager; meeting with our lawyer, tax accountant, and investment advisor. Unending to-do lists filled a notebook I nicknamed my widow journal. It became my bible. Meanwhile, thanks to Elle, Harry's blossoms and greenery thrived in a world beyond my grief.

As I tried to move forward after Harry's service, small, everyday occurrences became major setbacks. I was shocked at how many miscellaneous items Harry had routinely attended to without so much as a notice or a thank-you from me. For example, car maintenance was now my responsibility. After sitting in the garage for weeks, Harry's Buick developed a flat. I needed to buy a new tire and replace the old one before I could sell what had become an unnecessary second vehicle. Home maintenance, however minor, such as changing a recessed light bulb or removing a dead rodent from a mousetrap, could reduce me to tears. And what was worse, the tears were laced with an irrational anger directed at Harry for leaving me with the job.

It was after an unusually disgusting task involving a dead mouse followed by a free fall into despair that I finally considered myself a possible candidate for grief therapy. My therapist, a sharp woman with boundless patience and a stellar reputation, encouraged me to join a grief group made up of other widows. My first meeting became my last. It wasn't that the people weren't supportive. They tried to be. But the average age of the other women was fifty-five, and from the start, I sensed judgment. I internalized the subtle message that instead of being angry at my husband's fate, I should consider myself lucky that he had survived into his eighties. I should have looked for another support group with older widows, but I could not muster the energy. Then out of pure contrariness, I gave up the therapist as well. Clearly, I was not a good example of how one should deal with traumatic loss.

The word *should* had always bristled me, especially when it followed the word *you*. For as long as I could remember, advice couched in those words fueled my journey in the opposite direction. Contrary Miss Mary was a moniker that I proudly accepted when I was young, and now as a lonely, old person, I viewed my contrariness, even though immature, as a connection to my authentic self.

Accepting widowhood was a task I had been avoiding

with gradual withdrawal. By November, when trees had lost their leaves and the darkness of night cut into the supper hour, I began my hibernation in earnest and with the intention of sleeping through the first holiday season without Harry. Invitations from friends arrived, and I accepted one from Claire for a seat at her Thanksgiving table. The day was quite lovely, the food delicious, and the company warm. But along with the care package of leftovers, I brought home a case of melancholy. So when Millie asked me to spend the holidays with her at her condo in Maui, I declined. She would have been great company, but mustering the interest and energy for travel was beyond my spirit. I knew I was incapable of faking a week of Christmas aloha. Instead, trying to deny the holidays altogether, I spent the days in my undecorated home with a stockpile of unread library books and a determination to avoid as many sappy Christmas carols and television shows as possible. In the midst of it all, winter arrived with a vengeance as cold as the blood that ran through my veins. I wrote very little. I slept a lot.

Today, however, I had accomplished a minor coup. Making peace with Silverwood Park, although emotionally exhausting, had been mildly successful. The flood of memories associated with the park and Harry's memorial had not totally knocked me off-balance. Reconnecting with Elle had been therapeutic in a personal way, and her offer of help with the gardening meant I could avoid the guilt I would have eventually developed over neglecting Harry's flowers.

A familiar malaise, however, seeped into my spirit with the darkness of the evening. I felt a bit like one of Harry's buds that worked desperately to poke its head out of the rotting leaves only to get nipped by a late, unexpected frost.

I chastised myself for the melodrama. Then I justified

it. Seeing the glass half full, not one of my sterling qualities, required a healthier outlook than I was able to sustain. Weary of my shaky attempts to attack life head on, I knew deep in my bones that before I set my head on the pillow, I would be able to manufacture enough excuses to spend the next day, Sunday, as it was designated, a day of rest.

6

*T*otally disgusted with my Sunday's sloth, I rose Monday morning with a dull headache and forced myself to pick up a pen and fill three pages in my morning pages (MP) notebook. The first two contained sentence after sentence of self-disappointment. Self-loathing of my surrender to laziness alternated with self-loathing of my own self-loathing. Finally, by the third page, a switch flipped, and I found myself setting up meager goals for the day. I exchanged my MP notebook for a small notepad and jotted down a to-do list of errands that needed attention.

Showered and dressed, I was stuffing the notepad into my handbag when commotion coming from the driveway drew my attention out the window to a rusty SUV that Elle was loudly backing into the driveway. I stepped through the side door into the garage and activated the electric garage door. Outside, Elle was opening the hatchback.

"Wow, you got right on it!" I said as I surveyed the load in the back of her car.

"I pulled all-nighters and finished my final papers on Saturday. So yesterday I went shopping with your money. Can I leave the mulch in the garage until I clean out the beds?" asked Elle.

"Anywhere that's not behind my car. I'm about to leave," I replied. "What have you got here?"

"Mulch, mulch, and more mulch. And a couple of bags of potting soil. Think we should wait a bit to get the bedding plants in case of frost. Oh, and wait 'til you see these," she added, going around to the passenger side, opening the door, and removing a huge pot of blooming pansies. "I thought these would look fabulous on your porch right now. They should do fine in the cooler weather."

"They're beautiful, Elle."

"I'll buy some annuals and a couple of hanging baskets later. Maybe some tomatoes and peppers, too. What do you think?"

"Great, Elle. Everything. Just great," I said, realizing how much I really meant it. With no expertise, I had no idea what needed to be done or what timetable was best. "Perhaps my yard is not destined to be the derelict on the block, after all. How's the money holding out?"

"Here are the receipts," said Elle, pulling scraps of paper from pockets in her jeans and doing a quick total in her head. "I put a dent in what you gave me."

"I'm headed out on errands, and I'll make sure to stop at the bank for cash. There's lemonade in the fridge and snacks in the cupboard. Help yourself. Sorry, no pop. The back door is unlocked, so you can go in any time you need a break. How long do you think you'll be working?"

"I expect most of the day," Elle replied. "I want to get a good start."

"Maybe I'll see you later," I said as I climbed into the Volvo and rolled down the window. "If you leave before I get back, just lower the garage door. Code is the same as last summer, 0430. Hopefully I'll be back before you go."

With strength that belied her slender frame, Elle heaved a bag of potting soil out of the hatchback and dropped it flat on the garage floor. She was hoisting another as I slowly backed the Volvo past her and down the driveway.

Time evaporated as I checked off my destinations: bank, post office, gas station, drugstore. Impressed with my productiveness, I summoned enough courage to cross the threshold of the local library, something I hadn't done in weeks. I dodged Gayle, the head librarian, to avoid any inquiries regarding my prolonged absence or the launching of my next book. Quickly scanning the display of new additions, I claimed two, one mystery and one memoir, then took them to the self-checkout and dug a library card out of my wallet.

Still bruised by the hit that Harry's death had taken on my ability to enjoy a good read, I was hoping for a different result from my experience at Christmastime. Alone, while other families enjoyed holiday traditions together, I had hunkered down with enticing books. But delicious prose blurred behind tears, and intricate plots challenged a grieving brain. Thoughts wandered, and the need to continually reread proved exasperating. Finally, I gave up and dropped the half-read books into the drive-up book return. With hope for a better outcome this time, I quickly checked out the books, then slipped out before Gayle could emerge from the break room.

My next destination, Target, confounded me. I entered with the single purpose of picking up the reprint of the photo taken at my birthday luncheon. But instead of going directly to the photo desk next to customer service, for some unknown reason I grabbed a bright red shopping cart and headed to the center of the store. Wandering haphazardly through the rows, I amassed an impressive assortment of paper products, light bulbs, laundry supplies, personal items, and grocery staples. I resembled someone on her way to open and restock a summer lake cabin. Finally, my cart filled with new purchases, I detoured over to the service counter and claimed my photo on the way out.

China Fare, my last stop, was an intimate eatery with only a few tables. I decided on takeout and placed an order for two in case Elle had not left for the day. Pondering the menu, I decided on Harry's and my tradition, sesame chicken, vegetable lo mein, potstickers, cream cheese puffs, and extra rice. Within ten minutes, Mr. Lee handed me a packed and fragrant brown paper bag and asked, like always, if I wanted chopsticks. I declined, like always, thanked him, and headed home.

"Amazing," I called out to Elle, after turning into my driveway and surveying the work that she had accomplished during the few hours I had been gone. Many of Harry's favorite bushes and flower gardens had been cleared of dead leaves and debris. Surrounding the front patio, clusters of newly exposed day lilies protruded at least three inches above newly raked earth. On the side hill, shoots of hyacinths, daffodils, and tulips poked through the black dirt.

"Looks like the squirrels didn't get all the bulbs after all. Harry would have been happy. Great work, Elle! I can't believe all you've done today!"

"Wait 'til I spread the mulch. That will really give things a clean look," she replied.

"Ready for a break? Chinese is hot," I said, popping the trunk.

"Yum!" Elle set down her rake, brushed off her jeans, and walked over to the Volvo. Reaching into the trunk, she grabbed a huge Target bag in each hand and lugged them to the house. "Looks like you've had a productive day, too."

"Haven't done a Target run in months, obviously," I said as I opened the door to the back hallway and held it for Elle. She stepped inside and set the bags on the floor. Then she turned toward a collage of photos that were held by magnets to a huge piece of metal that Harry years earlier had attached to the wall.

"Wow! Is this Harry? He's so young!" she said, pointing to the photo in the center.

"That's one of my favorite pictures of him," I said. "It was taken at Gooseberry Falls. He loved the North Shore."

"I miss him."

Her simple acknowledgment, expressed so directly, cleared the house of unspoken grief.

"Me, too," I replied.

As Elle headed to the bathroom to freshen up, I unpacked and stowed perishables from the Target bags and then opened and arranged takeout boxes on the kitchen counter. We mounded our plates and took them and glasses of lemonade into the dining room and sat opposite each other. I hadn't eaten in that room in months. The table could comfortably seat six, but two worked nicely, just as it had each evening with Harry. Elle opened packets of sweet-and-sour sauce and squirted the contents liberally over her cream cheese puffs before devouring them with gusto. Everything tasted as good as it smelled. Sharing the meal with a hungry, appreciative guest was an added bonus.

"I think I can get all the beds cleaned out today," Elle said. "When it's safe, I'll plant annuals. They will really add color."

Conversation about final papers and summer plans kept Elle talking. I enjoyed vicariously eavesdropping on her life and relaxing and laughing in the company of someone young, fresh, spontaneous.

"There is only one thing worse than my cramped apartment and that's the roommate from hell. I finally told Felicia that I'm not renewing my part of the lease," Elle said.

"So now she's looking for someone to take my place— preferably someone deaf and not allergic to all the molds growing in her bedroom and on her shelves in the refrigerator. And don't even get me started on the dirt bags that she drags home every weekend."

"So what will you do?" I asked.

"I hate to say it, but I'll have to move home until I can find something affordable. Hopefully an efficiency with no roommate."

"Where's home?"

"My mom and two of my sisters live in Lindstrom," she said. Anticipating my concern about losing a gardener, she added, "It'll be a bit of a drive, but our agreement won't change."

Lindstrom, a small community about forty miles north and east of the Twin Cities, seemed like a fairly long commute to me, but I kept that thought to myself and simply responded, "Sounds good."

After we finished eating, Elle efficiently rinsed and placed the dirty dishes in the dishwasher, while I refrigerated the leftovers.

"Well, I'm going back out to see what more I can accomplish before it gets too dark," said Elle. "Thanks for the great dinner, MJ."

"You are most welcome."

After Elle disappeared into the garage I turned my attention to the remaining Target purchases. Finally, the counter was clear except for a photo envelope containing the snapshot of my smiling writers' group. I carried it into my office. Opening "Marguerite's Birthday Book" to the first blank page, I attached the print to the center with black, old-fashioned photo corners. Above it I wrote, "April 30, 2015—Age 80." For the life of me, however, I could not compose a caption that summarized the day.

7

I was running out of delaying tactics. Morning pages, simple housekeeping tasks, and three loads of laundry had occupied the morning. Having completed errands the day before, I now had checked off all items on my to-do list except one. Facing the inevitable, I picked up a red pen and *Seldom What It Seems* and worked with an editor's resolve on one more revision. Results were pitiful. I hated the three-inch stack of printed sheets. I hated the characters. I hated everything about the lifeless plot that eerily reminded me of my equally lifeless existence without Harry. I straightened the pages, dropped them back into the manuscript box, and closed the lid. Hearing the ring of the doorbell, I headed to the front door.

"You wouldn't let me buy you a birthday present, so here's a little something I'd like you to borrow," said Millie, poking a manila envelope through the small slot of the partially opened storm door. Instead of taking the envelope, I opened the door wider and invited her in. She stepped over the threshold and into the front entry. Dressed in a pair of light pink capris and a floral sweatshirt, Millie theatrically thrust the envelope into my hands.

"Here!" she said.

"What's this?"

I unclasped the cover and slid out the contents: a book, map, brochures, newspaper supplement, and small notebook. I heard a clink and looked down at the floor. A silver key ring lay at my feet. Millie, with remarkable dexterity, gingerly bent over and retrieved it. She grabbed my right hand, deposited the ring and the attached keys firmly into my palm, and closed my fingers around them.

"My condo in Kihei is empty. Just waiting for someone to air it out. A perfect writing space. I've written my best stuff on the lanai."

"Oh, Millie! I couldn't!"

"Of course you can," she replied. "All you need is a flight to Maui. Take a friend if you'd like. Only it can't be me. I've got blood clot issues at the moment."

"No! How serious?"

"Just a nuisance, but flying is out. I'll be spending the entire summer here, I'm sorry to say, so the condo is open. Some say it is too hot in Kihei in the summer, but I love it. The crowds in Maui are down, and the only things missing are the whales. Just promise me you'll think about it. Gotta run," she said. Without giving me a chance to respond, she abruptly opened the front door and stepped outside. She headed to her car as quickly as she had arrived, and as an afterthought called out, "Look at the brochures. And the book. And I've written some thoughts in the notebook. Seriously, check them out."

"You're a good friend," I yelled back as Millie climbed into her Lexus. She responded with a quick wave and backed out of the driveway.

I opened my fingers and examined two keys that were held together by a simple, metal ring. *B314* was clearly printed on one; the other was marked *POOL*. Next to them dangled a small silver charm in the shape of a plumeria. I quickly dismissed Millie's invitation as a kind, but totally inconceivable, gesture and deposited the keys and the travel materials on the entry table. Then I returned to the office to verify that all the bills had been paid.

Thankfully, a long-term relationship with an astute financial planner had left Harry and me, if not wealthy, then at least sustainable barring no health crisis to undercut the principal. An insurance payout from a policy we had never wanted to use now supplemented the comfortable nest egg. Having to live from one Social Security check to the next was not my reality, a blessing not shared by all widows, and I gratefully acknowledged that fact each month with every check I wrote. Yet, I found myself sitting in front of an open ledger, anxiously analyzing cash flow, and dreading the time when I would be too blind or demented to handle financial details without help.

Fifteen minutes later, I stood up, spontaneously grabbed a windbreaker, and headed out the door for a close-up of Elle's gardening. The newly mulched landscape provided a fresh, neat foundation for new bursts of growth. Along with the spring flowers that had survived the winter, ferns and hostas were emerging from their dormancy and showing signs of vitality, thanks to the warming sun.

For me, Elle's meticulous attention to the flower beds was therapeutic as well as cosmetic. Inspired, I retrieved a small, wrought-iron cafe table, no easy feat, along with two matching chairs that for two years had been gathering cobwebs in the back corner of the garage. After some scrubbing and a little drying time in the sun, the grouping returned to its summer home, the patio outside the front door. Fresh and inviting, the seating arrangement beckoned me to take an afternoon break. I stepped inside only long enough to pour a tall glass of iced tea.

On my return with beverage in hand, I passed the front

entrance table, grabbed *Hawaii,* the book Millie had included in the manila envelope, and headed to the patio. Both Harry and I had read and enjoyed James Michener's tale decades earlier. Harry had been fascinated by the geological formation of the islands described eloquently in the beginning of the book. I had scanned those pages with less interest but became totally absorbed when the story turned to the migration of humans to the islands, beginning with the earliest Polynesians. Michener's fascinating story described an evolving Hawaiian culture further influenced by whalers, missionaries, sugar cane developers, pineapple barons, and ethnic groups that emigrated one after another. With creative precision, he had braided all elements into a giant, enjoyable read.

The Hawaiian Islands held a prominent spot on our retirement's bucket list of travel destinations. But as fascinated as we were with the history of Hawaii, Harry and I reasoned that we should prioritize rigorous international travel first, while we were still mentally and physically able to deal with the complexities of foreign languages, unfamiliar currencies, and strenuous schedules. As we checked off countries in Europe and Asia, Hawaii gradually worked its way up the list. We imagined that soon the two of us would be ready to take a more leisurely vacation involving snorkels, fins, and the coral reefs of a chain of islands many considered paradise. For us, the question was not if we would make the trip to Hawaii but when. Sadly, we had waited too long.

Now, I had been gifted a generous invitation. Going without Harry to Millie's beautiful Maui, however, seemed inconceivable, almost a sacrilege. With a measure of sadness, I imagined the excitement we would have shared while preparing for such a getaway. Instead, I was alone, anticipating with dread the anniversary of his death.

Anniversary! What kind of word was that for a day that I had no desire to remember? Eleven days away, May 16 was already pressing on my chest.

The uncomplicated pleasure of reclaiming the patio space shriveled as familiar anxiety returned. I closed Michener's book and stared at the clumps of sprouting day lilies that outlined the patio blocks and visually softened the space. Unconditionally, the lilies returned every year, no matter how cold the winter. In a month or so, stalks would boast a plethora of golden buds. Each in its own time would bloom gloriously for a day or two and then shrivel and drop back into the dirt, while another would open up to take its place.

Harry had started with three small plants he had purchased at a nursery. "The first year they'll sleep," he told me. "The second year they'll creep. The third year they'll leap!" The years passed and Harry's plants multiplied. He separated and transplanted new growth, and eventually the entire patio was framed in golden blossoms.

"Strong, beautiful," Harry once said. "Just like you," he added with a silly smirk.

"Love is blind" was my reply.

At the time, I had not the heart to tell Harry I felt neither strong nor beautiful. Unlike the proliferous day lilies that produced many offspring, Harry and I had been unable to sustain new growth on our branch of the family tree. Our daughter Emma had died. Now with Harry gone, I had become the sole surviver hanging on to a withering stem.

Like an uninvited houseguest who arrives unexpectedly and stays too long, an all-too-familiar wave of anxiety triggered a flush of heat. I uncrossed my legs hoping to subdue the twitch in my ankle. I grabbed the edges of the table and breathed deeply over and over to steady an increasing pulse. Finally, with equilibrium somewhat restored, I stood up and started walking, down the driveway, down the street, over to Freedom Park to a bench under a giant oak. It was there that I reached a decision. I must go somewhere, anywhere, soon. Before May 16.

I reentered the house and sat down with the rest of the information from Millie. In the notebook she had detailed everything a traveler needed to know about Maui: airport shuttle services, car rental information, sightseeing options (complete with personal reviews). Grocery stores, farmers markets, drugstores, coffee shops, and beaches were numbered and described in a flair that was all Millie. Corresponding numbers appeared in ink on a map of Maui. Brochures from the Maui Visitors Bureau advertised sightseeing opportunities, everything from snorkeling, horseback riding, and zip-lining to tours of the dormant volcano, Haleakala, and daylong trips to the town of Hana. A supplement of *The Maui News* highlighted restaurants and activities ranked best by the locals.

But most impressive was a photo that slipped out of the notebook. It was a snapshot taken from the lanai of Millie's condo with "A PERFECT PLACE TO WRITE!!" printed boldly on the back. It appeared that her oceanfront condo enjoyed an unobstructed view of the Pacific Ocean. What would time on that lanai feel like? I longed for the Marguerite of younger years who would have jumped at the chance to find out.

All I knew for sure was that I needed to mitigate the oppressiveness of May 16. Slowly, I felt a subtle stirring of possibility. I stared at the cover of *Hawaii* as I garnered strength. If Polynesians could traverse an ocean by canoe, certainly I was capable of getting there with the help of Delta.

"Sorry, Harry," I said with a growing resolve. "I just might be going. Alone."

8

I continued to vacillate between "No way do I want to travel so far without Harry" and "I must go now!" I opened my MP notebook, dated the day's entry, and began to write. *Ten more days! Should I go?* What followed was a heady list of pros and cons. But once again, by the third page, my subconscious took over, and I began to tap into a disturbing undercurrent of anxiety. *I fear that if I stay home, I might curl up and disappear.* What was spilling from my pen was an overreaction, but long ago I had learned to take seriously any thoughts that presented themselves on the page.

Intellectually, I knew the ineffectiveness of trying to leave grief behind. Like a travel companion, it also boards the plane; and just like carry-on luggage, it arrives at the destination. Prescription: relocation? I knew it bordered on quackery.

I was not expecting to be healed in Maui. I fully understood that paradise would not cure me of anything. Besides, widowhood was a condition, not a disease. The only way to mitigate the condition, I decided, was to do whatever it took to resuscitate my writing.

Somehow, my passion for Harry and my passion for

writing had become so intertwined that, hand in hand, both had slipped behind a shadowy veil. Without the two loves of my life, I was disappearing as well, slowly and silently. After my utter failure with therapy, I had reached out to no one, real or spiritual. And without support, a giant piece of me was turning to dust, just like Harry.

Yet, occasionally there was a faint glimmer of hope. At the strangest times, I sensed Harry's presence. It was as if he were directing me to give his essence preferential standing over my emboldened inner critic. Years earlier when I had set out to write my first book, he had been my loudest cheerleader. Now, there were fleeting moments when I could sense his encouragement to fight the negativity that was rendering me silent.

Over the course of the day, I sought his guidance regarding management of the upcoming anniversary. I threw out questions to the void and opened myself to a response. I waited patiently for answers that, as usual, never materialized during the light of day.

9

*I*nspired by a dream in which I was afloat in rhythmic ocean waves, I awoke in a spirit of gratitude for Millie's invitation. Like a wrapped Christmas present, her gift was enticing my spirit with possibilities. A sense of foreboding was being replaced with a stirring of excitement.

May 16 would arrive whether I was in Minnesota or Maui, so within my morning pages, I contemplated spending the day in each. In Minnesota, my friends would be ready to help me survive the date of Harry's death; yet, the familiar surroundings would constantly remind me of the horrors of the previous year. In Maui, I would be alone, but alone with tropical distractions. Neither option gained higher ground from this analysis. But giving Maui a subtle sway was a gentle voice from an inner child who giggled at the opportunity. That younger self rarely had qualms about independent thought or action. Quickly, before momentum faded, I investigated airline websites for availability and prices to Hawaii. Finally, I phoned Millie.

"Hi, Millie, MJ here. Can we talk?"

"About Maui?" Millie asked. Before I could answer, she added, "I'm tellin' you, girlfriend, it'll reinvigorate your soul."

We agreed to meet at Silverwood Park. Two hours later, I pulled into the lot next to the park building and entered the cafe. Elle immediately greeted me from behind the counter, and we chatted as she pumped my cup of Mississippi Mud. Just as I turned to find a table, Millie arrived.

"Aloha,'" she said with a smile before turning to Elle and ordering a small decaf. We sought out a sunny table on the patio. "So, let's talk." When she saw that I was carrying the manila envelope with her Maui materials, she added, "You're not giving those back, are you?"

"I'm so sorry that I was not more appreciative of your offer yesterday. You took me by surprise," I said.

"Seriously, MJ, it's a great place to write. There's a light on the lanai. It's warm. No mosquitos. You can write into the night. Or early morning—that's more your style. Either way, with the ocean and trade winds, the sounds, the smells, you'll love it. Believe me."

"I seriously need to work on my book. It's a mess," I confessed.

"Listen, luv, it isn't easy. When Owen left, it was good riddance. Even so, my life was upended for awhile. You and Harry—you were soulmates. I can't imagine what you're going through."

Hearing Millie drop Owen's name surprised me. I thought she had easily moved on after their messy divorce. Once it had been finalized, she ceased her rants about his spending sprees and womanizing and forbade her friends to speak of him at all.

"Oh, Millie. I wasn't much of a listening ear for you back then. I had no clue," I said. "I'm sorry."

"No problem. Some people like to talk, some don't. I didn't, and I know you don't either. I get it. Besides, I did move on. And since Owen and I never traveled to Maui together, there is not one memory of that cad on the island—one more reason to love Maui." After a long swig of coffee, she asked, "Back to your book. Aren't you coming up on a deadline?"

"I'm way past. And the book—it's not coming together. At all!" Telling Millie the truth opened a pressure valve. "Oh, it's written. It's just bad. Really bad. Nothing like the others."

"What does Georgia say?"

"She wasn't very impressed with what she read early on and hasn't seen the last half at all. She has no idea how dreadful it is. She backed off for awhile because of Harry, but she's losing patience."

"Sounds like you need a working vacation." Millie looked at me expectantly.

"That's why I wanted to talk to you, Millie." I paused. "I can't believe I'm saying this, but I'm seriously thinking about going. And soon. I'd like to spend May 16 in Maui. Is that possible?"

"It's easy. Buy a one-way ticket. Get there. Settle in. See what you think. And when you want, come home. The condo is open until mid-October, when my nephew and his wife are using it."

"Mid-October! I'm not thinking of an extended stay," I said.

"Why not? Got something better going on here?"

"I was thinking more like a couple of weeks."

"You don't have to decide now," she said.

"The idea of booking a one-way ticket does sound enticing," I said. "But will I have trouble getting a seat at this late date?"

"No worries," Millie replied. "There's always a seat for a singleton. I've booked one-way often. It keeps options open. Book it. Throw some things in a suitcase. There's even a Target in Kahului for anything you forget."

"Kahului?" I said, acquainting my tongue with the unusual name.

"You will fly into Kahului, a town in the valley. My condo is in Kihei, a relaxed little town in South Maui, a quick drive from the airport. You'll find everything very easy, MJ." Millie spoke as if my decision had been made. She explained in detail the amenities of her condo and the logistics of traveling around the island. Next, she opened the small notebook to the page of her favorite haunts and expanded on her written comments. I interrupted only briefly with questions.

"Thought I'd mention that I'll be over tonight to mow the grass." I looked up when I heard the familiar voice. Elle had approached our table without either of us noticing. "Wow, looks like you're planning something big," she said, glancing at the unfolded map of Maui on the table.

"Yes, I think I am," I replied and then spontaneously asked, "Elle, would you by any chance be interested in housesitting?"

"What an inspired thought," Millie said as she took another swig of coffee.

10

*F*or me, the trip became real on May 9 when I purchased a one-way airline ticket for May 13 to Kahului, Maui, MSP to OGG. Just as Millie had predicted, seats were available for anyone who did not consider a middle seat near the rear of the airplane a deal breaker. Desperate to be in Maui before May 16, I booked one. Over the weekend, I focused on details that needed attention before my midweek departure.

With the aid of adrenaline, I prepped the guest room and bath for Elle. She intended to bring her own sheets and towels, so I folded and stored the guest room linens and cleaned out the bathroom drawers. Next, I emptied the closet of rarely worn clothes and set aside several bags for the thrift shop. Finally, I turned my attention to the dresser and desk that for years had housed a miscellaneous assortment of Harry's things. Shortly after his death, I had weeded through each drawer with a box for donations on one side, a trash bag on the other, and a box of tissues in my lap. Now only a few sentimental items remained, including one of Harry's favorite T-shirts. I placed his wallet, watch, and stack of personal letters in a wooden cigar box, one of the few remaining treasures from my father, and closed the lid.

I inspected the T-shirt. Worn and washed many times, it looked like a perfect candidate for the rag bag; its teal color had grayed, and the neckline ribbing was irreparably frayed by the stubble on Harry's chin. Screen-printed on the front of the shirt was a stylized red heart that represented the occasion, a fundraising race in honor of a coworker with a serious heart condition. Harry, one of the runners, had been given the largest size by mistake. During the 10K, he had worn it over his running attire. Later, it became a favorite nightshirt that he refused to give up. When I had sorted through Harry's belongings shortly after his death, I initially tossed the T-shirt into the trash bag, then inexplicably retrieved it. Now, I was still unable to throw it away, so I set it aside.

I scrutinized the bare room that would soon be Elle's and declared it ready just as she knocked at the door. She followed me around the house and took mental notes as I explained the trash and recycling schedules and the peculiarities of the air conditioner, washer, dryer, water softener, kitchen appliances, and thermostats. Finally, I revealed my hiding place for cash, a stack of twenties reserved for gardening supplies and house-related incidentals.

"I can't tell you how excited I am to live here while you're gone. But I'd like to wait until Friday to move in, if that's okay. This week's really hectic with my new internship," she said, referring to her summer position at the University of Minnesota. "That means the house will be empty for a couple of nights, but I'll stop in daily to check on things and work on the yard."

"Whatever fits your schedule is fine by me," I assured her as I handed over a set of house keys.

Actually, Elle's schedule worked best for both of us. Internally, I was relieved that the move-in process would be accomplished when I was not around. For me, anxiety always accompanied change, and I was experiencing enough of that already. Plus, Elle deserved an opportunity to settle in free of oversight.

After Elle left, I scanned the day's mail and discovered among the circulars a postcard from Pat announcing her upcoming book launch on June 20. Another graphic novel was almost ready for distribution. On a whim, I drove over to the nursery and picked out a beautiful hanging basket studded with purple, orange, and red petunias and headed to Pat's home. Sweaty and exhausted from a long run, she was standing in her driveway when I drove up.

"They're gorgeous," she said with her usual enthusiasm when I stepped out of the car and handed her the flowers.

"Congratulations on your book! You'll be making a lot of teens very happy," I said, referring to her loyal following.

She described her hope for a rain-free June 20, the day she had reserved a county park pavilion for her book launch. She enthusiastically described her plans for the event and for a string of book signings throughout the summer. I envied her excitement, accomplishment, and tireless spirit, attributes that for me had drained away. Somehow Pat, the busiest of the Write Women, continued to successfully juggle demands of authorship with full-time employment.

"Millie told me you're gettin' out of Dodge. Good for you! Hold these," she said as she handed the basket of petunias back to me. "I've got something for you." She disappeared into the house. Shortly, she reappeared with a small brown case with the word *Delta* written on the front. "I was given two of these when I flew first class to Arizona and back last winter for work. You need one," she said as she exchanged the case for the flowers. "At least you'll need the earplugs, and maybe the eye mask."

I unzipped the case and inside discovered an assortment of travel accessories intended for elite Delta travelers.

I thanked her, wished her well with the book launch, and just in case I did not make it back for the launch, extracted a promise that she would set aside an inscribed copy for me.

Finally, the last item on the latest to-do list could no longer be avoided. With a deep breath, I picked up the phone.

"MJ?" the voice asked.

"Hi, Georgia. Your wayward author here. Do you have a moment?"

"Good to hear from you." Georgia paused. The ball was back in my court.

"I wanted to let you know that I will be relocating temporarily," I said.

"Tell me" was all she said.

As cheerfully as I could, I described my travel plans and emphasized my commitment to working on the manuscript in Maui. I asked if she would stay with me until I had a decent book to show her.

"You've got it," she said without any qualifiers. "It's good to hear energy in your voice, MJ." She pivoted the conversation away from the manuscript and toward the details of the trip. "Do you really want to go to Maui alone?"

I tried to sound self-assured. "Yes. It's a working vacation."

Georgia ended the conversation with a deadline extension, a pep talk, and a restatement of her willingness to read the manuscript in any form, at any time, even now.

"Not yet," I said. "But thanks. You are the most supportive slave driver an author can have. Really, Georgia. Thanks."

We ended our conversation. But instead of relief, a familiar heaviness returned. Georgia's willingness to be supportive and to extend the deadline, once again, sat squarely on my chest. I knew she was busy with other authors. Nonetheless, I felt a deep sense of duty to uphold my half of our working relationship. Over the phone, I had verbally recommitted to resuscitating the manuscript, and that responsibility had cracked open a mental entrance-way for self-doubt and procrastination. Shrugging off the sensation, I checked Georgia's name off the list and headed upstairs to pack.

Millie's guidelines were simple: cool, casual clothes, maybe a sundress or two, and definitely beach attire. My choices, plus a last-minute inclusion, Harry's teal T-shirt, easily fit into a suitcase that, fully packed, weighed in at thirty-six pounds, well below Delta's fifty-pound limit. Writing supplies, manuscript, MP notebook, and a small digital voice recorder that I used to capture fleeting thoughts or unusual sounds fit nicely into a carry-on. Lightweight personal items loosely settled to the bottom of my favorite tote.

I considered it a good omen that "TSA PreCheck" was prominently displayed at the top of the boarding pass when I checked in online for my flight. After I printed the pass, I unplugged my computer and slid it into the padded pocket of my roller bag, then folded the boarding pass and slipped it into an outside pocket of my tote. I was packed.

Tomorrow the house would be Elle's. Checking for anything that needed attention, I walked through each room for one last scan. "Marguerite's Birthday Book" sat open on the corner of my desk, and the photo of five smiling women at Muffuletta stared up at me. With the intention of returning the book to the cabinet in the living room, I closed the cover. But my fingers lingered on the smooth black walnut. Carefully, I reopened the cover and located the first entry, "April 30, 1940—Age 5." The photo captured a precocious, curly-haired child flanked by two smiling youngsters. What had possessed me to stick out my tongue? Under the picture the caption read, "Marguerite's Fifth Birthday Party With Jimmy and Sandra in Davis, Minnesota, 1940."

I reexamined each youngster in the photograph and studied the backdrop, a two-story stucco and wood house with bold, black numerals, 671, running lengthwise alongside the front door. Did I remember the house? Did I remember sticking out my tongue at the exact moment that the camera clicked? After sitting quietly for several minutes, I picked up a pen and a blank notebook and began to write.

APRIL 30, 1940—AGE 5

I guess birthdays are as important as Easter because Mama says that I can wear my Easter dress today. She sewed it up with her treadle. She keeps talking about gingham. All I know is that the pink squares on my dress are the same color as my sweater, and I feel special when I wear them together. Sitting with Jimmy and Sandra on the top step of my house, I follow Papa's directions and smile for one last photo. It is the first birthday that I can remember.

At age five, *magical* was a word as foreign to me as the Norwegian Nana spoke quietly to herself when she thought no one was listening. But *magical* proved to be the perfect adjective for my recollections. Part memory, part yearning, descriptions of a five-year-old's birthday party flowed easily from my pen. I wanted to continue, to flesh out the scene, to tap the essence of the day. But I needed to get to bed and, hopefully, to sleep in preparation for a long day of travel. Carefully, I untied the frayed grosgrain ribbon that held the album together and unthreaded the pages. Then, with the intention of finishing my story in Maui, I took the page with the picture of my fifth birthday party and set it aside.

Spurred by the gentle nudge of nostalgia, I began turning pages, studying photos of birthday after birthday, reading captions, and scrutinizing miscellaneous comments. If an entry stirred me, I separated it out and added it to a growing stack that would accompany me on my trip. I allowed instinct to be my guide. Eventually a select number of pages was prepared for travel, and the small cardboard box that I found to protect them was fastened with rubber bands and packed inside my tote alongside the notebook that contained my story. I glanced at the clock: 12:10 a.m. I set the remaining pages of the birthday book next to the walnut cover, dropped the grosgrain ribbon on top, and headed to bed.

11

*C*laire, my transport to the airport, arrived at 6 a.m., with Ginny along for the ride.

"You've got everything you need for the summer in this bag?" Ginny asked as she pulled my suitcase down the driveway to the open hatchback.

"Who says I'm staying for the summer?" I replied as I followed with my carry-ons.

"No one," replied Claire, with a disapproving glance in Ginny's direction.

"Millie said her condo was open all summer. I just assumed," said Ginny. "Millie also said you're not going to want to return once you get there."

Obviously, I had been the center of conversation some-time earlier.

"Get in the car, Ginny," said Claire sternly.

"Here," said Ginny from the back seat as we backed out of the driveway. "A few snacks for the plane. They won't feed you, you know. Can't believe you can fly cross-country, or halfway 'round the world in your case, and get nothing more than a measly bag of pretzels."

The mention of halfway 'round the world bluntly reminded me of the long travel day ahead. I accepted and opened the brown paper bag from Ginny and discovered an odd assortment of single-serve packages of chips, crackers, cookies, and fruit snacks alongside a small tangerine and a stick of beef jerky. Ginny must have raided her grandchildren's treat drawer.

"Thanks, Gin. I didn't think to include any snacks."

I wedged the bag into my tote. Just when I was starting to feel like a kindergartner heading out to meet the school bus for the first time, Claire added, "No news is good news, MJ. Stay in touch when you feel like it. But we won't be hounding you. Will we, Ginny?"

Ignoring Claire, Ginny replied, "Well, you could at least text us when you get there."

In less than thirty minutes, we arrived at curbside check-in, and twelve minutes later I was standing on the other side of security and peering around for a place to kill the extra hour that I had allowed in case of congestion. I bought a cinnamon chip scone and a cup of coffee, settled in at the gate, and pulled out Michener's *Hawaii.* Eventually, boarding began for what I hoped would be an uneventful trip. The first leg proved to be just that.

Any concern I might have had about making my connection in Seattle disappeared once I deplaned and located an overhead board with flight information. A delay had pushed the departure of my flight to Kahului back two hours. The change provided plenty of time for a leisurely lunch, a bowl of delicious clam chowder, which I augmented with selections from Ginny's care package. By the time I boarded the plane to Maui, I had spent more time in airports than in the air and had reread a good chunk of *Hawaii.* And I still had over 2,700 miles and five and a half hours to go.

Opting for earplugs and an eye mask instead of inflight entertainment or interaction with fellow passengers, I settled in as comfortably as one can in an airplane's middle seat and tried to nap. Thanks to Pat's thoughtful travel items, I blocked out all distractions. Exhausted from a hectic week and a late night of final preparation, I welcomed the quiet. Images of a small five-year-old with a protruding tongue danced in the darkness behind my mask. Soon, bubbles surrounded the child. I heard laughter. The child faded away, and so did I.

I awoke startled and dry mouthed but somewhat refreshed. As I removed the eye mask and dug out the earplugs, the tiny woman seated next to me by the window smiled. A few minutes later, she turned and asked, "Is this your first trip to Maui?"

"Yes," I answered. "How about you?"

"I am returning home," she said. "I have been visiting my beautiful hapa grandchildren in Seattle for the past four weeks. I love them dearly, but I am very ready to return to Maui."

"Hapa?"

"Their mother—my daughter—is Japanese, and their father is haole—white. Hapa children are of mixed ethnic ancestry. I tell them to be proud. That they are double blessed. Perhaps it is easier to feel that blessing in Maui than in Seattle." She paused and added, "My name is May."

Surprised by her openness, I replied, "Nice to meet you, May. I'm Marguerite."

"Marguerite," she repeated slowly as if to taste the name on her tongue.

"It's French," I added.

"So, you are French?" she asked.

"French and Scandinavian," I said. "Norwegian actually."

"So to an extent you are hapa, too," she said with a smile.

We chatted about superficial things, including the inconvenience of arriving two hours later than scheduled.

"We will miss sunset," May said after she checked her watch.

"Really? The sun sets early in Maui."

"We are near the equator so the time varies little during the year. Right now the sun disappears into the sea about six forty-five." As an afterthought, May added, "I hope my sister checks the arrival information before she heads down to the airport. Do you need a ride to your hotel? We would be happy."

"That's very kind, but my friend scheduled a shuttle service for me." I described Millie and the generous offer of her condo in Kihei.

"You will be staying with her then?" asked May.

"No, actually Millie is back in Minnesota. I'll be by myself, which is good, because I have much work to do on my next novel. Millie tells me her condo's lanai is the perfect place to write." I skipped any details concerning Harry or the anniversary of his death.

May seemed genuinely interested in chatting with an author and asked astute questions about the writing process.

"You sound like someone who has studied the craft," I said, hoping to find a writer's connection.

"Oh no," May said. "I could never write. But I love to talk story."

"I love to write them, or at least I used to when it wasn't so difficult. Millie tells me that Maui will reignite my creativity," I said.

"Wonderful things happen in Maui," said May with firm assurance.

Near the end of the trip, flight attendants collected the Hawaii Department of Agriculture declaration forms that all travelers were required to fill out. In exchange, they offered maps of the island. I took one and opened it up.

"Do you mind?" May asked. She began to circle locations and make notations on my map. "These are hidden treasures." Ethnic grocery stores, bakeries, an out-of-the-way labyrinth, botanical gardens, and a heritage park were highlighted in May's neat penmanship.

"This is where I live," she said, pointing to one of the circled areas on the map. "My sister Fern and I share a house with our father. Upcountry. It's so beautiful. Cool." She pointed out small towns close to her home on the western slope of the dormant volcano Haleakala. "You must visit Makawao and Kula. Maybe you will drive to the rim of the crater?"

"Honestly, I haven't thought much about anything except getting to the condo."

At the top of the map, she printed MAY WANTANABE and below it her phone number.

"Everyone needs a local contact," she said matter-of-factly. "I will be yours."

In response, I wrote my full name, Kihei address, and cell phone number on a page torn from a notepad and handed it to May.

"Look, Maui!" May invited me to lean into her space and glance out the window. All I saw was the darkness of twilight. At her urging, I leaned a bit farther until I was able to see a large, dark land mass dotted with pockets of twinkling lights. "Home," she added.

After a gentle landing, May and I exited the plane and parted outside a women's restroom. After an exchange of best wishes, she continued on to baggage claim, and I turned into the restroom. Studying the reflection in the mirror, I hardly recognized the frazzled-looking woman who was staring back at me. The day's travel had taken its toll. I could do nothing about the dark bags under my eyes, so I applied fresh lipstick and pulled a pick through the matted curls that were already beginning to frizz in response to the humid air. Then I joined the other stragglers who were heading to baggage claim.

At the bottom of the escalator, a young woman in a floral dress held a white sign with BURDICK printed in bold lettering. As I approached, she sought confirmation that I was the Burdick she had been assigned.

"Aloha! Welcome to Maui," she said as she placed around my neck a lei of purple orchids that matched the flower tucked behind her ear. The lei was Millie's thoughtful addition, I assumed, since she had insisted on making the shuttle reservation. "Your luggage should arrive at carousel two," the hostess said, motioning to the second of four carousels that were only steps away. "After you collect your pieces, we will take you to the shuttle."

In short order, my suitcase slid down a chute, landed on the carousel with a thud, and traveled along the conveyer belt in my direction. As I attempted to grab the handle, a strapping young man with a scruffy beard reached over and hoisted my bag off the belt and set it upright beside me.

"Good to go?" he asked, in case I needed help with another piece.

"This is all. Thanks so much," I said as I raised the handle.

"Enjoy Maui," he said as he grabbed a huge backpack off the belt. He disappeared into the sea of people who were pulling luggage toward the curb.

I paused to appreciate the cool breezes that were blowing through doorless exits before heading over to my hostess. She called out to a gray-haired man in a matching floral shirt. He approached with a greeting and relieved me of my luggage. I followed him to a white van parked at the curb and joined four other travelers who were also heading to the Kihei/Wailea area. As our luggage was loaded in the back of the van, we exchanged pleasantries and climbed in for the final leg of our journey.

Assured that people and luggage were securely stowed, the van's driver, a young man with an engaging smile, climbed into the driver's seat and offered a warm aloha. He merged the van into outgoing traffic, and in short order, we exited the airport. The next few turns wove through Kahului, a much smaller city than I had imagined. "Even in paradise," commented a young woman to her travel companion as she pointed to a huge store with a familiar red logo. I smiled as I recalled Millie's assurance that I would be able to buy at the local Target whatever I had forgotten to pack. After we left the lights of Kahului behind, the night sky darkened the landscape and obscured any visuals.

We traveled through the valley for a few miles. The smell of salt filtered through open windows. Everyone in the van oohed simultaneously with the first sight of the ocean. As if to welcome us to the island, the clouds parted and reflected rays of a half moon shimmered off the crest of easy waves. Shortly, the van stopped at the Menehune Shores, and a gray-haired couple climbed out.

Next was my turn. The van pulled into the Maui Sunset and deposited me and my luggage in front of the office, which, as expected, was closed for the night. Thanks to Millie, I did not have to deal with the lockboxes that held condo keys for late arrivers. Instead, I simply fished her keys out of my tote and proceeded to the elevator, which was right where she had described. I ascended to the third floor and followed an open-air walkway to B314. One of Millie's keys easily turned the lock. I dragged my suitcase and carry-on over the threshold and dropped my tote on the floor. I had arrived.

Millie's condo was a feast for the senses, thanks to the cleaning service that had prepped it for my arrival. A

pleasant floral scent emanated from a beautiful arrangement of tropical flowers in a tall crystal vase. It stood next
to one of several artificial candles that flickered throughout
the condo and invited me inside. From an iPod attached
to the entertainment center, slack key guitar music played
on an endless loop. I passed through a wide aisle with the
kitchen on one side and a built-in desk and bookshelves
on the other. It opened into a living area with a rattan
couch, love seat, coffee table, and entertainment center.
Each well-chosen piece of furniture and artwork emanated
quality and good taste, just like Millie's home in Minneapolis. I was most excited to check out her famous lanai, so I
opened the drapes and searched for the remote to switch
on the outdoor light.

Millie's lanai, her favorite writing space, lit up with the
press of a button. She had described it beautifully. Opening the sliding glass doors, I stepped through and instantly
knew that Millie had been right. Even in the dark of night,
this space, with the soft lapping of the nearby ocean and
the delicious fragrances of flowers and salt, was a slice of
paradise. I rested my arms on the railing and peered down
to inspect the pool and hot tub, both glistening with the
reflections of flaming tiki torches. A few nighttime swimmers, some quite young, were splashing and laughing
at what appeared to be the shallow end of the pool. The
nearby hot tub sat empty, the water, flat.

Except for the pool, the grounds seemed amazingly
quiet for eight thirty in the evening. I removed my watch,
which was still on Minneapolis time, 1:30 a.m., and adjusted
it back five hours. No wonder I was so tired.

I reentered the condo, latched the deadbolts on the
doors, and dragged my luggage into the bedroom. The
focal point of the room was the beautiful, celadon-colored
Hawaiian quilt Millie had chosen for the queen-sized bed.

I scanned the room and saw touches of her in every acces-
sory, from the small trinket box on the bedside table to the
exquisite, floral prints on the wall. I quickly unpacked the
suitcase and jumped into a much-needed shower. Clean
and exhausted, I pulled Harry's T-shirt over my head,
turned on the overhead fan, switched off the lights, and
slid into bed.

12

I awoke disoriented. The only light in the room was from the clock radio that registered a red four o'clock. Slowly, I pieced together all the confusing information—my relocation, the time difference, the dull caffeine headache. Grateful that Millie had suggested that I bring coffee for the first morning, I brewed a pot and took a mug onto the dark lanai. Even at this early hour, the temperature of the moist, still air was comfortably warm. Except for an occasional lamp or flickering TV, most condos in the A building on the other side of the pool remained dark.

Having slept soundly for over seven hours, I had no intention of returning to bed. Instead, I reentered the condo and planted myself at Millie's desk with my MP notebook. Easily filling three pages, I recorded the happenings of the previous day. I described May in great detail and reflected on all the people that had in one way or another eased my journey. Even the scruffy guy with the backpack garnered an accolade. *It took a village to get MJ to Maui!* I wrote.

Within the morning pages, I explored my present state. I had assumed I would hunker down once I finally arrived in Maui. That continued to be my basic plan, but May had piqued my curiosity about the island she called home. Not inclined to drive Upcountry, I was, however, ready to check out Kihei. My motivation was simple: I was starving. The only edibles in Millie's kitchen were a few spices, nicely sealed in glass jars to discourage the attraction of bugs, and a small cluster of bottles containing olive oil, rice wine vinegar, and soy sauce. Seattle's clam chowder was a distant memory, and Ginny's care package had been whittled down hours ago somewhere over the Pacific Ocean. I retrieved my tote, dug out the wrinkled brown paper bag, and emptied the contents on the granite countertop. An individually wrapped rod of beef jerky and a small box of raisins staved off hunger while I focused on Millie's detailed notes. "The car rental agency will gladly pick you up, but it doesn't open until 8 a.m. If you get up early, like I always do, you can walk an easy route over to the town center (check the map!), grab breakfast at one of the cafes that I have starred, and hang around until the agency opens."

I opened the map and checked out the inset focused on Kihei. Millie had drawn dotted lines and arrows from the condo to the town center and printed comments next to the eating establishments. Next to one, she had written, "Try malasadas." Malasadas were a mystery, but the name of the restaurant, Home Maid Cafe, stirred an already growing appetite.

When had Millie become a morning person? That had been my question when I had read her suggestion back in Minnesota. Now I was experiencing firsthand the effects of a five-hour time change. I was eager for breakfast, and sunrise was still over an hour away. I organized my writing materials and computer on Millie's huge built-in desk, synced up with her Wi-Fi and printer, and dressed for the day.

Retrieving a notebook, a favorite pen, and the cardboard box that contained pages of the birthday book, I refreshed my coffee cup and turned on the lanai's overhead light. Nestling into a padded chair at the glass-topped table, I breathed in the early morning quiet, broken only by the lapping of the ocean and an occasional coo of a mourning dove. After retrieving from the box the desired page from the birthday book, I reintroduced myself to the curly-haired five-year-old in the photo and closed my eyes. Once again, bubbles. Children laughing, running. A camera.

Images crystalized. Were they memories or reminiscences that Mama had shared over the years? It didn't matter. I opened the notebook that contained the beginning of the story that I had written in Minnesota. After rereading the introduction, I began to write. For the first time in months, the words gushed out of my pen almost too quickly to be captured on paper. Faded and foggy memories of the past morphed into recognizable images on the written page. Obviously, my brain had been working on the details while I had traveled and slept.

Intriguing is the organ that never shuts down. Like the overnight cleaning crew that works in the dark of night, emptying wastebaskets and tidying up for the next day, the brain during sleep rids the unconscious of unnecessary trash. It polishes creative nuggets and readies them for their grand entrances during the waking hours. The writer's job is simply to be receptive. During my productive years, when I needed to conjure a complicated yet believable pathway for a protagonist, reliably a twist or turn would present itself upon awakening. I had learned to trust the fact that much of the story's crafting took place while I slept.

Unlike other novels, however, *Seldom What It Seems* had been excruciatingly difficult from the start, like a nauseous pregnancy followed by a painful childbirth with nothing to show at the end but an offspring dead on arrival. I had feared that my aging brain was no longer up to the task of weaving an intricate story, but my morning's attempt at re-creating a decades-old tale offered a slice of hope. I set down the pen, switched off the light, and sat in peaceful darkness.

Millie's lanai had already lived up to its designation as the perfect place to write. Even though my first attempt at writing in Maui had nothing to do with my manuscript, the fact that I was writing at all reaffirmed my decision to travel, according to Ginny, "halfway 'round the world."

Oh no! Thoughts of Ginny reminded me of my failure to check in. Picking up my cell phone, I composed a simple text and sent it to the Write Women.

Aloha. Arrived. Flight late but good. Paradise here. Your lanai is all you said it would be and more, Millie! Thanks, all—ride to airport, snacks, earplugs, eye mask—and this BEAUTIFUL *space to write! Most important, your support!*

An obnoxious rooster, or maybe two, announced the arrival of a new day. Shortly after, the first rays of morning sun quietly appeared. Incrementally erasing the darkness, they revealed what I had been unable to see since my arrival. A well-manicured lawn, studded with palm trees, extended from the condo buildings to the ocean's edge. A mounded area of turf was sculpted and trimmed into giant letters spelling out MAUI SUNSET. Beyond, gentle waves of blue, turquoise, and aqua stretched to the western horizon. Slightly to my right and across what looked like a bay, rugged volcanic peaks rose from the ocean. The brownish-black slope appeared undeveloped except for a vertical line of white wind turbines that snaked up the mountainside. The eastern mountainside was greener and perhaps wetter, judging by the dark clouds that hovered over what, according to the map, were the West Maui Mountains. They had been present all night, simply out of sight.

Finally, it was nearing 6 a.m. Following Millie's directions, I set off on quiet Uluniu Road that ran parallel to the ocean. Hens and chicks greeted me. When I had nothing to offer, they meandered across the road and disappeared into the brush. Roosters, perhaps the same ones that had crowed so noisily an hour earlier, now quietly ignored me as I passed them by. On my short walk, I passed single-family homes, small condo buildings, and a gated area with a VFW building and a large advertisement for an upcoming steak fry. Soon I turned into what Millie had called Azeka's, Kihei's two-block town square that housed businesses, stores, restaurants, a post office, and plenty of parking spaces. South Kihei Road, a main thoroughfare, ran right through the middle.

I easily located the Home Maid Cafe. A few early risers were already enjoying breakfast either inside the small cafe or around tables on the front patio. Malasadas, I discovered, were small Portuguese doughnuts without holes. I ordered a standard egg and bacon breakfast and added a six-piece order of malasadas to go.

"Sugar or cream?" asked the gray-haired woman behind the counter. As far as I could tell, she was one of only two workers in the cafe.

"Excuse me?" I asked, confused because I had not ordered coffee.

"You have to try the cream-filled ones. They're the best," said a young woman in line behind me. Deeply tanned and casually dressed in shorts, tank top, and worn flip-flops, she appeared to be a local authority on malasadas. With skin as white as the Minnesota snow, I must have looked like a new arrival.

I thanked her and turned back to the the woman behind

the counter. "Three of each," I said as I handed her payment. I chose an outside table and awaited breakfast. In a notebook, I jotted down my first reflections of Maui, ending with a description of the four chickens that were hanging around the perimeter of the seating area. Obviously, they were the reason for the sign that read: "Do not feed birds. Especially chickens!!!"

With a plate in one hand and a box in the other, the woman who had taken my order now placed both in front of me. "Fresh and hot!" she said, referring to the malasadas, which had been deep-fried in oil and either rolled in sugar or shot with a thick cream. The small doughnuts sat in a square takeout container with the top open. "You might want to let them cool a bit before you close 'em up," she added.

I thanked her and picked up a fork for the eggs and bacon. After a few bites, I could no longer resist the fragrance of the deep-fried delights. I picked up a warm malasada and took a bite. Delicious cream oozed out of tasty, fried dough. I finished it off and then decided to compare it to one rolled in sugar. Both were delicious, not greasy or heavy. But the young woman was right. Cream was the best. Without hesitation I ate a third with my eggs before placing a strip of bacon and the second half of an English muffin in the takeout container with the three remaining malasadas.

Breakfast seekers continued to arrive. My spot on the patio provided great people watching. A steady stream of humanity exited the cafe with boxes of malasadas, breakfast sandwiches, and/or coffee. Several workers climbed into company vans or pickups filled with equipment. Not everyone in Maui was on holiday.

I gave my table to a family with a fussy toddler. The blond mother sported a painful-looking sunburn, and she winced as she tried to pry her clingy child away from her body and into a booster seat. Sunscreen—one thing I had forgotten to pack!

The car rental agency punctually opened at 8 a.m. A young, female employee quickly processed my reservation, and after commenting on its great mileage, she offered a Toyota Prius. More interested in the ease of parking I would gain from its compact size, I accepted. After a quick survey of the vehicle and a tutorial on the keyless start, I headed out.

"Aloha! Another beautiful day in Maui. Sunny and seventy-four. High of eighty-six degrees today. Enjoy." The soothing Hawaiian voice flowed from the radio on the dash. "Hawaiian music, Maui style," the female announcer added.

If eating malasadas with feathered companions was not enough, the strumming of slack key guitars on KPOA, the local radio station, confirmed that I was a long distance from Minnesota. I drove to the end of the parking lot, and instead of turning north toward the condo, I turned right onto South Kihei Road. In no time at all, I was passing a string of beautiful beaches, one after another, some with picnic areas, playgrounds, and lifeguard stations. Even at this early hour, beach umbrellas and colorful beach towels dotted the sand. I gravitated to a lot that offered plenty of off-street parking and crossed South Kihei Road to a sign that advertised the beach: KEAWAKAPU. A shaded path between two condo buildings led to an expansive stretch of golden sand already inhabited by an array of early-morning beachgoers.

Kicking off my sandals, I headed down to the water's edge, where compacted sand provided ideal conditions for a morning stroll. I was not alone. Many likeminded walkers and a few joggers smiled and extended greetings in passing. When I reached an outcropping of volcanic rock at the south end of the beach, I realized I could easily pick my way through the lava and reach another beach and then another if I were so inclined.

A surprising number of people had already staked out patches of sand for a morning at the beach. Some supervised energetic children who were either playing in the shallows or building creations with an interesting assortment of sand toys. The people who chose to swim studied the waves and then timed their entrances to avoid getting tumbled. A few with boogie boards floated beyond the crest of the surf and tried with varying degrees of success to ride a wave back to the sand. Everyone appeared relaxed, happy. Why wouldn't they? They were among the lucky ones to be enjoying the beach during a workday. I vowed to return another day with a beach chair and sunscreen.

Thirty minutes later, I was back in the Prius and beginning the four-mile return trip to the Maui Sunset. This time I paid greater attention to essentials, such as grocery and drugstores, coffee shops, restaurants, and an urgent care center which I hoped would not be needed. The journey was interrupted twice with stops at Times Supermarket for some groceries and Longs Drugs for sunscreen, the morning edition of *The Maui News,* and an empty three-ring notebook.

Avery, the receptionist in the office at the Maui Sunset, greeted me pleasantly when I introduced myself and registered my car.

"There's an orientation every morning for newcomers," she said. "At 9 a.m. You're a little late for today's but maybe tomorrow? It's held down at the pool with our activity director, Patti. She can fill you in on all the island activities and set you up with tours."

I thanked her for the information, which I quickly discarded. I had no interest in anything organized.

"Also," Avery added, "grocery carts are available to help you transport things to your condo. Just look under the stairs. The carts are stored inside on ground level."

That was welcomed information.

"There!" I said as I finally unpacked the last of my groceries and folded and stowed three reusable cloth shopping bags. The refrigerator was now satisfactorily stocked with the basics, a few irresistible deli items, and a pint of passion fruit sherbet. Two bottles of red wine, the first alcohol I had purchased in months, sat next to a fresh supply of Kona coffee. Fruits and vegetables still remained on my shopping list, but a run to Millie's favorite farmers market would have to wait. The lanai was calling.

I iced a glass of water, grabbed my laptop, and retrieved the notebook that contained the story of my fifth birthday. Spreading out at the table on the lanai, I created a Word document for the story I had written before dawn. The process proved a bit challenging and required a fair amount of deciphering and editing. Obviously, my morning brain had been traveling faster than my fingers. Much like priming a pump, the physical act of typing the story prompted additional, dormant images to spring to life. The story expanded, and for some reason Mrs. Fullerton presented herself. I relished her arrival and continued to write. Finally, I was ready to print.

Unlike many writers, who create and edit directly on their computers, my process usually began with longhand. My most creative thoughts flowed from a ballpoint pen into a lined notebook. Sometimes my brain worked faster than my fingers. At other times, *flow* was too generous a word. There was a reason for naming the first attempt a rough draft. My first copy usually captured the essence of a thought or story, but at this stage, it resembled a messy jigsaw puzzle. Words were crossed out, written over, or encircled with arrows pointing to their new locations. The next step involved tidying up, and the computer became the great organizer. The typed story took on a more professional look and was saved for future work, which usually included several more revisions. Then it was critically tightened and scrutinized for mistakes in grammar and mechanics. Finally, I declared the revision process complete. The last step involved printing a hard copy, because, after all, I was old school. I had to see the words on paper. The process was time consuming, but when it was clicking along, I hardly noticed.

The morning's writing had been surprisingly pleasurable and offered a bit of hope. Unlike the torturous attempts of the last few months, the experience on Millie's lanai offered my soul an inkling that I might someday enjoy writing again. The huge missing piece, however, was Harry's cheerleading.

The clock on the computer and a simple calculation confirmed the reason why my legs twitched and my core needed a stretch. Hours had passed. During that time, thirty feet below on the grounds of the Maui Sunset, a steady stream of people had enjoyed the pool, shuffleboard courts, and lawn. I had not moved except to grab a Cobb salad out of the refrigerator and to refresh a water glass. Finally, within my computer was saved a somewhat polished story titled with the date and caption from the birthday book. Narrated by a five-year-old child, the recollections were based on fuzzy memories that had been expanded to include suppositions and probabilities. I printed the pages, passed them through Millie's hole puncher, and dropped them into the new three-ring notebook. With little forethought, I grabbed a Sharpie and printed MARGUERITE on the spine.

MARGUERITE—AGE 5
April 30, 1940
*"Marguerite's Fifth Birthday Party
With Cousins Jimmy and Sandra
in Davis, Minnesota"*

I guess birthdays are as important as Easter because Mama says that I can wear my Easter dress today. She sewed it up with her treadle machine. She keeps talking about gingham. All I know is that the pink squares on my dress are the same color as my sweater, and I feel special when I wear them. Sitting with Jimmy and Sandra on the top step of my house, I follow Papa's directions and smile for another photo.

"Hurry, Papa! Mama's got bubbles!" I want to hand out my party favors, bubble pipes. I wiggle as Papa takes forever to snap us with his new Kodak Baby Brownie.

"Sit still. Just one more," he says. He has already taken lots of photos of me opening presents and blowing out birthday candles.

Jimmy and Sandra sit like stones for Papa, but just before the shutter clicks, I stick out my tongue to make him laugh. Finally, he says, "All done," and the three of us race into the front yard, where Mama set a huge bowl of bubble solution on the brown grass. I pass out the bubble pipes as she pushes up our sleeves. In no time at all, Jimmy and I blow all sorts of bubbles that sparkle in the sun. Sandra is still a baby (she hasn't turned three yet), so we try to show her how. Her first attempt is awful. She sucks in instead of blowing out. I talk her into trying again, and this time she blows a stream of shiny balls that catch the breeze and dance across the yard. The best bubbles are the biggest and the ones that last the longest. We chase and try to catch them in our hands. Sometimes Jimmy and I blow them in each other's faces. By the time Auntie Marilee comes to pick up Jimmy and Sandra, all of us are sticky and slippery wet to the elbows.

"Looks like a successful party," says Auntie.

"I'm afraid the bubbles got a bit messy," says Mama.

"I'd call it good clean fun," Auntie says. The adults laugh. "Thanks, Celeste. You, too, Louis." Then she gives the order, "Gotta go, kids. Come get dried off."

As Jimmy wipes off his wet hands and arms on a terry cloth towel, Aunt Marilee bends over and whispers in his ear.

"Thanks for inviting me to your party," Jimmy says to me in a voice so low he sounds like a cow.

"What do you say to Jimmy?" Mama asks me.

"You're welcome," I say.

"And for the gift?" Mama reminds me.

"Thanks for the harmonica. And the paint set," I say, turning to Sandra, who jumps into her mama's arms and asks to be carried home.

Jimmy, caring not a whit about the thank-you, grabs his bubble pipe and takes off running.

"Thanks again. I actually napped. First time in ages. Talk to you tomorrow, Celeste," Auntie Marilee says before turning toward home with Sandra atop her swollen belly.

"Greet that brother of mine. Tell Raymond we expect to be the first call he makes once that baby arrives," says Mama as Auntie waddles down the sidewalk.

"Marilee looks so uncomfortable. I hope this baby comes soon," says Papa.

Mama agrees, then turns directly to me and says, "I declare this party over!"

"I declare this party successful!" says Papa, winding the film in his new Brownie.

Later at supper, I wonder, "Am I five now?"

"Let me think about that," says Papa. "You were born at three in the afternoon, so yes, I guess you are."

"Now," Mama says, "let's think about bedtime. It's been a long day, what with no nap."

I hate naps. I'm five years old, and next fall I will be a kindergartner. I'll take a rug to school for rest time, but I won't have to sleep if I don't want to.

"Naps are for babies," I say, "and for Mrs. Fullerton." After a pause I add, "How old do you have to be before you can nap sitting up? Or is Mrs. Fullerton just odd that way?"

"When you're as old as Mrs. Fullerton and have no one around to help with the chores, you have the right to nap any which way, whenever," says Papa.

"You look like you could fall asleep sitting up right now, Marguerite Jonella," adds Mama. "Early bedtime tonight. For everyone. I'm exhausted!"

"Me, too," Papa says. "How about you, MJ?"

Papa is the only one who calls me MJ. I don't mind. In fact, it makes me happy to hear him say it. It's like we have something special between us.

I crawl into bed, and after goodnight kisses, I listen to Mama and Papa talk quietly in the living room. I'm cozy, and when I'm not remembering my party, I think about Mrs. Fullerton, who is alone in her big house across the street. I think Mrs. Fullerton is probably the oldest person I know. Sometimes she knocks on our front door and gives us yummy baked breads or sweets. Mama always says, "C'mon in. I was just ready to put some coffee on." I don't drink coffee, so Mama pours me a glass of milk. Then the three of us sit around the kitchen table and munch on date-filled cookies or Swedish coffee cake or rhubarb custard pie, whatever Mrs. Fullerton brings.

I'm not sure if Mrs. Fullerton cooks for the pure joy of it or because she likes the act of giving. There's no one at her house to feed. Her husband is "in the ground but thankfully here in Davis. Tyler isn't." I heard her say it. When I asked Papa what she meant, he told me that Mrs. Fullerton's son Tyler was a soldier in the Great War, and no one is quite sure what happened to him. Maybe Mrs. Fullerton bakes often just to be ready in case he surprises her someday. I think she must get tired of waiting.

Mrs. Fullerton always asks me lots of questions when we sit with Mama around our kitchen table. She likes to know how old I am. She always asks about kindergarten, even though I have no idea what kindergarten is like. I haven't started yet.

"Run along now," Mama always says after I've finished my treat and milk. After I leave, Mama and Mrs. Fullerton talk in softer voices. Sometimes I notice that when Mama gets up to refill Mrs. Fullerton's coffee cup, she reaches for a box of tissues and sets it down right between them.

Once Mama asked if I would like to return a bottle of vanilla to Mrs. Fullerton. It was the first time I was allowed to cross the street by myself. I walked to the end of the yard, looked both ways like I'm supposed to, and then ran across while Mama watched. Mrs. Fullerton, even though she was slowly swaying back and forth in her porch swing, didn't see me coming. Her eyes were shut. It took two tries of calling to her before she jerked, snorted, and opened her eyes.

"Caught me nappin'," she said with a chuckle that jiggled the skin under her chin.

She didn't look like herself until she picked up her silver-rimmed glasses and fitted them on her nose and around her ears. She smiled at me and asked, "So, Marguerite Jonella, how is kindergarten?"

13

*T*he Pinot Noir was a treat, but I was careful not to call it an earned reward. That designation would have given the soothing, red liquid too much standing. Yet, a silent toast to my first full day in paradise seemed in order, so with glass in hand, I stepped out onto the lanai. Strong trade winds that had whipped palm fronds and upended beach chairs earlier in the afternoon had relaxed into comfortable breezes. This truly was paradise, I decided.

Standing at the metal railing, I studied the trajectory of the sinking sun and wondered if a set of palm trees near the beach might obscure the view. Down on the grass, activity increased as people strolled toward the water's edge in anticipation of sunset. To guarantee an unobstructed view, I decided to join them.

The elevator stood empty when I stepped inside and pushed the button for ground level. On its way down, it stopped on the second floor and opened for an elderly man and woman. Both sported bronze tans and offered congenial greetings. He tenderly assisted her as she navigated her walker over the threshold.

"Did you just arrive?" the gentleman asked me.

Not sure if he was noting a new face on the premises

or simply surmising by the whiteness of my skin, I replied, "Late last night."

"So this is your first sunset. Should be a beautiful one. Just enough clouds," he said.

"Enjoy," his companion added as the elevator came to a stop on ground level and opened for all of us.

He held the elevator door, then nodded for me to exit first. I stepped out, hesitated for a moment to orient myself, then followed a family of four through a tunnel-like walkway that led to the pool, shuffleboard courts, and the immense stretch of manicured grass between the condos and the beach. I joined the stream of condo inhabitants who were ambling toward the shoreline in search of a good vantage point for the evening's sunset.

Instinctively, about halfway to the beach, I kicked off my sandals and wiggled my toes in the cool, comfortable grass. The thick, short turf resembled a golf green. Millie had explained that the strip of greenway closest to the beach was actually a public park tended by the groundskeepers of the Maui Sunset. So immaculate were both that I found it difficult to establish when I had exited one and entered the other.

On the southern edge of the green space, a small public parking lot provided slots for the locals. Singletons, families, and pets spilled into the welcoming green space and joined the vacationers near the water's edge. Excited canines, off leash and roaming freely, resembled schoolchildren at recess. Comfortable with what appeared to be a familiar ritual, they raced around kite flyers, members of a yoga class, and a circle of twelve-steppers. "God, grant me the serenity . . ." wafted in the air.

One elderly dog with a graying muzzle plodded over to me as I walked toward the edge of a grassy berm that dropped two feet down to the sandy beach. His black and white markings and the build of his hindquarters resembled a border collie, but his square head and solid shoulders did not quite fit. He stopped in front of me, so I held out a hand for him to sniff. Like an old soul, he looked up with entrancing, cobalt-blue eyes. His owner, a short, stocky, middle-aged man in a faded T-shirt and shorts, strolled over.

"Looks like Frankie has made a friend," he said.

"Frankie?" I asked.

"Like Mr. Blue Eyes Sinatra," he added with a chuckle.

"Ah," I said. "Looks like Frankie is enjoying the evening."

"Favorite part of his day. He gets to see his pals. Just can't keep up with 'em anymore," he said, gesturing to the other dogs who were running in circles around the open space. "We come almost every night. Right, Frankie?"

Frankie seemed unfazed by the attention. He slowly moseyed off with his owner a few steps behind. I scanned the heterogeneous crowd. A cross section of the world, all ages and ethnicities, occupied the grassy berm above the sandy shoreline. Simultaneously, in hushed unison, everyone turned west and paused as the brilliant globe fell into the sea. Someone on a lanai behind us blew a conch; a deep, sustained "Ummmmm . . ." announced to all within earshot that the sun had disappeared.

The crowd dissipated, too soon, I thought, because the beauty continued for the patient few who stayed to gaze westward. The gentleman in the elevator had been correct in his prediction. Once the sun vanished below the horizon, the clouds became costars in the night's production. Reflected light transformed them into striations of gold, peach, and red. Within minutes, the glow spread across the horizon and upward until every billow joined in the celestial fire. Slowly, the sky morphed from tints of warm to shades of cool: reddish golds to pinks, pinks to lavenders,

lavenders to deep purples, and finally, darkness. Those who had remained with me on the berm peeled away and, with the aid of cell phone flashlights, retreated toward the flickering tiki torches that surrounded the pool. A young couple walked back with arms around each other. I wondered about their story. One thing for sure, they had avoided our mistake. Harry and I had waited too long.

By the time I reached the condo, I was enveloped in a familiar melancholy. Like a dark gauze, it draped over me, distorting my view and allowing through its loose weave just enough air so I would not suffocate. I wanted to pour another glass of wine. Instead, I retreated to the bedroom. With the help of the TV remote, I searched for a channel that would drown out the quiet. Dispensing with dinner, I set the TV's auto shutoff for sixty minutes, climbed into bed with my companion, the Maui Visitor Channel, and closed my eyes.

14

*O*nce again, I arose in the dark, this time after a fitful night's sleep. Coffee and my MP notebook accompanied me to the lanai. Forgoing the glare of the overhead light, I chose indirect illumination from the lamp in the living area and sat down for my morning ritual. Morning pages began as any journal might with a chronological recollection of the preceding day's events. I described the sunrise, the malasadas, the beach, the sunset, the story of five-year-old Marguerite, and, equally important, my gratitude for my written accomplishment. But as often happens when I write whatever streams out of my pen, a word unexpectedly appeared. With Harry's anniversary only a day away, I would have expected the word to be *grief* or *depression* or *sadness*. Instead, the word *fear* popped up, and like an unavoidable head-on collision, no diversionary maneuvering was able to deny its presence. I was quite sure that the glorious sunset of the preceding day had kick-started my descent into despair, and to be so overtaken by something so beautiful saddened and upset me.

Worse, I had chosen to remove myself from my people, my tribe, those willing to drop everything and to arrive at my doorstep when needed. Last night I had needed them, like those first few nights after Harry died when the Write Women, despite my meek protestations, took turns sleeping on my couch until I could face an empty house alone. Right now, I needed their companionship. I needed their living examples of crazy normalcy. I needed them to cajole me, to cushion me from the world. But I was alone and had no one but myself to blame for choosing solitude for the anniversary of Harry's death. As I wrote, I questioned not only my decision-making but also, to a degree, my sanity and definitely my ability to handle May 16, which was now only a day away. I had hoped to fill the day with exploration and beautiful, tropical distractions. But I had no plan. *If a sunset can dissolve me,* I wrote in my morning pages, *I fear, what else?*

I closed the day's entry with a chastisement for self-pity and a reminder of Mama's advice for negative thoughts: "Name them. Claim them. That's important, Marguerite. But then you must put them high on a shelf, so you'll need a ladder to get them down." In my MP notebook, I had named them and claimed them, but the written words also confirmed that I had not stashed them out of reach.

Sunrise helped. The south and western sides of the island awoke as streams of sunlight peeked over the top of Haleakala. Feeling a bit disoriented, I opened up the map with May's notations, located the airport, and reconstructed the route the van driver had taken to Kihei in South Maui. I studied South Kihei Road and discovered names for all the lovely beaches I had passed the day before.

The map made it easy to see why this Hawaiian island was nicknamed the Valley Isle. Two volcanic land masses, Haleakala and the West Maui Mountains, met in the valley between. According to May, viewing Haleakala's dormant crater at sunrise was a breathtaking activity. She had suggested that, if interested, I should make the trek to the crater's rim early in my visit, while my body clock was still waking me before dawn. Although I was up in time to make the trek, neither driving up the switchbacks alone nor going with a tour group appealed. I had traveled to Maui to write, I justified, so a round trip to the crater's rim at sunrise was nixed for an effortless drive to Millie's favorite farmers market. After downing a day-old malasada, I grabbed a reusable shopping bag and headed out.

"It's Aloha Friday / No work 'til Monday . . ." The catchy tune streamed from the radio as I pulled into a small parking lot next to the farmers market. Golden papaya, so unlike the dark green, unappealing fruit available in Minnesota, sat in shallow crates on tables in the sun alongside ripe pineapples and bananas. As I pondered my selection, a worker offered his assistance and selected two papayas, one ready to eat immediately and one that would fully ripen in a couple of days. He suggested serving the papaya with a slice of lemon, so I dropped a small one into my shopping basket along with a pineapple that he guaranteed would be sweet and juicy. I moved into the tent, where I perused and selected an array of veggies, jelly, honey, and bread.

The shopping experience was a welcomed distraction. I returned to the condo and immediately cut and seeded one papaya and served half of it with a squeeze of lemon. Smooth and delicious, it disappeared easily, so I returned to the kitchen for the second half. Having run out of delaying tactics, I grabbed the dreaded manuscript and headed out to the lanai.

To the uninformed, the stack of pages looked impressive. Even the title, *Seldom What It Seems*, suggested the likelihood of a decent read for those who loved intrigue. I attempted to reread it with fresh eyes as if the characters were appearing for the first time. Thirty pages in, as a reader, I felt betrayed. As the writer, I was embarrassed.

Years earlier, with help from teachers and other supportive writers at the Loft Literary Center in Minneapolis, I reconfirmed what I already knew. Creating something worthy with written words was not easy. It required shaking off fears, lowering one's head, and plowing forward until characters took form and the plot developed into what might eventually become a rough draft. Next came fleshing out, editing, deleting, and rewriting, followed by more editing, deleting, and rewriting, until the final piece was a tightly honed work of art. At some point, the writer was the one who declared the finish line crossed, which meant, in my case, a manuscript was ready for Georgia's eyes.

Coming up with a decent rough draft was always the scary part for me. It required trust in my own creativity and strict determination to fight off battles with self-doubt, procrastination, and writer's block. Once the bones of the story appeared, however, I usually relaxed and began the enjoyable work of fleshing out description and plot and culling out the unnecessary. Bearing in mind my audience and what might appeal, I eventually picked up an editor's red pen and critically analyzed the story. I added fat and muscle when needed, then ligaments and tendons to hold it all together, until, finally, I had created a body of work that I felt others would enjoy. Until a year ago, the process had been exhilarating.

In contrast, *Seldom What It Seems,* from its inception, had been different and difficult. Assuming grief was the culprit, I slogged on for nine months hoping that time would remedy the defects. The most upsetting aspect of the rough draft was the voice, which sounded schizophrenic, untrustworthy, and unbelievable, even after multiple rewrites. Astute readers, I feared, might wonder if different people had authored different sections. Unfortunately, they would be right. Each page reflected whichever slice of the fractured Marguerite showed up to write on that particular day. No wonder I was unable to pull it together. The story was screaming to be euthanized, and I wanted it buried—all of it, that is, except the title. I loved the title, but that had nothing to do with the text and everything to do with Mama.

Retrieving the pages of the birthday book, I searched for a photo of Mama and picked up a pen.

MARGUERITE—AGE 10
April 30, 1945
"Marguerite's 10th Birthday
With Just the Five of Us"

A tenth birthday should be a day of gladness, and Mama and Papa try to make it so. So do Nana and Grampa. But Jimmy, Sandra, and Mikey have moved to Ohio with Auntie Marilee to be closer to her kin, so this is the first birthday I can remember without cousins to help me celebrate. Papa snaps the picture as I blow out the candles of my birthday cake in Grampa and Nana's apartment above the shoe store. Everyone around the table is smiling, but there is sadness everywhere. And no one mentions Uncle Raymond. Instead, the adults talk about the war.

I love dressing up, and today Mama lets me wear my new Easter dress, although I probably shouldn't call it that. Not this year. We don't go to church anymore. Mama says I can call it my dress-up dress, since it doesn't have to be Easter or even Sunday to wear it. It has lace and ribbon, even pockets on the sides. After she finished sewing it, she took me downtown to Papa and Grampa's store and let me pick out a new pair of patent leathers.

"Can't we go to church so I can wear my new outfit?" I ask Mama.

"You can wear your dress anytime you'd like, Marguerite, but we're taking a break from church," says Mama.

"Because they wouldn't bury Uncle Raymond?" I ask.

"It's complicated, Marguerite."

"He was selfish to leave Jimmy, Sandra, and Mikey without a daddy," I say.

"It's seldom what it seems, Marguerite," says Mama.

"But he'll burn in hell. Killin' yourself is a mortal sin. The Bible says."

"Nonsense, Marguerite. Jesus was the first to greet your uncle Raymond. Trust me on this."

"But the church says . . ."

"That's why we're taking a break from church for awhile."

"But what do I do with my sins, Mama? They're stackin' up without confession."

"We gave up church, Marguerite, not God. Talk to Him straight. He'll hear you."

"It doesn't seem that He could," I say.

"Things are seldom what they seem," Mama says again.

15

*T*he cell phone buzzed, and I glanced at the caller ID.

"Hi, Millie," I said with all the cheerfulness I could muster.

"Aloha, MJ. Just checking in. Hope this is a good time."

"It's a perfect time. Oh, Millie, I feel like such an ingrate. I meant to call you yesterday—to thank you. Your place is fabulous."

"So all's well then," she said with a slight edge of doubt. "Shuttle work out? Car rental?"

"Like clockwork," I said. "And I assume I have you to thank for my beautiful lei. Not everyone was getting one."

"All first timers to Maui deserve a lei," she said.

"Well, it's gorgeous."

Answering a slew of Millie's questions, I summarized my day of travel and my positive first impressions of Maui, the Maui Sunset, and her condo. I avoided any mention of my partial meltdown after sunset.

"Tomorrow's the dreaded day. Any plans?"

I hesitated. "I've been checking out the map and your notes. Think I'll try to find Kepaniwai Park. Is that how you pronounce it?"

"Sounds about right. Good plan. It's beautiful and easy

to find. Just remember to stay right at the fork once you head up the valley from Wailuku."

"Right at the fork," I repeated.

"I'll be seeing the gang after my doctor's appointment tomorrow. Any messages?"

"Doctor? Everything okay?"

"Fine, just routine. I know they'll want an update on you, so thought I'd make a quick call."

"Just tell them everything is good, and that tomorrow will be what it will be," I said.

"One more milestone." Millie paused before she asked, "Have you had a chance to do any writing?"

"Actually, yes, a little, but not on the manuscript."

"Oh?"

"That's a subject for another time," I said. "Aloha to everyone tomorrow."

"Stay in touch, MJ. We care," she said with an uncharacteristic softness that she quickly rectified. "Just remember the time difference! No calling after 5 p.m. Hawaiian time. I don't want you waking me up."

Millie's call buoyed my spirits. She sounded upbeat, strong, glad that I was enjoying her favorite places and her Maui home. After hanging up the phone, I realized I had unwittingly finalized my plans for Harry's anniversary. May had described Kepaniwai Park on the plane, and its history and purpose intrigued me. Millie had also listed it in her notes as a must-see. So, not wishing to look like I was floundering, I had blurted out the name of the park in answer to Mille's inquiry. Decision made.

I grabbed a Maui travel book from Mille's bookshelf and headed to the lanai. Within the Central Maui section, a short paragraph described Kepaniwai as a memorial park dedicated to preserving the island's heritages: Hawaiian, New England American, Chinese, Japanese, Filipino,

Portuguese, Korean, and Puerto Rican. Maui residents from each ethnic community had transformed small sections of the park into gardens and architectures characteristic of their respective cultures. Located in the lush 'Iao Valley, the park also offered pavilions for resting and picnicking. It sounded like the perfect place to distract me on May 16.

On the grounds below the lanai, people of all shapes and sizes were enjoying the afternoon sun and the cooling, brisk trade winds. Unsecured beach towels flapped like flags. One blew across the pool deck and landed in the water. It slowly sank before it was retrieved by a young boy with diving goggles. In the deep end, three women socialized. Each held onto a visor with one hand and a noodle, a long, tubelike float, with the other. Sun worshippers chose lounge chairs and baked to various shades of brown and red. On the lawn near the ocean, two men and a woman, all outfitted in short-sleeved wetsuits, unfurled huge, multicolored kites and fought to control them in the wind. When I checked a few minutes later, all had somehow launched their kiteboards and were now skimming the waves. Regrettably, I had missed their takeoffs.

According to Millie, the beach in front of the Maui Sunset, although a perfect place to watch the sunset, was less desirable than other Maui beaches for swimming. Here, the shallow water rolled over submerged rocks and deposited stones and bits of coral onto the grainy sand. Walking the beach barefoot was less than ideal, but for a person with water shoes, the shoreline was perfect for a solitary stroll. I followed Millie's advice and dug through her play closet, which contained an assortment of useful items for the beach: chairs, towels, beach umbrella, even a boogie board. Discovering water shoes in a variety of sizes, I retrieved a pair that fit and headed down to the beach.

Thanks to the footwear, I enjoyed both a walk in the sand and an occasional cooling wave that lapped over my toes. Out on the water, a fourth kiteboarder had joined the other three. All were skimming back and forth across the water's surface. Like acrobats, they took turns skillfully catching the wind in their kites and parachuting into the sky. Elle, who loved snowboarding, would appreciate the athleticism, I thought, so I located a shady spot on the grassy berm, sat down, positioned my cell phone, and recorded the show. After previewing the video, I sent it with a simple text message.

Aloha!

Within minutes the phone buzzed, and a message appeared.

Amazing! Thanks. Hope you are having an awesome time. All's good here.

The technology that provided instant communication across thousands of miles continued to amaze.

By the time I returned to the grounds of the Maui Sunset, the outdoor activities of the day were subsiding. Most people had vacated the pool. Some had disappeared into condos to get cleaned up and ready for the evening. I had already decided to view the night's sunset from the security of Millie's lanai, so I rinsed off my feet and immediately headed up.

After a bite of supper, I carried a dish of passion fruit sherbet to the lanai and settled in for the night's show. Dogs, some familiar, including Frankie, jumped from parked vehicles as locals joined vacationers for sunset. Once again, animals romped as their owners visited. Activities resembled those of the night before, right down to the twelve-step gathering. When the conch once again announced the sun's final seconds, I stood at the lanai's railing to view its departure.

Unlike the night before, however, the golden globe dropped out of a cloudless sky. Without any reflected brilliance, the horizon quickly turned gray and then dark. Thankfully, on this night, the darkness of the evening did not heighten my anxieties. Instead, an inner peace comforted my tired spirit. Without analysis, I welcomed the calm.

16

*H*arry's anniversary had arrived. Calculating the time change, I realized I had slept through the hour that marked his passing. This fact both surprised and comforted me. In Minnesota, noon was approaching, and a year ago at that moment, Harry's body was already cold. He had been dead one year and five hours. And I was still standing.

A letter to Harry filled my morning pages. With a box of tissues at the ready, I thanked him for finding me and loving me. I strengthened my resolve to honor him with pleasant memories as I showered and picked out a sundress. Retrieving my lei from the refrigerator, I placed it over my head. Its cool dampness and tropical fragrance stirred the senses as I gathered the day's necessities and headed to the car for the twenty-five minute drive to Wailuku, the county seat of Maui County.

Once I passed the farmers market, I angled west toward the wind turbines. Then at the base of the valley, I turned north. Apprehension about navigating city traffic subsided a few minutes later as I entered the outskirts of the sleepy town of Wailuku. Apparently, few residents stirred early on a Saturday morning. Within minutes, I passed two churches, a school, and a public library, all surrounded by lush, tropical foliage. When I stopped for a red light at the center of town, the cell phone's GPS directed me to turn left onto Highway 320. Within seconds, I was leaving Wailuku behind and heading uphill and into a rugged valley. Similar to Millie's reminder, the GPS instructed me to stay right at the fork. Immediately after the divide, the road narrowed and dropped downward before climbing again through deep vegetation and beautiful flowering trees. After a couple of minutes and several winding turns, the GPS squawked, "Your destination is on your left."

I turned onto a narrow paved road that led to the small parking lot of Kepaniwai Park and Heritage Gardens, then stepped out of the car and into the cool humidity of a tropical rainforest. Although the rising sun promised a beautiful morning, an earlier shower had left the pavement wet and the trees dripping. In the span of twenty-five minutes, I had driven from the arid west side of Haleakala into a rainforest. Having grown up in Minnesota, I found this sudden change in ecosystems remarkable.

Only a few cars occupied the park's small parking lot. I scanned the surroundings, then headed across the asphalt to examine an ornately painted replica of a Korean temple. Pausing often to investigate unique gardens and buildings, I circled through a Portuguese villa to areas dedicated to Native Hawaiians, American missionaries, Filipinos, and Puerto Ricans. Finding each site fascinating, I renewed my commitment to completing my reread of Michener's *Hawaii*, the book that so aptly described each ethnic group's migration, including the unique hardships and the extraordinary perseverance required of each wave of new settlers. Circling back, I paused for an extended time at a Chinese pagoda and read about Dr. Sun Yat-sen, a man whose influence positively impacted both China and Hawaii.

An elderly gentleman in the adjacent Japanese heritage site diverted my attention. With impressive agility, he crouched down and pulled weeds that were encroaching on a walkway that wound from a ceremonial teahouse to an immaculate Japanese garden. Next to him stood a woman. Her tiny physique and shortly cropped, gray hair reminded me of May. I almost called out her name. Then she turned. I had been mistaken. Disappointed, I finished reading the history of Dr. Sun Yat-sen before turning and walking toward my final destination, the Japanese gardens and teahouse.

"Marguerite?"

The voice had come from the hillside where a stone pathway disappeared behind giant philodendron. A woman descended into full view and smiled.

"May?"

Dressed in a multicolored tunic and white crop pants, she looked as fresh as the greenery that surrounded her. She walked over, and we exchanged greetings.

"Come. I would like you to meet my family." May ushered me to the man and woman on the other side of the pond. "Father, this is my friend, Marguerite. I met her on the plane Wednesday. Marguerite, this is my father, Keniji Sato."

"How do you do, Mr. Sato," I replied.

He smiled and remained silent.

"And this is my sister, Fern. Fern, Marguerite."

No wonder Fern had reminded me of May, I thought. The familial resemblance was remarkable.

"Hello, Marguerite," said Fern as she extended her hand.

"So, you decided to visit our heritage gardens," said May. "I'm delighted."

"They are beautiful. Thank you so much for suggesting that I come."

"You picked a good day," Fern said, glancing at the sun. "Often it rains."

"It is a beautiful day. Do you come here often?" I asked.

"Usually on Saturday mornings, we go to the swap meet. But today Father wanted to come here first. He loves to tend the Japanese garden. It is one of his favorite places," May said.

"So, we have you to thank for this beautiful place," I said, turning to Mr. Sato.

Again, he smiled but remained silent, and I wondered if he spoke English.

"Mauians of Japanese descent take responsibility for this area. Pick up trash. Pull weeds. We honor our ancestors," said Fern. "Let us show you."

Fern led me to a bronze statue of a diminutive man and woman, both dressed from head to foot in layers of clothing, large brimmed hats, and sturdy shoes, most likely for protection from the sun during long hours in the sugar cane fields. The woman held a hoe and the man, a blade. I read the dedication inscribed on a plaque positioned at their feet. The last line struck me: *Our tears of gratitude now transcend time to mingle with their tears of sacrifice.*

"Beautiful!" I said, appreciating the tender prose.

"Our grandparents emigrated from Japan. First our grandfather. Then our grandmother," said Fern.

"This is how we picture them," said May, gesturing to the statue of the field workers. After a pause, she added, "We are ready to take a break. Would you like to join us?"

"Yes, very much," I said.

"I'll get Father settled. You get the picnic," Fern said as she headed back toward her father, who was kneeling once more.

"Not really a picnic. Just a little snack," said May.

I followed her to a white Honda that was parked close to

my Prius. She opened the trunk and pulled out blankets, a wicker picnic basket, and a small cooler.

"Please excuse my father," May said. "He suffers from memory issues. He does not mean to be rude."

"Your father has a very sweet smile," I said as I picked up the cooler.

We rendezvoused with Fern and Mr. Sato at a table in one of the open-air picnic pavilions. After we draped the table and benches with blankets, Fern assisted her father as he slowly positioned himself on a bench, while May opened the cooler and pulled out small plastic containers and a quart of orange juice. Then she counted out paper plates, plastic cups, and napkins from a stash inside the picnic basket.

"This is one of Father's favorite snacks," May said, removing the plastic wrap from a block of rice that was similar in size to a bar of soap. The rice was wrapped in a thin, black layer of seaweed. She cut the contents in half and placed one half on the plate in front of me and the other on Mr. Sato's plate. Then she repeated the procedure for Fern and herself.

"Musubi," explained Fern. "Seared Spam wrapped in rice and nori."

"I've read that Hawaiians are big on Spam," I said.

"Delicious," said Mr. Sato. His voice was gentle and clear.

"I agree," I said after taking a bite. "This is a new taste experience for me. Do you know, Mr. Sato, that Spam was first produced in my home state of Minnesota? In Austin, Minnesota, actually—not far from the Twin Cities." I was babbling.

"Minnesota. Fort Snelling," said Mr. Sato.

May and Fern exchanged glances and smiles.

"Fort Snelling is about thirty minutes from my house," I said. "How do you know it?"

Mr. Sato took another bite of musubi followed by a swig of juice and a very long pause. I feared that I had either disrespected his privacy or challenged his memory.

"I trained at Fort Snelling—during the war," he said. "It was a long time ago."

Mr. Sato stared off. I feared that any lucid connection he had made was closing off. But after another long pause, he returned my gaze and locked his eyes on mine.

"I loved Minnesota. But the winter!" Mr. Sato faked a shiver and then laughed with such vigor that he shook the table.

"Father was trained in military intelligence," said May.

"At Fort Snelling?" I asked, bewildered that I had not heard of that part of Fort Snelling's history.

I had directed my question to May, but Mr. Sato answered. "Yes, your Governor Stassen was willing to take a chance on Japanese. Other states refused."

I tried to keep the conversation going. "Take a chance?"

"After Pearl Harbor, Americans feared us. But we were Americans, too. Nisei." It was as if Mr. Sato's brain had warmed up.

"First-generation Japanese Americans," I said, remembering the term introduced to me by a high school social studies teacher of Japanese descent.

"Yes, yes. My parents were born in Japan, so they were Issei. I was born in Hawaii, so I am an American citizen. Nisei."

"And you went to Fort Snelling," I said, hoping he would continue.

"Many Nisei like me speak and read and write Japanese—and English—both. After Pearl, they sent us to Military Intelligence Service Language School—in Minnesota. To be translators," he said, with lengthy pauses. "Your Governor Stassen was willing to take a chance on Japanese.

Other states refused," he repeated. "Do we have more musubi?"

"It has been a long time since you have spoken about your training," said May as she unwrapped another block of musubi and set the entire piece on his plate next to two slices of pineapple.

Ignoring her comment, Mr. Sato focused on his snack, so May turned to me and asked, "How are you liking Maui? Have you been able to see much of our beautiful island?"

"Until this morning, I have stayed around Kihei, just relaxing mostly. But I am so glad that I ventured up here today. I can't tell you how much it means to see you again and to meet your family." Then before I even realized I could, I told them about Harry and his death and how visiting with them was making the first anniversary of that terrible day bearable. May and Fern listened intently and offered condolences. Mr. Sato continued to devour the musubi.

"Marguerite is an author," explained May to her family. "She is in Maui to work on her next book." She turned to me and asked, "Are you finding our island conducive?"

"So far my experience with writing has been mixed. I'm still having trouble with the book. But I'm revisiting some personal memories from the past and writing about those instead. That has been very enjoyable. So, all things considered, I guess I am finding your island conducive."

"Good. Write your stories before you can no longer remember," said Mr. Sato, who had been silent for such a long time that I thought he had become disconnected from the conversation. After another long pause, he added, "We need to show this woman Kuka'emoku."

"Marguerite, Father. Her name is Marguerite," said May.

"Like the daisy," he said, referring to the yellow and white flower by that name.

"Yes," I said. "Like the daisy, Mr. Sato."

"And you can call me Ken," he said, "like—no flower I can think of." Then he let out a belly laugh, and the table rocked again. "Time to move."

"If you have time, let us take you up the road to 'Iao Valley State Park. It's not far," said Fern. "We would love for you to see it. No one should visit this valley without stopping there."

"I certainly have time, and it sounds wonderful," I said.

"We will drive," said May, repacking the cooler. "You can leave your car here. The state park is at the end of the road, so we will be returning this way."

The four of us climbed into the Honda. With Fern behind the wheel, we continued up the valley until the road petered out at the parking lot of 'Iao Valley State Park. Fern located a parking space near the park's entrance. As we approached the entranceway on foot, a large group of noisy tourists filed out of the park and headed in a steady stream toward a tour bus. We threaded our way through them to a display of large signs that described in words and graphics a bloody battle in 1790, when Kamehameha I defeated the Mauians in his quest to unify the Hawaiian islands under his rule. By the time we finished the history lesson, the tour bus had pulled away and the park had reclaimed its quiet ambiance. Fern and May led the way down a narrow asphalt path. Mr. Sato proceeded at a slower pace. I hung back with him.

"This is a sacred place," said Mr. Sato. As we walked, he lucidly explained the importance of the valley to the Native Hawaiians. He paused occasionally to point out tropical flowers or lush vegetation. When we arrived at a small bridge that traversed a rushing stream, he stopped about halfway across and gestured toward a towering pillar of rock covered in lush greenery.

"Kuka'emoku!" he said.

"Also known as The Needle," said Fern. "It's over 1,200 feet high."

"This is what happens to your lover when you defy your parents," said Mr. Sato clearly, as if he had said it a hundred times before. Quizzically, I glanced at May. She smiled and waited for her father to continue. Haltingly at first, he explained. "The gods, Maui and—"

"Hina," prompted Fern.

"Hina—did not like the lover of their daughter 'Iao—so they turned him into stone." Mr. Sato smiled broadly as he pointed to the towering pillar.

"Ouch," I said.

"My daughter May married well," said Mr. Sato. "Did you marry?"

"Yes, Mr. Sato. I married a wonderful man," I answered. May placed her arm around my waist as if to apologize for her father's forgetfulness.

"And your parents approved?" he asked.

"My parents died when I was fifteen, but my grandmother, who finished raising me, approved of Harry and loved him very much."

"You have suffered much loss. You are of strong stock," said Mr. Sato. "Just like Japan, Minnesota has strong women." I appreciated the endearing compliment. I was equally grateful that his faulty short-term memory had not erased our Minnesota connection.

We continued over the bridge and ascended steps to a better vantage point of The Needle and the 'Iao Valley. Neither Fern nor May was concerned about their father's physical ability to climb the taxing ascent, but they lovingly positioned themselves behind and beside him in case he might stumble. Finally, arriving at the overlook, we stood in silence for several minutes. The lushness of the valley, accompanied by the sounds of rushing streams, affirmed the sacred history. It was easy to imagine why early Hawaiians chose this space to honor their gods and bury their royalty.

We descended and chose a fork on the path that led us down to a botanical garden. Often Mr. Sato stopped to examine and explain. He pointed out each species of tropical flower, plant, and fruit tree and described in great detail its characteristics and growing pattern. We stopped for a lengthy period in front of a water-filled plant bed, and, with passionate lucidity, he delivered a botany lesson on the planting and growing of taro, a plant that could breathe under water and whose leaves and roots were valuable commodities.

Abruptly, Mr. Sato announced, "We go now." Accompanying his declaration was a mental retreat. He remained silent as we walked back to the car and drove the return trip.

Back at Kepaniwai Park, I thanked my three friends for an extraordinary morning and turned toward my car.

"Please, wait," said May. She disappeared inside the Japanese teahouse and quickly returned with a beautiful orange flower on a long, thick stem.

"A bird of paradise," I said, recognizing its distinctive shape.

"We brought a floral arrangement for the teahouse this morning, but I think this flower should go home with you, in memory of your Harry on this day," May said.

"It's beautiful," I said. "What a thoughtful gift. It will remind me to think beautiful thoughts of Harry today. And it will also remind me of a lovely morning with your family."

"When the flower wilts, perhaps you will take it down to the ocean and set it adrift," May said with a smile.

Silenced by the lump in my throat, I nodded.

17

*I*ndicating a gradual adjustment in my body clock or perhaps simple exhaustion, I managed to sleep not only past 4 a.m. but also through the 5 a.m. rooster crows. The ocean was already sparkling in the sunlight by the time I settled on the lanai with a cup of coffee and my MP notebook. Harry's anniversary, the day I had been dreading for months, was now history. Immortalizing the day in my morning pages, I noted in great detail the serendipitous hours with May, Fern, and Mr. Sato followed by an afternoon of pleasurable reading intermittently interrupted by phone calls from each of the Write Women. Like sentries assigned to protect my mental health, each in turn had checked in.

Claire had called first. She attacked the anniversary head on by recollecting the morning of Harry's death from her perspective. I appreciated her forthrightness. It legitimized rather than minimized the tragedy and reminded me of her steadfastness during a time when I needed unwavering support. This time she was offering long-distance comfort. I was pleased that I could tell her about an outing that had reconnected me with May, the calm and gentle woman I had met on the plane.

"Good, so good," she said. "You aren't letting the day own you." She deflected my questions regarding the status of her next cookbook that centered on ingredients from the Saint Paul Farmers' Market. "Enough about that," she said. "I want to know what new taste experiences you've had in Maui. Tell me everything!"

I described malasadas, musubi, and the deliciousness of locally grown veggies and fruits. I avoided sharing the fact that most other meals had been purchased at the grocery store's deli and pitifully eaten in. She quickly answered my inquiries about her family with, "Fine, everyone's fine." Answering her questions about my emotional status, I finally convinced her that I was doing fine as well. Our upbeat conversation reminded me how easily cell phones with unlimited minutes could reconnect people, a thought I tucked away for the next lonely time.

Ginny had called next. In her familiar empathetic style, she gushed out condolences as if Harry had died that very moment. Thanks to my conversation with Claire, I felt grounded and did not let Ginny's emotionalism suck me into sadness. Instead, I thanked her for her concern, and then to pivot the conversation, I asked about Gary and the kids. She enthusiastically gave detailed updates on each of her three sons and seven grandchildren. Regarding her husband, she simply said, "Gary is doing well. Thanks for asking." A recovering alcoholic with six years of sobriety under his belt, Gary had tested Ginny's limits years earlier when his drinking compromised his health, his job, and his relationships with her and the boys. Ginny, a registered nurse, finally realized that her compassionate caregiving had enabled him long enough, so she strengthened her resolve and threatened him with expulsion from the family's home if he did not stop drinking. To the surprise of everyone, he decided it was time for treatment. His recovery experienced some bumps along the way, but he recommitted to sobriety after each relapse and was now active in AA. I described to Ginny the nightly gathering on the lawn and the Serenity Prayer that wafted on the wind.

"It's the part about 'wisdom to know the difference' that usually bamboozles me," Ginny replied, punctuating the comment with her usual laugh. The conversation ended much lighter than it began.

Pat had called at 3 p.m. Taking a different tack, she launched into congratulations. "Hip! Hip! You made it! You have arrived and are about to surpass the one-year mark. I'm just glad the date is no longer looming. Anticipation must have been hell!"

"You're right about that!" I said, acknowledging for the first time that the anticipation of the day had been much worse than the reality.

"Just so you know, I'm holding up a wine glass in your honor. Right now. Cheers!" Then with a softer tone, she added, "I realize there's no magic to being on the other side of one year, but maybe there will be fewer days of awful. That's what I wish for you, MJ."

My friend, Pat, the succinct one. I thanked her for the kind wishes. She was right. She confirmed what I had known in my heart. The twelve-month benchmark was only a point in time. Grief, although somewhat diffused by the passage of time, was destined to be a lifelong companion.

"Fewer days of awful—yes, I'll drink to that," I said as I held up a glass of guava nectar.

I asked for an update on her book release, and we chatted briefly. Thankfully, she did not pry into the status of my book. The only mention was in her sign-off: "Good luck with your writing." Our conversation, short and sweet, left me warmed and affirmed.

Millie had been the last to call.

"Aloha, aloha, aloha," she said as if she had totally forgotten the reason for checking in on Harry's anniversary. "Is the sun shining? Are you eating fresh passion fruit? Any problems with the condo?" Her questions stacked one on top of the other with no time for response.

Millie had little frame of reference for losing a trusted life partner. Owen certainly had not been faithful. But she totally understood being alone in the world with no children for support. Both of us were orphans in our eighties, so, in that regard, we shared common ground. During our conversation, her only reference to the year-old tragedy was a simple, "I'm glad you are one year out." Millie, although a bit flip about the erasure of grief with the passage of time, offered a gentle reminder with her upbeat spirit that I might think about dialing back my own tendency to take the world so seriously.

After I described the wonderful hospitality of May and her family, Millie said, "Glad you're soaking in the warmth of my beautiful island." Clearly, she was referring to more than the sunshine, and a confirmation came with her next statement. "I'm glad you're meeting some locals. Maui is filled with uniquely wonderful people."

As we ended our conversation, I thanked her once more for her generosity. "Maui is exactly what I needed." I expressed my appreciation not only for the use of her lovely condo but also for the gentle nudges that I needed to embark on the trip.

The descriptions of Harry's anniversary, including the morning with May's family and the supportive phone conversations with the Write Women, filled the required three pages of my MP notebook, but I lingered and continued to write as my heart caught up to my head:

The Write Women, once again, individually and collectively, have raised my spirit. I felt surrounded by them yesterday, just as I had the day that Harry died. They do not feel slighted that I chose Maui over Minnesota to spend May 16. They understand. Why wouldn't they? Just like I know them and how each would offer her unique assurances over the phone, they know me. All year they have patiently given their stubborn friend sufficient space to independently find her way through her hardest drama. Yet, they are always in the wings, cheering me on, ready to rush onstage if I freeze. They also understand that just because the one-year mark has been reached, the milestone does not arrive with a magic elixir for the grief of losing Harry. Yesterday these sisters of my own choosing gently reminded me that, lo and behold, I am still standing and deserve to take a bow. Harry's anniversary has been put to rest. I toasted him during a glorious sunset, and I promised him and myself that I would never again refer to May 16 as his "anniversary." That description gives the date too much prominence.

"I'm still learning, Harry!" I said, with raised glass.

And, I could almost hear him say, "Lovin' that about you, MJ!"

With reflections of May 16 captured in my morning pages, I turned my attention to not only the rest of May 17, but also my purpose for coming to Maui in the first place.

I headed down to the beach for an early morning stroll and some serious contemplation. Thanks to low tide, a wide swath of compacted sand allowed for an easy walk. The gentle lapping of the ocean and an occasional mourning dove were my only companions as I pondered my options for moving forward.

If my reason for coming to Maui was to avoid being

in New Brighton on May 16, mission accomplished, and I should consider returning home. A viable option was to book a return flight for the end of the week. That plan would give me a few days to further explore the island before flying back to Minnesota.

However, if an equally valid purpose for my travels was to tend to my craft, then I needed to start with a healthy dose of honesty. As a writer, I was out of practice, lazy, and lacking discipline. I needed structure, like the days when I was on top of my game. Back then I ushered in each morning with morning pages followed by a reading from one of many books on the craft. Only after these mental exercises were accomplished did I turn attention to the current manuscript. Then, to prime the pump, I sat down in front of the computer. Editing as I typed, I added the paragraphs that had been handwritten the day before. Once that was completed, I picked up a pen and notebook and continued the story in longhand, with a daily goal of at least eight hundred fairly well-chosen words. Slowly, the manuscript expanded as plots and subplots unfolded and characters presented themselves. At times, I felt more like a vehicle for their arrivals than their creator. Amazed, I learned to trust the process. Next came the rewrites, which were many, until each manuscript was sent to Georgia. Like a birthing coach, she knew what needed to happen before each book was ready for the reader.

By the time one novel was ready to launch, the next had germinated, and I was eager to transcribe new plots onto paper. At the end of the day, Harry usually found me in front of the computer, totally engulfed.

"Coming to bed, Luv?" he often asked.

"What time is it?" I usually responded, surprised once again by the evaporation of hours.

I sorely missed both the creative spark and Harry's

encouragement. For twelve months, exhaustion rather than enthusiasm had dictated each day. My brain's creative, thought-processing ability had atrophied. Worse, my love for writing had curled up into a tight, inaccessible space. The situation was understandable given the circumstances, but one fact was undeniable: As an author, I was in trouble.

By the time I returned from my stroll, a lukewarm decision had been reached. I tabled temporarily the plan to book a return flight to Minnesota. Instead, I decided to exercise my brain in Maui with a recommitment to a tried-and-true writing process. Millie's condo would become my writing space, as would nearby parks, beaches, and coffee shops. I could ease in, I decided. There was no reason to go home now. In fact, Elle had moved into the house with the intention of being on her own, for awhile at least. Sorting out the pros and cons, I warmed to my decision. As I traveled up by elevator to the third floor, I detected a subtle infusion of energy.

Back in the condo, I scanned Millie's bookshelves and discovered a nice selection of paperbacks dedicated to the craft of writing. Some I had read, a few of them several times. In fact, more than one had been a gift to Millie from me, I discovered, as I read inscriptions. Familiar authors, Welty, Goldberg, Butler, Cameron, and others, were all good choices. But, I wanted something with a little humor, so I selected Anne Lamott's *Bird by Bird* and settled into the lounge chair on the lanai. I had read the book several times, a chapter at a time during my morning writing ritual. Filled with advice for those passionate about writing, the book dispensed hearty measures of honesty, encouragement, and hilarity.

Stretching out with my lower legs in the sun, I read the preface of *Bird by Bird* as if for the first time. I focused on the sentences that Millie had underlined in pencil and tried to imagine what chord each had struck in her. A heavy line was drawn under one sentence in particular, and to further indicate its importance she had changed the period at the end to an exclamation point: "The act of writing turns out to be its own reward!" Yes, that line would resonate with Millie, the woman who cared not one whit about published success.

A metaphor from *Bird by Bird* triggered an underlying sense of guilt about my lack of attention to the basics. Lamott's father, also a writer, compared a writer's skill to that of a pianist's. A gifted pianist, he explained, practices basic scales daily before he or she moves on to more difficult pieces. A writer needs the same level of commitment to the basics to become accomplished in the craft, he continued.

I had become lazy. For a year, I had avoided practicing my craft. Instead, I had scrapped the basics and just plugged along on my next book with the goal of completion rather than perfection. Like a lazy pianist who unsuccessfully attempts to play a Rachmaninoff concerto with under-trained fingers, I had tried to write a book with a brain of mush.

Clearly, it was time to return to the basics. I had already taken baby steps. Since my birthday, I had started off most days with morning pages, and the result had been comforting. Plus, I gave myself credit for the two short writings I had composed about my childhood. "Write what you know," masters tell neophytes and rightly so. Writing about the past, I discovered, was a satisfying exercise on many levels. My life had its own plot, and with hindsight and reflection, I had been able to spin two brief slices into memoir without pressure or expectation. Writing memoir had never been a goal, yet now, with no audience to please, it was becoming an enjoyable and fascinating brain exercise that could continue. The pages of the birthday book

offered a wealth of fodder for additional writing. That possibility felt wonderfully appealing, which was a gift in itself.

But quietly like a rolling fog, a shroud descended over
my newfound excitement. It was not grief this time but
a heavy feeling of responsibility that was blanketing my
enthusiasm. Checking my watch, I grabbed my cell phone
and scrolled through my contacts. As the call was connect-
ing, I realized I had not planned what I intended to say
to the woman who had given me her private number so I
could call her anytime. This was the first time I was calling
Georgia on a Sunday.

"Hi, MJ. So good to hear from you. How are things in
Maui?"

"Good morning, Georgia. Oh, guess it's afternoon in
Chicago," I stuttered. "I'm so sorry to call you on a Sunday."

"No problem, MJ. I've been thinking about you," she
said. "I figured it was a tough week. Everything okay?"

"Maui is wonderful. Beautiful. Quiet." I hesitated, and
Georgia remained silent on the other end. "I've made a
decision, Georgia, and I couldn't wait even one more day to
discuss it with you."

"I'm listening," she responded.

"I want to pull the plug on *Seldom What It Seems.* Resus-
citation isn't possible. I want to bury it once and for all. It's
haunting me, and I need to get the monkey off my back."

"What are you saying? That you're retiring?" she asked.

"Retiring? Hopefully not, but there is no new MJ Burdick mystery on the horizon as far as I can tell. I'm letting
you down, and that's the last thing I ever wanted to do."

The conversation continued, waffling between professional concerns and personal ones. Georgia did not sound
overly shocked at my decision, a fact that sparked a tinge of
sadness. No longer an encourager to keep writing through
my writer's block, she accepted my decision without

protest, and we turned the conversation toward contractual concerns. Thankfully, no advance had been paid.

My guilt was partly assuaged when she told me that she was, in fact, busy with other authors. Subtle envy clouded my relief, until she added, "Never forget that I'm your editor. So your next manuscript, whatever, whenever, comes here first."

"Absolutely," I said.

After another apology from me, we flipped the conversation to more enjoyable topics. She and her significant other, Maureen, "Mo," had finally decided to tie the knot, and they were considering Maui as a destination for a February wedding. I congratulated her on two great choices, her future mate, whom I had met and found grounded and delightful, and Maui as a possible wedding location. The conversation ended on an upbeat note with both of us expressing gratitude for our friendship and a promise to stay in touch.

Relief! How could I express it? Like an anchor, my dead manuscript had hung around my neck. Finally, I had cut the chain. Released from the pressure that had consumed so many waking moments, and fitful dreams if truth be told, I stepped out on the lanai and breathed in fresh salt air. I extended the exhale deeply as if to purge all the pent-up anxiety and frustration that had taken up residence in my gut.

Barely noon, the remainder of the day awaited, and freshly exorcized from both the weight of May 16 and my writing commitment with Georgia, I was eager to embrace the afternoon. I flipped through the pages of the birthday book, selected one, and quickly slipped it and a notebook into my tote. After applying sunscreen, I headed down South Kihei Road by car in search of a beach park with grass and shade. I easily maneuvered the Prius into a newly vacated parking space beside Kama'ole Beach Park III, one of the Kam beaches that Millie loved. I grabbed my tote and a Tommy Bahama beach chair from the trunk and headed across the lawn looking for a shady spot with an ocean view.

Once settled, I studied the birthday photo I had selected. The simple caption written in my adolescent handwriting read, "Turning Fifteen With Mama, Papa, Nana." With Mama on one side and Nana on the other, I sat at a wooden table behind a two-tiered, chocolate layer cake aglow with fifteen candles. Papa must have been the photographer. The evidence clearly proved that a party had taken place. However, my mind recalled nothing of that day.

After a lengthy pause, I picked up a pen, opened my notebook, and began to write about the photo. My first draft was a simple history based on the obvious. During the rewriting process, one sentence spontaneously led to another and then another as submerged sixty-five-year-old memories bubbled to the surface. I was engrossed. As additional details presented themselves, they were recorded on any available white space, and arrows were drawn to their exact points for insertion. By the end, every page was filled with scratch-outs and overwrites. Although I owned the habit of being snidely critical of my work, on this day, I accepted with gentleness the disjointed tale. No deadline and no audience to please were additional bonuses.

The afternoon slipped away, and so did the shade. After repositioning my beach chair for the third time, I finally tucked my writing materials and an empty water bottle back in my tote and closed my eyes. The warm salt air, accompanied by the rhythm of the shore breaks, relaxed every muscle. Soon my head nodded. I could have remained through sunset, but I was thirsty and ravenous. The latter was a sensation that had been absent so long that it struck me as curious. I gathered up my paraphernalia and headed back to the car with no plan, until I recalled the Vietnamese restaurant in Azeka Shopping Center, next to the cafe with the delicious malasadas.

I had planned on ordering takeout, but as I waited for the hostess to return to the front counter to take my order, a server walked past with enticing glasses of creamy, Vietnamese iced coffee balanced on a black lacquered tray.

"A table for one?" asked the hostess.

"Yes!" was my reply, a rarity since eating alone in a restaurant had never appealed. This time, thirst and hunger overruled my natural inclination. When the server appeared, I immediately ordered an iced coffee and a large glass of water. I relaxed into my chair and perused the extensive menu.

Instead of burying myself in a book, my usual fallback when dining alone, I engaged with two youngsters at the next table as I sipped the refreshing drink and awaited food. The younger child, a pudgy, black-haired toddler sitting backward in his chair, carried on a game of hide-and-seek with me. Every time the older child lifted a menu that she had placed in front of her brother's eyes to block our lines of vision, he giggled uncontrollably when I came into view. The parents apologized for their children's boisterousness, and I took responsibility for egging them on. When the family's food arrived, the boy quickly turned around and, with adeptness that I had never mastered, picked up chopsticks and dug into his dinner.

The hostess, a middle-aged woman with silver-flecked, dark hair twisted into an orchid-studded bun, glided around the tables in a long, beautiful muumuu. Obviously, she knew many of her guests, including the family next to me. After a short conversation with the parents and a question for each child, she turned to me, smiled, and asked if I was a visitor to the island. Before she moved on, she had

extracted more details than I had intended to divulge—
my name, state of origin, condo location, and indecision
regarding the date of my return to Minnesota. She introduced herself as Vivian, a name I had not expected. She
welcomed me to her restaurant and thanked me for coming, then backed away so the server could present the main
dish, a grilled beef noodle bowl with spring rolls. By the
time I finished eating the tasty concoction, every table in
the establishment was filled.

When I passed the hostess stand on my way out, Vivian wished me a good evening and extended an invitation
to return. I complimented the food and assured her that a
return trip to her restaurant was entirely possible.

The sky was dark; the sun had set while I had been eating, a fact that stirred only slight remorse. There would be
more sunsets, I reasoned. For now, I was staying put. My
stomach was pleasantly filled. I had been extricated from
my manuscript. My soul had been soothed during an afternoon at the beach. Body, mind, and spirit in sync, I had
achieved momentary balance.

Even the caffeine in the Vietnamese iced coffee could
not prevent my totally relaxed body from falling asleep on
the couch as I watched a comedy classic, a television show
that I quickly discovered was neither funny nor memorable. I awoke only long enough at 11 p.m. to flip the channel and catch the next day's weather prediction, eighty-five
degrees and sunny, a forecast repeated for the next five
days. Half expecting blissful dreams, I climbed into bed.

The memory of whatever dreams I was experiencing
quickly escaped when the neighborhood rooster offered
his wake-up call at 5 a.m., an hour that most people would
consider ungodly. However, his crowing coincided with
my internal body clock's announcement that it was time
to get up and practice my writer's scales. Recommitted to a

regime that had served me well over the years, I spent the first hour writing in my MP notebook and reading another chapter from *Bird by Bird*. Warmed up, I positioned my laptop on the glass-top table on the lanai. As the sun returned to the island, I transcribed and revised my scrawls from the day before.

MARGUERITE—AGE 15
April 30, 1950
"Turning Fifteen
With Mama, Papa, Nana"

Mama, with curls pulled to the top of her head and tied with a wide ribbon, sits on my right with her left arm extended across the back of my chair. Nana, the only grandmother I ever knew and the one whose name Jonella I inherited, sits on the other side of me and smiles on cue. Three generations are positioned in a row at Nana's dining table with her favorite piece of furniture, a large hutch cupboard, visible in the background.

A stack of four dessert plates sits on the table next to a cake. There's a sadness in the number. Grampa is no longer with us. Pneumonia took him the same weekend the first storm of the winter barreled down on Davis. For the last five months, Nana has lived alone in their apartment above the store. Self-absorbed, I'm oblivious to the fullness of her grief. Besides, sixty-two feels like a ripe old age to me. But that isn't to say that I don't miss Grampa every day. His passing has left a huge hole in the family that no one else can fill. For me, he will always be frozen in time. Patrick Campbell, Grampa, family man, cordwainer, master storyteller. He took good care of Nana—and the rest of us.

When questioning Grampa was still a possibility, I hadn't bothered. Now I regret not asking him about everything, especially his younger years. What slant would he have put on his own life? Now I'll never know. What I do know about his youth comes secondhand from other people's lips, mostly Nana's. She sparkles when she tells me about his adventurous spirit and hardworking character and how both were seeded at a young age. Imagine, only three years older than I turn today—leaving a broken family behind in Saint Paul—traveling alone three hundred miles north by rail to Davis with no job prospect until the owner of a black-smith shop at the edge of town took pity on him.

Not one to dwell on difficult times, Grampa, my favorite storyteller, chose to share hopeful tales about better days. The earliest one I can recall involved his transition from blacksmith to cordwainer.

"Everyone needs shoes, Marguerite, and I learned early on that I preferred makin' 'em for people rather than horses," Grampa stated matter-of-factly.

Then he described how, during the hours he wasn't shoeing horses, he worked as an apprentice to a cordwainer named Albert Peterson. According to Grampa, Mr. Peterson's ability to turn leather hides into handcrafted foot-wear was a miracle to behold. His able fingers and eye for detail garnered respect from everyone within a fifty-mile radius of Davis. At first, Grampa was taught to repair shoes in the shop while Albert concentrated on crafting custom-fitting pairs for his customers. By the time Albert died, he had passed on to Grampa not only each skillful nuance of leather working but his grateful clientele as well.

Proud of his work, Grampa explained, "I'm not just a cobbler, Marguerite. Cobblers repair shoes. I'm a cord-wainer. I craft new." He wasn't bragging as much as express-ing respect for the profession.

Grampa's custom-made creations walked out the door on the feet of many appreciative patrons. Polished to a dazzling shine, each pair advertised to townspeople that Patrick Campbell was an artist in the truest sense of the word. My grandfather crafted the best-fitting shoes in the township. At least, that's how I see things.

My favorite stool sits in Grampa's shop. As a youngster, I'd climb up the rungs that held the legs in place and twist myself around to settle in. From this high vantage point, I could watch his fingers work the tools and leather as I listened to his stories. Not attuned to passing on gossip, though he heard his fair share, he crafted other tales as skillfully as the shoes in front of him.

"Have I ever told you what a sweet filly said to me when I fit her with a new pair of shoes?" asked Grampa when I was barely old enough to remember.

"But horses can't talk, Grampa."

"Oh, but they can, Marguerite. Haven't you ever heard of a horse tale?" He paused to make sure I had caught the pun and then added, "One must listen very closely, but those animals are smart and have much to tell."

Having secured an enthusiastic audience, Grampa would share a story he claimed he had heard from one of the horses he had shod. Undoubtedly, by the end of his telling, the horse tale had spun a lesson on kindness or gratitude or work ethic or something else I probably needed to hear. I always knew when a story was over. After the last word, he would look up from his work, catch my eyes, and wink. I loved the horse tales. But I have to admit that my favorite story is the one about Papa and Mama that Grampa told from his perspective.

"One afternoon, I believe his name was Louis French, limped into my shop and asked if I'd be willin' to make him a special pair of shoes. You see, Marguerite, this young Mr.

French broke his left leg when he was a sprout, and it never grew quite right. All his growin' up years he'd been teased about being gimpy, and now as a man fully grown, the unevenness of his gait was givin' him too much hip pain. He figured that buildin' up his left shoe an inch or so might help. Once I took a look and did some measurin', I agreed and offered to give it a try. But there was one problem. Louis didn't have an extra dime, much less the money that a new pair of shoes would cost. He was determined, though, and we struck a deal, a handshake agreement. He offered to do whatever odd jobs I needed done until the debt was paid. He was so happy with his new shoes. I remember the day he tried them on and walked smoother than ever across the floor.

"I was impressed with Louis. He came to work every day as promised and never turned up his nose at a chore, no matter now lousy, and I threw him a bunch, like cleanin' the biffy, washin' windows, shovelin' snow off the roof. When I told him his debt was squared, he stuck around like a pesky fly until I agreed to take him on and pay him what I could. He wanted to apprentice in the shop, just like I had done with Albert, so I taught him what Albert had taught me, plus all the tricks I'd picked up since. Louis took to it all natural like. He appreciated fine leather, and his fingers worked like gears on a fine machine. After a few years, no one could tell whether new shoes were made by Patrick Campbell or Louis French.

"Somewhere along the way your mama caught his eye. There were eight years between 'em, so I was a bit surprised. He'd watched her change from an awkward little kid to a beautiful flower with boys buzzin' all around. But most of all, I think he was attracted to her independent nature. So with the same drive he used to learn the trade, he courted your mama. I don't think she believed his sincerity at first.

Then came the Crash of '29. Businesses all over the county were closing, and his family was one of many that left Davis. But not Louis. He refused to go anywhere. He set up house in a small room above the diner and spent every waking hour with me in the shop.

"Your papa proved his worth to me and your mama, and by the time she accepted his proposal in '32, we were holdin' our own as far as the business was concerned. We took a wild gamble and bought this building for a fair price from Amal Larsen's widow. Now we had space. Plenty of room for a small store out front and the shop behind. Louis and I divided the second floor into two small apartments, one for Jonella, Raymond, and me, and one for your mama and papa.

"The thirties were lean years. But when you have a trade, Marguerite, you have somethin' to barter. Shoes for beef, shoes for lumber, shoes for milk and bread and eggs. We found a way to make it work. While Louis and I worked in the shop, your mama and Nana became damn good salespeople in the store. They'd measure customers' feet, and if we didn't have the right size in stock, they'd order readymades from mail-order catalogs. Raymond helped out, too. He'd come straight to the store after school to run errands, wash windows, mop floors—the kinds of chores your papa used to do. We became what we advertised, Marguerite. 'The Campbell Shoe Company, A Family Business.'"

Since I had heard the story many times, I waited for the punchline I knew was coming. "And, there was one shinin' star arrived smack dab in the middle of the Depression." Then he would pause for at least ten seconds, look me square in the eye, and say, "YOU! Marguerite, my little daisy!" Then he would punctuate the end of his story with a wink.

18

*N*eatly transcribed into a Word document, the story of my fifteenth birthday captured a snippet of family history rather than details of the day. Satisfied, I saved the document and powered off the computer. Yet, the comforting warmth of the reminiscences lingered along with unanswerable questions. I wondered if my yearning to write had originated from some genetic connection to Grampa, my favorite storyteller. I knew for certain that I had him to thank for what little information I had gleaned regarding the family before my arrival. Perhaps because of the Depression, Mama and Papa, and Nana to some extent, had focused on the future not the past.

I returned to the snapshot of my fifteenth birthday and fixed my eyes on Nana's face. She had suffered great loss by the time the photo was taken, first Raymond by suicide, then Grampa. Yet, in the picture she wore a smile, perhaps a facade plastered on so her grief would not detract from her granddaughter's birthday celebration. I wished she had talked to me and shared her pain after Grampa's death. We had talked about so many things but not about her personal grief. I witnessed only her stoic example.

Memories of Grampa's passing left vague and intermittent images: a cold winter morning . . . Mama returning from the hospital as I was finishing my breakfast . . . hearing that Grampa was "gone" . . . being asked if I wanted to stay home from school . . . feeling guilty for wanting to go and be with friends . . . Nana, buttoned up, dry eyed, with a lace hankie stuffed up her sleeve just in case . . . our little family of four headed to St. Mark's Catholic Church for a funeral mass . . . feeling uncomfortable in the church that wouldn't hold a service for Uncle Raymond or allow him to be buried in the Catholic cemetery . . . burying Grampa next to Uncle Raymond in the town's other cemetery . . . tossing artificial daisies onto a sunken casket.

The birthday's snapshot was anchored on the page by black photo corners, which were now over sixty-five years old. I focused on Mama. Instead of looking at the camera, she was smiling at me. The camera caught her perfect profile, her head and neck artfully framed by the scalloped neckline of her blouse. Mama's flawless complexion and expertly tweezed brow were only slightly diminished by the graininess of the decades-old photo. Although the image was black and white, I conjured the butter yellow of Mama's blouse with the soft peplum and the worsted skirt and leather pumps that more than likely completed her outfit. Mama was beautiful. In the photo, she was forty years old.

Smiling at the camera in front of fifteen glowing candles, I had no way of knowing that neither Mama nor Papa would live to see my next birthday. Perhaps if I had known, I would have convinced Papa to let me take a photo of the two of them.

Finally ready for a respite from nostalgic recollections, I returned to present time and directed my focus toward the activity on the water. Once again, the afternoon trade winds had increased in strength and so had the waves. From the lanai, I watched as two novices about fifty feet offshore attempted with varying degrees of success to balance on stand-up paddleboards. Oh, to be young again.

During the rest of the afternoon, memories of Mama and Papa flitted by. The year I turned fifteen had been a pivotal time. I tried to imagine how life might have been different if any number of changes had been made one sunny afternoon in September: if we had decided to drive to Fargo on another day, if Papa had driven a bit slower or faster, if we had stayed a little longer or started back earlier, if the drunk driver after crossing the centerline had not chosen the same ditch as Papa for his diversionary maneuver, if I had not fallen asleep in the back seat. Medical personnel attributed my survival to my relaxed state. I escaped with contusions, a broken leg, a lacerated spleen, and a non-life-threatening concussion. Mama and Papa died at the scene, twelve miles south of Davis, and the drunk driver survived with a few broken bones and, perhaps, a guilt-laden hangover.

Due to the head trauma, I recalled nothing of the accident and little of the months previous, judging from my lapses in memory regarding my fifteenth birthday party. However, I strongly recalled my grief-induced anger at an unfair world.

Nana was my rock. She quietly buried Mama and Papa next to Grampa and Raymond. For the simple memorial service, she enlisted a Presbyterian minister/friend rather than the priest who had denied Raymond a Christian burial. The service was held in the hospital's chapel so I could be in attendance. I was certain that Mama would have approved. Once I was discharged from the hospital, Nana tended to my healing, both physical and emotional.

Nana cradled me when a family of four bought and

moved into our beautiful home on Holly Avenue, the one that Papa and Mama had scrimped to build when I was three, the one with trees and a backyard. Nana never took offense at my poor-me vibe, even though I refused for weeks to unpack my belongings after I moved in with her and took up residence in the small bedroom that had been Uncle Raymond's. Oblivious to Nana's grief over losing a daughter and son-in-law, I was consumed by my own.

A phone rang, interrupting my memories. Confused by the unfamiliar ringtone, I finally realized the sound was coming from the condo's landline, whose number I had given to no one.

"Hello?"

"Is this Marguerite Burdick?" a woman asked from the other end.

"Yes," I responded, not knowing whether to be concerned.

"This is Avery from the office. There is a woman down here asking about you." I heard some indistinguishable mumbles in the background. "Her name is May Watanabe. Would you like me to direct her to your condo?"

"I'll be right down," I said.

I descended via elevator to the ground floor and headed toward the office. May was standing outside on the hot cement. We greeted each other, and before I could ask, she explained the reason for her visit.

"I have lost your phone number," she said. I would learn later that it had disappeared during one of Mr. Sato's midnight attempts at tidying up.

"It's so good to see you. Is everything all right? How is your father?" I asked.

"Everyone is well," May replied.

"Good. Please come up. The lanai is so much cooler. Do you have time for iced tea?"

May accepted the invitation. Together, we entered the condo, slipped off sandals, and proceeded to the lanai with glasses of tea.

"I should have done this the first time," May said as she entered my contact information directly into her phone. "I have looked all over and cannot find the number you gave me on the plane." She described her father's middle-of-the-night purge of anything he did not recognize, including the page with my phone number. She looked up and added, "Father keeps asking, 'When are we going to see the Minnesota lady again?'"

"Your father is very engaging. So knowledgeable about the vegetation at the park," I said, recalling our exploration of 'Iao Valley. "I appreciated his patience with all of my questions."

"Yes, there are things he has not forgotten, mostly from his past. His short-term memory, on the other hand, is challenged. I recall that his brain warmed up that morning, and for whatever reason, the memory of you stuck. Maybe because of your connections to things he does remember. Minnesota. Fort Snelling."

"Dementia is such a mystery," I said.

"All I know is that Fern and I are very thankful that he remembers you and wants to see you. We are going to the swap meet on Saturday morning. Father used to sell his flowers and vegetables there. He still enjoys walking around and seeing the people. We are hoping you will join us."

"I'd love to."

May offered to drive down to Kihei on Saturday to pick me up, but I assured her I was ready and eager to strike out on my own and would meet her family at the time of their choosing. Using the map of the island, May pointed out the location of the swap meet, a simple drive back into Kahului. We agreed to meet at the ticket booth at 8 a.m.

"Now that our plans are taken care of, tell me, Marguerite, how is your writing going?" May asked.

"Actually, quite well," I answered, before giving my response any thought. "I'm doing some cathartic writing. Recalling my childhood and youth. I'm surprising myself with memories long forgotten—or just buried deep."

"Sometimes it is helpful to turn around and see from a new perspective the path that one has traveled," May said.

Before I could contemplate or respond to her simple yet profound statement, like a woman on a mission, she jumped up, bused her glass to the kitchen sink, retrieved her sandals, and opened the door.

"I will tell Father that we will see you on Saturday. Thank you, Marguerite."

"It is I who should be thanking you," I said as we walked toward the elevator.

19

A few sentences in my morning pages hinted at new possibilities:

For me May's visit was serendipitous, an unexpected and welcomed interruptor of solitude, just like my short conversation with Vivian on Sunday night. And now, I actually have an engagement entered into my calendar for the end of the week. Maybe I'm not destined to spend my remaining years as a dried-up curmudgeon after all. Perhaps the usefulness of my year-long, self-induced hibernation, the protracted solitude that had become my defense against a painful world, has expired. PERHAPS. My speech is dominated by this adverb. "Conceivable, but not certainly so" according to Webster. I have looked it up many times. The word offers hope. If only I could grow to love uncertainty. Perhaps . . .

By the end of the third page, I had described my desire to seek out human contact, with locals especially. The only way to accomplish this was to get out of the condo. But first things first. It was time to practice my scales.

After contemplating some inspiring thoughts from Anne Lamott, I turned my attention to pages of the birthday book. If judged by the final product, the hour-long writing session that followed the reading was unproductive. The work amounted to a few scratched-out paragraphs conjured from the photos of my sixteenth and seventeenth birthday parties. Obviously, Papa, now a memory, was no longer the photographer. Friends must have snapped the unfocused candids. Both pictures included only partial glimpses of the birthday cakes that Nana had painstakingly baked and decorated for each occasion.

Just like the birthday photos, recollections of my high school years were grainy at best. Impacted by both a head injury and the grief of losing Mama and Papa, I lived the subsequent years in a blur. Perhaps memory loss was nature's way to anesthetize. *Perhaps*—there was that word again. Defeated by my inability to add backstory to the photos, I put down my pen.

Clear, however, were two important considerations. First, I was definitely in need of replenishing my storehouse of creative images and ideas; second, outside the condo was an island abundant with both. With renewed intent, I packed my tote and headed to the car.

I landed in a nearby cafeteria offering custom-made sandwiches and salads. A small table located on the patio became the perfect spot to enjoy a uniquely composed ahi salad while I planned my exploration of Maui. Between mouthfuls, I exchanged a fork for a pen and compiled a must-see list from activities described in a travel book. Millie's recommendations helped to hone and prioritize the many interesting options.

Exploring Lahaina, a small town on the western edge of the West Maui Mountains, sounded like a worthy consideration. The area was described in the travel materials as a popular destination for tourists interested in shopping, dining, booking an activity on the water, or delving into the island's history. I was especially interested in the nineteenth century, when whalers frequented the port of Lahaina for supplies. The ensuing conflicts between sailors, Hawaiian leaders, and missionaries were legendary. Plus, the whaling industry's effects on the island's economy was something I wished to explore. According to the travel book, the courthouse of the whaling era had been repurposed into a heritage museum. A trip to Lahaina secured a spot near the top of my must-see list. Next to it, I wrote, "Full day!"

The road to Hana with its hundreds of curves, although a beautiful trek through tropical rainforests, held little appeal. I didn't see the point, since the travel book warned drivers to keep their eyes on the road. I added a notation to check with Patti, the activities director at the pool, about the details of hooking up with a small tour. On second thought, spending a full day in a van with strangers and no means of escape felt daunting, so I scratched out my notation and repositioned "Road to Hana." It now sat at the bottom of my list, right below "Haleakala at sunrise." Driving an hour in the dark to the crater's rim still remained unappealing. Driving up in daylight, however, continued to be a possibility. Both Hana and Haleakala were tabled for the time being; the simple fact that they remained on the list spoke to my increasing self-confidence.

The ease of driving on Maui had been a welcomed surprise. Although many cars shared the roads, reduced speeds and general politeness seemed to be the rule rather than the exception. Honking was almost nonexistent. (The only blast I had heard since my arrival was chalked up to a tourist's rudeness.) Drivers often deferred the right of way to others and regularly stopped for pedestrians regardless of the presence of crosswalks. These simple acts were living examples of the island's warm hospitality. Perhaps the locals would disagree with my positive assessment; my comparisons were based on experiences with rude behavior on Minnesota freeways and white-knuckle driving on snow and ice.

In addition to enjoying sane driving conditions, I no longer feared getting lost. With a mountain on each side and the valley between, the layout of the roads made sense, and I knew if I ever got confused, all I had to do was drive toward the ocean and recalculate or simply stop and ask a local for assistance.

Confident that I could jump in the car and drive, a favorite pastime with which I was becoming reacquainted, I scrutinized my must-see list. Instead of driving all the way to Hana, I still could drive a short distance down the Hana Highway, check out the large waves on the North Shore, and perhaps enjoy lunch at Mama's Fish House. According to a copy of the local newspaper that Millie had thoughtfully included in her travel packet, Mama's had been voted a winner by locals in several categories, including Best Ambiance and Best Place for a Celebratory Meal. I was intrigued.

A trip Upcountry could include a variety of options depending on how far I wished to drive: the cowboy town of Makawao, botanical gardens, a lavender farm, a winery. I made a mental note to ask May for recommendations. Museums, popular beaches, and eateries all found a position on my ever-lengthening list.

If Harry and I had visited years earlier, we would have snorkeled and swam at several beaches; hiked and camped in the crater of Haleakala; and possibly, Harry at least, biked down from the summit after experiencing sunrise together at the crater's rim. With manageable regret, I acknowledged the coulda, woulda, shoulda thoughts and refocused. My must-see list, detailed and lengthy, involved all parts of the island and included disparate suggestions, such as enjoying Polynesian entertainment at the Shops at Wailea, a high-end shopping area, and exploring a used bookstore behind an old sugar mill.

Two days earlier, I had contemplated an early return to Minnesota. How foolish and self-absorbed I had been! Millie understood me well and knew that Maui would be the comforting salve I needed to cushion me from my worst self. Now, here I was, munching a locally sourced salad and prioritizing a lengthy list of activities that definitely piqued my interest.

By the time I was ready to bus my lunch tray and refill my water flask, I had zeroed in on an easy activity for the afternoon. Accompanied by a map and a well-charged cell phone, I struck out for a tropical plantation, a destination I hoped would offer some sensory stimulation. Advertised as a place to discover and celebrate Maui's agricultural bounty, the attraction was not at the top of my list. But it was a good place to start, since it was located only a few miles away on a familiar road. I had driven right past it on my way to the base of 'Iao Valley.

When I arrived at the plantation, only a few cars and a tour bus occupied the substantial parking lot. I stepped inside the main building and found the huge gift shop equally deserted. A well-positioned sign advertised tropical express tours through the acreage.

"A tour is now loading," said a saleswoman who noticed my interest in the sign. "There are still a few spaces if you hurry."

Without forethought, I exchanged cash for a tour voucher and followed the woman's directions through the gift shop to the back door. Outside sat the express, a three-section trolley with bench seating. I climbed into the only unoccupied row in the rear of the last section and pulled out my notebook and pen.

"Ready to take notes, I see. Smart. I go on these things, then quickly forget everything they tell us. Hope we don't get sprinkled on."

I looked up to locate the originator of the comments. Sitting in the seat ahead, an elderly lady with wraparound sunglasses and a lime green visor smiled broadly over her shoulder. Without referencing my notebook, I replied, "Hopefully the clouds will produce nothing but wonderful shade."

"Wouldn't that be nice," she said before she redirected her attention to her seatmate.

The tour began, and the express moved quietly along an asphalt pathway toward groves of bananas, papaya, kukui nuts, coffee, and other tropical vegetation. With the help of a clear audio system, the guide, a young man who was also the driver, described the growing cycles, products, and uses of each. Just like Mr. Sato, he spoke with reverence about the earth and our need to protect her.

The plantation offered delightful sights and smells that I recorded with varying degrees of success in my notebook. By the fifth stop, this time to watch the husking and cracking of a coconut, a written description of several tourists had been added. At each stop, a middle-aged couple quickly jumped off the express and bustled to the front of the herd so the woman could position herself in front of whatever vegetation was highlighted. Oblivious to his interruption of the tour guide, the man cleared others out of the way so he could snap an unobstructed picture of his companion. In contrast, another couple never bothered to get out of their seats at any stop and took only pictures of themselves with the use of a selfie stick. He wore a T-shirt that read, "I survived the road to Hana." I wondered if they had bothered to capture any of the loveliness of that journey without their faces front and center. But as I described their playfulness and what appeared to be genuine affection for each other in my notebook, I ended my observation with a question: "In twenty years, would I want a photo of a beautiful waterfall or one with the person I loved in front of it?" My takeaway, I decided, was a reminder to be less judgmental.

Just like these two couples, I was one of the odds and ends that filled out the tour. Most of the people on the express, including the woman in the seat ahead of me, were easily identified as members of a large tour group. All sported name badges that dangled from lanyards around their necks. Most also wore lime green sun visors with "Maui Nō Ka ʻOi" printed across the brims. These were people who preferred traveling in a pack to traveling alone. I was sure that few of them, if any, would understand my need to do just the opposite.

By the end of the tour, rich images of scenery and people had taken up residence in my notebook and in my mind. After a short browse in the gift shop, I headed back to the condo. On South Kihei Road, I stopped spontaneously when I saw whole chickens sizzling and smoking on rotating spits in a church parking lot. After exchanging money for what the man in charge called "a plate lunch, huli huli chicken, one scoop mac, two scoop rice," I rushed back to my car and unexpectedly dissolved into tears. Feeling foolish, I hoped no one was noticing the curly-haired crazy lady crying over chicken, rice, and macaroni salad.

Flummoxed by my quick reversal to despair, I continued down South Kihei Road. The delicious aroma of soy sauce, garlic, ginger, caramelized sugar, and sesame oil must have triggered my reaction. Soy sauce chicken had been one of Harry's favorite dishes. My recipe, unlike huli huli chicken that was cooked over an open flame, roasted slowly in the oven in a covered pot until the meat fell off the bone, all the while permeating the house with the pleasant aroma of soy and ginger. I recalled Harry liberally spooning the sauce over the chicken and white rice and commenting, "I hope they serve this in heaven."

Somewhere in the recesses of my mind that memory had been buried, or so I thought, until the unique fragrance stirred it up. Once I understood the reason for my emotional blubbery, I felt a bit better. Nonetheless, I had been hopeful that untimely episodes like this, primed by something relatively inconsequential (this time a smell), were a thing of the past. Obviously, they were not.

Although I understood its cause, the most recent emotional eruption had not fully run its course. Although it was only 4 p.m., I immediately refrigerated the picked-over plate lunch, took a shower, pulled Harry's freshly laundered T-shirt over my head, and climbed into bed. Salty droplets leaked down both cheeks and dampened the pillow as I lay in the fetal position. Eventually, a good share of a box of tissues lay in soggy, scrunched masses atop the bedspread. Exhausted, I arose only long enough to check the locks on the door before returning to bed and pulling the sheet up to my chin.

20

*O*bjectivity accompanied the light of day as I dumped my anxieties onto morning pages:

I guess nothing happens in a straight line. My body seized up yesterday, a firm reminder to resist cockiness . . . I used to ache to dream about Harry, and I'd curse him for not returning. But to be honest, after my episode with huli huli chicken, I am thankful for a dreamless night. Exhausted, I slept the clock around with no interruption, and although I feel a bit bruised this morning, I've checked my pulse, and my heart's still beating . . .

Three pages later, the entry ended with a question regarding the tentative plan I was considering. *Am I up for a day in Lahaina?*

After a few encouraging pages from Anne Lamott, I decided to exercise my brain by writing about both the highs and the lows of the previous day. The pure act of cementing reflections on paper felt both rewarding (the highs) and cathartic (the lows).

The writing, accompanied by caffeine, yogurt, and papaya, buoyed my spirit. Although Lahaina deserved a full day of exploration, I decided instead to tackle an abbreviated trip. Lahaina Lite I called my day's approach. The plan required a seventy-minute round trip plus enough time to give the town a quick once over. As an unaccompanied traveler with the freedom to set or amend the day's agenda, I headed out.

Beyond Ma'alaea Harbor, the Prius joined a steady stream of vehicles that snaked northward along the western edge of the West Maui Mountains. The road, with mountains on one side and ocean on the other, cut through black, volcanic rock. In some places, wire mesh retainers had been rigged against the jagged mountainside to prevent boulders from sliding onto the roadway. In one spot, a man-made tunnel bored through the rugged terrain. Concerned that the unfamiliar drive might become treacherous, I was heartened when the road evened out and the small town of Lahaina appeared in the distance.

In full view, the glistening ocean resembled a playground. Near the shoreline, swimmers, some with surfboards or stand-up paddleboards, enjoyed glorious sunshine and white-tipped surf. Farther out, an array of sailboats, fishing trollers, catamarans, and excursion vessels dotted the water.

Across an expanse of ocean sat a neighboring island. That same landmass had intrigued me every night at sunset. From Millie's lanai, it appeared to nestle into the horizon like the mystical Bali Hai from the musical *South Pacific*. Each night after the sun dropped into the ocean, the far-off island disappeared behind pink and purple haze. Now that same island loomed large and green.

Eventually, the ocean disappeared behind homes, churches, and businesses. I had arrived. Lahaina, the whaling port that Michener so aptly described in his book, occupied a flat stretch of land between the ocean and the ascending West Maui Mountains. According to travel information, an easy walk down Front Street led to several historical places, including the Pioneer Inn, the prison ruins, the courthouse/museum, and a banyan tree that was advertised to be the largest in the United States. A short, two-block walk from my parking space brought me to Front Street. Bustling with shops, restaurants, and a steady stream of people, the main thoroughfare ran parallel to the water's edge.

The midday sun bore down. I browsed several shops in search of a flattering sun hat. Hot, sweaty, and still hatless, I eventually arrived at the historic banyan tree and plopped down on one of the inviting benches. The tree was magnificent, so huge, in fact, that the area below its giant, green canopy was designated a park. The shade had attracted many like me who were seeking a leisurely break from the sun.

Adjacent to the park sat the historic courthouse that now housed a museum. Once rested, I moseyed over to the building and did a cursory walk-through. When I realized the museum deserved much more time than I was prepared to give, I snapped a few photos and left with a commitment to return another day.

After a quick examination of a corner-shaped ruin of earthen blocks, a reconstructed remnant of the prison that centuries earlier had detained drunken, unlawful whalers, I headed toward the pier. I tried to imagine whaling vessels rather than the ticket booths that advertised all sorts of water activities, from sailing and snorkeling to glass-bottom boat trips and daylong fishing excursions. The empty slips suggested most of the boats were out for the afternoon. Eager to sell tickets for another day, young salespeople remained behind in tiny, hot booths.

On one corner of a nearby intersection sat the Pioneer

Inn. Green clapboard siding with white trim gave the small hotel a New England feel, although in Maui no window screens were required. At its entrance, a life-size statue of a smiling, peg-legged sailor greeted patrons. I watched as a mother of three positioned her children around the wooden statue. The eldest, an adolescent in board shorts, a Maui Built T-shirt, and flip-flops, was not cooperating and looked away with an expression of aloof discomfort exactly at the moment she snapped the picture. I tried unsuccessfully to muffle a chuckle, which only exacerbated the youth's embarrassment.

The sun continued to bake the pavement of Front Street as I headed back in the direction of my car. I ducked into Captured, one of a number of shops that occupied a small strip of real estate between the street and the ocean. A refreshing blast of air conditioning welcomed anyone who chose to step inside. Raising my sunglasses and docking them in the curls above my forehead, I stood in the center of the shop and quickly rotated 360 degrees to check out the unique shop. A colorful sign draped across the back wall announced, "It's all about the story, CAPTURE it!" A sign in the far right corner advertised "SNAP it!" with a giant arrow pointing through an open doorway. Wrapping around the far left corner of the shop were bookshelves under a sign that read, "The Beach READ."

"Aloha, welcome to Captured," said a voice from behind. I turned in its direction and found the originator, a young man who appeared to be in his late twenties or early thirties. Tanned with reddish brown hair, he sported typical beach attire, a black muscle shirt, shorts, and well-worn flip-flops. Pinned to his baseball cap was a name tag with "Mike" printed below his photo.

"Aloha," I answered.

"Have you been to our shop before?"

"No," I said. "But it looks intriguing."

"Like the sign says, it's all about the story. So we have many ways to enjoy 'em. Stories, that is." He gestured to racks and baskets containing T-shirts and other items of clothing screen-printed with caricatures of false bards and their fake quotes, such as "It's a Whale of a Tale!" attributed to Herman Melville.

"Sick humor, I know," Mike said as he held up one of the printed shirts.

The doorway under the "SNAP it!" sign led to a partially hidden lanai with an ocean view, the perfect backdrop for photography. I watched three young women, clad in swimsuits and cover-ups, as they posed against the railing and snapped selfies with their cell phones.

"People go out there," Mike said as he pointed to the lanai, "to take photos with their friends or families. If they get a good shot and want to have it printed on a T-shirt, postcard, mug, keychain, mouse pad, anything you see over on our displays, we can do that."

The young women stepped back into the shop and began comparing photos and perusing the displays as they decided how best to memorialize their Maui vacation. The options were endless.

"If you are camera shy but still see the need for a good story, we have a great selection of beach reads." He led me to the back corner on the left side of the store. Tall bookshelves showcased a collection of paperbacks. "Let me know if we can help you," Mike said. He excused himself to help the young women, who immediately surrounded him and flirtatiously peppered him with questions about ordering insulated travel mugs emblazoned with their favorite selfie.

I lingered at the paperbacks to scan the titles. Although a few bookshelves were dedicated to nonfiction, fiction dominated the collection. In each genre, books were alphabetized by the author's last name. As I often do in bookstores, I looked hopefully for something familiar. Surprisingly, five MJ Burdick novels sat prominently on the second shelf of the fiction section.

"Can I help you find something?" This time the voice from behind sounded a bit gravelly.

I turned and faced a man, an older version of Mike in height and build. His reddish brown hair sported a speckling of gray.

"I was just looking at your collection," I said. "E-books are fine, but I appreciate finding print copies." I glanced at a name tag on his chest that identified him as Rich.

"There are still many of us who love holding a book in our hands and turning the pages," he replied. "Can I help you find something?"

He followed my gaze to the second shelf. He frowned and began rearranging the MJ Burdick paperbacks in alphabetical order. I stood silently. Before he placed *Zero Degrees and Falling* in its proper place at the end, he glanced at the photo on the back cover and then at me. Then back again.

"Oh my god! You're MJ Burdick," he said.

"Guilty," I said. "Thanks so much for stocking my books. They must not be huge sellers if you still have five of them."

"It is a pleasure, Ms. Burdick," he said. "And, just so you know, your books are popular. I have extra copies in the back and try to keep several on display."

"Well, that makes me feel better," I said. "And please, call me MJ—or Marguerite."

"Marguerite," he said, rolling my name off his tongue. "Beautiful. And please call me Rich—or Richard. Your choice. It is not often that authors grace our shop."

"Nice to meet you, Richard," I said, confirming that we were now on a first-name-but-no-nickname basis. "I love the uniqueness of your shop. And your sign says it all. It *is* all about the story."

"Could I offer you a cold drink?" he asked.

Something wet and cold sounded undeniably wonderful. I accepted his offer, and he led me through the doorway and onto a lanai that ran the full width of the shop. On the end opposite the photo-staging area sat a high bistro table with three chairs. A cool breeze off the water and shade from an overhang more than compensated for the air conditioning we had left behind. Richard offered me a chair and then listed available beverages. Having secured my order, he disappeared, leaving me alone to appreciate the serendipitous turn of events.

"I'm afraid we're a bit on the casual side," he said a few minutes later as he cracked open cans of Minute Maid lemonade and poured the contents into large ceramic tumblers adorned with photos of the outside of the shop. Sitting down at the table, he added, "I don't even have a cookie to offer you."

"This is perfect. I hadn't realized how warm it was going to be in Lahaina, and I left Kihei without water."

"So, you're from Kihei?" Richard asked.

"Just visiting," I replied. "I'm staying in a friend's condo."

"Do you come to Maui often?"

"Actually, this is my first trip," I replied, before taking a long swig of lemonade. "This is so refreshing. Thank you," I added, trying to pivot away from any more personal questions.

"So what do you think of our island?" Richard asked.

"I can see why Mark Twain came for a short visit and stayed five weeks," I said. "There is something about Maui I can't quite put my finger on—besides the beauty, the calming ambiance. Maui is quite magical in that regard."

"It worked its magic on me back in '78 when I came to

Hawaii for a three-week, four-island vacation with some college friends. I loved all the islands, but Maui nō ka ʻoi," he said, repeating an expression I had seen printed on everything from beach bags to bumper stickers. "Maui is the best," he translated. "I returned the following year, found a starter job, met and married my wife Ani, then returned to Madison only long enough to pack up my stuff and head back to Maui. Have lived here ever since."

"So, you're a Wisconsinite."

"Well, used to be. I still have family there. Around Madison mostly. That's where I went to school."

"Go Badgers!"

"Are you a Badger fan?"

"Heaven forbid," I replied with a chuckle.

"Of course not. You graduated from—the University of Minnesota?"

"Yes, I did. Many years ago."

"After I read *Murder in the Student Section,* I researched you a bit," he said. "I love the local color in your books. I've read them all. They transport me right back to the Midwest."

"Truth be told, I was surprised to see copies in Maui."

"A mystery is a great vacation read," he said. "Plus, we get lots of tourists from the Midwest."

"Do you ever feel island bound or consider moving back to Wisconsin?"

"Yes to the first and definitely no to the second. Ani and I fly to the mainland every other year or so to visit relatives, but we are always ready to return."

"What do you like most about Maui?"

"You mean besides the beauty, the weather, the ocean, and the people?" he said with a chuckle. "You grew up in a small town not too far from Fargo, right?"

"Yah sure, you betcha," I answered with a smirk. "But I've

lived in the Twin Cities for over—sixty years!" I said after pausing to do the math. "I'm surprised you knew about my northern Minnesota roots."

"Like I said, I do my research on authors. Minnesota, Land of 10,000 Lakes, has a lot to offer. But be careful, Marguerite. Maui gets in your blood. Are you traveling with family?"

"Actually, no. I decided to come on my own," I said, wondering if Richard's research on me was recent enough to uncover information on Harry's death. I avoided the subject and asked about Mike, the friendly, young store clerk.

"Mike's my son. He was born on Maui, as was our daughter Kai, who should be back from break soon."

"So Captured is a family affair. I have a special warmth in my heart for family-owned businesses."

"Pretty much it is," he replied, "when we aren't doing our other jobs. Both Mike and I are web designers. That's flexible work, and it pays the bills. But I enjoy being in the shop, so I work in the back office and poke my head out every now and then. Mike works out of our print shop about a mile from here in cheaper real estate. He oversees that operation except for times like today when he comes down to deliver an order. He got shanghaied by his little sister to cover for her. Kai is really the creative spark behind the business. She also manages things. We wouldn't be able to handle the shop if it wasn't for her."

Richard was sharing personal information openly, and I felt a bit guilty for being so guarded with my own.

"Thelma and Louise are back, so I'm off." We both turned toward the voice at the doorway.

"Mike, come here. I want you to meet someone. Marguerite, this is my son, Mike. Mike, meet MJ Burdick."

We exchanged pleasantries. Mike was familiar with

my books, and it was from him that the dreaded question finally emerged. "When's your next book coming out?"

"I've taken a bit of a hiatus, so there's nothing new on the horizon," I said, forgoing any explanation. "Thelma and Louise?"

"My sister and our best salesperson," explained Mike. "They just returned from a very long lunch break, so I gotta go and get some of my own work done. Nice to meet you, Ms. Burdick." He disappeared through the doorway.

"You must be proud of your children. Mike is very personable," I said.

"They're great kids. Do you have children, Marguerite?"

Surprising myself with my own frankness, I said, "No, unfortunately. Our daughter died accidentally years ago. My husband passed away last May. So, I envy you your close-knit family."

"Oh, I'm so sorry," Richard said, without prying any further.

I interrupted the silence by asking Richard about the neighboring island that was clearly visible from where we sat.

"That's Lana'i. People take daily excursions by boat to golf, enjoy a ritzy lunch, or rent a jeep for a little exploration. The whole island used to be owned by Dole. Lots of pineapple. And if you look up that way," he said, pointing off to the right of Lana'i, "you'll see Moloka'i. If you drive up to Ka'anapali, you'll get a better view."

"Ka'anapali?"

"Ka'anapali Beach, a wide stretch of beautiful sand, lots of resorts. Whalers Village shopping center, restaurants, entertainment. Just up the highway about five miles. And there's lots more to see beyond that." He described the beaches and snorkeling spots between Ka'anapali and

Kapalua. "If you keep going, the road will eventually circle the West Mauis and end up back in Wailuku, but I'd recommend that somewhere around Kapalua you turn around and return the way you came. Otherwise, the rest of the drive gets pretty narrow and a bit scary for newcomers, and if there's an accident, you can be stuck for hours until the road is cleared."

My mind had drifted with the mention of Emma and Harry, but his warning about the narrow road returned my focus to our conversation. Richard spoke passionately about the island and ticked off a list of activities that would keep me busy for weeks. When he asked about my length of stay, he laughed when I explained that, as yet, I had not booked a return flight.

"Watch out, Marguerite!" he warned a second time. "Maui settles in like a quiet balm. Mark my words! She's hard to leave."

"Yes, a quiet balm. A perfect description, Richard. But at least I'll be returning to Minnesota in the summertime. I don't know how snowbirds ever get themselves back on planes in February or March."

We chatted leisurely until we finished our beverages. Then I thanked him for his hospitality and asked if I could meet his daughter on the way out. Richard led me back into the store and introduced me to two women who were busy refolding a messy stack of T-shirts. One was blond, and I immediately mistook her for Richard's daughter. Instead, he introduced me to a young woman with Hawaiian features and jet black hair that nearly reached her waist. "This is my daughter, Kai," he said. "And this is her righthand, Mel," he added, referring to the blond. "Together they keep the shop humming."

Immediately after discovering that I was an author, Kai

asked, "Ms. Burdick, would you have any interest in a book signing? We could set you up at a table. I believe Dad has a few of your books. We could order more."

"My daughter, ever the entrepreneur," said Richard. "Don't feel pressured if your intention is to get away from it all."

"Oh, please, Kai, call be MJ, or Marguerite. And to answer your question, let me think about it," I replied.

"Well, just let us know if that's something that might interest you," she said. "Have you taken your picture on our lanai?"

"I haven't mastered the art of selfies, I'm afraid."

"Then let me take your photo," Kai said. Leaving Mel to monitor the shop, she led me back to the lanai. She snapped away, first with my cell phone and then with hers, as I stood with the ocean as the backdrop. On my request, she took a shot of Richard and me and then shots of all three of us. Warm and engaging, she began calling me MJ, and within minutes we were exchanging contact information.

Savoring the spontaneity of the last hour, I strolled back down Front Street in the direction of my car. Lahaina Lite had been unusually enjoyable, and I found myself not quite ready to leave. Hoping to enjoy the lull before the dinner rush, I stepped into an eating establishment with a posted menu offering an enticing array of seafood entrees. The hostess led me past a rather dark bar area and onto a glorious deck where she offered a choice of tables, all with huge umbrellas and great ocean views.

A family of three sat nearby. Armed with spoons, they were poised to attack a giant slice of ice cream pie covered in melted chocolate and whipped cream. The woman asked if I would take their photo and then handed me an iPad. On the third attempt, I snapped a perfectly composed shot of the family. It highlighted their wide-eyed little boy eagerly navigating a spoonful of ice cream to his mouth.

"There's a unique shop down Front Street," I suggested. "Its name is Captured. The owners can print your photo on practically anything—postcards, T-shirts, mugs. You name it. It's a family business, and they're wonderful."

The woman seemed genuinely interested in preserving the moment on a souvenir and asked for directions to the shop. Imagining Kai with a thumbs-up gesture, I smiled as I filled in specifics.

After I had cleaned my plate of every delectable morsel of mahi mahi, rice, and island vegetables, the waitress reappeared.

"Would you like to finish off your meal with a piece of hula pie?" she asked.

"Hula pie? It that what it's called?"

"Macadamia nut ice cream in a chocolate cookie crust, chocolate fudge, macadamia nuts, and whip cream, of course," she said. "It's our signature."

"I'll have to return. With friends," I added with a laugh as I handed her my credit card.

The return trip to Kihei passed quickly. No longer feeling the need to glue my eyes to the road, I relaxed and appreciated the scenery as I drove the route in reverse. Quicker than expected, I reached the valley and the road straightened out. I passed familiar beaches, the farmers market, and the church parking lot with giant rotisseries of huli huli chicken. This time, when the smoke and aroma wafted through the open car windows, I drove on unaffected and thankful that the perfect afternoon remained unspoiled.

My conversation with Richard had buoyed my spirit. He had shared unique and interesting information about the islands. But more important, he had unknowingly created a soft space for me to open up about Harry and Emma. In hindsight, 1 realized that answering Richard's questions directly had been much less exhausting than my usual conversational dance filled with deflections when questions became personal. During our conversation, my flight instinct had not kicked in, surprisingly. Instead, 1 had let down my guard a bit. 1 congratulated myself for taking baby steps toward forthrightness. Not wishing to analyze my growth any further, 1 simply inhaled a deep breath of fresh air.

The sun was swiftly dropping toward the horizon as 1 drove homeward along the ocean. When 1 reached the Maui Sunset, 1 parked and joined other sunset worshippers who were migrating to the shoreline for the best view.

Frankie was ambling along. 1 called him by name, and he lumbered over for a pet. His owner followed a few steps behind with Frankie's unhooked leash in one hand and a Coors Light in the other. 1 had been in Maui one week and already 1 was recognizing regulars. Wise, old Frankie showed up almost every night and was quickly joined by his short-legged friend, a dachshund who raced with the big dogs for a couple of circles around the grass until he tired. Then he sought out Frankie, who was content to simply stroll and sniff.

The usual human contingent, condo owners, renters, and Kihei townspeople, gathered at the shoreline. 1 kicked my sandals off my hot, tired feet and walked across the man-icured lawn in their direction. These were the same people 1 had observed going down for sunset night after night. 1 admired one elderly gentleman in particular. His nightly ritual involved painstakingly pushing his walker step by step toward the ocean. Tall and sinewy, he looked as if he might have been an accomplished athlete in his younger days. Tonight, he stopped occasionally to pat dogs or chat with people. Finally, arriving near the ocean's edge, he repositioned his walker and plopped down on the attached seat. A wine bottle appeared from his backpack, and he poured its contents into plastic cups and offered them to anyone in his vicinity. I gladly accepted, and we settled in among a menagerie of vacationers, locals, and four-legged friends for the night's show. Free-flowing conversation and laughter turned strangers into new acquaintances. As the blowing of the conch announced the end of another day, everyone turned west for the sun's final descent. Eventually, my new friend Art stood up. He reclaimed and stacked the plastic cups and stuffed them into his backpack along with the empty wine bottle, turned, and slowly headed back toward his condo.

I was learning that the evening ritual of honoring the sunset was as consistent and reliable as the sunset itself. Many people stopped whatever they were doing to face west as the sun dropped into the ocean. It was as if we were members of the same club, brought together by Mother Nature, who offered a daily time-out. No longer just a beautiful visual, the setting sun had become a meditative pause, a time to breathe, a time to focus on the present, and a time to not worry about the future. It offered a subtle lesson regarding human insignificance. Art and I would eventually be gone, replaced by others who would gather on the shoreline to watch the same sun set into the same ocean.

After another spectacular show, I returned to the condo, opened the refrigerator, removed a covered plate of huli huli chicken, and settled in for a bite. Tired, but relaxed, I declared the day over.

21

*H*awaii's climate and divergent ecosystems were especially fascinating to me. Substantial rainfall continually refreshed streams, waterfalls, and tropical rainforests on the windward side of the volcanic mountains of Haleakala and West Maui. Hana, the small town on the eastern side of Haleakala, was nestled in this dampness. In contrast, Kihei was positioned on the leeward or western slope of the volcano where winds were drier. Since my arrival, sunshine had been the order of the day in Kihei, so I was surprised when I awoke to a storm on my eighth morning in Maui. Pelting rain and gusty winds prevailed, making the lanai uninhabitable.

Up until now, the only precipitation I had experienced in Kihei was liquid sunshine, an intermittent mist that blew in from some unknown source, even though the sun was shining and the sky was cloudless. This gentle, cooling spray never interfered with vacationers' activities. But today's heavy, dark clouds and torrential rains socked in Kihei. Already, rainwater was pooling in low-lying areas and flooding the nearby roadways. Howling winds, whipping with a force that would have uprooted trees in my

New Brighton neighborhood, drew me to the sliding glass door. In awe, I watched as stately palms defended themselves by bending their flexible trunks. No doubt these towering trees had survived many a storm.

I scanned the horizon and saw only bleakness. The weather called for hunkering down, an acceptable choice, since I was eager to tackle another story inspired by a page from the birthday book. I thought about Richard's unique business, helping vacationers permanently memorialize their trips to Maui, and realized that Mama had given me a similar opportunity with my life when she gifted the scrapbook. The small pages wisely limited inclusion to only one photo and caption per year. Choosing my favorite moment had been challenging. The process had required self-discernment, an introspective spirit that Mama encouraged. Flipping through the photos, I analyzed my reasoning for picking each one. Then I concentrated on my rationale for separating the pages. For the most part, the pages left behind in Minnesota covered years of stable living, when the highs and lows evened out. In contrast, the pages chosen to accompany me to paradise represented defining moments when events, most out of my control, had altered the trajectory of my life.

For the most part, I had no trouble recalling the defining moments, the years of promise, heartache, pain, and joy, but each was remembered with a strange degree of superficiality. It was not until I began writing in the voice of whichever Marguerite was celebrating the chosen birthday that I began unearthing memories buried under years of inattention. Facts frozen in time by a photographer's lens became the starting point. As I wrote, the obvious gave way to suppositions, which gradually peeled back more layers until emotional underpinnings were exposed.

The process, much like writing a whodunit, required

piecing together the plot and developing the characters. But in this very personal tale, I was the central character, and the plot was my life. I was also the audience, an audience of one, and I vowed to be nonjudgmental, and when that was impossible, at least somewhat forgiving. With that understanding, I was becoming free to write whatever flowed out of my pen, a posture that enjoyed the additional bonus of silencing my inner critic. The voices of Mama, Papa, Nana, and Grampa, the strong stock from which I grew, took its place. Their encouragement nudged me forward as I mined deeply to uncover not only long-forgotten happenings but also their effects on my soul.

I welcomed the pelting rain and relaxed into the morning with my companions, the pages of my birthday book and a notebook. Finally, I zeroed in on the snapshot chosen to represent my eighteenth birthday. Staring at the photo, I dug deeply into my memory bank. When the story began to unfold, I picked up a pen. Hours disappeared as I reclaimed memories of high school friends, especially Alan, the guy who unwittingly reignited a feistiness in me that I thought had been extinguished.

Pings from my cell phone occurred moments after I saved the edited story in a Word document. I unlocked the phone and opened a text message from Kai, which was accompanied by several photos of our visit the day before. She had cropped and edited the originals, and the results were stunning. I acknowledged their receipt and added a short note of thanks.

Hunger sent me to the kitchen to cobble together a meal from fruit and leftovers. I turned on the television in search of a weather forecast. Although winds were subsiding, a continuation of rain was predicted, so I scrapped any plans that would have taken me away from the condo.

Quickly calculating the five-hour time difference, I called the landlines of the Write Women and left messages on answering machines for all of them. Evidently, my friends were out and about. Either alone or together, they were busy as usual, and I saw no need to bother them on their cell phones. On the other hand, when Elle did not answer the home number, I called her cell. She picked up on the third ring. She was heading by foot to the student center on the Saint Paul campus of the University of Minnesota. We talked while she walked.

"The gardens are shaping up," she said, "and I'm loving your house. It's so quiet, and I'm even getting up early enough to have breakfast on the patio. The sky is so beautiful in the morning."

I smiled at the thought. The same sun that I had been enjoying every evening was having a similar effect on Elle in the morning. It had been there for me, too; I simply hadn't noticed. Perhaps both of us had needed a change of scenery. She peppered me with questions about Maui and seemed genuinely interested in my reactions as a tourist without a sidekick. Her statements commending me on my independence buoyed my spirit. Then she updated me on the latest storm to hit the neighborhood.

"Our place is fine, except for the loss of power for about four hours," she reported. I smiled at her use of the plural possessive. "I just had to clear some debris and hose down the patio—and I have a favor to ask."

"Shoot."

"I'd like to clean up Harry's greenhouse and get it back into operation. What do you think?"

Trying to get in touch with how I felt, I paused for a moment. My initial thought was great, go for it. But I hesitated just long enough for Elle to sense a reluctance.

"Or I could just leave it alone. Whatever you want, MJ," she said.

"Your plan would have pleased Harry," I said.

"But what about you?" Elle asked.

"It pleases me, too," I said, realizing how derelict I had been with Harry's favorite space. The greenhouse, home to mice and crickets and absolutely nothing green, stood in the backyard as a constant reminder of his departure.

"Don't worry. I'll be totally responsible for it, even after you get home," she said. "Do you have any idea when that will be?"

"I have no return date figured out yet," I said. "Sorry I can't be more specific. But I want you to know that you're welcome to stay as long as you need, Elle, whether I'm there or not. No hurry, really." I was surprised to hear myself hand out an open invitation with no reluctance.

"Wow, MJ. That takes the pressure off. I've been looking for apartments, but everything's so expensive."

By the time we ended our conversation, the rain had lessened to a steady mist. A few diehards in rain ponchos headed out for walks along the beach, and a family with two rambunctious children had slipped into the shallow end of the pool. Content to remain in the condo, I did some light housekeeping and threw in a load of laundry. If the time had not been midnight in Minneapolis, I would have called Millie again and thanked her once more for my home in Maui. Instead, I printed out the pages of my newly created Word document and filed them with the other stories in the expanding three-ring notebook.

MARGUERITE—AGE 18
April 30, 1953
"The Four Evers Say Goodbye, Davis!
Hello, Twin Cities!"

Four high school seniors crowd behind a birthday cake with eighteen blazing candles. We call ourselves the Four Evers, and in no way can we conceive of futures without the presence and support of each other. With graduation only five weeks away we are already dreaming of September, when all of us will be heading to the Twin Cities, three hundred miles southeast of Davis. Phyllis and I have been accepted into the same nursing program at the University of Minnesota in Minneapolis, and Monica and Rene, both good Methodists, are headed to Hamline University across the river in Saint Paul.

Phyl, Monica, and Rene are eager to be liberated from parents they consider smothering. But smothering is not how I portray Nana at all. If anything, patient and supportive are better descriptors. I can't imagine leaving her.

Since the accident, she has given me space and time to lash out at my circumstances. After an afternoon of drinking, a thoughtless adult got behind the wheel of a car. In an instant, he dismantled my world. He stole my parents and my idyllic life and left me broken in body and spirit. No one understands except Nana, who has been forced to endure her own personal loss. She is now childless. Yet, she somehow offers forgiveness, a trait that I admire but do not understand and one that I cannot even attempt to emulate.

A few months ago, my friends spent the better part of an evening ranting against their living parents. With an eruption of anger, I lashed out at their ingratitude and stopped them short with obscenity-laced judgments, which I immediately regretted. The obscenities, at least.

The whole outburst inspired from my best friends nothing but pity, a reaction that cut deeply. Since then, except for an occasional heart-to-heart with Phyl, I pretty much keep my feelings to myself, especially when grief-induced anger is involved.

At times, I feel stuck. If I am going to get a degree, I need to leave Davis, but gone is my naive belief that the world is a safe space. Just like my friends, I want to be giddy and excited at the prospect of going away to school. Instead, a frightening sea of insecurity churns behind my carefully constructed facade. Sometimes I let the terror take hold, and my usual reaction involves retreating into a self-protecting cocoon. During those scary times, Nana intuits and gently pulls me back.

"Nana, there are diploma schools cheaper and nearer," I say.

"Marguerite," she replies, "the university is a baccalaureate school. You mustn't settle."

"But the U is expensive and so far away. And it'll take so long."

"Leaving home is the natural order of things," Nana says. "And you have your scholarship."

"But the scholarship doesn't cover everything."

"It goes far enough. Your papa would have wanted the insurance money used this way. Your mama, too," she adds, her eyes locked on mine.

"But the money could help both of us if I stayed."

"No need to worry about me, Marguerite," she says as a firm reminder that she does not want to be used as rationale for my reticence.

"It's not just the money, Nana."

"I know," she replies. "We've been holdin' on to each other real tight. And that's been good. But it's time to let go, Marguerite. Just a little. We'll both be more than okay."

She makes it sound like we have been sharing the burden of grief, but I know Nana is the one who has been supporting both of us. As if she is reading my thoughts, she adds, "Never forget that you come from strong stock, Marguerite. You must never be too frightened to cut the cord."

Most of my recollections of the months after the accident are blurry at best. However, I know that while dealing with her own grief, Nana sheltered me from the duties of closing out Mama's and Papa's lives. She lessened my burden and honored as many of my wishes as possible as she settled their finances, distributed their personal effects, and sold the home I loved. Although Nana's example inspired, I could not summon the wherewithal to follow. While she quietly moved forward, I curled up in a ball. Nana hardly winced when she sold the store. Clearly, with Papa gone it had to be done, but when the papers were signed, I cried for days.

I moved in with Nana, right from the hospital. Without hesitation she turned over Raymond's old bedroom, packed away memorabilia, and let me redecorate and set it up as my own. When I was ready, we steamed off striped wallpaper and replaced it with muted yellow paint. Then she quietly backed away as I organized and displayed my eclectic collection of books, records, posters, and treasures in a fashion that resembled a cluttered cocoon.

I have endured many a pity party in my room without Nana's interference. If the door is shut, she gives me space, and if she needs me, she always knocks. I am all the family that she has left, and that makes me leery about leaving Davis. I chastise myself for using Nana rather than my own insecurities as justification for my reluctance. Underneath it all is a hidden grief over losing the MJ who would have longed to spread her wings and fly.

The shoe store was recently converted by the new owners to a Benjamin Franklin five-and-dime. Nana negotiated the sale of the building with the stipulation that she and I be allowed to live rent free in her apartment. The new owners, who live in a home that overlooks the Red Lake River on the northern edge of town, were fine with that. They rent the other apartment, my first home, to an elderly gentleman named Mr. Herman Schultz. He seems very attentive to Nana, and I wonder if she might give him some encouragement once I leave in the fall. I hope she will find someone to bring her, if not the happiness she deserves, then a little enjoyable diversion. Once I asked if she might consider sharing company with Mr. Schultz after I leave, and she matter-of-factly responded, "Heavenly sakes, no. Why would I? I've lived a woman's life since your grandfather died, and I have no need for any other man. Pass the mashed potatoes, please."

End of discussion.

I guess I have Alan Thorsen to thank for giving me the final push toward a life bigger than anything Davis could offer. A tall, husky farm kid with an ego bigger than his shoe size, Alan spent a good portion of our last date describing his great plans for the two of us once we graduate. He has enlisted in the Marines so he can "see the world, possibly even Korea." He wants an adoring, faithful girlfriend waiting for him when he returns to the family farm. I care about Alan and hope the world will be a kind place for him, that he can come home in one piece, but I have no intention of cementing my future to his. While we cruised around in his pickup, I tried to explain that my world is opening up, too, and that I am going to accept my scholarship to the University and leave Davis in late August. He got all moody. At first, I thought he just needed time to process. But now I'm not so sure.

Tonight is prom. Dressed in a lilac formal with white, open-toed pumps, I wait, first eagerly, then impatiently, for him to knock on the apartment door and pick me up for our last high school formal. As the clock ticks on, I notice Nana stealing glances out the front window and down the street. She's worried about Alan's safety; I fear something altogether different.

A phone call confirms my suspicions. The caller is Jeremy Dunleavy, my chemistry lab partner. Yesterday during lab, we chatted about prom. I chastised him for choosing to go stag to the biggest social event of the year, and he chastised me for going to prom with "such a prick."

Now Jeremy is on the line and saying, "I'm your prom date. I'm on my way. Be ready!"

"What?"

"I'll explain later."

I look up at Nana, who appears as confused as I. Jeremy must have called from the phone booth at the corner because within what seems like less than a minute he is knocking at the door.

"It's okay," Jeremy says. As an afterthought, he adds, "Sorry, I don't have a corsage."

When I refuse to budge until he gives me the entire story, he describes how Alan swooshed into the dance with a girl from East Grand Forks. Their arrival set everyone abuzz, especially Phyl, who was furious. She sought out Jeremy, and together they fashioned a plan.

"Aren't you the one who told me I shouldn't go stag to my senior prom?" he reminds me.

While Jeremy makes a convincing argument for giving Alan a taste of his own medicine, Nana hastily plucks an artificial gardenia from the centerpiece on the table. She ties it with a satin ribbon and hands it to Jeremy for me, then fashions a single rose into a boutonniere for me to pin on his lapel. "Go, go!" she says as she gestures toward the door.

I arrive at the high school gymnasium on Jeremy's arm, much to the surprise of everyone except Phyl. Alan, his ego badly bruised by my entrance with Jeremy, exits with his date, even before the Grand March. For me, the evening is memorable, as every prom should be, just not in the way I had anticipated.

The high school gymnasium becomes the setting for some final lessons before graduation. First, since Jeremy and I find it impossible to avoid gossipers, I discover that I'm totally ready to leave Davis and high school drama behind. Second, I am convinced that I really need to be much more discerning when I choose my next boyfriend. And probably most important, I learn that thoughtful guys like my friend Jeremy do exist. What's needed is chemistry of a different sort to bring a good fit my way.

But first things first. On to Minneapolis!

22

A few stray puddles were the only reminders of the preceding day's storm, thanks to the grounds-keepers who had descended on the green space shortly after dawn to rake up palm fronds, seedpods, and other debris. Immaculate once again, the area was buzzing with activity, especially around the tennis and shuffleboard courts. Maui's vacation life had rebounded and was once again on full display.

Feeling a bit housebound, I headed out for a walk along the sand and found a perfect spot near the shore to unfurl a beach mat, plop down, and attempt some writing. But the ocean's beautiful iridescence lured my eyes away from my notebook. I closed the cover and focused solely on the water. Outrigger canoes from a nearby canoe club skimmed across the surface. Farther out, a continuous parade of cat-amarans and small vessels filled with snorkelers and scuba divers were heading from Ma'alaea Harbor to Molokini, a small crescent-shaped crater that protruded out of the sea. If that was not enough, a monk seal, oblivious to me and other humans, played in the shallows. It was as if God had blown a whistle and declared, "Time-out is over; back to fun."

I was torn between two alternatives for the day. I could jump in the car and explore another corner of the island or continue reminiscing on paper, an experience that was becoming both energizing and cathartic. Since I had scheduled an outing the next day with May's family, I easily convinced myself to devote the rest of the day to writing. Staying in the condo for a second day in a row, however, did not appeal. When I discovered that my supply of ground coffee needed replenishing, the decision was finalized. With laptop stuffed into a tote, I headed out by car to Lava Java, a coffee shop whose coffee I hoped would be as enticing as its name.

Spontaneously, I bought an entire pound of coffee. As the server ground it to my specifications, I realized that my subconscious had no intention of returning to Minnesota any time soon. I ordered an iced Americano to go, wandered outside in search of a small table in the shade, and opened my computer.

I reread with fresh eyes what I had written the day before. The recollections only strengthened my appreciation for Nana. Her gentle nudges had tapped my courage. With her support, I had allowed neither injuries from the accident nor grief over Mama's and Papa's deaths to deter me from moving forward into an uncertain future. The winds of change had whipped me around, but somehow the eighteen-year-old version of myself had rediscovered her own resilience. Leaving Davis and Nana, although difficult at the time, had been a crucial step in the right direction.

Sipping the refreshing Americano, I contemplated resilience and my present need and want of it. Was resilience a finite gift bestowed at birth to be parceled out as needed throughout life? If so, my allotment had been used up long ago. Perhaps it was reserved for the young. When I was a child, I resembled one of yesterday's palm trees that survived the torrential rain by bending with the wind and disbursing nature's fury through its airy fronds. When did I become a blue spruce, easily toppled in strong winds after the soil around its foundation became saturated and soggy?

I pulled a notebook and a page from the birthday book out of my tote. Scrutinizing the photo for 1954, I began to write. Two hours and one iced Americano later, I closed the notebook and reflected on the years before the car accident. As a child, I had thrived as little miss drama queen. I had enjoyed retelling happenings with such embellishment that others in attendance would fail to recognize them. Mama was the best audience. She chalked up my expansion of the truth to imagination and creativity and encouraged me to secure my stories in journals that she carefully wrapped and presented to me as unexpected gifts.

Being orphaned by a car accident, however, was both dramatic and tragic. After opening night, no one wanted to attend a repeat performance of MJ's rendition of that drama. Phyl, Monica, and Rene, my best friends, were self-involved with their own dramas, and I quickly learned to keep my intensity and depression to myself. Of the three, Phyl was the one who accepted me and stuck with me. Decades later, I agonized over a detailed letter of gratitude and enclosed it in a card mailed just in time to reach her in Maryland before she died from breast cancer at the age of sixty-three.

What could I learn from studying Nana's response to tragedy? The deaths of Mama and Papa had been Nana's loss as well, but somehow she moved quietly and undramatically forward, as if she had been awaiting another bout of grief as a natural consequence of living. Nana was a calm round hole. I was a dramatic square peg who refused to sand down the rough edges. After the accident, I selfishly forced her to endure my dramatic responses to life's cruelest moment. She met each one with a loving embrace.

Eventually, I learned to tone it down for Nana's sake. But that only accomplished the relocation of my grief. Eventually, the worst of my drama settled in my gut, where it took up residence and ate away at my storehouse of resiliency. At the tender age of nineteen, the gently swaying coconut palm was morphing into a blue spruce.

MARGUERITE—AGE 19
April 30, 1954
"A Birthday Box From Nana"

Almost seven months into our nursing program, Phyl snaps a photo while I open my birthday package from Nana. Inside the box, I find an angel food cake wrapped in brown butcher paper and cushioned by now-stale kernels of popped corn. Hidden in the popcorn, I also uncover a small box of candles, a purple Hallmark birthday card with a handwritten note, and a black jewelry box containing a pretty star sapphire on a delicate silver chain. More than likely because this birthday is my first away from family, Nana has pulled out all the stops, and I love her for it.

After opening my birthday box, Phyl and I skip the Friday afternoon tea at Powell Hall and catch a city bus for a meetup with Rene and Monica at Milo's, a small cafe on University Avenue. The two of us arrive first and settle into an empty booth near the window. Twenty minutes later, Rene shows up without Monica.

"Sorry to be late. Happy Birthday, MJ!" she says as she removes her coat and deposits it on a nearby coatrack before sliding into the booth beside me.

"Thanks," I respond. "Where's Monica?"

"She sends her regrets. She had a big blowup with Rollie last night, and he called just when we were leaving. She sent me ahead and told me to wish you a happy birthday just in case she doesn't make it."

"Oh, for pity's sake," says Phyl.

"Hey, I'm just the messenger," says Rene.

"Well, I'm ready to celebrate, so let's order," says Phyl.

Milo's is known for its humongous malts. Mine arrives in two containers. Half of the thick chocolate mixture fills a tall malted milk glass and is topped with a mound of whipped cream and a cherry. The other half is still in the frosty metal container in which it was blended. Both are placed on our table and flamboyantly slid in my direction by a waitress who repeats the process for Rene and Phyl. She returns less than a minute later with the rest of our food. "Well done, cheese, pickles, hold the onions," she sings as she places a burger in front of me.

For the next hour, we laugh, catch up, and scoff at our year-old resolution to explore the Twin Cities as a foursome. Since October, we have rarely seen each other.

"Yep, great plans we had," I say, "before classes, homework—"

"And clinicals," adds Phyl.

"When winter hit," says Rene, "I had enough trouble just getting to class. It's warmer now, but it still takes hours to go anywhere off campus. Bus schedules are horrible."

"One of us needs to get a car," says Phyl.

I remain silent. Savings from my summer job at the *Davis Times* newspaper are long gone, and there is no way I will ask Nana to fund one more thing.

"I'll work on it," Phyl adds when neither Rene nor I respond.

Car or no car, our Four Ever friendship suffers from a deteriorating condition that just might be terminal.

Rene confirms the diagnosis with an announcement. "I have news. I've decided to transfer to Moorhead State at the end of the school year."

Phyl and I pause midchew and wait for an explanation for our friend's transfer to a school 250 miles north.

"I'd like to be closer to home. And they're supposed to have a good program for teachers."

"I didn't know you wanted to be a teacher," Phyl says.

"Well, I'm not sure I do. But I don't want to work in an office, and I can't imagine being a nurse. So, I'm going to give it a try," she says matter-of-factly.

Phyl catches my eye and communicates a look that screams, "Heaven help her students!"

"What does Monica say about you leaving?" asks Phyl.

"She's so busy trying to become Mrs. Rollie Ferguson that we've barely talked."

At the end of the meal, Phyl orders a cupcake and places on top several candles absconded from Nana's birthday package. Then she passes off her camera to our waitress, who snaps a few pictures while Phyl encourages patrons and waitstaff to join her in a rousing rendition of "Happy Birthday."

The evening's enjoyable, I guess, but sadly different from other birthday celebrations at home. Once Phyl and I say goodbye to Rene as she climbs aboard a city bus heading east, a sick, growing feeling in my gut proves that life has changed. The childlike magic of April 30 has ended. With no family to help me celebrate, the date has become an interruption for my busy friends.

As we wait for a bus headed toward Minneapolis, I half listen to Phyl's incessant chatter. I love her for trying to make the day special, but inside I feel hollow. Skin and bones mask a familiar emptiness that I fear might be my lifelong condition. And, to make matters worse, I find myself questioning my decision to go into nursing. I long for the passion and commitment that Phyl exhibits every day. She soaks up every bit of information and can't get enough of living, breathing patients. I, on the other hand, am terrified that I will screw up.

For as long as I can remember, Phyl has wanted to be a nurse just like her oldest sister Nadine, who was inducted into the US Cadet Nurse Corps in 1943. Phyl often bragged about her sister, the one who looked so beautiful in her gray flannel uniform with red trim.

"She even gets in free at the movies if she's wearing it," Phyl whispered to me in our third grade classroom at Franklin Elementary.

I was duly impressed. At recess, we schemed about how we would join the Corps when we were old enough. Then the war ended, and everything changed. But a nurse continued to be my answer whenever any inquiring adult asked what I wanted to be when I grew up. Now, I wonder why.

I peer out the bus window as Phyl continues her monologue, a diatribe against Monica's life choices, until the cupola on top of Powell Hall comes into view.

"We're home," she says, with an enthusiasm I wish I could share for the building that contains both my dorm room and my classrooms.

We exit the bus and turn toward the five-story building on Essex Street. Powell, filled with new friends and stern, good teachers, has been my residence for the last seven months, but I'm not ready to call it home, especially today. I long for my tiny bedroom in Nana's apartment. Sadly, I have outgrown the privilege of hiding away, so I trudge forward with head down until days later when Phyl returns from the drugstore with a package of newly developed photos.

"Sorry, your photographers weren't very good, and my damn camera is a piece of junk," she says as she scatters the pictures on my desk and culls out the ones taken on my birthday.

The blurry and overexposed photos in a sad way represent my current existence and my indistinct future. I ache for my youth. I remember Papa, who photographed his daughter much like he handcrafted shoes, with tender precision. While other men were physically stronger and more agile, he traveled through the world at a slower pace, pausing often to ease his hip pain. With the eye of an artist, he discovered beauty in the slightest of things, like a stone polished smooth by the rushing Red Lake River, a hand calloused by a lifetime of labor, or a daughter's joy on her birthday.

"I used to look at my leg as a problem," Papa once said when I asked him how he had learned to cope with his disability. "It wasn't always easy, MJ, but if I hadn't needed special shoes and hadn't come to Grampa Campbell's shop, then there's a real possibility that my path would never have crossed your mama's. So, disabilities can be blessings. They send us in a different direction, and sometimes that's good."

Wondering if perpetual sadness is now my disability, I spread out and study the photos that capture a birthday party that should have been joyful. Phyl's choice for my birthday book is the snapshot of the three of us mugging for the camera as our crazy waitress points it at us and yells, "Cheeeeeeseburger!" But once Phyl heads down the hall, I pick up a different photo, the picture of an opened box from Nana containing gifts lovingly protected by popped corn. Pleased with my choice, I tuck the photo safely away until it can be given a permanent home, the first blank page inside "Marguerite's Birthday Book."

23

*T*raffic was light as I drove into Kahului in search of the swap meet. The GPS led me to a huge parking lot with a surprisingly large number of cars. On foot, I followed a steady stream of shoppers to a fenced-in area with a sea of tents. Although it was barely 8 a.m., people were already exiting with bags of purchases and huge bouquets of gorgeous flowers.

The ticket booth stood at the top of an asphalt path that led down to rows of open-air tents. I used my cell phone to snap pictures of the bustling scene, then switched to video mode to capture a panoramic view and the harmonious chorus of wind chimes. Shells, glass, wood, and metal danced in the gentle breezes and beckoned me inside.

"Marguerite!" called May as she, Fern, and Mr. Sato approached from the parking lot. "I hope you have not been waiting long."

"Good morning, everyone. No, I just arrived. This looks like quite an adventure."

"Thank you for coming," said May. "This is a highlight for all of us, especially Father."

"It's a beautiful morning, Mr. Sato. Thank you for including me."

More intent on entering than socializing, Mr. Sato remained silent.

"We are glad you joined us," said Fern as she led her father to the ticket booth. She helped him retrieve two dollars from his pocket, which he handed to the cheerful lady in the ticket booth.

"Aloha, Ken. Aloha everyone," she said as she handed him four tickets.

May and I followed Fern and Mr. Sato, who walked a slow but steady pace into the swap meet and down an aisle of tents that showcased jewelry, paintings, woodwork, clothing, and an array of trinkets. Hanging from tent poles, dresses and cover-ups in brightly colored Hawaiian prints swayed in the breeze. Occasionally, I darted in for a closer look. I was especially intrigued by one tent that displayed children's books about Hawaiian sea life. The writer/illustrator sat on a high deck chair surrounded by stuffed turtles and whales. Engaged in conversation with an eager child, she inscribed a book as she talked. Another tent offered all sorts of lightweight articles made from parachute nylon: bags, backpacks, hammocks, and more. For sure, something from that vendor would make a perfect gift for Elle. After making a mental note, I moved quickly to rejoin Mr. Sato, who seemed to be gaining speed and zeroing in on a destination.

We entered an aisle that offered fresh fruits, vegetables, and cut flowers. The quality and quantity were impressive, especially the beautiful bouquets that were selling for the unbelievable price of five dollars. I examined one with a spectacular and hardy bloom that grew off a thick, woody stem.

"Protea."

It was Mr. Sato's first word to me. Hearing his voice, I turned my head and was greeted with a gentle smile.

"You must see our protea," he said. He turned to May and added, "She must see our protea." Before May could respond, he turned into the next tent and began examining onions.

"He disappears for awhile, but then he returns," May said.

"That must be hard" was my feeble response.

"Some days are better than others. I'm not sure why. Fern and I have learned to enjoy his lucid moments for as long as they last."

Just as I was fumbling around for an adequate response, Fern said, "A picnic table just opened up. I'll take Father over. May, will you get the lumpia?"

"Lumpia?" I asked.

"It's a Filipino egg roll," said May. "Father's favorite. Our neighbors used to bring us freshly fried lumpia regularly until they moved. Now we wait until Saturdays."

May stood in line for lumpia, while I took beverage orders and sought out a stand selling guava juice and lemonade. We rendezvoused at the picnic table. Mr. Sato's lucidity dramatically improved once the food arrived, and he greeted me as if he were seeing me for the first time. Fern and May accepted his turnaround with little acknowledgment. I, on the other hand, was amazed at the peculiarity of dementia. While enjoying the snack, we discussed a plan for the rest of the morning.

"We are hoping you might be free to come home with us and see Father's gardens after you finish shopping," said May.

"I'd love to see your gardens, Mr. Sato," I replied.

Totally focused on his treat, Mr. Sato remained silent. Fern and May discussed logistics. Finally, after I assured my hosts that I felt comfortable driving back to Kihei from Upcountry alone, we settled on a plan. Fern and Mr. Sato would browse a bit and head home. May would help me search for some unique gifts, then ride with me and give directions.

"We are actually on the grounds of the University of Hawaii Maui College," May explained about forty minutes later as we walked through the parking lot toward my car. May directed an easy exit and immediately pointed out another notable destination across the road. "That is the Maui Arts & Cultural Center. When Father was better, we often attended events there—concerts, plays, films, art exhibits. There is much going on. You might want to check it out."

"One more thing to add to my list," I said.

May continued to navigate. I drove through Kahului, a town that was beginning to feel like familiar territory.

"Continue on this road and you will eventually get to Hana," she said after we left Kahului behind and headed toward the North Shore.

"Not today," I said.

"No. Today, we go Upcountry. It is a little cooler and so beautiful. You will see," she said as she directed a turn onto Highway 37, which cut through open fields. The smooth, straight roadway gently ascended the northern side of Haleakala, the dormant volcano that loomed ten thousand feet in the air. My ears popping was the only clue that we were climbing. We passed turnoffs for the towns of Pukalani and Makawao. "Straight, straight," May said. She also ignored a turnoff that began a steeper ascent to Haleakala National Park and the edge of the crater. Our road, now curvy and narrow, continued up the western slope of Haleakala. We entered a unique ecosystem in which cacti, eucalyptus, bamboo, and cattle coexisted.

May shared a bit of family history while I drove the winding road. Her parents had moved Upcountry after they married. "Father raised flowers and vegetables. For years, his farm supplied local supermarkets, even after Mother died. When his memory began to fail him, he knew it was time to scale back. Thankfully, he sold most of his fields when he was still able to negotiate a fair price. Now, we live on what is left."

"How long have you lived with him?"

"Four years ago I sold my house and moved in with Fern and Father."

"Where was your home?"

"We lived in Kahului, not too far from the college. But after my husband died and my daughter moved to the mainland, I saw no reason to stay. I wanted to be closer to Fern so I could help with Father."

I had felt her empathy at the Heritage Park on the one-year marking of Harry's death. That morning she had eased my loss without mentioning her own. "I'm so sorry about your husband, May."

"We have much in common, Marguerite."

I wanted to hear more, but abruptly May changed the subject.

"This is Kula," she said as we entered a small village. "Actually the whole area around us is Kula. The 'heart of Maui,' Father likes to say."

Through a small opening in the trees, I looked down the mountain and spotted tiny buildings near the coastline miles away. We had driven much higher than I had imagined.

"That's Kihei," said May, reorienting me. "There's no direct road from here down to Kihei, so when you return, you'll have to retrace the route back through Kahului."

"I think I'm getting the lay of the land," I said.

We drove on, and the road continued to narrow. Finally, May directed me to turn onto a gravel road that was only wide enough for one car. I slowed to a crawl as we crossed small rickety boards that bridged a dry culvert. Just when I was afraid I might have to drive straight up volcanic rock, a driveway appeared.

"We're home! Just back the car into this space," she said, gesturing to a stretch of gravel.

I followed her directions. We stepped out into a refreshing coolness that must have registered ten to fifteen degrees less than the temperature in Kahului. Nestled into the property was a modest, one-story house flanked by two other structures, all connected by a walkway of crushed rock. One building appeared to be a large garage and the other, a small, freshly painted cottage. Blooming tropical vegetation in brilliant oranges, yellows, reds, and greens adorned every available space.

Fern greeted us, but Mr. Sato was nowhere in sight. Once inside the house, I looked around and tried to mask my surprise. I had expected a minimalistic ambiance, then internally reprimanded myself for the stereotypical assumption. Instead, flat surfaces displayed books, photos, artwork, and houseplants of all varieties. Matted and framed magazine and newspaper articles covered the walls. Four small-scale, wooden chairs and a round table sat squarely in what I imagined was the living room. It felt more like a library or a museum or a hybrid of both. The only other pieces of furniture were an easy chair and lamp in one corner. The room inspired my curiosity, and I was excited.

Before I could inquire about the treasures around me, Mr. Sato appeared and announced, "I must show you my gardens." He quickly led me back outside. Without pause we followed the pathway of crushed rock lined with beautiful stalks of bird of paradise and other spectacular blooms. Mr. Sato, as if on a mission, did not stop until we reached his destination.

"Protea!" he said. He led me through an array of magnificent flowers that surpassed anything I had seen on the island. Some resembled red and orange pincushions with stamens that rose from the center and exploded like fireworks into contrasting, bright pigments. Most had bracts as beautiful as their flowers. The leaves alone were works of art—some fuzzy, some spiky, some iridescent as the sunlight passed through them. Each variety had been carefully labeled with hand-painted signs. Mr. Sato led me through well-maintained flower and vegetable gardens and a small orchard of fruit trees. I was astounded that the compact plot of land could produce such abundance.

During the tour, Mr. Sato's vocabulary loosened with each sentence. He spoke with quiet reverence as he cradled each blossom or piece of ripe fruit. Once again, he resembled the teacher who had led the narrated tour of the 'Iao Needle. He described as a blessing the perfect growing conditions of Upcountry Maui. He emphasized that protea could be dried so the flowers could be kept indefinitely. "A blessing continued," he said.

We retraced our steps and returned to the house, where May and Fern were ready to serve tea at the round table in the living room. Once we sat down, an artfully arranged plate of strawberries and lychees with sliced papaya and bananas was passed. Surprised that I had never tasted a lychee, Fern demonstrated how to quickly peel the tough skin to uncover the sweet, juicy white fruit. Totally distracted by his tea and fruit, Mr. Sato retreated once again. Although I was sadly disappointed to see him drift away, May and Fern, familiar with his periods of silence, appeared unaffected.

Enticing memorabilia surrounded us while we sipped tea, and it took every measure of self-control to remain in my chair and not jump up to study each piece. Unable to resist any longer, I pointed to a framed picture on a nearby bookshelf and inquired about it.

"Would you like to tell Marguerite about the picture, Father?" asked May, hoping to draw him back.

All of us waited patiently for a response that I thought might never come. Eventually, Mr. Sato spoke, slowly at first, with measured words and lengthy pauses between sentences.

"This is my wedding day," he said, staring at the young couple in the framed photo. "The marriage was arranged. She arrived from Japan shortly before the ceremony. I had only met her briefly. I was lucky. She was lucky. Sometimes you know when you see someone for the first time that it will be good, and that is how it was."

"Lovely," I said. Moisture collected in Mr. Sato's eyes, and I feared I had dampened his day by asking him to relive memories of the past. Quickly, however, a blank expression erased the sadness. He had retreated again. I turned to May and Fern. They were exchanging forlorn glances.

"I can't thank you enough for a wonderful morning. I have enjoyed it all—the swap meet, the tour of your gardens, and the delicious tea and fruit. But I think it's time to head back."

"You wait," Mr. Sato said abruptly, surprising me but not his daughters. He rose and walked out the front door.

While Fern retreated to the kitchen to wrap up a care package of fruit for me, I moved over to the wall and studied a framed map of Maui.

"We live right here," said May, touching her finger to the glass. Then she dragged it along my route back to Kihei. "Really there are only a couple of turns. Left out of the driveway. Follow the road until it ends. Turn right and you'll be on the main highway that goes through Kula and down. Turn left toward Kahului when you reach the highway near the ocean. Easy."

"Seeing the map helps," I said.

"If you get disoriented, just head down to the ocean."

Next to the map hung a collage of framed newspaper clippings. The headline of one caught my eye: "Inductees arrive at Fort Snelling for intelligence training." I scanned the article.

"Father was very proud of his training in Minnesota." May's use of the past tense pulled at my heart. "Sometimes he remembers."

"It would be a wonderful story to hear," I said.

"You would consider coming back?"

"Of course."

"Good. Now let us see how Fern is doing."

May led me through a small doorway to the kitchen. Unlike the living room, the kitchen was sleek, modern, and functional. Dark wooden cabinets wrapped in a U shape around a gas stove with a built-in wok and a huge exhaust fan. Stainless steel countertops, uncluttered except for a butcher block of knives and a ceramic crock filled with cooking utensils, had been wiped spotless.

"So this is where you cook all the wonderful vegetables your father grows," I said.

"Fern is the chef," May replied.

"May is my sous chef," Fern added with a chuckle. "We are fortunate. The garden overflows year around. We would like for you to take this home." Fern handed me a cardboard box filled with lychees, strawberries, bananas, onions, three papayas in different stages of ripeness, a bunch of freshly washed greens, and two ripe tomatoes.

"Such hospitality! Thank you. I'll certainly enjoy everything," I said.

"Father and Fern have bedrooms down that hall," said

May as she led me to the side door. "I live in the cottage. Let me show you."

After depositing the box of produce in my car, I followed May to the cottage. She opened the door and gestured for me to enter. Her uncluttered private space was decorated in soothing blues and greens. A unique blend of Japanese artwork and family photographs graced the walls and side tables.

"I wanted you to see the rest of my ohana."

"Ohana?" I asked, unfamiliar with the word.

"Ohana—family," she said. "These are my grandchildren, Jacob and Lilly, and their parents—my daughter Rose and her husband Jerome," she said as she handed me a small framed photo displaying a handsome family of four.

"Your daughter and grandchildren share many of your features," I said.

"Perhaps life would be easier for them if they resembled their father," she responded as she set down the frame and reached for another. "This is Mr. Wantanabe, my husband." In the photograph, a young Asian man in a suit and tie stood erect for the camera with a beautiful bride standing at his side.

"And this is you on your wedding day? What a beautiful couple," I said.

"We were young then. We had a good life," she said as she set down the picture frame. "I regret not taking more photos."

May dug through her desk and retrieved a detailed map of Upcountry and with a red pen drew my return trip.

"For you to keep in the car," she said as she folded up the map and handed it to me.

May walked with me to the Prius where Fern stood waiting. As I thanked them again for the enjoyable morning, Mr. Sato returned from the garden with a huge bouquet of protea and bird of paradise and verbal instructions for their care. Once again he was lucid.

"You come again," he said.

"I would enjoy that very much. Thank you for the beautiful flowers."

I carefully placed the fresh cut flowers next to the box of veggies and fruits. When I waved goodbye, May and Fern waved back, but Mr. Sato had already turned toward his garden. A few minutes later, I was coasting down the final descent and approaching level ground. I turned toward Kahului and followed May's directions until I located the road that led me back to Kihei. The return trip had been amazingly easy. As I walked across the parking lot of the Maui Sunset, I gazed up at Haleakala and pictured my friends in their lovely spot halfway up the volcano.

A multitude of new sensory experiences had filled the day, and something I had heard resonated in my head. "I was lucky. She was lucky. Sometimes you know when you see someone for the first time that it will be good . . ." Attraction was not considered a necessary ingredient for a successful match in an arranged marriage. Yet, Mr. Sato, even though he was plagued by dementia, verbalized the importance of attraction and the good fortune that the right mate brings to one's life.

All afternoon, I returned to Mr. Sato's comment. By evening, I was reflecting on the good fortune Harry and I shared. By the time I climbed into bed, I was eager to commit the next day to the writing of at least part of that story.

24

*C*onfirming that Sundays in Maui were family days, intergenerational gatherings once again livened the beach parks along South Kihei Road. In anticipation of an extended stay, I had prepared a small picnic with plenty of water before heading out with notebook and pen to stake out a place in the sand. The day promised to be a hot one, especially since the cooling trade winds had taken their own vacation. Since I was beating churchgoers to the beach, I had expected to easily locate a parking place. Such was not the case. Already people were swimming, relaxing in the shade, tending charcoal grills, and setting out table-cloths and picnic supplies for Sunday at the beach.

I turned into the parking lot of an inviting beach and patiently waited as a bronzed young man dripping with seawater jumped into his jeep and backed out of a prized space. After pulling into the vacated spot, I unloaded. Determined to get a little sun, I lugged my beach chair and overstuffed tote down to the sand and staked out a lovely spot about thirty yards from the lifeguard stand.

The ocean fascinated me. With envy, I watched as young children ran in and out of the waves with carefree aban-don. Adults, some still wearing hats and sunglasses, deftly entered the water and swam a few yards past the shore breaks to calmer water. Finally, spurred on by discomfort from the heat, I headed toward the ocean to join them.

When swimming in Minnesota, I eased into lake water to give my body time to adjust to the cold. The ocean's shore breaks, however, were not conducive to a slow, methodical entry. After observing more experienced swimmers, I followed their example and waited for a set of huge waves to wash ashore. During the lull that followed, I quickly swam beyond the shore break to the smooth water beyond. The shock of the temperature change, from the heat of the sun to the coolness of the water, wore off immediately, and soon I was bobbing as carefree as the others. The saltwater added to my buoyancy, a rare and delightful experience for someone who lived half a continent away from the nearest ocean.

Refreshed, I exited the water, although a bit less gracefully then I had entered. All in all, my dip in the Pacific had been successful. As I plopped back into a beach chair and pulled out my notebook, my inner voice chastised me for waiting ten days to enjoy one of Maui's simple pleasures.

The atmosphere pulsed with sensory images, the ocean's beauty and activity, the scent and taste of fresh saltwater, the laughter of people of all ages at play. I first attempted to describe everything with words and filled several notebook pages. Eventually, I pulled out a small digital voice recorder, something I often used to capture fleeting thoughts or unique sounds. This time, I recorded rhythmic shore breaks that crashed upon the sand and quietly receded into the surf.

The goal for the day was to write about Harry and the beginning of our relationship. Inspired by Mr. Sato, I was determined to record as much as I could recall while my aging brain was still lucid. Before leaving the condo, I had sorted through the pages of the birthday book and had chosen the photo that reminded me of our rocky beginning. Pulling it out of my tote, I focused on the couple in the photo. Although well established in her nursing program at the university, the woman in the snapshot was naively unprepared for the next defining moment of her life. The man sitting next to her could only be described as a mystery. Conjuring the memories, I picked up a pen and notebook and wrote as quickly as I could. Every detail of my twenty-first birthday flowed easily onto the page.

I was interrupted only once, when an unusually large set of breakers sent inattentive waders sprawling. One young woman in a revealing, hot pink bikini theatrically screamed as a wave swallowed up her designer sunglasses. She had been taking a selfie in waves she assumed would remain only thigh high. Instead, a rogue wave crested on her head, ripped off her sunglasses, and drenched both her and her cell phone. She, like me, was probably an ocean novice who did not understand the importance of the warning "Never turn your back on the ocean!" In contrast, a gray-haired woman entering the water at the same time spotted the freakishly large wave. Holding a snorkel and set of flippers tightly to her chest, she dove under its crest and popped up on the other side, where she easily donned the snorkeling equipment and swam over to the rocks.

The interruption had been educational and entertaining. Thankfully, I had positioned my beach chair a safe distance from the water, a good lesson for the future. My writing materials remained safe and dry. Sunbathers closer to the water's edge, however, were not so lucky. I jumped up to help a family retrieve an array of sand toys that were now afloat. Meanwhile, the woman whose sunglasses had disappeared into the swirling water gave up the search and turned her attention to the task of removing sandy grit from her cell phone. Eventually, everyone was resettled, and life at the beach continued.

I glanced down at my Minnesota skin, now aglow under sunscreen that was no match for the direct rays of the sun. I gathered up my belongings, moved back to the grass, and spread out on an unoccupied slice of shade. Munching on a peanut butter sandwich and Mr. Sato's strawberries and lychees, I edited what I had written, then stowed my writing materials and relaxed into the rhythm of the waves. Like a soothing mantra, the ocean lulled me into deep thought.

Someone who had long ago discarded the white-clothed father figure in the sky, I spent the next few minutes imagining the ocean in front of me as the perfect visual for an ever-present higher power. To deny its strong existence was foolhardy and draining, a hard lesson learned by the woman with the sunglasses and cell phone. But those who relaxed in its care, like the snorkeler, breathed easily knowing that all would be well. The analogy worked for me because the ocean epitomized Mama's God.

"You are God's creation, Marguerite, so relax into your nature," she said more than once when I verbalized self-critiques that bulleted dismaying aspects of my body and disposition. It was her way of reminding me that God does not create junk. As I grew, I vacillated between railing against my uniqueness and flaunting it. As a gawky child with frizzy hair and a significant gap between my front teeth, being comfortable in my own skin was an ongoing challenge. As I grew, I was often threatened by over-sized feelings that felt too intense for my adolescent brain. I simultaneously envied and scorned my friends' abilities to live happy, superficial lives. I chose instead to be authentic, and only a small group of friends tolerated my moodiness and self-absorption. They chalked up my melancholy as a byproduct of my parents' deaths, but I knew that the seeds for darkness had been present all along. Now here I was, an old woman gazing at the ocean and experiencing an unusual comfort. Mama had been right. I needed to relax into my nature, to make peace with the darkness, if I wanted to prevent drowning in a sea of grief. I accepted the unique sensation. On this morning, I was right where I was meant to be.

I considered the silent commune my Sunday morning worship service. "Thank you!" was my simplest of prayers. I stuffed belongings back into my tote and headed to my car and then to the condo. Exhausted by both the sun and mental introspection, I jumped into the shower and then into bed for an afternoon nap that lasted almost three hours.

After waking, I ordered a pizza, then awaited its delivery while I viewed the setting sun from the lanai. Finally, realizing that my three-hour nap had killed any possibility of a good night's sleep, I opened my computer and transcribed the scrawls from the beach. Once I had the installment in legible format, I printed the pages and filed them with my other writings inside the three-ring notebook. Because the beginning of my relationship with Harry spanned two birthdays, I turned my attention to the photo of my twenty-second birthday and wrote as quickly as I could until I had filled page after page with unfiltered and unedited details. I stopped only for a bite of pizza or swallow of water. Finally, at 4 a.m., I headed to bed.

I almost missed the morning. The red numerals on the clock announced eleven o'clock. Friends back in Minnesota were most likely preparing dinner. A caffeine headache drove me to the kitchen to prepare a fresh, steaming cup of Lava Java. With mug, computer, and notebook, I settled in at the table on the lanai and began the lengthy rewriting process.

For the better part of the next two days, like a person possessed, I reworked and edited the second installment. Delving into untapped emotion, I fleshed out memories and honed the prose until I was convinced that the recollections on the pages honestly reflected my sensitivity at the time. The completed story chronicled a journey that began with a series of false starts and ended with a commitment. Finally, after sunset, I watched as the pages of a love story stacked one upon another in the printer's tray.

MARGUERITE—AGE 21
April 30, 1956
"A Surprise Birthday Dinner at Cafe Marc
With David Henry Burdick III"

The arm of a lanky, dark-haired man is casually draped across the back of my chair as the two of us lean together to make it easier for our server to snap the photo. I am caught midlaugh. After inquiring about the origins of my initials, my companion tells me that although everyone calls him Harry, his real name is David.

"David Henry Burdick III, actually. After my father and grandfather. Sounds pretentious, right?"

"Perhaps I should call you David Henry?"

"If you do, I am calling you Marguerite Jonella," he says with a laugh.

We continue our conversation as Harry and MJ. He's relaxed, and in turn, I settle in. We talk as if we have known each other for years rather than the eleven days since Phyl's marriage to Harry's roommate John.

Harry and I had been the only guests in attendance at Phyl and John's wedding. Although the couple's intention was to elope, Phyl had insisted on a maid of honor, me, which pushed John into recruiting a best man, Harry. Shortly before 3 p.m. on the chosen day, Phyl and I rendezvoused with the guys outside a small Lutheran church in Northeast Minneapolis and waited for the Good Friday midday service to finish up. After the churchgoers emptied the building, John located the pastor who had agreed to perform the ceremony. The nuptials and the signing of the paperwork, which took less than fifteen minutes, were followed by an intimate wedding dinner for four at Cafe Marc, a posh dining establishment close to the church. Afterward, the bride and groom headed off in Phyl's Studebaker, leaving Harry stuck with the responsibility of delivering me back to Powell Hall.

Now, less than two weeks later, Harry and I are back at Cafe Marc. So far, thanks to Phyl, the evening has surpassed any expectations I might have had for a Tuesday that also happens to be my birthday. I had been scheduled to work an evening shift at the hospital, which Phyl decried as "a lousy way to spend a birthday." Without my knowledge, she had tried unsuccessfully to recruit someone to switch shifts with me. Finally, even though I balked, she insisted that I allow her to work in my place. Right before she was ready to leave for the hospital, she instructed me to put on my cream-colored, wool sheath and await my birthday surprise.

When I absolutely refused to budge without knowing what she had planned, she confided, "Well, it was supposed to be a double date with John and me, but now it looks like it will be just you and Harry, and he'll be here soon, so get ready!"

With a mixture of excitement and skepticism, I asked, "Harry? Did you drag Harry into this?"

"It didn't take dragging, MJ." Then Phyl paused slightly

before adding, "Harry's been thinking about asking you out, and a double date seemed perfect. It was going to be so fun—the four of us. But now I have to work—for you! So don't be testy. Just say thanks and get ready."

I wasn't sure how much of what Phyl was telling me was accurate and how much was Phyl being Phyl, a great embellisher of the truth, especially if the story fit her purpose. But at that moment, I wanted to believe that Harry had been thinking about me. I had been thinking about him ever since the wedding. He had impressed me as someone several cuts above my other dates, immature, ego-driven guys who seemed obsessed with partying. Suavely self-assured, perhaps because he was five years older, Harry seemed comfortable in his skin, and an evening with him, I admitted to myself, was a perfect birthday present. I thanked Phyl with a big hug, then reached into my closet and pulled out my favorite sheath.

Harry arrived on time, and when we walked down the sidewalk, he touched the small of my back to steer me in the direction of his black and white Oldsmobile. A strange spark of electricity passed into my core, and I wondered if he had felt it, too. It was a new experience, a connection not felt with other dates, university students who hardly excited me and who grew less appealing the longer I spent with them.

Now, coincidentally, Harry and I are seated at the same table that we shared with the newlyweds. Happy to be in his company, I hope he is enjoying himself, too, even though John and Phyl are not part of the evening.

"You're deep in thought, MJ."

He looks at me quizzically like he is open to hearing whatever is on my mind. Not wanting to sound needy, like the girls I detest who require constant reassurance, I do not ask him the question that bubbles under the surface,

"Did Phyl and John push you into this date?" Instead, I say, "This is a wonderful place to celebrate a birthday. The food is delicious."

"There's a dessert I'd like to try, but it requires a bit of a wait. Are you in any hurry?" The question relaxes me a bit. I am not eager at all for the evening to end. While we wait for the mystery dessert, our conversation bounces back and forth. We share bits of our histories and plans for our futures. Surprising myself, I tell him about Nana and Mama and Papa and the accident and why Phyl is like a sister to me. He tells me about his family and growing up in Grantsburg, Wisconsin, with an older sister who shares some of Phyl's mothering tendencies. I tell him about nursing, a vocation I am learning to befriend. He tells me about coming to the University of Minnesota to study wildlife management and obtaining a degree in horticulture instead. I tell him about my work at the hospital; he tells me about juggling his work in a research lab by day and his graduate classes in architectural engineering at night.

In what seems like no time at all, a baked Alaska with several flaming, seven-inch candles is flamboyantly delivered to the table and placed in front of me. Gracefully swirled, golden meringue hides a base of chocolate cake and a block of peppermint ice cream.

"Happy birthday, MJ. Make a wish!" Harry says.

"How did this happen?" I ask, not clear when Harry placed the order for the spectacular dessert.

"Magic," he says.

Making a silent wish for more magic, I blow out the candles.

MARGUERITE—AGE 22
April 30, 1957
"Harry and Me ~ Looking Forward Together, Finally"

For the second year in a row, Harry is the only other person in my birthday photo. One might think his presence is logical, since my date with him a year earlier was perfect. But a relationship takes two people being of the same heart at the same time; and Harry and I, like two riders on separate cars of a Tilt-A-Whirl, seemed to be continually thrown in different directions. Shaken and a bit bruised, we each needed to get our feet back underneath us. When he and I finally could walk a straight line, thankfully we headed in each other's direction and met in the middle. Let me explain.

Shortly after my perfect date with Harry, my hope for a continuing relationship quickly evaporated. Like an adolescent schoolgirl, I thought about Harry incessantly and ached for the sight of him or at least a phone call. Two weeks later, I learned sideways from another nurse that not only was Harry dating someone else, he was attached. The whole revelation alienated me from both Harry and my best friend Phyl, whom I blamed for setting up the blind date in the first place. *Blind* was the operative word, and I chastised myself for that condition. I came to believe that David Henry Burdick III had been tossed in my path as just one more life lesson.

The bruising began during a conversation with another nurse as we stood in a light drizzle at the same bus stop after our split shifts had finally ended for the day. Exhausted, I was glad to have finished my last stint at Miller Hospital for awhile and was looking forward to my rural nursing practicum in Glen City, Minnesota. In contrast, my coworker Judy had only one thing on her mind. She was anxious to get back to her apartment and prep for a date with her boyfriend.

"Where do you find the energy to go out after a split shift?" I asked.

"Well, it's either a late date or none at all," said Judy in a voice that sounded more excited than tired. "Tonight, we're doubling again. My friend Rose is waiting for her steady to finish up his night class, and Rich is waiting for me to get home. We make it work. Thank heavens for late movies is all I can say."

"How can you stay awake? I'm exhausted."

"Once I shower, I'll be raring to go. Harry, on the other hand, he'll probably sleep through the feature again. Makes Rose furious. Can't blame him, though, after sitting through night classes in engineering, of all things. Must be boring as hell."

"Harry?" I said, hoping against hope that there could be two nighttime engineering students named Harry.

"Harry Burdick. Do you know him?" Judy asked. "Nice guy."

"I don't think so," I replied, trying not to react to the kick in my gut. My answer was truthful, since clearly I did not know Harry at all.

"We're going to see *Giant*. Rose and I aren't crazy about westerns, but Elizabeth Taylor's in it and, of course, James Dean. What's not to like there . . ." Judy prattled on about the movie. When her bus approached, she changed the subject. "I probably won't see you again before you leave, so good luck in Glen City. See you next fall," she said as she climbed aboard.

The bus lurched forward and proceeded down the avenue, leaving me alone with hurt and rage at Phyl for setting me up like a country bumpkin with a man who was attached to another woman. Certainly I had suffered much greater heartbreak in my life, especially when Mama and Papa died, but their parting had not induced self-loathing. As I stood in the drizzle, my memory rewound to prom night and my embarrassment at the realization that I had been stood up. My relationship with Alan and now my encounter with Harry brought me face-to-face with my own stupidity. Years had passed since prom night, and I was still as naive as ever. I remembered being furious with Alan. But thanks to Jeremy, I regrouped quickly and even managed to greet Alan aloofly when he flounced his last-minute date in front of me. That night, I had felt not a twinge of jealousy, only palpable relief, the ease one feels when a heavy rope has been detached from around one's neck. In contrast, the new information about Harry was spawning jealousy-laced anger that reinforced what I feared to be true. My sensibility regarding men was awful and definitely could not be trusted. I was the one who had placed the rope around my neck this time, and like a noose, it was tightening. I had no one to blame but myself.

My bus arrived. As I settled into a seat, I stared out the window and ran various scenarios in my head. Harry had been coerced into taking me out on my birthday. That was why I hadn't heard from him since that night. When the evening was over and he'd done his duty, he probably told Rose all about the mercy date, a favor for his ex-roommate John and his new wife. Rose might have been mildly annoyed with the arrangement but would have given her boyfriend a pass because he was helping out good friends who weren't able to give some poor girl a pleasant birthday evening. Perhaps in the end, I had provided both of them a good laugh.

John and Phyl must have known about Rose. So why did Phyl lie and say Harry had been thinking about asking me out? Was this the only ruse she could come up with to convince me to go out that evening? She knew, of course, that I was naive enough to believe her.

Rose. Of course she would have a beautiful name. She was probably gorgeous, too, voluptuous with thick, straight hair that contoured smoothly into a bob or pageboy. Instinctively, my fingers combed through tame damp curls that were already turning to frizz, thanks to the steamy bus. By the time I disembarked in front of Powell Hall, I had beaten myself up. During the birthday dinner at Cafe Marc, I had feared Harry felt trapped into spending an evening with me, and now I knew that was exactly what happened. Hadn't Mama always told me to trust my gut? Thankfully, I hadn't further embarrassed myself with Phyl or any of my other friends by gushing about the evening and my adolescent infatuation.

I fought the urge to phone Phyl and to call her out for betraying my trust. But, I had endured a long day, a split shift from 7 a.m. to noon and then 3 to 7 p.m., with studying in between. I was exhausted and hardly able to construct thoughts into logical sentences. I knew I was no match for quick-talking Phyl. I avoided confrontation and, right after a late supper, climbed into bed. Sadness and hurt accompanied the anger. At that very moment, Harry was enjoying an evening with his girlfriend. I tossed until exhaustion finally allowed my mind to shut down.

Packing for my summer nursing assignment filled much of the next day, especially after a call from Louise. We were two of the four student nurses who had been assigned to the same hospital in rural Minnesota for the summer. Louise had finagled temporary use of her family's car and offered to drive all four of us to Glen City, if we could be ready by 4 p.m. I had intended to take the bus on Sunday, but going a day earlier by car with friends sounded like a much better alternative since I was especially eager to leave my personal mess behind.

After clearing my early exit with the dorm director, storing the belongings I was leaving behind, and tightly packing the rest, I met Louise, Joy, and Elizabeth on the curb. We wedged suitcases and boxes into every available space and headed to our destination, a rural township fifty-five miles west. Giddy with nervous excitement, heightened even further by our accelerated departure, we took turns pondering our futures as Louise drove. In the crowded back seat, I penned a simple note to Phyl to explain why I had left sooner than I had intended without saying goodbye. I omitted any mention of Harry or Rose. I addressed and stamped the envelope and asked Louise to pull over at a mailbox en route.

The first glimpse of Glen City was disappointing. It was even smaller than Davis. The four of us stowed our belongings in two double rooms in Mrs. Porter's boardinghouse, conveniently located across the street from the hospital, and handed over the car to Louise's brothers, who farmed a few miles away.

None of us had thought to inform Mrs. Porter that we were arriving a day earlier than scheduled. Although she offered to rustle up a quick dinner for us, we declined and asked for directions to the nearest restaurant, which turned out to be the only eatery in town. The four of us walked to the diner, a mom-and-pop place, and were offered plasticized menus. My eyes scanned the limited selections, then spotted the words that were capitalized near the bottom: NO ALCOHOL SERVED! The unavailability of alcohol was a nonissue since all of us had been firmly taught that it was inappropriate for student nurses to imbibe publicly within the city limits of the town in which we worked.

With our fountain Cokes we toasted to a summer of new experiences, then devoured plates of comfort food, meat loaf with mashed potatoes, canned corn, biscuits with homemade strawberry jam, and lemon meringue pie. On the short walk back to the boardinghouse, I sensed a level of familiarity. Just like in Davis, the pace in Glen City was slow, the air was fresh, and the people who passed us on the street actually looked us squarely in the eyes and smiled. Unbeknownst to us, most of the locals were already privy to a great deal of information, thanks to Mrs. Porter, who relished her role as the town's authority on anything related to newcomers. They could guess we were the new nurses who would help in their hospital. Townspeople were happy about that, and I was happy to be away from the Twin Cities. Prescription: relocation was going to treat my present depression and offer a new perspective.

My summer of nursing in Glen City was a mixed blessing. Surprisingly, my favorite shifts took place in the emergency room, where I assisted the doctor in charge as he (all doctors in the hospital were men) triaged and treated patients who arrived after farm accidents, auto crashes, or sudden onsets of illness. Those times demanded total focus. After each person was stabilized, I welcomed the fact that in some small way I had helped and was now free to turn over the patient to other nurses. Then I enjoyed time alone to savor the lingering adrenaline.

One of the doctors, however, unnerved me, at least at first. Dr. Rohr informed the new nurses that we were students and were expected to stand whenever he walked into the room. In contrast to his authoritarianism with us, his bedside manner was soothing and paternal, especially with his pediatric patients, whose parents trusted him explicitly. He was an aging pillar of the community, and I found myself craving from him a positive comment or any sign of appreciation. Louise and Joy found him off-putting and egotistical. I realized that if I needed emergency care, I wanted him to be the doctor on call. He earned my respect, and I yearned to earn his. With each shift under his tutelage, I became more skilled and self-confident.

But just as my professional life grew, so did the festering over my personal life. Shortly after arriving in Glen City, I received a newsy note from Phyl that started with a regret that we had been unable to get together one last time before I left for the summer. Then she gossiped about our mutual friend:

> *Monica was in the Cities on a shopping spree, buying her white wedding dress and prepping for the big day. She was quite insufferable. Very mad at me since I refuse to ask for time off to go up to Davis for the wedding. How about you? Are you going? I made the mistake of asking her if Arnie knew about the abortion. She almost took my head off and swore me to secrecy. "Rollie never existed" was all she said before changing the subject . . .*

The note prattled on for three pages, with a brief paragraph regarding John and his seminary studies but no mention, whatsoever, of Harry.

I had not received a wedding invitation from Monica. Perhaps it had been sent to Powell Hall and was in the process of being forwarded, or maybe I had been left off the guest list entirely. That was a possibility. Most likely Monica was still festering about the fact that Phyl and I had been unwilling to help her with her "little problem." Even though we warned her, she blamed us for the outcome of a shady abortion that, in all likelihood, will make childbearing in the future difficult, if not impossible. Rollie paid for the procedure, then disappeared from her life.

I hypothesized Monica's motivation for meeting up with Phyl in Minneapolis. Either she was offering an olive branch or just looking for an opportunity to gloat about finding someone smarter and richer than Rollie, someone who could offer her a church wedding and reception that would make the society column in the Davis newspaper, something that Phyl's wedding had not. Thankfully, I didn't care about any of it and was happy I had not been pulled into Monica's latest drama.

Neither fear of pregnancy nor the need to clandestinely acquire a diaphragm were among my worries, since my personal life in Glen City totally lacked romantic relationships. If there was a promising bachelor under the age of fifty within the city limits, I had not met him, although I had been subjected to flirtations from a single grocer who had to be over sixty. Calvin was recovering in the hospital from a skin infection that he had ignored for months until the sores developed into an ugly, oozing mass. Thanks to him, I was forced to hone another crucial nursing skill, the ability to swiftly deflect inappropriate advances.

A fair chunk of the town's male population had been decimated by World War II. Too many parents had lost sons; one family had lost a daughter. A monument with the names of the dead stood in the town's square surrounded by clay planters filled with red and white geraniums, green spikes, and miniature US flags.

Many of the eligible males, those too young for the draft in the forties, now worked the family farms. They rarely came to town, except on Friday nights to hang out, do their shopping, or catch a movie. Both of Louise's brothers fit that description. One of them, Frank, became infatuated with Joy and took her to an occasional movie at the Grand, a theater that offered fairly current movies but hardly lived up to its name. I happily worked at the hospital on Friday evenings, with no desire to become entangled with single men who seemed only interested in finding women to share their beds and help with chores.

As the weeks passed and my obsessive thoughts about Harry failed to diminish, I journaled daily and filled page after page with dramatic angst. Placing physical distance between me and my problem, I eventually realized, was a terrible prescription for a cure. Like unwanted bedbugs that stow away in a piece of luggage, my depression had secretly journeyed along. Was I suffering from a diagnosable mental illness? I hoped that was not the case, although indisputable sadness was attacking my well-being. Once again, I grieved the loss of Mama and Papa and longed for their wise insights. Nana would have offered unconditional support, but she would have found my depressive state alarming, so I suffered alone.

I corresponded with Phyl but intentionally omitted any mention of Harry or our evening together that she had arranged. Although that scenario needed closure, I was committed to handling my exchange with her firmly and in person. In my journal, I rehearsed the exact wording of my confrontation, complete with comebacks for Phyl's imagined responses.

Closure with Harry was another matter. No amount of journaling clarified to my liking the ambiguous nature of my insecurities. Harry had agreed to a pity date to be kind and to help out John and Phyl. He had not misled me in any way. He had failed to be forthcoming; yet, he was not obliged to tell me of his other relationships. Clearly, I needed to let him off the hook and direct my anger back at myself for taking a simple date and exponentially expanding it into a fantasy based on warped perception and unspoken dreams. But that was my head talking. When I probed deeper, I exposed a layer of hostility toward Harry that was both confusing and disconcerting.

Loneliness left my insides cold, even during Minnesota's summer heat. I had felt the chill before, after Mama and Papa had passed. Never wanting to feel that depth of loneliness again, I had slowly built a layer of self-protection over my wounded heart. Now Harry, or rather the thought of Harry, had pierced that crust, and I hated him for it. Which of my defects had allowed him to become such an all-encompassing thought? I wanted not only treatment for this mental failing but also protection from relapse. Finally, after hours of writing I made shaky peace with the idea that some questions may never have answers.

When my commitment to Glen City Community Hospital came to an end in mid-August, I was conflicted. I said goodbye to colleagues who had become, perhaps not trusted friends since I had kept my personal concerns close to the vest, but special friends nonetheless. Glen City, a self-supporting farming community with decent people, had provided the perfect environment for the internal work I needed to do. With a margin of success, I had spent my summer shoring up my damaged crust. Hardened once again, I was ready for unfinished business in the Twin Cities, but only after a visit with Nana. I headed directly by train from Glen City to Davis.

Nana was excited to welcome me home. In anticipation of my arrival, she had prepared a delicious soup flavored with pork spareribs, potatoes, and finely chopped kale, parsley, and onions. It had been simmering for hours on low heat in a big stockpot, while Nana awaited my arrival by train. After exiting the town's only taxi, I glanced up at Nana's apartment and spotted her familiar wave through the window. But when I crossed the threshold, Nana's stature alarmed me. She seemed smaller, somehow, and definitely frailer. She hesitated slightly before gently reaching out for a hug. When my arms encircled her, I felt nothing but bones and tried to cover my alarm.

"Nana, how are you?" I asked as evenly as possible with hope that my generic question would provide space for her to open up.

"First things first," she answered. "I have soup ready. You must be hungry from your trip."

"Actually, I am very hungry. Let me wash up first," I said as I headed for the bathroom. Behind the closed door, I opened the medicine chest in search of any clues to what was ailing Nana. Aspirin was the only drug in the cabinet.

"Delicious!" I said after I downed a spoonful of broth and accepted the bread basket Nana was offering. We chit-chatted through the meal. Anytime I asked her a personal question, she answered simply, then pivoted the conversation back to my plans for the fall. She wanted to hear all about my nursing experience in Glen City and what lay ahead before graduation in the spring. Finally, I had waited long enough.

"Okay, Nana. Without your support, I never would have become a nurse. Now let me help you. What's going on?"

She spoke slowly. "Well—after a checkup, Dr. Thorsen sent me to Fargo. Now—the doctors there want me to go to Mayo Clinic in Rochester."

Masking my fears, I asked about the diagnostic tests that had been done. Instead of pivoting this time, she answered each question as clearly as she could, stopping only once to retrieve a file folder with her notes, doctors' reports, and test results. Systematically, we discussed the information. No longer evasive, Nana answered every question. I sensed her relief, as if she had been patiently waiting for the opportunity to share her concerning news with me in person.

"Family is a place to be vulnerable," Nana had said,

offering me a space to open up after Mama and Papa died. Now she was the one opening up to me. I suspected she wasn't sharing her innermost fears, probably to protect me, but she was willing to verbalize her commitment to getting to the bottom of what was making her feel crummy and then to do whatever was necessary to regain her health.

We spent a great deal of the next day making expensive, long-distance phone calls to her Fargo doctors and to Mayo Clinic, which led to the scheduling of an assessment in Rochester that would take several days to complete.

"I'll get a car and drive up to get you," I said, worried about her stamina.

"Nonsense, I'll take the train," she said, concerned that my offers of help would conflict with the beginning of my final year of coursework.

We compromised. Nana would ride seven hours on a train to Minneapolis. I would somehow find a car, pick her up at the station, and drive her to Mayo Clinic in Rochester, Minnesota, ninety miles farther southeast. I insisted that she allow me to stay with her in Rochester for as long as it took to get a diagnosis. She agreed to the last part only after I assured her that my presence would help both of us. Being in Rochester with her, I argued, would give me the opportunity to witness cutting-edge diagnostic care.

Fearing that her needs were intruding too much on my responsibilities, Nana urged me to return to Minneapolis as soon as possible, so a day later I was back on the train. I was anxious to talk to my teaching supervisors and find out what accommodations might be allowed. Nana was my top priority. I wanted to focus on her appointments and aftercare, which would, more than likely, extend into the first weeks of the fall quarter. If necessary, I was prepared to drop out temporarily. I was surprisingly content with that possibility.

Exhausted, I slept sitting up during the last three hours of the train ride back to the Twin Cities. Using some of the cash Nana had thrust into my hand after she hugged me goodbye, I took a cab from the train depot to Louise's apartment, where I took up temporary residence while I worked out the details of my impending absence.

The hectic few days leading up to Nana's appointment were eased by the kindness of teachers and staff at the university. They understood that when a nurse is needed by her family, that's where the nurse should be. Dropping out of school was premature, I heard. They encouraged me to move back into Powell and let the fall quarter unfold with the understanding that I might miss valuable experiences that I would have to make up. "Those details we can attend to at a later time." This quote came from one of the teachers I had misjudged as uncaring, stern, and overly critical three years prior.

The only remaining concern was the acquisition of an automobile to take Nana and me to Rochester. Buying a car, even a used one, was financially out of the question. I looked into renting, but the daily rate was outlandish. Finally, out of alternatives, I picked up the phone and called Phyl, described my predicament, and asked if either she or John would be available on the evening before Nana's appointment to pick us up at the train station and deliver us to Rochester.

"Of course," said Phyl without thinking twice or checking her schedule. "I'll talk to John. I'm sure one of us will be free. You can count on it," she said. She asked about Nana, expressed heartfelt concern, and never mentioned my lack of correspondence over the summer. Her unconditional support stirred a shudder of guilt for the ill feelings I harbored.

On the day of Nana's arrival, I took a city bus to the

train depot and waited for Nana's train to pull into the station. I gathered her up along with our small suitcases and headed to the curb where John was standing next to the old Studebaker. He greeted both of us, then opened the passenger side door and helped Nana into the front seat. I slid into the seat behind her, while John stashed our luggage in the trunk. Nana was finally on the last leg of her trip.

"Phyl had to work tonight or she would have ridden along," said John. "But she sent a picnic of sorts. It's in the basket next to you, MJ."

I was thankful for Phyl's forethought. I opened the basket and found ham and cheese sandwiches on whole wheat bread. I passed one up to Nana, who quickly unwrapped the brown butcher paper and took a bite. She had not eaten on the train. "Too hard to get to the dining car," she said. I uncapped a bottle of orange juice and forwarded that as well. With a sandwich in one hand and a bottle in the other, she looked armed for the journey and for whatever the outcome would be. Less than two hours later, we were settled into a hotel room, with our luggage unpacked and the contents of Phyl's basket, a loaf of bread, small jar of peanut butter, carrot sticks, apples, ginger cookies, and picnic utensils, spread out on the table between us.

"Phyl, bless her heart, packed plenty of nutritious treats to keep us going for awhile," said Nana. "Help yourself, Marguerite. I'll just take one of these cookies, then I have to start fasting for tomorrow's blood test."

Nana was showing not a hint of apprehension about the days ahead, and when I asked how she was feeling, she said, "Worrying about things I can't control is just wasting energy—but I'm glad you're here, Marguerite." She reached over and patted my hand. I was glad, too, and happy when she quickly fell asleep. The day's travel had worn her out.

The next morning she awoke refreshed and ready to get to the bottom of things.

The Mayo Clinic staff impressed me with their thoroughness and attention to all aspects of Nana's health. All specialties were conveniently located, and we easily moved from floor to floor, building to building, and even back and forth to the hospital for tests and biopsies. Some procedures were routine, like simple blood draws. Others were invasive, sometimes uncomfortable. At the end of the fourth day, the diagnosis of cancer in the lymph nodes was confirmed. Nana took the news in stride and immediately questioned the doctors about treatment that involved surgery to cut out as much of the cancer as possible and radiotherapy. She was ready to begin.

I latched on to the good news. Even though the cancer had spread, so far it was only detectible in two spots. Nana was not surprised at all by the diagnosis. In all likelihood, her pain had been signaling for weeks the onset of a life changer. She focused on moving forward.

Nana's indomitable spirit was no surprise. The woman with the strength to carry on after burying family member after family member had no plans to abandon me and join the dead anytime soon, at least not without a good fight. Thankfully, her doctors refrained from including a timeline with her diagnosis; rather, they focused on Nana's positive attitude and her aggressive response to symptoms. "Both will add years to your life," Dr. Wheaton, a young and charismatic oncologist, told her. His words encouraged both of us, and when I had a moment with him out of Nana's earshot, I thanked him. He responded with something I already knew: "Your grandmother is a remarkable woman."

Once Nana was able to walk independently after her surgery, she grabbed my hand and firmly said, "It's time,

Marguerite. Return to school. There's nothing more you can do here. I'll let you know when they're done with me, and you can help me get back on that train to Davis." When I protested, she added, "I want a graduated nurse in the family, and that's not going to happen if you waste your time here." Her sentiment was reinforced by one of my favorite nurses in radiology, who promised to keep an eye on Nana during her therapy. "There will be times when your presence will be critical," she said. "But now is not one of them. We'll take good care of her."

Once more, Nana and I compromised. I agreed to go back to school, but only after she was settled into transitional housing and transportation to and from the clinic for her radiotherapy had been arranged. Two days later, we relaxed in identical rockers on the porch of Nana's rooming house and waited for Phyl to pick me up per our arrangement by phone the previous evening.

Considering all she had been through, Nana was in great spirits. "There's something to be said for being able to put a name on what sickens you," she said. "I hated the not knowing. I'd rather have it be a nasty virus—cancer is such a beast—but it is what it is. Now, you study hard, Marguerite, and I'll work hard, and we'll both be in fine shape to celebrate that graduation of yours come spring."

Expecting to see Phyl's cream-colored Studebaker at the prearranged time, I panicked when a black and white Oldsmobile pulled up and a dark-haired, lanky guy emerged. Harry strolled up the front walk and announced, "This must be the place, and you must be Marguerite's grandmother," as he extended his hand to Nana before turning to me. "Nice to see you again, MJ."

I wanted to run, but I stood up and offered introductions. "Hello, Harry. I hadn't expected you. Yes, this is my grandmother, Jonella Campbell. Nana, this is Harry

Burdick, a friend of Phyl and John's." I couldn't bring myself to say a friend of mine.

"How nice of you to help my granddaughter," said Nana.

"My pleasure," replied Harry.

After some chitchat that involved the weather and road conditions, Nana offered Harry a beverage. When he declined, she turned to me. "Looks like it's time then. Off with you. I want you back in the Twin Cities before dark." I bent over and kissed her goodbye as Harry reached for my suitcase. "You've been a godsend, Marguerite," she whispered. She directed her next comment to Harry. "Drive safe."

"That I will," said Harry. "It was nice to meet you, Mrs. Campbell."

"Likewise," she replied.

My mind reeled. Once again, Harry had been roped into helping Phyl, this time getting her off the hook for a commitment she had been unable to fulfill. Once again, I felt like a bothersome child being passed off from one adult to another, and to make matters worse, for the next two hours I was going to be trapped in a car with Harry.

I waved goodbye to Nana from the front seat. She waved back from her spot on the porch. As we drove past the stately homes on Pill Hill, I turned to Harry and said coolly, "I'm sorry that Phyl was unavailable and that you were called in."

"I wasn't called in," he replied, matter-of-factly.

I turned and looked at him.

"I've been wanting to talk to you, but you are a hard person to track down," he said. "I'm sorry about your grandmother's illness. If you don't mind my asking, how's she doing?"

He had driven all the way from the Twin Cities to help me, so he deserved an answer. I described Nana's diagnosis and treatment plan. Harry listened as he drove and followed up with gentle questions. I considered verbalizing my utmost fears, that Nana's disease most likely would kill her, then stopped myself and directed the conversation back to safer topics. I asked him about work and his classes, and he asked me about my summer's nursing assignment.

Conflicted and terribly uncomfortable, I felt the rise of silent panic anytime our conversation moved beyond the superficial. Harry's motivations for driving to Rochester remained a mystery, and I avoided any questions about his exchange with Phyl. I wasn't sure I'd hear the truth, anyway.

Plus, there was the issue of Rose, someone I wasn't supposed to know existed. It was as if her specter was occupying a seat in the Oldsmobile, most likely the one right between us. I fought to keep myself in safe territory. I never broached any subject that would relate to other relationships or how he spent his free time. I also avoided any mention of our dinner together and the void afterward. But even within these boundaries, I could feel myself getting sucked into a vulnerable place. The Harry of old, the man who had attracted me quickly and firmly months earlier, was resurfacing with each compassionate response, especially those regarding Nana. With each mile, my resolve to remain detached from someone who was involved with another woman continued to erode.

Harry escorted me into the entry of Powell Hall, set down my suitcase, and asked for a pen, which I dug out of my handbag. After requesting my phone number, he scrawled each digit of Powell Hall's main switchboard into the palm of his hand, then quickly turned and disappeared into the night. Our time in the car should have been the perfect opportunity to address some of the issues that had been smoldering for months, I thought as I watched him walk out the door. I had squandered the chance to ask about Rose. And what was worse, after a single car ride and a request for a phone number, butterflies were drawing me back into a naive schoolgirl fantasy that was bound to lead to heartbreak.

Gutless, I had lacked the self-confidence to speak openly with Harry. I was not going to let Phyl off so easily. After a class we shared the next day, she and I sat down for our first face-to-face conversation in months. Her first questions involved Nana, and I answered as thoroughly as possible. Then I pounced.

"Why did you have Harry pick me up?"

"Honestly, I was going to drive down and get you, MJ. But Harry insisted. He was at the apartment when you called, then said, 'I'll go.'"

I looked at her skeptically. "Oh, come on, Phyl. Don't treat me like a child—again. I know you roped him into taking me out for my birthday. He has a girlfriend, for pity's sake. And now this trip to Rochester—what were you thinking?"

Now it was Phyl's turn to be at a loss for words. "Oh, MJ, I'm so sorry about your birthday. John and I—well, we just hated Harry's girlfriend and wanted him to spend some time around other people without her, and your birthday was coming up. Then the whole work schedule thing, and I had to cover for you—and you were balking—we just wanted you to have a nice birthday."

"So you let me think he was interested in asking me out?"

"Well, maybe that was a bit misleading. But he seemed happy to join the party when we set up the surprise."

"But he hadn't expected the two of you to drop out."

"That's probably true. But he told me afterward that he

was glad he'd met you. And he asked about you—where you'd gone this summer."

"Oh, stop!" I said disgustedly.

"No, really, and I wouldn't be the least bit surprised if meeting someone like you was what undermined his relationship with Rose."

Her name hit me like a brick.

"She's a case," continued Phyl. "All sweet and clingy when she's with Harry, then bitchy beyond words when he's out of earshot. John saw right through her, but you know Harry. Too nice. Thank heavens he'd finally had enough."

"What?"

"He broke it off weeks ago. Midsummer. She was mad as hell, and he thought he had a stalker on his hands for a while, but she finally latched on to some other poor fella."

She paused while I digested her comments and then continued, "I'm telling you, MJ, he insisted on driving down to Rochester. Insisted! I told him he could ride along with me if he wanted, and he told me he wanted to go alone. It's the God's honest truth! So what happened?"

"He picked me up and drove me home," I said, not sure how to answer her question.

"And—?" She waited for details, and when nothing else was forthcoming, she asked, "So what do you think?"

"I think I can't spend any more time talking," I said. I stood up. "I'm so far behind, and I really gotta go."

"I am sorry, MJ. About your birthday. You know that, right?"

"You're forgiven." I looked Phyl squarely in the eyes to reinforce that she really was forgiven, since failing to tell each other the whole truth was a condition from which we both suffered.

Later that evening, the operator of the main switchboard buzzed my room, the signal that I had received a phone call which was being forwarded to the telephone at the end of the hall.

After flying down the hall with concern that the call might be about Nana, I answered breathlessly, "Hello, this is Marguerite French."

"Hi, MJ. It's Har—." A male voice was competing with some sort of racket.

"Harry?"

"I . . . you might . . . me . . . ?" Only a few of his words were distinguishable until he shouted, "Can you come down?"

"Where are you?" I yelled back.

"At the pay phone in the lobby," he answered.

After hanging up, I rushed back to my room, quickly exchanged sloppy study clothes for a cotton sheath and cardigan, ran a brush through my untamable curls, and applied a fresh coat of lipstick. Then I headed down the stairs and toward the laughter and chatter of a large group of women who were milling around the lounge area. I spotted Harry, the only man in the lobby, casually leaning against the wall by the pay phone. He was wearing a white dress shirt, open at the neck with sleeves rolled up to the elbows. It was neatly tucked into a dark pair of trousers. He met me halfway and then guided me out the front entry in search of a quieter spot.

"This is better," he said. "Can we start over?"

I thought he was referring to our incomplete phone conversation, but then he extended his hand for a shake.

"Nice to meet you, Marguerite Jonella French. My name is David Henry Burdick III. Feel free to call me Harry."

"Feel free to call me MJ," I replied.

"So, MJ, would you like to go out for a cup of coffee? Burger? Dessert?"

"Have you been talking to Phyl?" I asked.

"Not lately, why?"

"Not important. Yes, coffee and dessert sounds good."

"I know a great place for dessert," he said as we exited Powell Hall.

We sat across from each other in a big padded booth surrounded by rich mahogany in the bar area of Cafe Marc. The highlight was not the pecan pie, which was deliciously rich and gooey, but the ease at which we were replacing the memory of an evening tainted by misunderstandings with another, happier one. Harry opened up. He made a point of mentioning a former girlfriend named Rose, who had complicated his life. He assured me that the relationship was over, and that he didn't want any secrets between us.

"I don't want any secrets either," I said. After a pause I added, "I knew there was a girl named Rose."

Harry reacted with a bit of surprise but thankfully did not ask for details.

Much like a painter who reuses an old canvas, with each bit of honesty, I whited out the dark shadows that clouded the past few months. Then upon the fresh surface, each bit of sharing added a fresh, bright color to a new design. We talked and laughed for much longer than we had intended. Concerned about the dorm's curfew, I gasped at the time. Harry sped down the city streets, illegally parked so he could race me up the walk, then planted a soft kiss on my lips before ushering me back inside, just in the nick of time.

If my trust in Harry was not totally rebuilt that evening, it became firm and unshakable three weeks later after he insisted that he be allowed to drive me down to Rochester, pick up Nana, and then turn around and deliver her to Davis, over 375 miles north. His consideration of her was extraordinary and, as it turned out, necessary.

Although Nana was excited about going home, three weeks of radiotherapy had taken its toll, and a train trip would have been insufferable. Instead, she enjoyed the luxury of stretching out in the back seat of Harry's car and sleeping most of the way. For me, the trip was an opportunity to spend extended time with Harry, a great improvement over the small slices we had been able to cobble together since our evening at Cafe Marc.

Once gently assisted up the stairs to her apartment, Nana declared the day's travel over for all of us. She was insistent. "You'll spend the night, and drive back tomorrow."

I welcomed the extra time to observe Nana as she puttered around the apartment. She moved about slowly but sure-footedly. Although surgery and treatments had weakened her body, her mind remained sharp and her spirit strong. When she stated that she was definitely capable of living alone, Harry and I seconded the opinion.

Watching Nana interact with Harry warmed my heart. They laughed as they set the table, while I reheated the casserole and pie that Nana's friend Edith had prepared as a homecoming surprise. While I gave the apartment a good once-over with dust cloth and mop, Harry hunted down a ladder and washed layers of grime off the outside of the windows.

"If Nana is going to be housebound for awhile, at least she is going to have a clean view," Harry said, calling her by the name she insisted upon.

That night Harry slept on the couch as I stretched out in my old bed. Amazed at all that had transpired since the last time I had slept under my lilac quilt, I filled pages of my journal before unwinding enough to fall asleep.

The following morning, Harry and I stocked Nana's pantry and refrigerator, portioned out leftovers for her, and returned a freshly washed casserole dish and pie plate along with our thanks to Edith, who assured us that Nana's friends would watch over her.

When she hugged me goodbye, Nana whispered in my ear just loud enough for Harry to hear, "He's a keeper, Marguerite!"

I do not like to say that I fell in love with Harry. Falling connotes loss of self-control, an exhilarating ride until the bottom is reached with a crash of broken dreams. I had experienced free fall during my first round with him. I hated the one-sidedness of that condition and did not want to repeat it. This time, I was not alone. Both of us were accepting the risk that accompanies the building of a new relationship. At first, I thought that risk-taking would be harder for me. But it was equally hard, if not harder, for Harry. He confided that there had been another woman, a fellow student during his undergraduate years, who he thought had wished to share a future with him. She had broken off their engagement at the end of their senior year and had returned to Upstate New York and her previous life without so much as an over-the-shoulder glance. She had left a deep scar. "A string of Roses," as he put it. "John was a friend through it all. And later on, Phyl. They were trying to help," he said, referring to their missteps in hooking us up. "I'm just sorry you were hurt in the process."

"Can we be done looking back?" I asked.

25

*R*ecalling Harry's entrance into my life was like dusting off an old videotape and rewatching a sappy love story. My brain was as outdated as a VCR, yet somehow, after a bit of fine-tuning, it had produced a relatively clear picture of how Emma's parents had found each other. I had planned to share our love story with our daughter when she was old enough to understand. But that time never arrived, and without an audience, I simply had filed it away like so many other memories that were now resurfacing thanks to my memoir writing. During the process, images had emerged, like the one of Harry leaning against the wall next to the pay phone in Powell Hall. There was no photo documenting that pose, yet there he was in vivid detail, the central character in the video that, once I got the machine to work, was running through my head.

The ringing of my cell phone quickly called me back to the present. It was Kai.

"Happy Memorial Day, Ms. Burdick."

"MJ," I reminded her. "I'd forgotten today was a holiday."

"Not for me, I'm afraid. Today is a busy day at the store. Actually I'm calling with a request. The photo of you and Dad on the lanai turned out so great. I was thinking that if it was okay with you, I'd blow it up into a poster and display it in our book area. 'An author stops by.' Something like that. Any thoughts?"

"I'd be fine with that, Kai," I said.

"Great." After a brief pause, she added, "Have you given any more thought to a possible book signing? We'd love to set one up. We could make it informal and just have you hang out and talk to people who come in."

"Truthfully, I haven't thought too much about it, but something casual sounds doable," I said.

"Would Friday work? Say noon to three? There'll be a cruise ship in port, so we should have a fair amount of traffic."

"Works for me," I said, a bit amazed at both her enthusiasm and my spontaneous reaction.

"Good, good, good. I'll do the promotion, so all you need to do is show up. And I'll get Dad to dig out copies of your books."

Kai thanked me again and ended the conversation with a promise to check in on Thursday.

The phone call spiked adrenaline. I almost felt like a writer again. Reenergized, I donned water shoes and headed down to the shoreline for a late afternoon hike.

As I picked my way around the rocky remnants of low tide, I contemplated the mysteries of the brain. In mine, eighty years of memories had been filed away. Recollections depended upon my ability to open the correct folders and dust off the images. Thanks to Mama, photos from the birthday book were triggering the process. Each year's carefully chosen picture and caption were greasing the pathway inward. And best of all, the written stories they were generating were reserved for a safe, nonjudgmental audience—me.

Having the ability to recover decades-old memories

eased my fear of impending dementia. Less than a month earlier, I absentmindedly had engaged the lock on a door-knob rather than a deadbolt, an action that had left me shaken and concerned about my aging brain. Since then, Mr. Sato, by his example, was teaching me to appreciate my situation. Watching him float in and out of lucidity was a lesson in the harsh realities of dementia. How scary to misplace memories, the stories that anchor a person's existence. Thankfully, that was not my present condition. I would continue to record my own stories, I decided, for as long as I was able.

Hunger and the lateness of the afternoon forced me to turn around and head back to the condo. I watched the evening's sunset from the lanai and offered a short prayer of thanks for Harry as the sun spectacularly set once again. Later that evening, I wrote about the culmination of our courtship, which seemed a fitting way to close out Memorial Day.

MARGUERITE—AGE 23
April 30, 1958
"First Birthday as MJB"

I am now Marguerite Jonella Burdick.

"MJB, just like the coffee," jokes Harry, the first of many times he will offer that comparison.

My life is nearly perfect. Mutual longing to build a future with each other ignited our relationship. The trajectory of our dreams, although not always a straight line, propelled us to the altar. Corny but so true!

Eleven months earlier, shortly after both of us received our degrees, John, now an ordained pastor, married Harry and me during a simple, midmorning ceremony near the roaring waters of Minnehaha Falls with Nana, Harry's mother Catherine, his sister Jane, and Phyl in attendance. After brunch, Harry and I, eager to spend four uninterrupted days and nights together, sped north to the shores of Lake Superior in what was now "our" Oldsmobile. The cold wind and intermittent rain hardly dampened a honeymoon spent cozily under blankets and a down comforter. Feeling loved and safe, I had only one regret. Mama and Papa had been absent from the most important day of my life.

When Harry and I returned to the Twins Cities, we settled into a two-bedroom rental in Northeast Minneapolis, a house with ample room for Nana, whose deteriorating condition is the only downturn in my new, wonderful life. Nana will continue to require additional trips to Mayo Clinic as new cancerous growths are detected and carved out of her frail body. Arrangements have been made to simplify things for her, and in turn, Harry and me. Surgeries will still take place in Rochester, but follow-up treatment will be done in Minneapolis, where we can transport and care for her more easily.

Harry, bless his heart, loves Nana. She is the only grandmother he will know since both of his refused to emigrate from Europe with their children. He has convinced her that the second bedroom in our apartment is specifically hers, not a guest room.

Her response is "until you need it for a little one."

"When there's a little one, we'll get a bigger house," Harry replies.

Their exchange leaves me warm and hopeful.

26

The phone rang early on the day following Memorial Day, but not before my writing exercises had been completed.

"Marguerite, this is May. I hope I did not wake you." After I assured her that she had not, she urgently described the reason for her call. "Father is very disturbed. Last night, he wanted you to come—immediately! We tried to explain that it was very late—nighttime—and we could not ask you to drive up in the dark. But he was unrelenting—pacing, pacing. Repeating 'Today I remember!' Over and over! Finally, Fern and I got him to bed. We hoped by morning he would have forgotten whatever was making him agitated. But after he awoke, same thing. 'Get Marguerite! We must talk story.' Perhaps if you are free, you could come?"

"Yes, of course I will come," I said, concerned not only for Mr. Sato but also for May, who sounded unusually distraught.

I dressed and headed out, easily finding the turns that led Upcountry. May, who had been watching for my arrival, met me at the car and expressed her gratitude as we walked together into the house. In the living room, Mr. Sato was standing over an open, black-lacquered box, the contents of which were strewn on the table.

Looking up, he dropped the papers that he was holding and quickly walked over to me. "Marguerite," he said. "Today, I remember. Today, we talk story."

Not sure how to respond, I simply said, "Yes, I would love that."

He offered me a chair next to the table. After asking if I might take a few notes, I reached into my tote bag and grabbed a notebook and pen. As an afterthought, I retrieved my digital recorder and requested permission to use it. Unfazed by the small electronic device, he quickly nodded and turned his attention back to the contents of the box. As unobtrusively as possible, I hit the record button and settled back with pen in hand.

Mr. Sato rummaged through an array of newspaper and magazine clippings, snapshots, and letters that he had removed from the box. He paused only long enough to retrieve several newspaper articles and photos that had been framed and hung on the living room walls. Perhaps overstimulated by the sheer number of objects in front of him, he stepped back and stood silently with his head bowed. I feared he was retreating, so I grabbed the wedding photo that he had been able to describe to me on Saturday and offered a simple statement.

"So this is your wedding photo."

He stared at the photo for at least thirty seconds before responding. "No, this is my parents' wedding photo."

I looked up at May. She nodded her head affirmatively, then exchanged smiles with Fern.

"They were a lovely couple," I said, hoping to prime the pump for more information.

Mr. Sato detailed again an arranged marriage and a love that eventually grew into a strong and lasting relationship.

Only this time the groom was his father, not himself. He described his father's arrival from Japan in 1906. "His passage was paid by plantation owners in exchange for a year's work in the sugar cane fields. The work was hard, the wages low. Some of the Japanese workers returned to Japan, but my father stayed." Six years later his bride, a woman he had never met, arrived, and the two were wed. "They were a very good match. Babies followed. Three daughters, none survived, then two sons."

With the help of a brain that was definitely clicking, Mr. Sato explained that his parents were Issei, the first generation to emigrate to America from Japan. He and his brother, both American citizens because they had been born in Hawaii, were considered Nisei. We had talked about this during our morning at the Heritage Park, but I let him repeat without interruption. Quietly and articulately, Mr. Sato continued, "Third generation, my daughters—Sansei." He was definitely tracking. He picked up a photo of a young man in a military uniform.

"Is that you?" I asked.

"This is my brother, Ichiro." Mr. Sato paused before continuing the story. "He was a soldier in the 298th Infantry Regiment of the Hawaii National Guard. Then came the bombing of Pearl Harbor and everything changed. A very scary time for Japanese in Hawaii—and on the mainland. Those who did not know us questioned our patriotism. They feared sabotage. Espionage. My parents lived in fear. Friends, priests, language camp teachers, journalists, businessmen were led away—some in handcuffs. Taken to immigration centers or jails, then to quarantine stations under military control. Many ended up on the mainland at internment camps. There was no reason to fear us. We were Americans! Loyal to our country!" His voice grew louder and more urgent with each sentence.

As if to regain his composure, Mr. Sato closed his eyes and took several deep breaths. May, Fern, and I waited in silence. When he opened his eyes, he stared down at the photo of his brother and continued softly, clearly, concisely, as if he had told the story a million times before. "I wanted to be like my brother. To go with him—to fight for our country with him, but I was too young to serve in the US military in '41. Even if I had been older, I wouldn't have been allowed. The draft was suspended for my race right after Pearl. But Ichiro was already a soldier. He was transferred with other Nisei soldiers out of the 298th and into the Hawaiian Provisional Infantry Battalion. They sailed from Honolulu on the SS *Maui* to San Francisco and were activated into the 100th Infantry Battalion. It was an orphan battalion—no regiment. Trained in Wisconsin— Camp McCoy." The information poured from Mr. Sato in a steady, detailed stream. "Nisei were strong soldiers—quick. The boys in the 100th proved their grit."

Mr. Sato dug through newspaper clippings and pulled out one that hailed the 100th as an exemplary battalion. The text described how later at Camp Shelby in Mississippi the battalion received its colors and motto, "Remember Pearl Harbor."

"After Pearl, few trusted American soldiers of Japanese descent. Nisei needed to work harder—be stronger— quicker—braver. Many, many of the One Puka Puka sacrificed their lives."

"One Puka Puka?" I asked.

"*Puka.* Hawaiian for hole," explained Mr. Sato. "One Puka Puka is 1-0-0. One hundred."

Then, as if he had led the battalion himself, he described in detail the 100th's contribution to the Italian campaign. He recounted combat with Axis soldiers on September 29, 1943, near Salerno in southern Italy, followed by a bloody push through Benevento, attempts to capture Monte Cassino, fighting in Rome, and, finally, movement into northern Italy. Mr. Sato handed me yellowed newspaper clippings, one after the other, in which war correspondents extolled the courage, skill, and tireless spirit of the Nisei soldiers of the 100th. One article described how their sacrifices earned the tag the Purple Heart Battalion. Another article detailed the battalion's attachment to the all-Nisei 442nd Regimental Combat Team.

Mr. Sato's voice softened. "Ichiro died in January 1944, during the Battle of Monte Cassino," he said, never taking his eyes off a clipping that described how the soldiers held their ground against heavy machine-gun fire. "The letters stopped," he added, picking up a tightly bound stack of envelopes from the bottom of the box, adjusting the twine, and setting it back down.

"I'm so sorry," I said, imagining a mother's, father's, and brother's pain. I was not totally surprised to hear that Mr. Sato's brother had not survived, but I was taken aback by the way he dropped that piece of information and then quickly moved on. I wanted to hear details. How was the family notified? Were his remains returned to Maui or buried in Italy? How did the family move on? Interrupting with personal questions, however, seemed inappropriate, so I simply listened.

Thankful for the recorder, I gave up note-taking as the story turned to horrific battles of the 442nd in France and Germany. I settled in and listened, totally captivated by Mr. Sato's knowledge, eloquence, and passion. His only difficulty, or perhaps it was mine, involved the chronology of events as he jumped from one military campaign to another with each newspaper clipping. He described in great detail the exemplary service of the 442nd during the remainder of the war. Yellowed newspaper clippings described how

Nisei earned great respect from military leaders and how their undeniable bravery and sacrifices helped to ease racial tensions and discrimination back in Hawaii and in other parts of the United States.

When Mr. Sato appeared to be winding down, I asked about his military service. He brushed off my question as if his story was less important than his brother's.

"Eventually, Americans of Japanese descent were allowed to enlist in the US military. I signed the day I turned eighteen," he said. "I wanted to join the 442nd, but because I could speak and write Japanese, I was separated and sent to Fort Snelling for training at the Military Intelligence Service Language School. My parents were relieved. I was not happy. I wanted to go to Europe. I arrived in Minnesota in the winter. Oh, so cold. So unlike Maui. But the training was good, and I got along. Afterward, I was sent to the Aleutian Islands to decode intercepts. Then bombs were dropped, the war ended, and I finished my tour in postwar Japan." Mr. Sato had summarized his military experience in a few sentences after taking almost three hours to describe his brother's and that of the One Puka Puka and the 442nd. He looked up at Fern and declared, "We must have tea."

"Actually, Father," said Fern, "it is time for lunch."

"Yes. Lunch would be good," he said as he haphazardly returned memorabilia to the black box and closed the cover.

Obviously, the history lesson was done for the day. I turned off the recorder and stowed it and the notebook in my tote, then helped Mr. Sato return the framed newspaper articles and photos to their original locations in the living room.

Meanwhile, Fern placed chopsticks, a large bowl of rice, and a small bowl of salt-pickled cabbage on the table and then instructed Mr. Sato and me to sit down. She retreated to the kitchen and within minutes reappeared with May and four steaming bowls of soup. In each bowl, slivers of pork, carrots, mushrooms, cabbage, spring onions, and a hard-cooked egg had been artfully arranged atop noodles and a clear broth. I followed Mr. Sato's lead and stirred my soup with the accompanying chopsticks, but try as I might, I was unable to replicate his technique for picking up the slippery noodles and transporting them to my mouth. Fern, witnessing my plight, got up from the table and returned with a fork, which I gratefully used to capture and twirl the delicious broth-soaked ramen. Determined to improve my skill with chopsticks, I followed May's tutorial and practiced on the meat and vegetables. Amused at my attempts, Mr. Sato offered encouragement and further instruction. Throughout the meal, he remained engaged, until the conversation turned to Japanese cuisine.

"Mirin and miso have never found a home in my kitchen, but that's all going to change," I said as I followed Mr. Sato's lead and picked up the soup bowl and drank every last drop of the delicious broth.

"Mr. Sato . . ."

"Ken," he interrupted.

He had asked me to call him Ken back at our first meeting, but I had hesitated to use a first name for this dignified gentleman. Now, dishonoring his request seemed disrespectful.

"Ken," I continued, "you are an incredible storyteller. Thank you for sharing your knowledge and experience with me."

"I wanted you to hear Ichiro's story. His sacrifice proved our family's patriotism." Then he quietly added two sentences that became the succinct lesson of the day. "We must never allow racism to turn us against each other.

When we know each other and respect each other, fear cannot survive."

He abruptly stood up, announced that he was going to check on his gardens, and headed out the door. I looked to May and Fern for clues to help me sort out the morning.

"I am overwhelmed and so grateful that your father was able to share Ichiro's story with me," I said.

"We are glad as well," said Fern. "It is an important part of our family's history."

"After Pearl Harbor," continued May, "terrible wounds were inflicted on my grandparents by those who did not know them. After working for many years in Hawaii and living honorable lives, their loyalty to America was suddenly questioned. Like most Issei, they were fearful that they might be judged treasonous and that Grandfather might be taken away. So they stripped their home of Japanese books and family treasures. They burned everything that might cast suspicion or suggest that they were more loyal to Japan than America. We discovered the box in 1973, after our grandmother died. We thought it contained family heirlooms she had hidden away, but as you saw, it was filled with memorabilia about the war and our uncle's battalion. The box remained unopened to us until after her death."

"She never shared the contents with you?" I asked incredulously.

"No. Ichiro was their firstborn son. His life was our grandparents' greatest sacrifice," said Fern. "After his death, Grandfather made clear that no talk of the war was ever allowed in his home."

"Even as small children, we were told never to ask our grandparents questions about our uncle," said May. "No one ever spoke of him. Grandmother processed her grief in silence. We now think she poured her tears into this box," she said, motioning to the treasure that was much more than a lacquered box.

"Yet, they allowed your father to enlist."

"According to Father it was hard for them," continued Fern. "But he was strong willed and pleaded to their patriotism. His older brother Ichiro was his hero, as were all the other Nisei fighting for America. Father always felt his service was less important than his brother's and never spoke of it while we were growing up."

"After Grandmother's death, we discovered the box," said May. "Father became obsessed with the contents, spending hours poring over every word. He sought out survivors of the 100th and traveled, even as far as San Francisco, to speak with some of them. Eventually, he pieced the entire story together."

"What an important story! And your father is such an engaging storyteller. I feel honored to have been given the chance to hear him tell it," I said.

"For years, Father was invited into classrooms to share what he had learned about the 100th with Maui students. Over time, he started turning down the teachers' invitations," said May. "We thought he was just tired, so we did not read too much into his decision, until my daughter's family came home for a long visit. When my granddaughter Lilly asked him to tell the story in Ichiro's box, he asked, 'What box?'"

"That confirmed for us his dementia," said Fern. "Later, we realized that at some point, Father had taken the box to the garage and stacked it among the storage."

"We were certain the story, like so many others, was lost to dementia," said May.

"Until yesterday," I said.

"Yes, yesterday. Memorial Day," said Fern.

"So strange," said May. "The radio was streaming

patriotic music all day, and Father started whistling and then singing along, every word clear. Last night he disappeared, and we feared he was confused and had wandered off. Fern and I were frantic. We found him in the garage, furiously pulling down cardboard boxes until he found Ichiro's box. He kept screaming, 'Today I remember!' Over and over, and then, 'Call Marguerite!'"

"But why me? I don't understand," I said.

"We don't understand, either. Perhaps he needed fresh ears—someone who also tells stories," said Fern.

"Someone who understands the power of story," added May.

When I walked out to the garden to say goodbye to Mr. Sato, Ken, my friend, he responded, "Please come again!" as he bowed and handed me another glorious long-stemmed bird of paradise.

"This will remind me of Ichiro," I said.

"Thank you for coming. We talk story again, Marguerite."

"I'd be honored."

27

*E*xhausted and anxious, I returned home from my visit Upcountry. Technologically challenged, I knew I would not be able to relax until I had successfully transferred the digital recording of Ken's narrative to my computer. I had been entrusted with a fragile treasure. The recording had beautifully captured not only a knowledgable and passionate account of great historical significance but also Ken's distinct vocabulary and cadence. Finally, the narrative was safely transferred and saved.

The next morning, I awoke groggier than usual. I attributed my lethargy to the stress of the previous day. Even though the plan for the morning was to write about Nana, emotions that had been stirred up during my visit with Ken, May, and Fern still haunted me. Dominating my morning pages was an internal discussion that attempted to identify and find a home for lingering sadness:

I am grateful and a bit overwhelmed the more I think about it. Ken wanted me to be his audience yesterday. Why me? May thought it was because I believe in the power of story. Which I do. But how did Ken sense that? I should have asked. I'm left with just one more ambiguity. His story was powerful.

Strong in detail and rich in passionate truth. Racism. Cruelty. Spawned by fear, of course. A nation's blemish. Many are still hurt by it. Loyal Muslim Americans forced to suffer after 9/11. Hapa grandchildren—what do they encounter? When do we learn Ken's lesson: "When we know each other and respect each other, fear cannot survive."

Confounding dementia, Ken was able to convey every detail of the One Puka Puka yesterday. Amazing! Affirmative glances from May and Fern, plus the newspaper clippings, confirmed the accuracy of every point. I don't think the return of his lucidity on Memorial Day was coincidental. The patriotic music. His singing. Keys to unlocking his brain?

Ichiro died tragically, so far away, proving his loyalty to the good US of A. His parents and Ken hid their grief, pushing it down as if not talking about it would help them move on. To this I can relate!! Deaths that arrive quickly and tragically leave survivors reeling. Mama, Papa, Emma, and now Harry. Gone in a blink. As an adolescent, I found it hard to speak about Mama and Papa's deaths with anyone other than Nana and then hardly above a whisper. At least when Emma died, I had Harry. But then he left for good, rather than for the forty minutes that his bike ride should have taken. The last thing he said was "Let's have coffee at Silverwood when I get back."

Ichiro's mother—I feel a strange kinship to this woman, someone I will never meet. Her meticulous accumulation of newspaper clippings and memorabilia (not to mention her son's letters!) must have helped her sort through her grief when no spoken words were allowed. Revisiting the past—a source of comfort—she had a black-lacquered box. I have a birthday book.

War and death occupied my thoughts as I headed northward along the beach. But midway through my morning stroll, my mind settled on Nana and my thankfulness for her love and example. For her, death had taken its rightful place and had waited until she had lived a fruitful life, a blessing that Mama, Papa, and Ichiro had not been given. Yet, lingering illness and pain occupied much of her final years. Through it all, with a mind as sharp as the day she was born, Nana had managed to coexist with her condition even as the end approached. With a mixture of sadness and warmth, I recalled her undeniable strength and spiritual peace. For the rest of the day, anxious to transpose feelings onto paper, I wrote, edited, reworked, and edited again. Still, by the end of the day the story did not include the end of Nana's life. That is the way the end of life is preferred, I decided, reminiscent of an ellipsis rather than an exclamation point.

MARGUERITE—AGE 28
April 30, 1963
"Celebrating in Our New Home!"

Not until this, my twenty-eighth birthday, could I imagine the extent to which a person might simultaneously anticipate and dread the passage of time.

"Let's get you standing up for the photo, MJ," says Harry, "Get in there, Nana."

"No," replies Nana. "Let me take a picture of the two of you," she says, reaching for the camera.

"First, the two of you," says Harry as he snaps a couple of shots of Nana and me, unmistakably pregnant.

Then he hands off the camera to Nana and exchanges places with her.

All three of us know that this birthday might be the last

one shared with Nana. Her cancer has become a formidable opponent, which now is aggressively attacking vital organs. She becomes weaker each time the doctors carve out another cancerous piece. I have altered my prayers. Now I pray for her to live long enough to enjoy her new great-granddaughter or great-grandson. She speaks about the joys of watching her family grow, first with the addition of Harry, whom she considers a grandson, and soon the baby, who seems to be a miracle after years of hoping.

We pose for several more photos until the doorbell rings and the guests arrive.

"Happy birthday, MJ!" says Phyl with her usual flourish.

"And happy housewarming," adds John as he passes two bottles, cabernet and sparkling grape juice, to Harry.

"Oh, Harry, you've outdone yourself," says Phyl as she sprints around the house peeking through doorways. "Where's the nursery, MJ?"

The house is Harry's creation. For years, he hunched over blueprints and tweaked our dream home until every square inch radiated the perfect mix of beauty and functionality. I thought the house was just that, a dream, relegated to carefully drawn sketches that Harry used to hone his architectural skills. Then last summer, he drove me to a subdivision in the nearby Saint Paul suburb of New Brighton.

Harry parked in front of a wooded lot and declared with a crescendo of excitement, "I can picture our home right here with those pines in the back and the birches along the side. It will flow right into that hillside," he said as he gestured. "With the driveway here. And patio here. The plate glass windows will let in the morning sun. We'll have to take out some of the scruffy growth, but we'll put in flowers and vegetables. This whole area is being developed, MJ. Schools will follow. I think this is where we should be. What do you think?"

I laughed.

"Is that 'Harry, I love it!' or 'Harry, you're crazy!'?"

"It's 'Harry, let's do it!'"

Taking a financial leap of faith, we bought the land and broke ground for a one-level, contemporary home. Harry the architect became Harry the general contractor. Under his supervision the construction crew worked nonstop during autumn to get the structure up while the weather permitted. Over the winter, Harry turned his attention to the inside work, making sure every square inch was finished with precision.

Brightened by sunlight streaming through large picture windows, Harry's creation is modern, smooth, and sleek, the perfect backdrop for the teak dining table and chairs and the master bed and dresser, our only new purchases of furniture other than the crib and changing table in the nursery. My pregnancy, confirmed shortly before Christmas, spurred Harry on. His goal was to move in by my birthday, so Nana can live out her final months and Baby can begin his or hers in the home that he created for our family.

"We want a grand tour!" says Phyl.

While Nana takes a seat in her favorite chair by the window, I follow behind as Harry leads our guests around the sprawling main floor. *Oohs* from Phyl increase when she steps into the nursery and then into Nana's bedroom, which includes a private bath. John compliments Harry on design elements that will be crucial for Nana, extra-wide doorways for wheelchair accommodation and a shower that can be easily accessed. Finally, when Harry leads John down the stairs to the unfinished basement to check out less exciting construction details, Phyl and I exit the tour and return to Nana.

"Everything's lovely," says Phyl to Nana.

"Everything's perfect," replies Nana.

It is perfect, and I am heartbroken that Nana will have such limited time here. By my way of thinking, life has dealt her a dirty deal; yet, with a smile that disappears only occasionally when her body involuntarily winces in pain, she is serene. Her quiet strength is a standard I admire and one I fear I will never possess. I want our baby to be nurtured by this woman, to receive through Nana's touch the comfort of loving security, and through osmosis, the spiritual strength that perhaps skipped a generation with me.

I want our baby to come home. Then I want time to stop.

MARGUERITE—AGE 29
April 30, 1964
"A Family of Four"

Emma Celeste Burdick, now eight months old, highlights this birthday. She arrived dramatically three minutes after midnight on August 15, 1963, after a long, grueling day of labor. Her boisterous wail demanded attention. When she was placed in my arms, she slowly reduced her volume to a whimper and finally settled down. I looked down at her beautiful, scrunched, little face and heard my inner voice say, "Finally, Marguerite, you have done something perfectly." Within minutes, Emma was able to cast a spell of enchantment over three fairly reasonable adults. In no time at all, she learned that soothing voices and gentle rocking were only a fitful cry away. Now, she has added smiling to her repertoire. Consequently, all three of us are mesmerized.

Nana continues to hang on, much to her doctors'

amazement. When they comment on her perseverance, she attributes her strength to Emma, who gives her "a shot of positivity." Nothing can diminish my gratefulness for a healthy child, a loving husband, Nana's continued presence, and our new home, which has become the perfect nest for both beginning and ending life.

In stark contrast to my contentment, violence has rocked the world. One month to the day after Emma was born, four other mothers were forced to endure unbelievable loss when their daughters were killed in the bombing of the 16th Street Baptist Church in Birmingham, Alabama. Hearing the news, I grabbed a sleeping Emma out of her crib and held her tightly. Having lost parents, grief is no stranger to me, but gazing down at sweet Emma, I could not fathom how parents reconcile losing a child, especially to a violent act of hatred and bigotry. Less than three months later, the wonders of television offered minute-by-minute updates on the killing of America's president, followed by the shooting of his alleged assassin. News, something I can no longer ignore, reports disturbing views of the world that Emma will inherit. Witnessing my distress, Nana wisely encourages me to pour out my concerns onto paper. I find the simple act of writing cathartic, and thanks to Nana's help with Emma, I am able to dedicate a small slice of each day to written contemplation.

Shortly before Emma's birth, I resigned my nursing position at the Minneapolis Clinic. I have no intention of returning anytime soon. My vocational choice, one that has never felt like a perfect fit, is now proving beneficial. I have learned the necessary skills to take care of Nana and, hopefully, keep her home until the end. Her strength has diminished steadily these last few months. Now she needs assistance to transfer from chair to bed or toilet, and when skilled nursing is required, I can perform many of the procedures at home. Concerned that her medical needs overburden me, she finds innumerable ways to help out with the housekeeping and cooking when her health allows. Most important, she is a godsend when it comes to Emma, who happily enjoys hours in Nana's arms.

Harry continues his work in horticulture research, but he and two likeminded friends are putting their heads together and considering expansion in a new direction. Combining their passions for architecture and horticulture, they are in the early stages of creating a business that designs greenhouses of all shapes and sizes, from small hobby greenhouses to educational, institutional, specialty, and multiroom, research-centered greenhouses. I enjoy watching his excitement; but honestly, I glaze over as he talks about heating, cooling, ventilation, irrigation, climate zones, and sick rooms and am grateful that he has found Ben and Jay to share his passion.

No matter how tired he is when he gets home, Harry manages to squeeze in plenty of one-on-one time with Emma. From the day we brought her home from the hospital, he has read to her, often from the newspaper. He recites the news of the day, the weather report, and the sports section aloud and with inflection as if they were bedtime stories. Her reactions to his vocal modulation and his facial expressions vary according to his purpose, and the results are quite comical. He can elicit either giggles with a dramatized rendition of the rainfall predictions or yawns with a play-by-play summary of a University of Minnesota Golden Gophers basketball game delivered in a soft and steady cadence. We are slowly stockpiling favorite children's books for the time when Emma no longer finds the newspapers amusing.

Outings instigated by Harry include indoor stroller rides through Apache Plaza, a nearby enclosed shopping mall, a perfect destination during subzero weather. When skies are clear and temperatures rise, he bundles Emma up, and we head outdoors to explore our neighborhood, which, like Harry predicted, is dotted with new construction. Fatherhood suits Harry. He is unflappable, even if Emma is wailing unconsolably for some unknown reason. In such moments, I am reminded to express my appreciation to Anna for raising a sensitive son and to Jane for treating her little brother with the patience that he now bestows on Emma.

Even though tending to a new baby and an ailing grandmother can be exhausting, I sleep solidly every night knowing that all is good right now. When I find myself eagerly looking forward to the next stage of Emma's growth and development, I pull back and remind myself to stay in the moment, relax, and enjoy.

MARGUERITE—AGE 30
April 30, 1965
"Happy Birthday—Nana's Final Song"

I have a habit of holding on to calendars. Filled with daily schedules, they also become the depositories for miscellany, such as the appearance of Emma's first tooth after three nights of fitful sleep or Nana's final decision to discontinue her trips to Mayo Clinic. I am quite certain that next January, when I stow the calendar for 1965 in my box of memorabilia, it will include the details of Nana's passing. I believe her goal is to live beyond today, my birthday, so as not to tinge April 30 with sadness.

Unlike 1964, a year of relative tranquility within the Burdick home, 1965 is clouding over with unease. Heartbreak is settling in like an uninvited guest that arrives too early and, I fear, will stay long after Nana has left us. Unlike the abrupt and unforeseen loss of Mama and Papa, Nana's slow retreat is sadly expected. At times, I feel like she has a foot in each world. I sense that she is torn between staying with us, which is where I want her to be, and heading to the light and whatever lies beyond, which she is certain will include a reunion with Grampa and her children.

"I'm not afraid to be dead," she says, wincing in pain. "Heaven knows, my body is no longer useful. It's the dying—I'm having trouble with the process. But all will be well in the end, Marguerite," she says as she grabs my hand and holds on tightly until our eyes meet and I nod in agreement. Yet, I disagree in my soul. For me, the end of Nana's suffering will be the only redeeming aspect of her passing.

Nana's faith is unshakeable, and unlike Mama and me, she somehow has been able to forgive the church for condemning her only son for what it considers the mortal sin of suicide. As long as the church continues to relegate to fiery Hell those who do not live by its standards, I will remain unable to muster Nana's ability to pardon the institution. Yet, I help her to mass each Sunday when she is able. Thankfully, she has connected with a liberal Catholic congregation that focuses more on service to others than condemnation of "others." The priest makes house calls and has promised to administer last rights when the time nears.

"That's all I need, Marguerite. Then you can take me back to Davis and plant me right there in the spot between Grampa and Raymond."

"Don't you want a service in Davis?" I ask, thinking of old friends who would probably wish to pay their respects.

"No service, MJ," she says so emphatically that I am inclined to believe that, although she has forgiven the church in Davis, she has not forgotten or healed from the deep wound it inflicted.

In her customary fashion, Nana hates that her neediness now requires so many of my hours plus the expense of additional nursing help during the night. We have hired Stella, a friend and nurse, to help with nighttime medications, toileting, and repositioning. A godsend, she arrives five days each week at 8 p.m. and tends to Nana until 6 a.m. so Harry and I can enjoy some alone time and restorative sleep after Emma is settled for the night. My nightly prayer is simple. Hating to believe that a higher power responds to those who plead the loudest, I ask for nothing and merely offer up gratitude for another day with Nana.

At times, Nana's pain is unrelenting. Together, the doctors and I constantly work to maintain a delicate balance between medicating it and reducing the unwanted side effects of the drugs. Her comfort is our major goal. No matter how we treat it, though, pain is a constant companion, and too often it negatively impacts her quality of life.

I try to approach Nana's nursing needs clinically, as any good nurse would do, in vain attempts to combat the consequences of her disease. But my professionalism crumbles as I witness each of Nana's personal losses, when the simple act of holding Emma becomes too painful, for example. At these times, I return to my primary role—granddaughter— to the very woman who nursed me, loved me, raised me. We hold each other. Reminisce. Laugh. Cry. She needs both relationships from me, and in return, she shares her spiritual strength and undeniable trust that the end of life is not the end. With the anticipation of a child waiting for her birthday party, she talks so confidently about those who will be meeting her once she passes. The fact that I will be excluded from the grand reunion stirs a quiet melancholy. Focusing on Emma and Harry is the only remedy.

Grief is like a dragon with two methods of attack. I have confronted both. Even though I was groggy, I have a distinct memory of the night it roared into my hospital room when Nana shared the truth: Mama and Papa had not survived the accident. Like a giant beast, it raced full on, striking and shattering me. Thankfully, Nana was there to pick up the pieces. This time the dragon has been cagey—hiding in the shadows—an unwelcome companion slowly sauntering forward, gaining strength, and finally demanding our full attention. It has taken up residence in our lives.

Gone is the numbness and the denial. Clearly, Nana is no longer an active participant in this world. Instead, she has become an observer from her bed, wheelchair, or rocker in the living room. Together and individually, we grieve each of her losses. She is ready to go, just not today. But I don't think I will ever be ready to say a final goodbye.

She manages a few bites of the birthday dinner that Harry has plated: takeout baked rigatoni, tossed salad, dinner rolls, and chocolate cake. In her usual manner, she compliments the aroma of the pasta before struggling to get a forkful from her plate to her mouth. She accepts my help but declares herself full before a quarter of her small portion is eaten, then smiles when the birthday candles are lit and tries valiantly to add her voice to Harry's rendition of "Happy Birthday."

28

I awoke early, skipped my morning writing rituals, and chose instead to write about Nana. *Nana is my rock, my pillar,* I wrote, confident of the use of present tense. The more I wrote, the more I felt her presence, her gentle reassurance, her imprint on my soul. I was astounded that after all of this time, Nana's essence was resurfacing as easily as if I had called her from an adjoining room. She was returning as closely as she was allowed. Or perhaps she had been present all long, and I had been unaware. Either way I was receptive to the mystery. The ringing of my cell phone interrupted my contemplation.

"Hi, MJ. It's Kai. Are you enjoying the sunshine?"

"Hi, Kai. Yes, it's gorgeous," I said, failing to mention that I had been so self-absorbed that I had barely noticed the weather.

"I'm just calling about tomorrow. Thought I would confirm."

"Noon to three, right?"

"Perfect. And again, nothing for you to do. We'll have it all set up. Oh—Dad wants to talk to you. I'm giving him the phone. Bye until tomorrow. Can't wait . . ." her voice trailed off.

"Hi, Marguerite," said Richard. "I'm so glad you're coming tomorrow."

"I'm looking forward to it."

"Parking can be a bear, so I thought I'd give you the address of our print shop. There's plenty of parking there, and Mike can drive you over to the store. Also, Ani would love to meet you, but she won't get done teaching until after three. She was hoping you would hang around and have an early dinner with the two of us."

By the end of our conversation, I had accepted Richard and Ani's dinner invitation and had written down the address of the print shop. The casualness of the upcoming book event required little preparation beyond the laundering of my favorite sundress and linen jacket. While the washing machine whirled, I returned to my writing with the hope that Nana's essence would continue to be my day's companion.

MARGUERITE—AGE 31
April 30, 1966
"Gooseberry Falls, North Shore—Endings and Beginnings"

My birthday surprise this year is a weekend getaway to the North Shore of Lake Superior. We haven't been back since our honeymoon. Harry's reasoning for an extended celebration, he says, is because my birthday falls on a weekend, but I think deep down he wants to create a new memory that does not involve Nana's suffering. Last year's birthday dinner was the last meal she enjoyed. After that she refused anything but a cup of tea with toast and jelly. When I gently coaxed her to eat, she repeated, "I have everything I need, Marguerite."

Even when movement caused great pain, Nana insisted on getting out of bed each day. She enjoyed sitting upright in her favorite recliner in the living room so she could enjoy the sights outside the picture windows. It was in that chair that she passed, quietly and unceremoniously, with Emma busily constructing Lego towers at her feet and Harry and me enjoying our morning coffee at a nearby table. The end had been more peaceful than I had ever imagined. My sadness was muted by an intense wave of relief that Nana had died under her own terms, in our home, and under the watchful eyes of her small family.

I continued to process my grief in a red leather journal, Nana's last gift to me. At first I hesitated to mar the clean, white pages with ink. Then, inspired by one of my evening courses in creative writing, I decided that Nana's gift would be the perfect place to record stories of her. I dedicated Emma's nap time to writing, and after a few months, the journal was filled with not only silly and fun anecdotes but also important life lessons that only Nana had been able to teach. After the journal was filled, I inscribed the front cover to Emma and stowed the book safely in the cedar chest until a time, probably her teen years, when connection to Nana's wisdom might help Emma through some growing pains.

I have fallen in love with the process of writing, and like any other skill that requires daily practice, the more consistency I give my hobby, the more creative depth I am able to tap. In correlation, the frenetic tendencies that have often punctuated my life are slowly giving way to a calmer approach that both Harry and little Emma sense and appreciate. Life for the Burdicks can be a bit chaotic, but at this very moment, the day is a snapshot of peacefulness.

The North Shore is lovely. Harry and I laugh as we remember our honeymoon and how briefly we explored anything beyond our cozy bed in the cabin. This time, we are bundled up for the crisp, chilling wind that blows like a natural air conditioner off Lake Superior. Taking turns carrying Emma on our backs, we explore a lighthouse, several waterfalls, and miles of trails.

I am struck by the contentment that accompanies staying in the present. Harry, on the other hand, is forward gazing. More goal oriented than I, he seizes opportunities to push me out of my comfort zone. And today's topic, as we hike along the newly defrosted terrain of northern Minnesota, involves major movement.

"Green Space is at the stage where I have to decide if I can go all in with Ben and Jay," he says as he hoists Emma off his back and lets her run a few steps ahead of us on the trail.

Going all in, he explains, would require resigning from his day job in the lab and devoting one hundred percent of his work time to the greenhouse company that has been in developmental stages for years.

"For a while, perhaps a long time," Harry points out, "we would be financially pinched, but I really believe in it, MJ."

I turn and focus on his face, glowing with the expectancy of a soon-to-be parent with a child on the way.

I want to say "Go for it!" just like I did when he proposed building our home. I want to say, "Thank you for allowing me to have a voice in the decision." But I hold back, until I am reminded of Nana and how Harry never questioned or resisted the fact that marrying me meant a package deal that included taking care of Nana until her death.

We are interrupted by the need to corral Emma as we approach the rushing water of Gooseberry Falls. As we plant ourselves on a huge boulder warmed by the April sun, I peer over at Harry. Realizing that nothing I say will be heard over the thunderous roar of spring runoff cascading through the rocky gorge, I catch his eye and give him a thumbs-up. He smiles back and hands off his camera to a young woman who snaps a photo of the three of us, the one that eventually finds a home in my birthday book.

Later, with Emma asleep in her carseat, we talk about logistical and financial considerations relating to Harry's job change. As we drive northeastward along the shoreline of Lake Superior, I suggest that, perhaps, I should return to work. Such a move would lessen the financial strain. "But if I go back to a clinic or hospital, who will take care of Emma?" I voice the question aloud but keep other concerns to myself. I know that I am using Emma as an excuse for my own anxieties. Although I am thankful for my nursing degree and the skills that helped Nana, old insecurities resurface at the mere thought of returning to a paid nursing position.

Knowing me too well, Harry senses my reticence. "You're a good—no—great nurse, MJ, when you have to be. But you've told me that nursing fits you 'like a pair of baggy trousers cinched together with a belt of clothesline rope.' That's an image that's hard to forget," he adds with a chuckle. "Maybe it's time for both of us to take risks and follow our passions."

"Whatever mine is, I'm willing to bet it doesn't come with a paycheck," I respond.

"So we live like paupers for awhile. Starting tomorrow." He parks next to an enticing eating establishment on the main street of Grand Marais. "Ready for a birthday lunch?"

Little Emma, blissfully unaware of her parents' latest defining moment, opens her eyes, looks around, and answers for both of us. "Yes!"

29

*A*fter completing early morning writing exercises, I headed out for a short walk to mentally prepare for the day. Water-soaked sand, left behind by the gently receding tide, provided a firm, wide path. As I headed north, I contemplated my first book event in over a year. Perhaps *event* was too strong a word for Kai's informal meet-and-greet. I had no presentation to prepare, but if asked to do a reading, which I did not anticipate, I could fall back on a selection from my latest book, *Murder at the Eagle's Eye*, a convoluted mystery set in a fictitious river town that resembled Wabasha, Minnesota.

Facing readers and their questions after such a long absence might have been a disconcerting thought. Instead, I was surprisingly calm and objective, especially after I reminded myself that today was all about my published work and not about the implosion of *Seldom What It Seems*. Audiences at book events had always energized me with their enthusiasm, and I had every reason to believe that today would be enjoyable. With that reminder, I inhaled deeply. Thanks to a cup-filling respite in tropical Maui, I was beginning to understand that, even though I was not quite ready to jump back into the creation of another quirky, Minnesota-based mystery, my love of a good story had not expired and neither had my love for an appreciative audience. As I turned and headed back to the condo, my cool composure dissipated. Excitement rather than dread, thank the heavens, took its place.

Recognizable terrain during my second trip to Lahaina eased the trip, and the GPS led me right to the print shop. Mike stopped whatever he was doing and chauffeured me through late-morning traffic to Captured, where he double-parked long enough for me to jump out. A large poster attached to the front window of the store advertised the day's event. A photo of Richard and me on the lanai was positioned above the invitation, "Chat with a mystery writer!" Details followed. Diagonally positioned across one of the top corners, a recently added banner announced, "TODAY!"

Kai, looking stunning in a maxi-length, tropical sundress, greeted me enthusiastically and then ushered me over to an area that had been cleared to make room for a round table and several chairs. On a nearby counter, a smaller version of the poster sat on an easel next to a display of MJ Burdick mysteries.

"Will this work, MJ? We'll be offering lemonade and bottled water, too, but we'll take care of that," said Kai. "And I should have asked, will it be okay if people want to be photographed with you?"

"No problem," I said, dropping my tote into an empty chair.

"Marguerite, you are here." Richard approached from the back with a plumeria lei draped over his arm. He was dressed more formally than the last time we had talked. Instead of a T-shirt and shorts, he was wearing a mint green linen shirt and long, dark trousers. "Thank you for coming," he said as he placed the lei over my head and arranged it to his preference. "Perfect. Now, is there anything else you need?"

"This is lovely and smells heavenly," I said as I raised the flowers to my nose. "Thank you so much. And no, I think you've thought of everything."

"Kai has thought of everything," Richard corrected with a grin. "Don't give me any credit."

As if on cue, Kai deposited a stack of bookplates on the table.

"Dad and I were afraid that we might run out of books. His inventory was lower than we thought, and there wasn't time to have more shipped. So we printed bookplates with your photo and today's date. We left room for you to add an inscription. Then if we don't have the book they want, we can order it and have it shipped to them, and they can leave with the personal inscription and paste it in later."

"As I was saying—," said Richard with a laugh.

"Yes, Kai has thought of everything," I said as I sat down at the table and retrieved my favorite extra-fine Sharpie from my tote.

"And this is MJ Burdick," said Kai less than a minute later. She directed an elderly couple to seats at the table and offered beverages. We were still fifteen minutes away from noon, but the event had begun. The wizened gentleman introduced himself and his plump, animated wife as "the Olsens, with an *e*" and explained that they were yearly vacationers from Hudson, Wisconsin.

"We noticed the poster earlier and decided to hang around Lahaina until you arrived. We've read all your books," he said.

"We love the settings. So familiar to us," added Mrs. Olsen, who reminded me a bit of Mrs. Fullerton, our neighbor and my mother's friend in Davis.

We chatted about Wisconsin, Minnesota, and Maui and

then about storylines, characters, and settings. Mr. Olsen's eyes traveled over to the display of MJ Burdick mysteries, and I braced myself for the question.

"Do you have a new book out?" he asked.

"No," I said apologetically. "I've taken a bit of a breather since my husband died."

Immediately, I felt the shame of using Harry's death as an excuse, but then Mrs. Olsen reached over and patted my hand. "Honey, you take as long as it takes." Briefly voiceless, I thanked her with a nod.

I picked up my pen and inscribed a bookplate for the Olsens with a message of gratitude for both their interest in my books and their compassion. "Since I don't have a new book for you," I said, handing them the bookplate, "perhaps you might like to place this in one of your favorites." Mrs. Olsen, appreciative of the gesture, quickly slipped the bookplate into her handbag.

"Keep writing," said Mr. Olsen as he carefully rose and steadied himself before helping his wife out of her chair. "It's been a pleasure."

"It has," I responded. As I watched him unsteadily maneuver to the door and then pause for a spasm of coughing, I wondered if I would be able to produce another book in Mr. Olsen's lifetime.

A steady stream of shoppers moseyed into the store. Some were merely curious, pausing for a moment or two before continuing their stroll down Front Street. Others sat down to chat, while others eavesdropped as they browsed the store. I enjoyed talking with convivial vacationers from the anchored cruise ship. Their glimpse of Maui, I sadly realized, was limited to a single day. Many swooshed in just long enough to buy a book, snap a photo with an author, and/or collect a signed bookplate.

Some shoppers were familiar with my books, especially

if they were from the Midwest. My first question to them was always, "Where's home?" I inscribed bookplates for walk-ins from Minnesota, Wisconsin, Washington State, New Jersey, California, Alaska, Canada, Maui, and China. Even though the books were not written as a series, new readers often wanted to purchase my first. Thankfully, Richard had a decent stack of *Murder in the Student Section*, my first and his favorite. Several people asked me to step out on the lanai for a photo. Not fond of having my picture taken, I smiled cheerfully and tried to ignore the possibility that my face might be printed for eternity on mugs, magnets, or whatever.

Readers familiar with my novels predictably asked about my next release. Unlike my comment to the Olsens that cast blame for my unproductiveness on Harry's departure, I devised a stock answer: "Well, there's much work to do before I can release my next book. I don't have a date yet." There was truth in that remark, I justified.

The afternoon flew by. At 3 p.m., three people, an older woman with a golden tan and striking silver bob, a young man whose facial hair made any estimation of his age unreliable, and a middle-aged man, remained in the chairs around the table. Their technical questions regarding process and publication led me to believe they were writers, and when I inquired, they eagerly shared their latest projects. We talked about different genres, and for the first time, I was asked if I had ever considered writing memoir. The question came, surprisingly, from the youngest of the three, the man whose facial features were hidden by a thick, well-trimmed beard. Before I had an opportunity to respond, he added, "Self-perception can also be a mystery."

"You are wise to learn that so young," said the older man. The discussion continued for another twenty-five minutes. During that time, a petite, attractive Hawaiian woman with a sprinkling of gray throughout her thick, shoulder-length, black hair entered the store and positioned herself so she could listen to the book discussion without intruding. Finally, after I personally inscribed a bookplate for each of the writers and wished them well, she walked over and extended her hand.

"Hello, Marguerite," she said. "I'm Ani."

"So nice to meet you," I said, noticing for the first time how much she and Kai resembled each other. A few laugh lines and wrinkles had carved their way into Ani's dark complexion, but her sparkling eyes and graceful posture had been passed on to her daughter.

"I'm so thirsty," she said. "I'm getting some bottled water. Can I refresh your lemonade?"

"I'd love some water, please."

She returned to the table with the water, handed me a bottle, and seated herself in one of the chairs.

"I eavesdropped," she said. "I loved the discussion."

"Weren't they interesting? The men both live on Maui, and they swapped contact information. I hope they'll stay in touch."

"So today was worth your time?"

"Most definitely. And hopefully it brought in some business. This is a very unique shop."

"It is, and the kids and Rich have worked so hard to make it go."

"And you teach?"

"Right now students are on break, but I'm a tutor. So for me, summers are busy with helping kids catch up or further excel. I was listening to your exchange with the young man with the beard. You were very encouraging," she said.

"If young writers need anything, it's encouragement."

"Hi, Mom. Isn't she great? I think our afternoon was a success. Don't you, MJ?" asked Kai, joining us.

"Well, I'm not sure what constitutes success, Kai, but it was most enjoyable from my perspective." I took a long swig of water. All of a sudden I was very thirsty and tired.

"Ani," Richard said as he stepped out of his office, "you're here. Didn't see you come in. MJ, that last trio—you were very accommodating. It sounded like a writers' group."

"A writers' group," Kai repeated slowly. Everyone could see the wheels turning in her head.

"Before Kai signs you up to lead a weekly gathering, we need to get you out of here," said Richard as he flashed his daughter a smile. "I just called down and reserved a table with a view."

"Will you be joining us, Kai?" I asked.

"Don't I wish. No, I'm here 'til closing. But thanks so much, MJ. It was great. Thank you. Thank you." Then she reached in for a surprise hug, the culmination of an enjoyable afternoon.

I accompanied Richard and Ani down Front Street. We strolled past the giant banyan tree and into a shopping area with stores and restaurants. Eventually, we entered an establishment whose hostess greeted Richard and Ani by name. The young woman led us onto the veranda and seated us at a table with a magnificent ocean view. With an unexpected sense of relief and accomplishment, I gazed at the water and relaxed into the chair.

Happy hour was in progress. When I passed on alcohol, Ani suggested virgin lava flows for both of us. The cooling and delectable drink featured pureed strawberries swirled like molten lava through a blended mixture of bananas, pineapple juice, and coconut milk. Richard ordered appetizers, poke made from fresh ahi tuna, as well as wonton and basil-wrapped shrimp. Easy conversation accompanied the delicious food and drinks, and by the time entrees arrived, we had covered a variety of topics from business to personal, including Ani's concise summary of her upbringing on Maui, her college years on Oahu, and her attraction to a vacationer from Wisconsin.

"The rest is history," said Richard.

"Marriage, children, teaching—the years have gone so fast," Ani said. "When the kids were ready for college, Rich and I insisted that they pick a school on the mainland to broaden their perspective."

"Both went to the University of Washington," said Richard.

"And thankfully, both returned to Maui," said Ani.

"You should be very proud," I said as I extolled their virtues.

"We are," said Ani. "Do you have children, MJ?"

Richard winced slightly as if he should have informed her.

"My daughter Emma died from a freak sledding accident when she was seven," I said, offering more information than I usually extended.

"Oh, I'm so sorry," said Ani.

"It was a long time ago," I said.

"But loss like that never goes away," said Ani, speaking as if from experience. "We lost our third child, Kale, when my pregnancy was six months along. I find myself asking so many questions. How old would he be now? What would he look like? What would he have chosen to do with his life?"

"Yes, I find myself grieving new losses at each stage of my life," I said.

"New losses?" asked Richard.

"Well, like my latest, never getting the chance to be a grandmother when all my friends rave about the experience," I replied with a newfound openness. "But who knows? Maybe Emma wouldn't have married at all, or maybe she would have chosen not to have children like so many couples."

"But the not knowing—that's something I grieve," said Ani.

"Exactly," I responded to the woman who understood.

The conversation shifted as the sun approached a thick cloud bank that stretched above the horizon. Looking west, we spotted the anchored cruise ship and smaller watercraft that were ferrying exhausted vacationers back to their floating hotel before its scheduled departure. Such a short time in Maui, I thought.

"Looks like tonight's sunset will be earlier than usual, judging by that cloud bank," said Richard.

"That's the one thing I have trouble getting used to—the early sunsets—compared to the long summer days in Minnesota," I said. "But I love how everyone pauses to appreciate the setting sun here, even if it drops behind clouds."

"Sunset is different every day," said Ani. "Always a time to pause. I try not to take it for granted."

We chatted as we watched the sun disappear. Slowly the upper edge of the cloud bank lit up as if a painter had outlined it in a thin line of iridescent orange. Tiki torches were lit. Evening had begun.

"I think it's time for me to make my way back to Kihei," I said.

"We kept you so long," said Ani as we walked back up Front Street to Richard's car. "You'll be driving home in the dark. Would you like Richard to drive you home? I could follow and give him a ride back."

I assured both of them that I was perfectly comfortable driving back to Kihei in the dark now that the route was familiar. When Richard dropped us off near the print shop,

Ani and I located our cars, and the three of us headed out in three different vehicles. Thirty minutes later, I reached the turnoff to Kihei, which easily led to the parking lot of the Maui Sunset.

The day's human interaction had been heartwarming and exhausting. A warmth of satisfaction accompanied me over the threshold. Protea and birds of paradise in a crystal vase on the counter welcomed me home.

30

*A*s usual, thoughts from my head transitioned within my morning pages into feelings from the heart:

Driving myself around the Twin Cities meant I was free to follow a whim or fashion a quick escape if I felt so inclined. Deciding to fly alone to Maui has taken that freedom to a higher level, and as a result, unique opportunities have unfolded. I probably never would have been seated next to May Wantanabe on the airplane if I had been traveling with a friend. And who knows if yesterday would have transpired with Richard and his family if I had been involved with travel companions when I entered Captured for the first time . . . How close I had come to declining Millie's offer to use her condo! What a mistake that would have been! At first, accepting her invitation felt so out of character. But accepting an opportunity for adventure is very much in character for the Marguerite of old. Out of character is the meek, little caterpillar I had become, the one content to sleep away the hours within the safety of a hardening cocoon . . . So stop wasting precious energy trying to create a new Marguerite. Focus on reclaiming the Marguerite of old . . .

By the time I closed my MP notebook, the simple act of matching words to my stream of consciousness had worked its magic once again. Brain drain completed and reenergized as a result, I headed to the beach for what was becoming a daily stroll.

Reflecting on my conversation with Ani and Richard, I thought of Emma while I picked my way around driftwood. Had she lived, she would be celebrating her fifty-third birthday at the end of the summer. She would have enjoyed snorkeling, hiking, camping in the dormant volcano of Haleakala, and certainly driving the road to Hana, all the things Harry, she, and I would have done together if we had been allowed the opportunity. And if Emma would have survived to experience the death of her father, the two of us would have comforted each other as we dealt with the loss of the same special man. But I had no memories of an adult Emma, and no amount of conjuring was ever going to change that. Yesterday's exchange with Ani acknowledged once again the gravity of losing children. I had been given seven years with my daughter; her son had never breathed. I longed to find the blessing in my situation.

Photos had captured every stage of Emma's short life, thanks to Harry, who became as dedicated a photographer as Papa. But after Emma's death, the photo albums that documented her growth were relegated to the cedar chest, right next to the red journal that was filled with memories of Nana. Revisiting the photos and the memories they represented offered comfort to me, but Harry found them painful, so I learned to peruse the albums by myself when he was not around. The cedar chest, much like Ichiro's box, became my receptacle for unspoken grief. Only two favorite photos of Emma remained in view, a professional one on the mantle and a small candid shot in a collage of photos of departed family members that hung above my desk.

I had pulled out the photo albums only once since Harry's death. Instead of bringing comfort, they only exacerbated my grief and aloneness, so I had returned them to the cedar chest, where they remained out of sight. Now, an overwhelming yearning to see Emma's face descended.

When I returned from my walk, I retrieved pages from the birthday book and selected the ones with photos of Emma. In 1963, she showed up as a bulge under a maternity top during our housewarming/birthday party. In 1964, she sat on Nana's lap—Emma, a squirming eight-month-old, and Nana, a picture of adult gentility. By 1965, Emma had grown bigger and stronger, while Nana appeared shrunken and withered. In that photo, I was holding Emma since Nana no longer had the strength. Emma's smiling face was tilted toward Nana, whose wistful expression revealed a quiet sadness. I was smiling at both of them.

The birthday photos of the next four years pictured our small family of three. In 1966, toddler Emma sat between us on the rocks alongside Gooseberry Falls. Safe and secure, she had no inkling that her parents were making life-altering decisions that would change their careers and lives. She was simply loving the stimulation and the thrill of the rushing water.

I picked up the photo of 1967, stared at it intently, and set it down. After sufficient time away, I returned to the photo, studied it once more, and uncovered memories inspired by a chocolate blotch on the end of Emma's nose.

MARGUERITE—AGE 32
April 30, 1967
"A Chocolate Nose and Gifts From Second Read"

April is the perfect month for a birthday, especially if you live in Minnesota. Everything about April screams spring— the lengthening of the days, the budding of the daffo- dils, the opening of an ice cream parlor in nearby Apache Plaza. After a casual birthday dinner in a family-friendly restaurant in Northeast Minneapolis, Harry declares that the dessert course will be served at Apache, so the three of us head north on Silver Lake Road. The newly opened ice cream shop, located in the interior of the indoor shop- ping center, offers brownie sundaes. He orders two and a chocolate cone for Emma, who is quickly learning to love birthdays with all their surprises. Harry hands me a sundae and begins a robust rendition of "Happy Birthday." Emma squeals with joy when shoppers pause to add their voices to the song.

"Sorry, MJ, no candles. Fire restrictions," he says.

Before I am allowed to take a bite, Harry corrals a young man who is leaving a nearby bookstore and asks him to take a picture of our family. By the time the photo is snapped, Emma has managed to coat her nose in chocolate. As we sit on a bench and finish off Harry's creative alternative to birthday cake, we predict a profitable summer for the mall's new ice cream parlor.

Emma downs her ice cream and spends the next few minutes running around a raised display of blooming tulips before returning to her stroller and climbing in. She is ready for a ride, and Harry and I gladly accommodate. As we have done so many times before, we stroll around the indoor shopping center and talk. With each pass, I look longingly into a bookstore. Stacked with used books and appropriately named Second Read, it stands in stark contrast to the huge, sleek department stores that anchor the mall.

Finally Harry says, "You shop. I'll keep walking and pick you up on the next pass."

When I enter the bookstore, the middle-aged shopkeeper enthusiastically greets me and offers his assistance. He points out first editions, classics, Newbery Medal-winning children's books, *New York Times* bestsellers, memoirs, how-to manuals, cookbooks, and rare finds from estate sales. Although the organization appears haphazard to me, he knows each book and where it belongs.

I pull my bulky sweater close to my body as I explore tight aisles jammed with books of every genre and condition. Like an offspring of Alice in Wonderland and Willy Wonka, I disappear into stacks containing all sorts of delicious reads. For thirty minutes, I relish the quiet and explore every nook until Harry enters the store with Emma asleep in her stroller. He waves to me, but instead of pushing her stroller in my direction, he seeks out the shopkeeper, who leads him to the checkout counter. From underneath, the gentleman pulls out a red canvas tote with Second Read screen-printed on the front and exchanges it for Harry's cash.

"Happy birthday, MJ," Harry says as he turns around and hands me the tote. "I had Ray pull together some reference books for my wife, the writer. I figured you could use something besides your dictionary."

Flabbergasted at the surprise, I open the tote and remove each book. Three giant hardcovers, a thesaurus, a college writing handbook, and a manual of style, weigh down the tote, while a paperback rhyming dictionary and a book by Eudora Welty sit on the top.

"I threw in the novel for fun. My treat," says the shopkeeper, who is now on a first-name basis with my husband.

"Thanks so much for your help," says Harry. "Ray, this is my wife, Marguerite."

"Nice to meet you, Marguerite," he says, extending his hand. "Ray. Ray Ingvold. Happy birthday!"

"So you've been my husband's personal shopper. Your choices are perfect. Thank you," I say as I examine each book.

"Glad to help a writer. Who's this little pumpkin?" Ray asks as he circles the counter and bends over a sleeping Emma.

"This is Emma," Harry whispers, "who is totally worn out."

"Aren't they cherubs when they sleep? I have three of my own," Ray says, tapping a family photo that is taped to the side of the cash register. "Twin boys, Ian and Fletcher, fraternal as you can see. Better they don't hear me call them 'cherubs.' They'll be sixteen next month. And the little one is Peggy. That's my wife, Mary," he says, pointing to each one. The photo curls up from the bottom as if it has been posted for decades.

"I think we enlisted Ian earlier to take our photo," Harry says as he scrutinizes the photo.

"Probably. He's around here somewhere," says Ray. "Both boys help out in the store."

After we leave the bookstore, I experience a peculiar warmth, like I have become reacquainted with an old and dear friend. The feeling intrigues me until I can finally give it words. Ray reminds me very much of Uncle Raymond. The two share not only comparable names but also a rare sensitivity.

"Let's come back soon when Emma is awake," I say as we walk to the car. "I want her to get to know Ray. And I have to set him straight. I'm not a writer, just a person who . . ."

"Loves to write," says Harry.

31

$\mathcal{N}$ixing my early morning ritual, I declared my third Sunday in Maui a respite from the usual. Practicing my craft and hiking the beach would be replaced with—I had no idea.

I showered and slipped into a tropical skirt and matching T-shirt, recent purchases from a small shop in Kihei, then headed down to the pool to confer with the activities director, Patti. From the lanai, I had watched as she held daily informational sessions for new arrivals on the pool deck. So far, not interested in committing to an island activity or a mini tour, I had avoided the sessions. This morning, however, I caught her as she was setting up and peppered her with questions about the island's North Shore. Young, energetic, and knowledgable, Patti was the perfect ambassador for Maui. By the time newcomers had assembled for the organized presentation, I was heading to my car with a list of suggestions for exploring new territory.

Maui's weather forecast for the day, eighty-six and sunny, was a repeat of the day before. A now-familiar female voice on KPOA radio promised "another beautiful day on Maui!" I rolled down the windows of the Prius. "So boring . . ." she added with a laugh.

"Who doesn't love this kind of boring?" I asked out loud.

Once I passed the familiar turnoff that led Upcountry, I entered new territory and joined a steady line of cars that backed up outside of the small town of Pa'ia. At the edge of town, I slowly drove past a paved area filled with vehicles, the choicest place to park, I realized belatedly. My little Prius crawled along a main thoroughfare dotted with restaurants, surf shops, and boutiques. Window displays and outdoor racks offered artwork, crafts, clothing, and decorative home goods. A tan, long-haired, surfer type jaywalked in front of my car and jumped into a small vehicle with a surfboard protruding out of the sunroof. He, plus the tie-dyed fabrics, macramé creations, and tinkling wind chimes gave Pa'ia a hippie, sixties vibe. Not finding a single available parking space along the street, I drove along. In no time at all, Pa'ia was visible only through my rearview mirror.

Soon the road curved left toward the ocean, and I drove past the entrance to Mama's Fish House. According to Patti, this restaurant was considered by locals and tourists alike to have the greatest ambiance and the freshest fish on the island. "You will pay dearly for both, but trust me, you'll have no regrets. Reservations are needed and sometimes hard to get. You'll need to plan ahead," she had said.

I looked longingly at the turnoff for Mama's as I proceeded down the road toward my intended destination, Ho'okipa Beach Park, or more specifically, the lookout above the park, the perfect vantage point for viewing both surfing and windsurfing. Huge waves and a rocky reef gave the beach its well-earned reputation: For experts only! The lookout was a popular spot, and a steady stream of vehicles took turns occupying the small parking area. I carefully pulled into a vacant space and got out of the car for a better view. Below were the stunning turquoise-blue water and loud, crashing surf of Ho'okipa.

According to Patti, surfers and windsurfers followed strict protocols regarding the time of day and the numbers that could share the waves. Mid- to late morning, I might get to watch both, she had said. Sure enough, in the distance multicolored sails caught the wind and propelled windsurfers and their boards across the waves. Stabilizing my arms on the wooden fencing that was positioned to protect the viewers from the edge of a rocky cliff, I recorded the spectacle. Then I turned my attention to a cluster of surfers off the point. Attuned to the ocean's rhythm, guys and gals, some appearing quite young, straddled surfboards and patiently waited for the perfect wave. When a giant set arrived, several of them pivoted their boards, stretched out upon them, and paddled furiously to catch the largest waves. Latecomers peeled off, leaving one or two to ride it as long as possible and as close to shore as the rocky reef would allow. I could only imagine the skill necessary during winter when monster surf pounded the North Shore.

I was mesmerized by the powerful waves and the skill of the surfers who caught them. An hour slipped by unnoticed. At one point, I exchanged my cell phone for Millie's binoculars and focused on a single surfer, a young girl who seemed unfazed by the waves and the rocks. With dark hair and a trim body, she reminded me of Elle. She waited a long time before she picked a wave to her liking. I recorded her takeoff and ride and immediately sent the video via text message to Elle. Within minutes, the ping of the cell phone announced a reply, "Amazing!!" followed by a sticker of a surfer.

Elle, athletic and fearless, would appreciate Maui's water sports, I thought as I recalled her conversations with Harry about downhill skiing and snowboarding. Now, I had a strange yearning to share with her the artistry of the athletes in front of me. For the first time since my arrival, the absence of a travel companion registered as a loss. With the exception of other strangers at the railing, I had no one with whom to share the memory of sun-sparkled water erupting over and over into huge, white-tipped swells that thunderously crashed upon the rocks below. Sadly, the sights, sounds, and fragrance of salt could not be adequately captured by a cell phone camera. Instead, hoping to create an enduring memory, I concentrated on each sense.

Thirst lured me away from the never-ending show. Back at the car, I swigged from a water bottle as I consulted my notes from Patti. If I continued driving in the same direction, I would eventually arrive in Hana, a trip that would involve "four hundred to six hundred turns, depending on who's counting," Patti had said. My decision to forgo that trip remained intact. Instead, I decided, I would check out a town in Upcountry that both May and Patti had suggested. I backtracked to Pa'ia and turned onto Baldwin Avenue, a road that led Upcountry. Ten minutes later, I arrived at the cowboy town of Makawao. I had no trouble finding the Mexican restaurant Patti had recommended and was soon enjoying steaming fish tacos freshly prepared with sautéed ono.

Fortified, I poked in and out of shops and galleries that lined the town's main street. They offered an eclectic mix, everything from designer jewelry, artwork, and fashions to Western wear, baked goods, New Age crystals, and natural foods. Posters announced an upcoming event, the 60th Annual Makawao Rodeo, scheduled over the Fourth of July weekend. Hitching posts along Baldwin Avenue also added to the town's cowboy tradition, a clear distinction from the surfing mecca of Pa'ia, six miles away.

My unique shopping experience culminated at a fine arts gallery. A stunning gold pendant caught my eye. A stylized plumeria on a delicate snake chain cast its spell from under the glass of a locked display case. Beautiful in its simplicity, the piece represented much more to me than the designer's probable intent. When the salesperson draped the necklace around my neck and fastened the clasp, I scrutinized the beauty of the flower. Gold petals overlapped in such a way as to create a tiny opening in the center that invited the skin of my throat to show through. As my body turned, the flower remained securely in position as the chain gently moved through the small loop of gold on the back. The design reminded me of a wooden trinket box Harry had crafted in his workshop and presented to me one Christmas. "For the things that inspire you," he had said. When I asked about the small hole he had drilled in the cover, he said, "An opening for possibilities." In short order, I separated myself from a chunk of savings and left the gallery with a velvet box.

Back at the car, I paused to get my bearings. Consulting the map May had given me plus the GPS on the cell phone, I calculated that I was already several miles Upcountry and only fifteen minutes or less from May's. Spontaneously, I left Makawao and drove to Kula, where I stopped at a bistro and picked up a specialty cake described as coconut mango.

Ken looked up from his protea to check out the crunching of gravel. He recognized my car and waved, both good signs that he might be enjoying a lucid day. He placed his hoe upright against a wheelbarrow and headed over just as May greeted me from her porch.

"I know I should have called," I said. "But I was out exploring and found myself close, so I wanted to drop in."

May was the first to respond. "We are glad you did. Aren't we, Father?"

"Of course. Hello, Marguerite," he said, with no prompting.

"It is a very good day for you to come," said May, before directing me to the main house.

Fern opened the front door, gratefully accepted my gift of cake, and ushered all of us inside. "We will have tea and cake," she declared, before disappearing into the kitchen.

Once more the four of us circled the table in the living room, this time enjoying hot tea and slices of a cake that Fern described as "heavenly." Ken surprised me with his enthusiasm for the dessert as well as his willingness to engage in conversation with a Minnesotan.

"So, you do not live far from Fort Snelling," he said, recalling our previous conversation.

"It's about a thirty minute drive from my house. I live in a northern suburb of Saint Paul—New Brighton."

"I have memories of your state, especially Minneapolis and Saint Paul," he said, "although my time there was short."

"Fond memories, I hope," I said, fishing for more details.

"We arrived in the winter. Before Christmas 1944?" I realized his question was directed at himself, so I followed the example of May and Fern and waited. "Yes, December 1944," he continued. "The temperature was below zero. I'd never heard of such a thing. I thought I would never be warm again," he said as he feigned a shiver and then laughed just as he had done at Kepaniwai Park. "At the time, I wanted so much to be in Europe with the 442nd."

I knew that Ken's proficiency with the Japanese language had determined his assignment to military intelligence training in Minnesota. But on the day he had shared his brother's story, he had been reluctant to talk of his own. Hoping that he was opening up, I pulled out the voice recorder and asked again for permission before turning it on. I interpreted his shrug as an affirmative.

"How old were you when Pearl Harbor was bombed?"

I asked, hoping my question would not challenge his memory.

"Fifteen," he answered quickly. "Too young. One needed to be eighteen to enlist. By the time I reached that age, Ichiro was dead. I wanted to take his place."

"But you weren't allowed?"

Ken paused, and I feared my question had become too personal.

"What Father is not telling you is that once he enlisted, he scored very high on the Japanese proficiency test and was singled out for military intelligence," said May, who knew her father would humbly minimize his accomplishment.

"I was told I could help America in another way. To fight with my brain. So I went. To Minnesota."

"I never knew about this part of my state's history," I admitted.

"The language school began in San Francisco," explained Ken, "but in 1942, President Roosevelt issued 9066."

"Executive Order 9066 was the order that led to the internment of so many Japanese," Fern explained.

"After Japanese were rounded up, San Francisco was no longer a good place for the school. Too many Californians saw us as traitors. But your governor, Harold Stassen, agreed to take the school. Minnesotans would be accepting of Japanese Americans, he said. So it was moved to Camp Savage in Scott County."

"Camp Savage?"

"Camp Savage first. Then the school got too big and it moved again—to Fort Snelling— just a few months before I arrived. Fort Snelling," he repeated. He paused as if to picture it in his mind. "A large and very good place."

"Did you find Minnesota accepting?" I asked.

"Yes, that was mostly my experience. Some prejudice, yes, like everywhere. But Minnesotans are very patriotic.

People would look first at the uniform and most would see us as American. During leisure hours, we would go to Hennepin Avenue. Eat at a Chinese cafeteria." Ken laughed at the memory.

May removed a framed newspaper article from the wall and handed it to me to read. The write-up from the *Honolulu Star-Bulletin* described the Military Intelligence Service Language School whose purpose was to teach army personnel the language and culture of the country that bombed Pearl Harbor. Ken remained silent and finished his cake as I read about the tribute to Hawaiian-born Nisei. The article also explained the intricacies and benefits of codebreaking and the eventual acknowledgment by the military that soldiers with this skill more than likely shortened the war. At the end of the article was a list of Nisei from Hawaii who had been trained at the school. Keniji Sato was listed with an asterisk by his name. He had been one of the codebreakers.

"You were a codebreaker," I said, prompting him to continue.

Ken downplayed his involvement. "I was assigned to an Army unit and helped. But soon the war ended. I finished my stint in occupied Japan, then came back to Maui."

"And hardly talked about any of it," added May. "I discovered the newspaper article a few years ago," she said, referring to the one I had been reading, "in the archives of the Nisei Veterans Memorial Center in Kahului and had a copy framed for our wall."

"You and so many other Japanese-born Americans proved your loyalty," I said.

"Ichiro gave his life," he said.

"You never talked about your wartime contribution?" I asked, trying to mask my disbelief.

"War. No good. We never learn."

"Have you stayed in touch with any of the other men at the school?" I asked.

"Only one. After the war Ed returned to Minnesota, married a woman he had met during training, then stayed and became a teacher," he said. "The last time he visited Maui was 1998. Maybe if I give you his name, you could greet him for me, Marguerite."

"You could pick up the phone and call him, Father," said Fern.

"I suppose I could," he said. "I don't suppose there is any more of that delicious cake." Ken had a way of bringing the conversation to a close, as if his brain had exhausted its allotment of words.

By the time I left, another strand of Ken's life had been recorded. I secretly hoped that the afternoon's visit with this fascinating man would not be my last. His gentleness, humility, and enduring nature acted as magnets and inspiration.

On the return trip to Kihei, I tried to imagine what life was like in Maui on December 8, 1941, the day after the bombing, when without the benefit of hindsight, no one knew what lay ahead. Moving forward with trust must have challenged everyone.

32

*F*lipping to the first blank page in my MP notebook, I paused to make a mental calculation—June 1, 2015, a new month and my nineteenth day in Maui! As often happened when I spontaneously recorded whatever popped into my head, a string of questions followed:

Should I be reserving an airline seat for a return flight to Minneapolis? If so, when? What would I be returning to? What would I be returning for? Can I justify extending the trip? Is staying in Maui another feeble attempt to separate myself from the inevitable? And what is the inevitable exactly?

The pages of my MP notebook provided resting spots for mental concerns. Although today's questions were elementary, the answers were complex and continued to evade me. By the time I closed the notebook, only two facts had crystallized: I still had a fair amount of emotional work to do, and I still had no clear direction for the rest of the summer, much less the week or even the day. My conclusion for the time being, I decided, was a procrastinator's first choice. Today, I would decide nothing.

I picked up two pages of the birthday book, stashed

them and my writing materials into my tote, and headed by car to Kama'ole Beach Park III, or Kam 3 as the locals called it. After a refreshing dip, I retrieved a beach chair and the tote from the hatchback and staked out a relaxing spot in the shade.

The mesmerizing Pacific Ocean lulled me into further contemplation. As I watched a single sailboat skim across the water, I congratulated myself for making at least one important decision since my arrival. Although I had traveled to Maui to work on *Seldom What It Seems,* I had chosen to reminisce. Strangely, I was not experiencing an ounce of guilt for navel-gazing. Instead, story by story, the fragmented memoir was gently rebuilding my mental foundation. Revisiting each memory through an eighty-year-old lens was adding new perspective, and tapping into my ancestors' source of wisdom and strength offered an additional, unexpected blessing.

Of all the things I had lugged to Maui, pages from the birthday book were turning out to be the most crucial. The ones quickly culled out for travel had been well chosen. They represented, perhaps, not all of the defining moments of my life but definitely years most worthy of reflection. With that thought in mind, I pulled out two, the pages representing 1968 and 1969, focused on the photos, and began to write.

MARGUERITE—AGE 33
April 30, 1968
"A Birthday That Begins at Como Park Zoo
and Ends With a Change in Direction"

My birthday celebration begins with a family outing to Como Park Zoo in Saint Paul. Harry and I brace against the

April wind and refuse to admit that we are uncomfortably cold. Hunched shoulders give us away. On the other hand, Emma, bundled in a woolen parka with a hood drawn tightly under her chin, seems unfazed by the weather, even after a gust of wind catches her stray curls and blows them with such force that they straighten and cover one eye. Four months shy of turning five, our daughter happily poses for the camera by turning and offering a cheesy smile to the photographer, a young woman who volunteers to snap a photo of our family. As we stand shivering in the raw wind, she takes great pains to center the shot so that a baby giraffe and its mother can be included in the background.

Shortly after the photo is snapped, Harry stumbles and twists his ankle. To his great dismay, the rest of the day's outing is spent in the emergency room. At first, Emma is intrigued by the activity of the hospital. But soon, the newness wears off, and she morphs into a cranky malcontent. The sights and smells of the emergency room trigger a disconcerting response in my gut, and once Harry is released, I gladly leave the hectic atmosphere behind. For me, the afternoon offers a subtle confirmation; separating myself from any occupation related to healthcare is for the best.

Feeling terrible about ruining my birthday, Harry refuses to relax until he has located by phone a restaurant that will deliver. Eventually, we eat a birthday dinner of barbecued ribs and fries from TV trays, a novel experience that excites Emma, while Harry elevates and ices his foot on the couch. I reassure him that the day has not been ruined, quite the opposite. His unexpected need for medical treatment has strengthened my resolve to head in a different occupational direction.

A few days later, while Harry is wobbling about on crutches, I receive an offer that validates my decision to leave nursing behind. Weeks earlier, I had applied for a

position at a community newspaper in Northeast Minneapolis. A wimpy résumé listed my pitiful journalistic experience, writing for a school newspaper and working odd
jobs at the daily in Davis after my junior and senior years of
high school. Pertinent education included a smattering of
noncredit writing classes and editing workshops, all taken
purely for enjoyment. In all likelihood, I thought, landing
the job with these credentials was slim. I did not understand the reality; sometimes a warm body willing to work
for little compensation is all that is required.

After the phone call that confirms the job is mine, we
celebrate as if I had won a Pulitzer. Harry splurges and
makes reservations for the three of us at a revolving restaurant atop a hotel in downtown Saint Paul. He enjoys his
new role as a stationary tour guide by pointing out all sorts
of landmarks as they glide into view through the window
next to our table. Emma's favorites are the winding Mississippi River, the Minnesota State Capitol with its beautiful dome, and the distant skyline of Saint Paul's twin,
Minneapolis. Not comprehending her mommy's new job,
she considers the celebratory dinner a make-up birthday
party and insists on cake and ice cream, an indulgence her
father seconds. I love both of them for the gesture and joyfully blow out the candles. It isn't until later that I realize
the only snapshot I have of the evening is the memory in
my mind.

I love my new job, covering community events for the
small newspaper and writing whatever I am assigned,
everything from obituaries and community calendars to
feature stories. My boss, a patient mentor, supports me as
I resurrect and grease rusty journalistic skills and attempt
to learn new ones. The relationship is a win-win for both of
us. What I lack in knowledge, I make up for in enthusiasm.
Eventually, I negotiate the freedom to work from home, a

valuable perk, and in return, devote many more hours to the job than my part-time status requires.

The upside for Emma is seeing her mother motivated and excited about trying something new. Her life is also about to change. In September, she will be heading off to kindergarten. Just like her mother, she is eager for whatever lies ahead.

MARGUERITE—AGE 34
April 30, 1969
"Emma and Harry's Gastronomical Accomplishment"

Harry snaps the picture of Emma sitting beside me on a dining room chair. Both of us have our faces puckered midblow as we aim our breath at a ring of thirty-four candles that flicker around the edge of a very lopsided triple-layered chocolate cake. Emma and Harry's attempt to create a homemade birthday cake started out artfully, with a bake that produced nicely raised layers. But Harry was unaware that he should level off the rounded tops before stacking them. The gooey chocolate frosting between each layer acted more like grease than glue. Now fully decorated, the cake resembles a miniature Leaning Tower of Pisa.

"As an architect, I should have done better," says Harry.

"But wait 'til you taste it, Mommy. It's the best cake ever," says Emma.

"Yummy perfection," I say after taking a bite.

Emma and her dad take turns congratulating themselves for pulling off a birthday surprise without any outside help or interference.

It is hard to imagine life any better than this. Harry's fledgling company is growing wings, our drama queen

Emma is bringing home kindergarten tales that entertain nightly, and I am following my passion at the newspaper.

"I'd like you to do a follow-up feature story on the mall," directs my boss, after calling me into his office one afternoon in mid-October. He hands me an eight-year-old clipping, a feature story focused on the opening of Apache Plaza in 1961. "Check out the stores. Interview shoppers. How has the mall changed since it opened? Does it still fill a need? Take Emma along. See what's available for kids."

The 1961 newspaper article lauds the creation and opening of Minnesota's second indoor shopping mall on land that had been a pig farm. The new, climate-controlled mall, the article states, "offers shoppers the convenience of never having to step foot outside . . . Department stores and smaller specialty stores encircle a three-story-high court area, with multicolored clerestory windows beneath hyperbolic, paraboloid shells . . . The mall is destined to become a hub for the community . . ." It is upon this last assumption that I center my investigation.

The opportunity to research a feature story with Emma thrills me. Once her school bus returns her from morning kindergarten, the plan unfolds.

"We're going to Apache after lunch. So hurry and get washed up!"

"To see Ray?" she asks.

"Yes, hopefully we'll see Ray. Mommy's writing a story on the mall, and I need your help. I want a special paragraph on what's great at the mall for kids. What do you think? Will you help me?"

"Do we have to eat lunch first?" asks Emma as she flies to the bathroom.

"We'll need fuel for this job, so eat up!" I insist when she returns to the kitchen.

Emma plops down in front of a ham and cheese sandwich, apple slices, and a glass of milk. After she makes a
satisfactory dent in her lunch, we head to the car.

Emma is very familiar with Apache Plaza, or Apache,
as we call it. Harry and I shop there often. In addition, the
mall has become a recreational destination for the family.
We often take treks around the indoor courtyard, especially in winter when nasty windchill factors or icy sidewalks force us indoors. For Emma, a stop to visit Ray in his
bookstore ranks as high as a ride around the mall on the
indoor mini train.

"Ray-y-y-y-y-y," screams Emma as she races inside the
bookstore in search of her friend.

"Well, if it isn't my favorite kindergartner," says Ray,
hoisting her up and giving her a big hug before setting her
on the counter next to the cash register. "Did you bring
your mama or did you come alone?" he asks before peering
beyond her and winking at me.

"Mommy's coming. Only she's slow," says Emma.

"Hi, Ray," I say, finally catching up and extending my
hand for his customary handshake.

After pleasantries, Emma jumps down and heads to the
children's section, and I explain my assignment to Ray.

"You've come to the right place. Let me get my scrapbook." Ray walks to the rear of the store and retrieves a cor-
rugated box from under his desk. With two hands, he lifts
out a heavy, thick scrapbook, carries it back to the counter,
and lovingly opens it. "If it happened at the mall, it's in
here," he says as he pages through his collection of photos,
newspaper articles, handwritten notes, and an assortment
of other memorabilia that document the mall's life.

"This is incredible!"

I read about community events, celebrity visits, seasonal

activities, cooking classes. Each page documents the growth of an indoor mall that is establishing itself as the hub of the community.

"Take it for a few days," he says. "Maybe you can find something useful for your article."

Ray's understatement brings a smile to both of our faces.

I thank Ray for his generosity and arrange to pick up the scrapbook on our way out, then gather Emma and continue our research by carefully documenting the present state of the mall. We painstakingly cover every square inch, including the bowling alley in the basement. After interviewing an array of patrons and sales employees, including an elderly gentleman playing a piano in the center of the courtyard, I return home with a very tired Emma, open Ray's scrapbook, and begin to write.

The story begins as a tribute to a well-loved shopping plaza that has secured notable standing within the community. As I write, however, a more interesting aspect of the mall evolves. It centers on one particular shop owner who documents the mall's development, similar to a parent who lovingly records a child's growth and activities in a baby book. Ray's love for story and his unique bookstore give heart to the mall. So I write from that perspective and present my draft to Jim. After a quick read, he arranges for a staff photographer to take photos of Ray and his sons.

Eventually, the feature story lands above the fold on the neighborhood page. I can hardly contain my excitement when I see a photo of Ray, Ian, and Fletcher unpacking boxes of books from an estate sale. The caption reads, "Second Read owners unpack recently acquired first editions at Apache Plaza." Ray's enthusiasm for the article is only surpassed by his gratitude for the exposure. During our family's next visit, Ray directs our attention to the wall. The entire page of the newspaper with the article and picture of Ray and the twins has been framed and hung for all to see.

"I have you to thank for the uptick in sales, MJ," he says. "Promotion has never been my forte."

"Glad the article helped," I reply as I try to imagine how many books Ray would have to sell each month just to pay the rent.

Harry and I poke through the shelves while Emma sits at the children's table and draws one more of a never-ending supply of pictures for Ray. We reunite at the register. Harry clutches one hardbound historical fiction, and I balance a stack of paperback mysteries and memoirs.

"Sure you don't need some more hired help here, Ray?" Harry asks in jest as he peers down at the pile of books in my arms. "My wife could benefit from an employee discount."

Harry's comment may have planted a seed. A few weeks later, Ray asks if I would be interested in becoming an occasional fill-in when he heads out to weekend auctions and estate sales. Easily, I slip into my second job. On beautiful summer and autumn weekends, while Harry and Emma enjoy father-daughter activities, I immerse myself in books, some pristine with unturned pages and others weather beaten and frayed. Comfortable in my soul, I welcome the warmth of belonging.

On the wall next to the framed newspaper article about the bookstore hangs one of Emma's portraits of Ray, recognizable by his bald head, wire-rimmed glasses, and backdrop of books. It is captioned, UNCLE RAY THE BOOK MAN.

33

*R*ay's kind and gentle spirit had surrounded me the previous day at the beach while I wrote about the development of our friendship in the late sixties. Now, his name appeared over and over as I jotted down my morning thoughts. Finally, after closing my MP notebook and calculating the time in Phoenix, I picked up my cell phone. Ray's daughter, Peggy, answered on the third ring. Our conversation lasted less than fifteen minutes, but by the end, I had expressed what my previous note on a generic sympathy card had failed to adequately say. She and her brothers, Ian and Fletcher, had lost a generous, kind, and loving father, a man who had extended that love to Harry, to me, and especially to Emma. We loved him, too. I missed him, and I apologized to Peggy for not following my urge to fly to Phoenix one more time to visit him before it was too late. She understood. She apologized for not helping her father stay in touch with me, especially after Harry's death. With regrets expressed and released, we ended our call.

Spirit cleansed, I was ready to write. The next page from the birthday book jumped ahead fifteen years.

MARGUERITE—AGE 49
April 30, 1984
"A Birthday Amidst the Ruins—Apache Tornado"

Harry, Ray, Ian, Fletcher, Peggy, and I sit around a round table in a homey-looking Northeast Minneapolis restaurant. I am not smiling for the camera. It catches me midthought. My eyes give me away. Vacant and weary, they hint at my emotional retreat. Where am I?

It is my forty-ninth birthday, but no one is in a celebratory mood. In fact, a birthday dinner is an afterthought. On this particular Monday evening, all of us are physically and emotionally spent. We are finally taking a break after hours in Second Read frantically separating dry books from wet ones. Harry is the one who attempts to refocus the group on the birthday celebration at hand, but the rest of us are inclined to either rehash our stories of nature's vengeance or simply listen.

Four days ago, Fletcher and Peggy jumped aboard flights from Oregon and Arizona, respectively, as soon as they received the call from Ray with news that an F3 tornado had roared through Apache Plaza, with their father and brother inside. Everything considered, Ray and Ian fared much better than the bookstore. Ian dove under a counter when the winds roared through the mall's broken exterior and the lights flickered and died. Ray, less nimble, dislocated his shoulder when he tripped in the dark. The bookstore and many beloved books were heavily damaged by the tornado and also by a spring snowstorm that deposited three inches of melting slop days later.

Harry and I were fortunate to be together and at home when the storm hit. Uneasy, we headed for the basement when the sky turned an eerie green and the sirens sounded. We crouched over a transistor radio and listened intently as a weatherman announced that rotation had been spotted in a storm that was heading in our direction. Outside, the spooky quietness gave way to howling winds. At one point, Harry and I exchanged grimaces when a loud crack followed by a crash echoed from the backyard.

After the all-clear was given, we carefully emerged from the basement to survey the damage. Although power was lost, the interior of our home had survived without injury. Clutching the radio in one hand and a flashlight in another, Harry led me outside. A huge limb from a cherished shade tree lay on the ground, its branches splayed on the grass next to Harry's greenhouse. A once-beautiful oak now stood awkwardly erect with only half of its original canopy intact. Although the greenhouse had avoided damage from the falling limb, several windows had been shattered. The culprits, hailstones the size of golf balls, slowly melted on the lawn. Littered with debris and downed branches, our yard was a mess, but damage to the exterior of our house, at least what was visible in the dark, appeared to be limited to pockmarks from hail on the siding and fascia. We were stunned but relieved, until the weatherman reported that a tornado had touched down in nearby Saint Anthony. Apache Plaza had taken a direct hit.

In the distance, sirens from emergency vehicles pierced the silence. For years, I had recoiled at their sound, and on this night, they only added to my panic.

"Ray and Ian!" I gasped. I had left the bookstore four hours earlier after Ian had arrived to finish up and help Ray with closing. Both men were probably still at the store.

"Let's go," said Harry as he dashed back inside to get the car keys.

Instinct and concern overpowered common sense as we headed in the direction of the mall. Harry drove slowly through dark side streets and around downed branches until we approached the congested intersection of Silver Lake Road and Fourteenth Street. Neither the traffic signal nor the streetlights were working; so like others, we proceeded slowly and waited our turn at what had morphed into a self-regulated, four-way stop. We joined a slow-moving caravan headed south. About a mile from the mall, a police cruiser blocked the road, and two officers directed traffic. When we reached them, Harry rolled down the window.

"Is there any way to get through to check on our store and coworkers at Apache?"

"Sorry. Streets are closed to all but emergency vehicles."

With his flashlight, the other officer directed Harry to make a U-turn. Worried and frustrated, we slowly backtracked and returned to our dark house.

"Phones are out at Apache. Not a surprise," Harry said, after repeated attempts to call the bookstore. I dialed Ray's home number. The phone on the other end rang, but no one answered. Out of options, we waited.

"Should we call Peggy and Fletcher?" I asked. "Maybe they've heard from Ray."

"And if they haven't?" Harry said as he shook his head.

Harry was right. If they had not talked to Ray, any news from us would be alarming and premature. For the next two hours, both of us jumped each time the phone rang. Neighbors and friends called to check on our condition and update us on theirs. In each case, we quickly brought the conversation to a close to reopen the phone line. The bad news: we heard nothing from Ray and Ian. The good news: power in our home was restored after momentary flickers.

During the hours of waiting, I feared the worst. Losing Ray, Ian, or both would be unbearable. As the time ticked away, Harry remained positive and chalked up the absence of a phone call from them to the storm's aftermath. I appreciated his efforts to alleviate my fears, but only Ian's voice shortly after 2 a.m. allowed me to fully breathe.

"We're both okay. At the hospital. Dad dislocated his shoulder. They've taken care of that and don't need to admit him, so we are free to go. But Dad's car and my truck are still at the mall," he said matter-of-factly, as if he had experienced a minor inconvenience rather than a tornado and a trip in an ambulance.

"Tell them we're sorry to ask for a ride in the middle of the night." It was Ray's voice in the background.

"On our way," Harry replied after confirming the name of the hospital.

We drove to downtown Minneapolis via an indirect route that avoided the mall and the damage that extended in a hit-or-miss fashion into nearby neighborhoods. As we approached the emergency room entrance of the hospital, Ian flagged us down, then disappeared behind the glass doors. Shortly, he emerged with a nurse who was pushing Ray in a wheelchair. I jumped out and gave both men a hug.

"You are sights for sore eyes," said Harry.

"We are sights that will make your eyes sore," replied Ray without missing a beat. Then he added, "The wheelchair is just for show."

He gingerly raised the footrests with his foot so he would have room to stand. Ian and Harry eased him into the car, as I scrounged around in the trunk for blankets. Both men had left their outerwear behind at the store.

"It's been a long night, especially for you," I said. "We'll get you home."

"Can we go back to Second Read? I want to check on the damage," Ray said, ignoring my sentiment.

"No one's getting near the mall tonight," Harry said. "We've already tried. Besides, it'll be pitch black without power. We'll drive you home, then we'll bring you back to check out things in the morning."

Harry and I were not surprised when the phone rang early the next day. Ian called to report that his father was up and anxious to survey the damage. With Harry behind the wheel, the four of us slowly snaked our way to the mall amidst a lineup of gawker-filled automobiles. Daylight exposed damage that Harry and I had not fully realized in the dark. A single-car garage had been lifted off its foundation and deposited intact in the middle of a side street. Shingles, sheetrock, and shredded insulation littered yards and in some areas actually hung from trees like creepy Halloween decorations. Nature's fury had stripped one giant oak of every leaf and freakishly had skewered the thick tree trunk with a long wooden plank from no obvious source.

After finally arriving at a police checkpoint, Ray pleaded his case. He begged that we be allowed to pass since we had cars and a business behind the police tape. The officer acknowledged our concerns but firmly denied access. Harry detoured down a side street and circled back until he located a small parking space in the residential area adjacent to the mall. He parked the car, and we headed closer on foot. Four blocks later we reached the yellow police tape that surrounded what looked like a bomb site. Ray's moans and stricken expressions prompted me to slide my arm under his good one as Ian and Harry moved closer to the man who was witnessing in broad daylight the extent of damage to the mall.

"She's been crippled," Ray said. Then he looked up and shook his head. "No, no!" The multicolored glass windows surrounding the inner courtyard had disintegrated. What remained were spiky shards.

"It's a good thing Second Read is on the north end," Ian said to Ray with a note of optimism. "It's less damaged over there." He pointed to the northwest entrance closest to the bookstore.

Ray did not follow Ian's gesture. He was focused on the southern end of the parking lot. "I hope the store fared better than my car."

Ray's Chevy had been parked as usual at the edge of the south lot under a tree, a spot Ray chose whenever he did not have books to unload. "A nice walk—good exercise" was his explanation to anyone who asked why he chose to park so far away from the bookstore. The cars that had remained in the parking lot after closing had been tossed like abandoned toys. The tree under which Ray had parked was nowhere to be seen. His Chevy was lying on its side several rows over in a sea of broken glass. Even from a distance, we could see that every window, including the windshield, had either imploded or been shattered by flying debris.

After a momentary pause that felt eerily like a wake, we circled along the tape to get a better view of the north end of the mall.

"It'll be impossible to know until we get inside," said Ray.

"At least the structure on this end looks stable," said Harry.

"How about your truck, Ian?" asked Ray, searching the parking lot. "There it is. Looks like it survived. The saving grace was its location."

Remarkably, outside of some hail damage, which in a bizarre way almost enhanced the pickup's rustic character, Ian's truck appeared unscathed.

"Wouldn't you know. My piece of junk survived, and Dad's took the hit," Ian said. "I hadn't heard any warnings of rain, so I left the driver's side window open for air. That must have equalized the pressure."

With nothing else to be gained by staying longer, Harry and I insisted that Ian and Ray come home with us. Over bacon and eggs, we gained equilibrium and discussed possible scenarios for moving forward with the bookstore.

"I'm so sorry I got you into this mess," said Ray, who tried valiantly to navigate his fork with his left hand.

"My timing was lousy," added Ian.

Owning a bookstore had been Ray's dream, never Ian's, and in mid-November Ian had announced that he wanted to move to the West Coast before the start of summer. His upcoming plans set in motion major changes for the business. Ray approached Harry and me to see if we had any interest in becoming half owners of the bookstore. "For health reasons, I have to step back, and without Ian, I'll need help. How about it, MJ? Any interest in coming aboard full time? And Harry, I know investing in a book business is risky, but I'd appreciate if you'd give it some thought."

Although I had never dreamt of becoming an entrepreneur, the idea of sharing ownership of a place that had become a second home sped up my heart. I looked at Harry, expecting him to talk both of us out of a wild and crazy idea. But instead, he smiled. We discussed the financial, legal, and personal ramifications, and in February, two months before the tornado's arrival, the three of us signed the paperwork that established shared ownership of Second Read. On Valentine's Day, I resigned from my job at the newspaper and turned full attention to the store that I had loved for years, the one that now sat behind police tape.

"It'll be a setback, but none of us will lose our shirts," said Harry, reminding Ian of the insurance upgrade on the bookstore that was purchased the same day the partnership was finalized.

"We'd be suckin' air with the old policy," said Ray. "We

need to notify the adjustors," he added with a note of urgency.

"Done," said Harry. It was, in fact, the one thing that Harry had been able to accomplish.

"Have you called Fletcher and Peggy?" I asked. "It would be awful if they heard about this on the news."

"I woke them both up, I'm afraid," said Ray, who winced as he adjusted the sling that had slipped out of place.

"I think you should go home and rest that shoulder," I said.

"Listen to her, Ray. She's a nurse, you know," said Harry.

We loaned our second car, a used Buick purchased years earlier, to Ian, who delivered his dad back home. For the rest of the day, Harry and I turned our attention to the yard and neighborhood. I picked up debris and dragged broken branches to a growing pile of yard waste at the side of the driveway. Harry revved up an antiquated chainsaw. Finding it operational, he headed across the street and added his help to those clearing a gigantic, uprooted blue spruce that had toppled into the roadway. By the end of the day, our yard and most of the neighborhood had been cleaned up. The only telltale signs of the storm were fresh stumps here and there and huge piles of debris in each yard.

Cleaning up Second Read, however, was a greater challenge. Thankfully, the bookstore was located in a section of the mall that was judged to be structurally sound. Unlike the south end of the mall, where roofs had been peeled back, walls damaged, windows blown out, and merchandise destroyed, the north section sustained less damage. Eventually, we were given the go-ahead to assess firsthand the bookstore's damage.

With a mixture of hopefulness and dread, we unlocked the doors. The walls of Second Read had held firm. Located in the northern interior of the mall with no windows to the outside, the bookstore had been somewhat protected from the winds of the tornado. But nothing could stop the water that dripped through the ceiling in multiple places. Snowmelt from the second storm compounded the damage. Water, seeking the path of least resistance, not only dripped down from above but also seeped in from the mall's flooded courtyard. Ray, Ian, Fletcher, Peggy, Harry, and I worked tirelessly to retrieve and protect as many books as possible.

I had barely begun my role as entrepreneur, but already I understood why Ray considered the store his baby. Growing inside of me were instincts one might classify as maternal. Now, they were warning that this baby, the one Ray, Harry, and I shared, needed intensive care to survive, and I questioned whether we were equipped for the task.

Ray attempted to mask his heartbroken spirit. I watched as he culled water-damaged first editions with his good arm, examined them briefly, and then threw them in the trash. Witnessing his methodical process only compounded my sadness.

In spite of it all, April 30 has arrived. In some ways it seems like forever since the tornado; in actuality it has been four days. Harry insisted that we take a break from the cleanup to celebrate my birthday, and Ray and his children agreed. So, disheveled and filthy, here we sit in a cramped booth and try to smile for the camera as we celebrate a birthday that I can't quite wrap my head around. My mind is elsewhere. The spirit of the day is dampened by reality, just like too many of Ray's first editions. Then I think of Emma and gain perspective. I know for a fact that the fear of losing a child of brick and mortar is nothing compared to the reality of losing a child of flesh and blood.

34

I closed my computer, but the memories of 1984 followed me through the day as I ran errands in Kihei. Finally, hot and thirsty, I stopped for a break and a cooling treat: shave ice from a stand in the corner of a small shopping arcade. I ordered a heavenly concoction of macadamia nut ice cream encrusted with finely shaved ice and flavored with guava, passion fruit, and li hing mui syrups. So I could savor the refreshment, I planted myself on a shaded bench next to a small koi pond. Although the kiosks under the green metal roof offered an array of souvenirs, clothing, and jewelry, I chose to forgo shopping. Relaxing in the cool trade winds and enjoying shave ice were much better options.

The Hawaiian shopping area, I feared, was heading in the same direction as Apache Plaza after 1984. Before the tornado, the state-of-the-art shopping mecca in Minnesota had been a magnet for shoppers and the community. After the tornado, it became a weaker twin, rebuilt but never strong. Its grand allure did not return. No longer state of the art, it resembled a cold and uninspired version of its former self. Although a far cry from the cement, steel, and glass of Apache Plaza, this Hawaiian shopping center, with too few shoppers and too many boarded-up stalls, was also past its prime and showing its age, as we all eventually do. As I watched the koi swim in the pond, I wondered if their home would still be here the next time I visited Maui. I had not left and already I was harboring thoughts of returning. I recalled Richard's warning, "Be careful, Marguerite. Maui gets in your blood."

Back on the lanai, I studied the only remaining page from the birthday book. The year was 2002, a year within a new millennium, a year marking another defining moment. Easily, I wrote the story.

MARGUERITE—AGE 67
April 30, 2002
"Harry and MJ Burdick, Author, at Cafe Marc"

A much older Marguerite sits in a booth with Harry at our special place, Cafe Marc. Relaxed and happy, I smile and point to my birthday gift from Harry, a wooden sign for my office door, as the waiter snaps our photo. This birthday marks a year of transition for both of us. Harry is settling into retirement. As for me, the sign says it all: "MJ Burdick, Author." Each of us has reached another milestone when one of life's chapters closes and another opens. Harry has sold his share of Green Space, and with less remorse than expected, I have buried a bookselling business that has failed to thrive. He is happy, and, surprisingly, so am I.

Crafted by Harry in his woodshop and then casually wrapped in tissue paper, the birthday gift is a surprise.

"I'm nailing it on your office door as soon as we get home," he states.

"Does this mean you're going to finally let me see Nana's room?"

The room has been transitioned many times since Nana's

death, from a play room to a guest room, then to a den with TV and VCR. But somehow, it has always remained Nana's room. Since Harry's retirement in February, the cozy space has been off-limits to me while Harry banged away with tools and lumber behind its closed door.

"Yes, tonight is the grand reveal—when Nana's room will officially become the home for my wife's imagination," says Harry as he takes another bite of baked Alaska.

Nostalgically, we chose Cafe Marc to celebrate the day. We limited the birthday celebration to just the two of us, so we would be free to talk about our dreams for retirement. Since selling his ownership of Green Space, Harry has been spending the majority of his time at home. Surprisingly, once he made the decision to retire, he refused to look back. Instead, he has transitioned smoothly into projects that bring him joy, like woodworking, gardening, and spending hours in his greenhouse in the backyard. Now that my home office is ready for occupancy, he intends to begin drafting a solar-heated retirement home complete with indoor and outdoor greenhouses. Sensing my hesitancy, since I can't imagine leaving our home and all its special memories, he says, "By the time it is built, I guarantee—you will love it as much or more." What I love is his youthful excitement, reminiscent of the glee he displayed decades earlier when we moved into our present home.

"You make it easy to imagine that I will," I tell him.

"What kind of writing space should I create for you in our next home? Dream big."

"My dream would be," I say after a lengthy pause, "a brightly lit room, hopefully east facing, with a large writing space, comfortable office chair, an easy chair with a foot-stool in one corner, and lots of storage for files and manu-scripts. Cork on the walls, so I can pin up my inspirations—and most importantly, floor-to-ceiling bookshelves."

"For the woman who cannot part with a single book," says Harry with a laugh.

"You know they're my companions. I love to be surrounded by them."

At Second Read, the quiet, enjoyable hours after closing had been my special time to play with poems and plots in a corner that I had fashioned into a writer's nook. A wellspring of creative thought had emerged in that space, and when I got stuck, I simply plucked someone else's book off the shelves to help inspire.

Those were good years in many regards, but the mall withered. Even though it reopened nine months after the storm, Second Read, just like the mall that housed it, never prospered. Sales never fully rebounded. Once-loyal shoppers sought out other sources for their reading materials during the lengthy rebuilding phase. We lured some back, but even with concerted marketing, sales never measured up to our hopeful projections. Other stores in the mall experienced the same downturn. Each year brought a few more closures, until Apache became a cement and glass shell with only two chain stores remaining. Those were owned by corporations that could afford to hang on longer than the rest of us.

By the time Ray, Harry, and I retired the business, I was ready to transition from a lackluster entrepreneur to a hope-to-be-published writer with scores of poems and stories in three-ring notebooks. Due to his breathing issues, Ray was eager to move to Arizona to be closer to Peggy, and Harry was more than ready to get out from under a business that had become a financial burden. It was time to liquidate and move on. The process was much harder for Ray. He saw the end of Second Read as the end of life as he knew it. I felt sadness, too, but welcomed uninterrupted time to write at home, and starting tomorrow that will be in my new office.

"Ta-da! The office of my favorite author," Harry says after we return home. He opens the door, snaps on overhead and under-counter lights, then steps aside so I can enter my new writing space.

Two steps in, I stop and turn 360 degrees. Harry's design and workmanship are flawless. A large writing space for my computer and printer sit atop built-in drawers and file cabinets. Floor-to-ceiling bookshelves fill two walls and await my collections.

"There's even cork on the wall above my desk. Harry, I love it."

"Tomorrow, we go to the store so you can pick out your office chair and that easy chair and footstool you talked about."

"Everything's perfect, but . . ."

"But?" he asks with a hint of concern.

"Aren't you being overly optimistic," I add, pointing to the word "Author" on the sign for the door.

"It's just a matter of time," he says, sensing my need for reassurance. "Your stories are good, MJ. You just need to know that as much as I do."

Harry's words resonate long after he pounds the plaque into place on the door of my beautiful new office. And just like that, with time to fulfill our passions, Harry and I easily transition into retirement.

The remainder of the year unfolds like a fairy tale. My first major project involves transposing onto paper the story that has been running through my head for years. Inspired by a men's basketball game at Williams Arena (affectionately known as The Barn) on the Minneapolis campus of the University of Minnesota, the characters include several students who take the barnyard comparison seriously and attend the game dressed as cows, sheep, chickens, or pigs. Then ten minutes into the first half of a game against Ohio

State, the costumed students begin to drop like animals at the slaughterhouse. There is no blood, just death. The convoluted plot weaves through Minneapolis's Dinkytown, then the suburbs of the Twin Cities, and finally outstate Minnesota.

Each morning with sunshine warming my new office, I trust that the day will be productive, and each afternoon as I reread the day's work, I ask myself, "Just where did that come from?" The process works, and three hundred pages later, the mystery is unraveled. Once the rough draft is revised for what seems like the twentieth time, I am satisfied and ready to shelve *Murder in the Student Section* and began another Minnesota-based mystery.

About the same time, Claire enters my life. During a writers' workshop, we discover we are kindred spirits and begin a solid friendship. Besides Harry, Claire is the only person I allow to read my manuscript. She is also the first person to hound me about getting it published.

"You need a literary agent, and if that doesn't work, check out small presses," she says.

I repeat what the inner critic is screaming in my head, "No one will be interested."

"Then self-publish. I'm telling you, MJ, this is a great read."

She teams up with Harry, and they take turns buoying my spirit when rejection letters from literary agents, professionals with no interest in an aged, wannabe author, stack up in a pile on my desk.

"I can't even get the manuscript into anyone's hands, much less get someone to read it," I whine to Harry one day during lunch. "I'm done with self-promotion and marketing. I just want to write."

Just when Harry attempts to reword encouragement for the umpteenth time, the phone rings.

"I know someone, a friend of a friend actually, who wants to read your manuscript. I'm coming over. Do you have a clean copy you can give me?" Claire's triumphant announcement over the phone stirs both excitement and dread.

"Wants to?" I question.

"Well, is willing to," she replies.

"Maybe I should . . ."

"All you should do is pull out a copy. I'm on my way."

As I drop a clean copy of *Murder in the Student Section* into a manuscript box, I steady my nerves by reminding myself that the worst that can happen is another rejection. Then I contradict that argument with another revelation. A rejection delivered by a literary agent who has actually read the manuscript will crush my spirit. Still, I hand over the manuscript to Claire and nervously wait.

Nothing happens for weeks. I resign myself to the likelihood that the manuscript is sitting in the bottom of a black hole. Shelving all hope, I turn full attention to writing a second mystery set in Saint Paul's Midway neighborhood. Then, unexpectedly on a snowy afternoon, I receive a call from Jason Mahoney, Claire's friend of a friend.

"I read your story and like it," says Jason matter-of-factly, "but I'm no longer in the business."

As quickly as my heart rises, it drops again.

"But I could put in a good word with a friend who is looking for new authors," he adds.

How about old ones, I want to ask, but keep the words in my head.

"Her name is Georgia Pope, an editor with a decent press out of Chicago."

We work out the details. Then I hurry out to the gardens to fill Harry in on the news, before returning to my office to call Claire.

"Congratulations, your manuscript will be read by an editor!" she says.

"I'm trying not to get my hopes up. But if it works, I'll have you and Jason to thank for knowing the right people."

"It starts with writing a good story," Claire says.

As it turns out, Georgia Pope is one of the right people, and into her hands two months later I entrust my manuscript. Although a trip to Chicago is not necessary (editorial work could be handled via the United States Postal Service and the internet, according to Georgia), Harry and I choose to combine business with pleasure and head to Chicago to meet the person who has agreed to shepherd my story to publication. I need to visualize my editor and the publishing house and am surprised when a young, enthusiastic woman, dressed monochromatically in black with a stunning pearl necklace, greets us at Webster Publishing and introduces herself.

"Call me Georgia," she says as she leads us down the hall to her office, a space that is surprisingly inviting even though its basic framework is cement and glass. Three framed copies of colorful Kandinsky prints warm the walls, while large, potted palms bask in sunshine that streams through enormous windows. A floor-to-ceiling bookshelf further softens the office by showcasing a small but impressive book collection that I immediately find intriguing.

My first reaction to Georgia, however, is mixed. For some reason, I expected someone older. I imagined developing an author/editor relationship with someone of my own generation, someone who has honed skills over a lifetime. Harry might be having the same thoughts, I surmise, judging by his questions as the three of us sit down and talk. After Georgia explains the publishing process and answers my questions, Harry, in his nonthreatening style, probes deeper into Georgia's credentials and work history. I can tell that she is quickly winning him over. Personable and articulate, Georgia appears faultless except, perhaps, for her youthfulness. I decide to reserve judgment in that regard.

Georgia has been an editor for fourteen years and appears to be in her midthirties, about the same age as I when Emma died. If at age thirty-six I could endure the death of a child, I finally conclude, than certainly this thirty-something can oversee the birthing of my novel. An hour into the meeting, I am totally on board and confident that once a lawyer checks out the contract Georgia is offering, I will have no qualms about signing it.

When business concludes, we cement our bond over lunch at Georgia's favorite deli. Our conversation tiptoes into the personal. She opens up about her parents, who left Illinois and moved permanently to Florida after her father retired from the US Postal Service because of Parkinson's disease. Harry shares, among other things, that we are childless, that our daughter Emma died accidentally at age seven. I am okay with his openness and grateful that Georgia's response is a genuine offer of sympathy and not a desire for details. She ends our conversation with encouraging words regarding our partnership. By the time we are back on I-90 and heading home to Minnesota, the mood in the car is celebratory.

"I bet Emma would have grown up to be a lot like Georgia. Confident. Sharp. Accomplished," says Harry.

"I felt it, too. Undoubtedly, there is something special about Georgia."

The next morning, Harry pokes his head into my office and interrupts my work on the rough draft of my next novel. "How goes it?" he asks.

"Pinch me, Harry. I can't believe retirement can be this enjoyable."

"You're not retired, Luv," he says. "You are merely writing a new chapter." Then he casually heads out to his latest gardening project, the planting of raspberry bushes in the backyard.

35

*W*riting filled two days. With energy that comes when the end is in sight, I edited the stories inspired by the final pages of the birthday book. Content to sit on the lanai, I typed away and only moved when hunger, a dip in the pool, or sunset beckoned me away. Once an installment was completed to my liking, I printed a hard copy, passed it though the three-hole punch, and placed it chronologically in the ever-expanding three-ring notebook. I was done. The accumulated pages had become a memoir for an audience of one: me.

In the late afternoon, I watched the twelve-steppers assemble on the lawn. The trade winds had increased from cooling breezes to hold-on-to-your-hat gales. Simultaneously, a change in the ocean games was taking place. While stand-up paddlers rowed to the safety of the shore, kiteboarders readied their equipment on the grass in preparation for a late afternoon of wave running.

I tried to imagine winter on Maui, when humpback whales arrived after a long journey from Alaska. Breeches and tail slaps were common sights and sounds off the Maui coast beginning as early as November, I had learned. These magnificent creatures returned to safe Hawaiian waters to birth their young. Theirs was an annual trek. I could not blame them.

Should I choose to return for another visit, I had plenty of housing options that did not overtax Millie's hospitality. Several units at the Maui Sunset were available for rent. I had developed hot tub connections with several condo owners who were looking for good renters. They included a Texan named Linda, who spoke with a mixture of excitement and anticipated exhaustion about the upcoming arrival of a gaggle of grandkids; Alison, who enjoyed soaking away while her husband, Greg, supervised the installation of new tile in their condo; and my favorite, Gwen, a spinster—her description, not mine—who seemed to know everyone who entered the pool area.

Gwen, after sizing me up as a possible renter, offered a tour of her lovely condo, a first-floor walkout that had been freshly renovated. The cooling palette of aqua blue and cream definitely created an inviting space.

"I'm always on the lookout for good renters," she remarked. "I was thinking I had lucked out last winter. A woman from Phoenix—retired, single, getting up in years—she booked my place for an entire month. Not a scratch or broken dish the whole time. But I nearly choked when the electric bill arrived. She must have been running both air conditioners twenty-four-seven. In January! Why didn't she just open the damn sliding door and turn on the fans?"

"I can't imagine someone coming all the way to Maui and then sitting in a closed-up condo. Although, you have created a little piece of heaven here, Gwen. Maybe she never wanted to leave."

"Or maybe she just left without turning off the AC," Gwen retorted with a laugh. "Wish I could spend more time here myself, but too much doctorin' to do back in

Portland." Pivoting midthought, she grabbed an information sheet and business card off the desk and handed them
to me. "Fees and contact info," she said. "If you don't have
a love affair with air conditioning, I'd be happy to rent to
you. I'll even throw in a ten percent discount that I usually
reserve for repeat customers."

I thanked her for the information and told her I would
definitely consider her condo if I were ever to return. There
would be no better way to spend a slice of Harry's and my
retirement nest egg, I thought, as I mulled over possibilities
during a presunset walk.

Knowing I had viable options for returning made it
easier to ask the question: Was it time to leave? I had used
my time well. Although I had not been able to resuscitate
my book, I had reenergized my yearning for storytelling.
Returning discipline to my writing regimen had greased
the gears. Once again, both halves of my brain were working in tandem. Exploring my past on paper had returned
me to a safe place, a comfortable space that cushioned my
soul.

As the blowing of the conch once again announced the
setting of the sun, the unease returned. By the time darkness enveloped the island, another question surfaced. How
could I write about the defining moments of my life and
skip over the two most important, the losses of Emma and
Harry? There had been no page in the birthday book dedicated to April 30, 1970, three months after Emma's death.
And the page with the Write Women smiling for the waiter
at my birthday lunch still sat on my desk in New Brighton.
These two years had left two holes in my heart, one calci-
fied over with unspoken grief and the other still bleeding.
Their omission from my memoir left me feeling not only
unfulfilled but also disgusted. Overwhelmed and tired, I
climbed into bed with hope for restorative sleep.

36

$\mathcal{R}$estless and achy, I awoke before dawn and settled into a chair on the lanai with my MP notebook. With only a faint overhead light to brighten the darkness, I wrote. My mandatory three pages turned into five, then seven, then nine before I closed the notebook. Fleeting thoughts about Emma swirled around memories of Mama and Nana. "Next in the line of strong women," Nana had said as she rocked her great-granddaughter.

I turned off the light, sat in the darkness, and waited for the island to awaken. Was I in that line? I did not feel strong. And with Emma gone, the line would soon end. I opened my MP notebook and read the final line. *Do I exist only if someone lives on to remember me?* Not wishing to continue my introspection, I headed to the beach for an early-morning stroll.

"It's Aloha Friday / no work 'til Monday . . ." The song streamed from KPOA radio as I continued into a day that had started too early after a rocky night's sleep. With MP writing and a lengthy beach walk accomplished, the remainder of Friday lay ahead unstructured. Unlike the singer, I was not anticipating a work-free weekend, at least not in the emotional sense. Unlike most days, when finding homes for frenetic thoughts on the written page quelled my anxiety, this particular morning's writing exercise left a disquietude that even a leisurely walk along the shore had not minimized. Clearly, I had emotional work to do. I waited until a reasonable hour, called May, and asked if she and her family were available for a visit.

"Yes, please come. You can have lunch with us," said May.

"I was hoping that perhaps I could take all of you out to lunch. Perhaps at the Kula Bistro?"

"Such a wonderful offer, but Father is not tracking very well today. I think it best if we stay home. But come. Please."

"For a short visit, then."

When I arrived, I was saddened by Ken's condition. He paused briefly from his work in one of his flower gardens but offered no wave or smile.

"Fern will be back in a bit," said May. "She is delivering some vegetables to friends. In the meantime, why don't we have tea?" She led me toward the cottage. "It will be easier to keep an eye on Father from the front porch. Sit. I will steep the tea." She gestured to one of the matching rattan rockers.

The air's cool crispness reminded me that I had climbed to a higher elevation. By the time May returned to the porch with the teapot and cups, I had retrieved my sweater from the car.

"We are so thankful he does not wander," said May, pouring the tea and scanning the protea garden for the straw hat that covered her kneeling father's head. "And you, Marguerite, how are you? And your writing?"

May offered me a teacup, settled into a rocker, and waited as long as necessary for a response to questions that were not simply rhetorical. I had learned to expect her intuitiveness; yet, I did not know where to begin.

"The writing—that's been going well. I had feared I might never write again," I admitted. "Maui has provided ample time for reflection, and here on your beautiful island, I have regained my yearning." I described "Marguerite's Birthday Book" and how first Mama and then I had used the pages to document my life. "I brought some of the pages to Maui as a way to remember, to reconnect."

"And these pages have inspired your writing?"

"Yes, surprisingly they have. I've been recording my memories from the perspective of the Marguerite that each page represents," I said, hoping that I did not sound too much like a person with multiple personalities.

"And who is the Marguerite that sits across from me?" May asked.

"This Marguerite still has work to do." I described how, even though I had written about every other major turning point in my life, I still had not written about the two deaths that defined who I had become. "I think I might be able to finally write about Emma. But Harry, I'm not so sure. Widowhood is still such a mystery to me."

"Widowhood is a complicated grief," May said.

"You are living it, too," I said and then paused with hope that she would expand.

"The passage of time does not cure everything, Marguerite," she said matter-of-factly.

"You mean the loss, the loneliness?"

"All those righteous things, yes. But also the shadows. We must tend to those as well."

The crunching of tires on gravel interrupted our conversation. Fern parked her car and approached the cottage.

"Sit with Marguerite, Fern. I will bring you a teacup," May said as she stood up.

"Marguerite, so nice to see you. Did you come to see Father?" Fern asked.

"Actually, I came to see all of you. Rather a spur-of-the-moment thing."

May reappeared with a teacup for Fern and an extra chair. For the next few minutes, our conversation centered on light topics as Fern shared tidbits of gossip that she had gleaned during her vegetable distribution. But sadness enveloped the porch when she added, "Everyone asked about Father. I never know quite what to say."

After a quiet pause, I stood. "I think I'll walk out to the gardens and talk to Ken."

"Let me go with you," said Fern.

We walked to the edge of the protea garden. Ken was squatting and tenderly pruning plants. No one would have guessed his handicap until he turned around and addressed Fern.

"Okaasan, is it time for dinner? Do you need me to pick vegetables?"

"No, I think we have plenty," said Fern.

"Hello, Ken," I said.

He looked sharply at me, studied my face, and said, "I am Mr. Sato. Have we met?"

"You have a beautiful garden, Mr. Sato," I said, deflecting the question.

"Protea. They grow Upcountry where it is cooler." He turned away, walked a few paces, and crouched down once again.

"We will call you when it is time to eat," said Fern. "Do you still have water?" She picked up a stainless steel thermos and checked the contents. Then she poured Ken a cupful and stood next to him until he had drunk every drop. Afterward, he wandered over to a hedge and with his pruning shears cut three lovely birds of paradise and offered them to me.

"Thank you so much. They are lovely," I said. Without comment, Ken turned and walked back to the protea garden.

"He has come to calling either one of us Mother—Okaasan—when he is not tracking," said Fern as we walked back to May's cottage.

"That must be upsetting," I responded.

"Not really. We have become quite used to it. Upsetting will be when Father forgets how to take care of his gardens. That will be a very sad day."

After I convinced May and Fern that I could stay no longer, that I had writing that needed to be done, May walked me to the car. "I am sorry I could not be more helpful. You are seeking insight that I can not teach," she said, referring to our earlier conversation. "We must each become our own teacher."

"You have given me great food for thought," I replied.

"Best wishes, Marguerite."

May's enigmatic comments about grief, both the righteous aspects and the shadows, accompanied me down the mountain and throughout the remainder of the day. Even so, not one written word found a home on paper.

37

*S*hadows danced around my brain. Several times during my morning pages I tried to extricate the word and plant it in the notebook. Instead, it spawned another word, *fear*:

I doubt that May was referencing Jungian psychology when she mentioned the shadows as opposed to the righteous aspects of grief. Her sharp distinction confounds me. Shadows? What? And what's righteous about the reality of widowhood? Loss? Loneliness? I am trying to comprehend the gravity of a loss that seemed to compound rather than shrink with each passing day. The loneliness, well, one has to live it to understand. I finally have come to the conclusion that it will be my companion until death. On the one hand, I long for Harry's touch, his gaze, his voice. I miss him so much. On the other, I quake in fear that someday I no longer will be able to conjure any of these images . . .

Finally, on the fourth page of my MP notebook, I drew concentric circles. I wrote the word SHADOWS in the center of the innermost and smallest circle. In the next and larger circle, I penned GRIEF/LOSSES. I paused for a moment and then wrote LIFELINES in the circle that encapsulated the first two. The final and largest one that encircled the others was designated WIDOWHOOD. Then as quickly as the words presented themselves, I filled in two of the circles. Easy to articulate were the losses I recorded in the corresponding circle, everything from Harry's blue eyes and his loving embrace to the companionship and security I had never fully appreciated while he was alive. In the circle labeled LIFELINES, the words *memories, writing, meditation,* and *God* were written next to names of living, breathing people, then dead ones whose strength in subtle waves had been arriving at opportune times from some mysterious source. Nothing new or jolting presented itself as I recorded the words and names as quickly as they appeared. But I brainstormed to no avail the word SHADOWS. As I stared at the blank circle in the center of the page, nothing came to mind. Yet, as if to tell me that I was on the cusp of something, my autonomic nervous system kicked in. Shortness of breath. An accelerated pulse. A wave of anxiety.

A robocall from an unfamiliar number interrupted the experience and offered a welcomed reprieve. I closed the notebook and stepped away to check the caller ID. There was no going back. Seeking distractions, I left both my notebook and the cell phone in the condo, grabbed a beach blanket, and headed to the shoreline, where I spread out under a palm tree and settled in. On this day, the ocean's bottom was clearly defined, thanks to the calmness and clarity of the shallow water. Strips of submerged sand led ribbonlike around outcroppings of black lava to the deeper sea beyond.

Two divers, clad in black wetsuits, snorkeled above and around the lava. Each man dragged his own floating flag, which remained on the surface to indicate his location when he disappeared into the water. About thirty minutes later, one diver swam to shore and headed in my direction to reclaim flip-flops, which had been tucked under the berm for safekeeping.

"What are you searching for out there?" I asked as he bent over to retrieve his footwear.

"He'e—octopus," he said as he held out a mesh bag lumpy with his day's catch. "They like to hide in the rocks." After I checked out his catch, he scrambled up the berm and headed to his pickup in the nearby parking lot.

The shore was unusually quiet. Two young children, using boogie boards as flotation devices, played in the calm, shallow water while an overseeing adult sat nearby in the sand under a beach umbrella. Otherwise, most people, like me, had opted for spots atop the grassy berm, a perfect vantage point to enjoy a view of the ocean from either sun or shade.

Nearby, a young couple positioned their Tommy Bahama chairs to maximize the sun. They appeared to be locals, perhaps of high school age judging from a conversation about friends and school that drifted my way. Just as he began to regale her with a boastful story, she cut him off and pointed to the water. I looked in the same direction. A giant sea turtle, identifiable only after its small head surfaced for a breath, floated effortlessly in the water, then resubmerged and once again blended in with the rocks below. Eventually, it swam through a sandy-bottomed area that exposed the dark, underwater outline of its giant shell and flippers. I had been told to look for honu, green sea turtles, but did not know how to spot them. Now, searching for tiny dark heads breaking the surface, I spotted two others gracefully gliding over the rocks in search of algae. What else was I missing simply because I did not know where or how to look? The peaceful honu and the he'e were quiet reminders to pay close attention, lest we miss what is right in front of us.

The morning evaporated. The children were called out of the water. The high school couple, skin glistening from sweat and suntan oil, jumped into the ocean for a cooling dip.

Not graceful like it had been in the water, one sea turtle waddled up on shore to nap in the sun. It wanted nothing from people but peace. I, too, was feeling awkward and ready to find a quiet spot and sleep. But unlike the honu whose sleep would be restorative, I knew from past experiences that my napping instinct was an avoidance technique employed when anxious. It indicated not the natural order of things, but a depressive state that on this day I fought with a shower and a raid on the refrigerator. Finally, I settled in once again to write, not to fill in concentric circles, but to revisit two defining moments fastened together with interwoven grief.

MARGUERITE—AGE 35
April 30, 1970

No photo, no people, no caption—nothing. No page in the birthday book, not even a blank one, commemorates the date. The page's nonexistence stands as a testament to the void. I wish to forget the day. How can I celebrate without my little girl, now three months gone? It feels like a lifetime. I choose to erase my birthday, but there is no way to erase the day of the accident. January 18, 1970, is etched in my heart—ache, emptiness, abandonment. Even compounded, these sadnesses barely dip into my ocean of grief.

Emma is gone, stolen by an errant snowboard that flew into her temple during her final run down a favorite sliding hill. In an instant she disappeared, like so many I have loved. I want to join her, but I'm caught in a struggle to hold on to Harry with every ounce of my strength, lest he abandon me, too. He blames himself for not remaining firm. "It's time to call it a day," he had said. But who can resist little Emma's sparkling excitement and relentless pleas for just one more ride on her Christmas present from Daddy, a red-and-white-striped plastic saucer with leather hand grips. If anyone is to blame, let it be the snowboarder who didn't bother with a safety leash; but he is only twelve years old and a child himself. No. No one is to blame. A fluke. A horrible, horrible fluke. An inch either way, a second sooner or later—life would have continued in its usual fashion. But . . .

The image of Emma uniting with Mama, Papa, Nana, Grampa, and Uncle Raymond keeps me alive, but I want her here. We want her here. We need her here. In an instant, Harry and I are no longer parents. Our monikers, Mommy and Daddy, disappear into a dark grave alongside a tiny casket. Harry looks at me like I should hate him, and his recoil from outstretched arms cuts me to the quick. He takes turns raging at himself, then God, then me when he can't comprehend how I can find my God comforting. I'm not sure either. All I know is that Harry's God, omnipotent and judgmental, is the one I gave up years ago, replaced by an undying, compassionate essence that I so desperately need.

We are on a precipice, and any morsel of life that hasn't been swallowed up by grief is threatening to slip away unless we both hold on. Hold on, Harry! Don't abandon me . . .

38

I closed my notebook and forced myself to breathe. The crushing memories of January 18, 1970, had quickened my pulse. I scanned the horizon and focused on the rhythmic waves, then tried to match my breathing with their regularity. Once again, I headed down to the shore and chose a northward path along the sand until exhaustion, high tide, and rocky outcroppings forced me to turn back. How many generations of humans have walked this beach? As I passed an ancient fish pond, I imagined native Hawaiians living harmoniously with the land and sea until missionaries passed judgment and sugar barons seized opportunity.

Throughout history, along with the sun that rises and sets each day, the ocean has proved its trustworthiness. Although furious at times, it never abandons children of the land. When low tide takes the water away, no one worries that it might not return. So dependable that its movements are accurately forecast in tidal tables, the ocean stands in stark contrast to the human condition and my own insignificance. In a blink, humans lose each other for eternity.

Returning to the green space between the Maui Sunset

and the ocean, I paused with other singles, couples, families, and pets and watched as the sun disappeared quickly behind threatening rain clouds. I turned immediately and headed back to the condo. The morning's writing had picked at a scab that for decades had been shielding an unhealed sore. Then the afternoon's story had peeled that scab away, leaving an erupting, painful, oozing mass.

After measuring a reasonable pour of Pinot, I sat down again and picked up my pen. Not fully ready to venture back into the shadows, I began slowly. When an evening squall drove me off the lanai and into the dry security of the condo, with a fair amount of trepidation, I continued into dark territory.

MARGUERITE—AGE 35
1970 (Continued)

Losing a child, a tragedy that only grieving parents understand, should have been enough. Yet each day brings new fears that Harry, now cold and distant, is slipping away. Nothing I say or do diffuses the cloud of depression that alters his perceptions, and now guilt blankets both of us. His guilt is about Emma, mine is about writhing anger—anger at the world that would take my little girl in a heartbeat, just like Mama and Papa. Harry can't believe I don't blame him for allowing her one last ride down a snow-packed hill, for not protecting her, for not bringing her home. Do I? I choose my words carefully, asking him to join me in lashing out at fate, the real culprit that placed Emma in the fatal spot.

He refuses to join me on my side of our grief. Not his fault, never his fault, I say out loud. Yet, why didn't he bring her home? At times, I fear I am getting sucked into his reality. Deep down, underneath my rational thinking, lurks an unspoken anger, which I combat daily for fear of the consequences of venting, even in the security of the therapist's office. She pokes and prods, but my discomfort builds an artificial facade that I shore up daily. Far worse, I dare not write about my anger; my journal, my second therapist, becomes stymied as well. What if Harry pries and discovers unfiltered and hurtful suppositions and condemnations? No. Writing about Emma is not an option. Instead, I live with uncertainty, hurt, anger at the world, as well as anger at Harry for leaving me alone to pick up the pieces of our broken family.

Harry is sinking deeper into depression. Ben and Jay, concerned about their friend, carry his weight at Green Space, which enables him to retreat even further. About the time he begins to find his legs, his mother Anna dies from an unexpected heart attack, and he slides back even further. Two deaths, like two shots to the heart, totally knock him off his foundation. Complicating matters is Jane's ill health, which prevents her from traveling back from her home in Connecticut to offer big-sister support during a time of shared grief.

Harry wallows in sadness, and I am furious at him for not giving me that same opportunity. Furious? Did I write that? Yes! I want—no, I need—to wallow. Give me time to do that, I scream internally. Instead, I am forced to be the strong one for fear that my husband, after finishing off a bottle of wine or scotch, might decide to leave the earth to lessen his pain. I fear that addressing my fears directly with him will only add weight to his guilt-laden depression. I am helpless. And rage filled! Harry, you were supposed to fight for our family!

With truths unspoken, I straighten my shoulders and

place one step in front of another and head in a direction away from inner equilibrium and toward an uncertain future. It is a lonely journey. I hate when friends commend me for my bravery. What's brave about masking my own pain so my husband will not consider suicide? What's brave about feeling relieved when Harry turns away in bed? I have no desire to conceive a second child with a man I no longer recognize. And another hidden piece: can I trust myself to parent again?

Emma, I am so sorry for not protecting you!

The first year continues in a blur. In silence, Harry and I search for new definitions as individuals and as a unit. At times, I catch a glimmer of the man I fell in love with, the man who, without a second thought, welcomed Nana into our home and compassionately cared for both of us during her final years, the man who loved his daughter and would have given his life for hers, the man whose eyes sparkled when he talked about simple things like plants, green-houses, a new idea or design. Those eyes eventually rest on mine and search into my soul for forgiveness, not just pardon.

Ever so slowly, our wounds crust over with protective scabs. Thankfully, the scarring process binds us together rather than apart. We become attached by a shared ache and an unspoken resolve to meet each other, to extend our hands, to clasp each other, to hold on for dear life. My anger, the threat to our newfound equilibrium, is assigned a new home, deep and dark. It disappears behind a scab that I incorrectly label an impenetrable scar.

Then Harry died. The onslaught of grief does not sur-prise. After all, who in their eighties does not consider the possibility of losing a life partner? What I had not expected is the ripping open of a forty-five-year-old scar with anger oozing everywhere. How could you abandon me again,

Harry? This time you are not coming back. How do I forgive you for dying before me?

An image presents itself so clearly that it defies its age—
Nana in her kitchen, cooking a large cut of meat in a huge
covered pot. I hated that pressure cooker. The noise and
the billowing steam that accompanied the release of the
built-up pressure scared me so much.

"Stop it! Stop it!" I would yell.

"Nothing to worry about, Marguerite," Nana would
reply. "You just have to respect the pressure and release it
slowly before opening the lid. Open it too soon, and there's
a fair chance that the cook will suffer. Letting the valve do
its work makes a lot of fuss, but it's worth it in the end."

39

I awoke with a groggy headache. Maybe it was the writing of the night before or the wine—certainly the tears—that led to a night of fitful sleep punctuated at dawn by a vivid lucid dream. Attached to the ground by a single thread, I soared effortlessly like a kite in the night's sky. When I realized I could will my essence to turn in whichever direction I wished, I zigzagged with outstretched arms over the treetops and a sleepy village below. Bravely, I tested the length and strength of the thread that anchored me safely to the ground. I vacillated between wanting to sever the thread, so I would be free to travel beyond the village, and hesitating with fear that if I chose freedom, I might disappear into the unknown and never be able to return.

Was the cord securing me or holding me back? The question gave me pause as I asked it in my morning pages, especially since I had spontaneously used the word *cord*. *Perhaps the thread was actually an umbilical cord, necessary for giving life at a certain stage, and then cast off to shrivel when no longer necessary. What infancy am I entering and what growth is ahead? Am I ready to cut the cord?* As usual, I ended my three pages of writing with questions to ponder during my morning's walk on the beach.

Although another bout of rainy weather was forecast for later in the day, I struck out during a calm interlude. I carefully picked my way around debris from the previous storm and slowly headed south. The metaphor was inevitable. After Harry's death, the latest storm in my personal life, months had been consumed with the practice of avoidance. Ever so carefully I had been picking a path around boulders of grief. One foot in front of the other. Staying in the moment. Wishing not to remember. Trying not to anticipate. Surviving. Protecting a scab that had crusted over decades earlier after the departure of Emma. Emma— my little girl—our little girl—sweetness and light.

Tears for Emma, tears for Harry, tears for Marguerite began as a slow ooze behind my sunglasses. Mounding with each step and clouding my path, they obscured the slice of black lava that forewarned a half-buried obstacle in the sand. Catching my shoe on the corner of the rock, I tripped and fell to my knees. Shaken but unharmed except for a bloody scrape, I rolled over to a sitting position. Salty rivers cascaded down my cheeks—tears of grief, anger, guilt. Thankful to be alone, I remained in that position until I was able to slowly rise and make my way back to the condo.

The winds and rain returned with a new ferocity. I closed the door to the lanai and opened my MP notebook to the page with concentric circles. With precision, I printed two words in the smallest circle, *anger* and *guilt*. Then after a cleansing breath, I concluded my memoir with a conversation with Harry.

MARGUERITE—AGE 80
2015

Harry, I know you understand my need to purge. Your voice resonates in my head.

"Give it all you've got, MJ."

I'm trying, Harry.

"Release the anger."

You left me to face the world alone—again! I hate you for it.

"It's okay to say it."

It hurts to say it.

"It's okay because you love me."

I do love you.

"I'm sorry, MJ."

I am trying to forgive you.

"Trying is good enough."

I'm a work in progress, Harry.

"That's what I love about you, MJ!"

40

I awoke to a new day. After the anger-laced guilt, after the tears, after the written words, I felt hollow, weak, and also, strangely calm. I had followed two of Mama's suggestions: "Name them. Claim them. That's important, Marguerite. But then you must put them high on a shelf, so you'll need a ladder to get them down." The third step was the work in progress.

Named and claimed by the implementation of simple tools, a pen, a notebook, and a relatively healthy brain, the shadows, once lurking on the other side of consciousness, had been exposed by the light of introspection. Writing had tapped the hidden pressure, slowly, safely. A gentle satisfaction filled the void. With the memoir completed to my satisfaction, I was ready to turn my gaze outward. I contemplated what that meant during my beach walk.

My first thoughts involved the Write Women. Solid, fabulous friends! Each of us had confronted life-altering experiences. With each other's help, we had endured. Last year was my turn to be challenged, and my friends gave me the space I thought I needed. I missed each remarkable woman, and I could finally admit to myself that I was also missing Minnesota.

Summer was a great season to be in the Land of 10,000 Lakes. Having turned snow and ice into distant memories, the sun beckoned eager Minnesotans to the lakes, where they packed as many carefree activities as possible into long, warm days. Mired in grief the previous summer, I had somehow missed the season. I had spent endless hours treading water, not in a favorite lake, but at my desk sorting out details of widowhood in a desperate attempt to keep my head above the surface. Perhaps it was time to test the theory that buoyancy improves for those who simply relax.

Was I ready to book a flight home?

Hunger struck, and its arrival confirmed that my body was returning to a healthier normal. I exited the beach and began a return trip to the condo via Uluniu Road. Serendipitously, I detoured into Nalu's South Shore Grill and perused the posted menu. A decadent Hawaiian version of French toast with macadamia nut-encrusted Hawaiian sweet bread, lilikoi marmalade cream, and tropical fruits sounded enticing. After placing my order at the counter, I filled a glass of ice water from a self-service urn and planted myself at a quiet outdoor table. In less than ten minutes, the breakfast platter arrived. Thankful that a soothing calmness had quieted my stomach as well as my head, I savored every bite. Just like others who had awakened to the sun after a windy, rainy night, I was buoyed by the subtle assurance that the worst was over.

The delicious breakfast provided fuel for the day's agenda, which I schemed as I forked my last piece of pineapple. Totally satiated, I returned to the condo for a refreshing shower before heading out.

A drive into Kahului for printer ink ranked first on my list. As I entered the city limits, the ringing of my cell phone interrupted the pleasant ride. Once I parked in front of OfficeMax, I retrieved the phone from the bottom of my tote and checked the call history. May answered the call-back on the second ring.

"MJ, is that you?" she asked in a voice that sounded breathless and urgent.

"Yes, May. Is everything alright?"

"No. It's Father. He's gone."

"Gone?"

"For the first time in months, he showed no interest in going to service this morning. We could not convince him, so we left him home alone while we went to church. When we came home, he was nowhere to be seen."

A wave of relief accompanied the confirmation that Ken was missing, not dead.

"Do you think he got lost? Walked away from the garden—got disoriented?"

"No, he took my car. It was in storage in the garage, and he rummaged through my drawers until he found the keys. He shouldn't be driving, MJ."

"Have you called the police?" I asked.

"Yes, they are looking. Fern and I are driving around Upcountry."

"What can I do?"

"We wanted you to be alerted in case he might drive down to see you."

"In that case, I better get back. I'm in Kahului running errands."

"Just a minute." I could hear Fern's voice in the background. "Fern is wondering, since you are in Kahului, would you check the Nisei Veterans Memorial Center? It is one of Father's favorite places."

"Of course," I said. "What make of car should I be looking for?"

"A silver 2005 Toyota Camry. Do you need directions?"

"I'll use my GPS and give you a call if I need more information. Or if I find him."

"Thank you, MJ. We are so worried. Father hasn't driven
in over four years."

"Well, he couldn't have gotten too far. We are on an
island, after all," I said, trying to lighten the moment but
sounding insensitive and flippant instead.

"But there are many side roads Upcountry . . ."

"I know. I'm sorry. I'll head over right now."

The GPS directed me along a familiar route. But
instead of taking the turn that would have led to the
parking lot for the swap meet, I continued along Kahului
Beach Road. A short distance farther, my destination
appeared on the left. The small parking lot of the memorial center was empty. Of course. It was Sunday morning.
A posting on the locked doors described an upcoming
educational event entitled Maui's WWII Response. More
than likely, Ken had spent many hours here when he was
able, I thought, but today there was no sign of him or a
silver Toyota Camry. I canvassed surrounding streets in
hopes of spotting his car. Having no luck, I finally decided
to head back to Kihei.

My return route led me through Wailuku. I stopped for
a red light at a main intersection, then instinctively turned
onto the road that led up the mountain to the ʻIao Valley
State Park. Ken's love for the park had been so clearly evi-
dent on the day he introduced me to it. I drove as quickly
as I dared around puddles and debris up the narrow three-
mile road. Finally, I arrived at the park's entrance and was
met by a sign: BECAUSE OF STORM DAMAGE THE PARK IS
CLOSED TODAY. The only vehicles within sight were two
maintenance trucks and a van that was making a U-turn. I
followed its example.

Disappointed, I began the return trip down the valley.

One mile later, the entrance to Kepaniwai Park and Heritage Gardens appeared. Hanging from the front gate was a similar sign announcing its closure. I peered into the empty park as I slowly drove by. The next driveway on the right led up to a small house, which sat fairly close to the road. Two vehicles, a rusty pickup and a late-model sedan, filled the short driveway. Next to them, partially hidden by tropical overgrowth, sat a clean silver vehicle. I slammed on my brakes, shifted into reverse, and backed up to take a closer look. A metal Toyota insignia was clearly visible, so I pulled off the road and jumped out. On the passenger's seat of the Camry sat a straw hat.

No one in the nearby house answered my knock, so I turned to the surrounding rainforest and called out, "Ken, are you here? It's MJ. Where are you?" I listened closely for a response but heard nothing except the distant sound of rushing water and the rustling of wild chickens as they skirted the closed gate and entered the park. I returned to the Prius, grabbed my tote, and headed to the entrance.

Of course, after last night's storm, Ken would have wanted to check on his heritage site, I thought. Just like the chickens, I found enough dry ground on one side of the gate to pass through. Once inside, I scanned the park. The 'Iao Stream had flooded low-lying sections, and standing water was slowly draining from the parking lot.

The Japanese site sat on dry ground. I picked my way around soggy patches and headed in that direction. Finding no sign of Ken, I circled the teahouse. Its door was securely locked. I returned to the small stone bridge that spanned the creek bed. Just as I was pulling out my cell phone to call the police, a shuffling sound redirected my attention to the wooded area behind and above me.

"Okage sama de."

It was Ken's voice coming from somewhere out of view.

I approached the base of a steep stairway constructed from bricks of black lava.

"Ken? Mr. Sato?" I called as I climbed a few steps upward through green tropical vegetation. Then I spotted him. Ken was crouching on a step and calmly removing weeds that had grown in the cracks between thick, black rocks of lava. He glanced up as I stepped into view. Neither recognition nor fear registered on his face.

"Mr. Sato. It's Marguerite," I said as soothingly as possible.

"Marguerite, a beautiful flower," he replied with a hint of a smile.

"Your daughters are wondering where you are. May I call them?" I asked as I pulled out my phone as discreetly as possible and tapped redial.

Ken remained silent for several seconds before finally answering. "They should know I'm here. I come often. To pay respect."

"Can you tell me what you were saying? I heard 'okage'— something like that," I said, trying to keep Ken engaged until I could get May on the line.

"I found him," I whispered to May. "At Kepaniwai. He's fine. I can drive him home."

"We're coming," she said. "Are you okay to wait?"

"Yes, we're fine," I said before hanging up.

"Okage sama de," repeated Ken, as I pocketed my cell phone. "Did you notice?"

"Notice?"

"The steps," he replied. "Those at the bottom. Shallow. Wide. Like Issei who endured much hardship to give strong foundation to the next generation."

"The next generation—Nisei."

"Yes, Nisei. You know of Nisei? I am Nisei. Like these narrower steps, we carry the tradition onward, upward," he said as he motioned to the steps around him. "We appreciate—and in return, try to live honorably. Come," he said, extending a warm and surprisingly strong hand. Together, we climbed several more steps that rose more sharply the farther we climbed. The last step opened onto a small plateau on which a small stone pagoda sat on a five-tiered base. It was surrounded on three side by luscious vegetation still glistening from the morning's damp.

"Beautiful," I said in a tone hushed in reverence.

"The generations that follow Issei and Nisei have risen higher and higher. Prospered."

"There is great symbolism in the stairway," I said.

"We must never forget from whom we came," he said, turning around and gazing back at the base of the stairway. After a long pause, he added, "Okage sama de . . . Because of you, I am."

"Okage sama de," I repeated.

For several moments, both of us stood contentedly hand in hand, grateful for our respective ancestry.

When Ken became restless, we returned to the pond and tidied the ground that surrounded it by stacking broken branches and other debris into small piles. In less than thirty minutes, Fern's white Honda pulled up and parked haphazardly in front of the closed gate. May and Fern jumped out and ran toward us. After she greeted her father, Fern, realizing her forgetfulness, took a few steps back and quietly notified the police that Ken had been found unharmed.

Shortly, a white SUV with Maui Police printed boldly in blue on the side panels pulled up, and a uniformed officer stepped out. He greeted Ken, May, and Fern by name and then established to his satisfaction that Ken was unharmed by his morning's adventure.

"Marguerite found him," said May as she introduced me to Officer John Luka.

"Ken was behind the vegetation on the steps leading to the pagoda," I said.

"We were so afraid that he had driven to one of the trails and hiked in," said May.

"I think it's time for you and Fern to look into a tracking device for Ken," said Officer Luka. "We could help with that," he added.

"Thanks, John. Perhaps it's time," said May. "Fern?"

Fern, silenced by a mixture of relief and sadness, nodded in agreement.

The four of us exited the park. Officer Luka located May's keys in the ignition of the Camry, handed them off to her, and then walked Ken to Fern's car and securely buckled him in. Fern waved goodbye as she drove off with Ken sitting serenely in the passenger's seat as if he were merely out for a Sunday drive.

"Ken's lucky today," said Officer Luka.

"It's time. I know," May responded. "Thank you so much for your support."

"We can help you as soon as today," he said before getting into his vehicle and heading off.

"Was he agitated when you found him?" May asked as we walked toward our cars.

"No, actually quite the opposite. He definitely feels comfortable in this space. And I'm amazed that even in his confused state, he continues to teach and inspire." I summarized Ken's lesson about the symbolism of the stairway.

"I am so thankful you chose to search here. We are so grateful." Then, uncharacteristically for a woman who rarely displayed emotion, May leaned forward and enveloped me in a strong, sustained hug.

May led as we drove in separate vehicles down the valley to Wailuku. We parted at the first stoplight. She headed to the police department for advice on a tracking device for her father, and I, with a new appreciation for my uncomplicated life, turned south and drove peacefully down the roadway that eventually branched off toward Kihei.

It was not until I turned into the parking lot of the Maui Sunset that I realized I had not purchased the printer ink, the needed office supply that had sent me to OfficeMax in the first place. I postponed the printing of my latest and probably final installments of *Rewriting Marguerite*, the working title I had given to what had started out as a writing exercise and had turned into a memoir for an audience of one. Instead, I saved the manuscript to a flash drive and securely stowed it in a zippered pocket of my carry-on.

When sunset neared, I took from the vase the stalks of bird of paradise Ken had given me during our visits and walked down to the beach to honor the ending of the day. A spectacular show of peach and purple danced from cloud to cloud as the blowing of a conch shell announced the disappearance of the sun. I waited until lingerers retreated from the shoreline, then stepped down from the grassy berm to the sand. One by one, I set the flowers, so magnificent in their youth and now muted and shriveled, adrift in the quiet ocean. With each one, I said a quiet prayer of thanks for Grampa, Mama, Papa, Nana, and Emma, then for my beloved Harry, and finally, for the God that encompassed them all. When the last one floated off effortlessly, I turned and headed back to the condo after a final benediction.

"Okage sama de."

41

The Minneapolis-Saint Paul airport buzzed quietly as travelers searched for checked luggage and morning coffee. Easily spotted by its tropical luggage strap, my black suitcase was already traveling in circles at carousel three by the time I arrived at baggage claim. Bulging carry-ons housed my valuables, computer, flash drive, notebooks, hard copies of my writing, and the original pages from "Marguerite's Birthday Book." After retrieving my suitcase, now laden with tropical gifts, I awkwardly navigated everything through the sliding glass door. Elle's car was idling nearby at the curb. Seeing me, she jumped out, popped the hatchback, and ran over to greet me with a hug and a helping hand.

"Perfect timing. If you hadn't come out soon, I would have been forced by that woman to take another pass around the airport," she said, pointing to a uniformed traffic enforcer, who was sternly reminding drivers that they were in a loading/unloading zone not a parking lot. Elle lifted my luggage with ease and deposited each piece into the back of the car.

"Thanks for getting up so early," I said.

"No problem. At this rate, we'll get home before rush

hour begins," Elle said, referring to the house that had become a home to each of us and would continue to be ours, as we had decided during a phone conversation the evening before. I was ready for a roommate and so was Elle.

Home. It had been a month, but it felt like a lifetime since I had left. I smiled at the irony; it had taken me almost a month to revisit and write about the defining moments of my life. I was weary from the trip and the hectic final week in Maui. Once I had decided to book a return flight, I had gathered my Lahaina and Upcountry friends to the condo for a simple dinner and a chance to not only say thank you but to introduce them to one another. Then when sadness totally enveloped me after the last goodbye, I sought out Gwen and booked her unit at the Sunset for an extended stay beginning in November. Just like the humpbacks, I would be returning. Confident that a second trip to Maui would provide opportunities to enjoy items on my lengthy list of Maui activities—perhaps a sunrise at the rim of Haleakala or a drive to Hana and most certainly a whale watch—I flagged the page and stashed the notebook in my carry-on.

Elle peppered me with questions about Maui as we drove north. Between answers, I concentrated on the metropolitan skyline of Minneapolis. Familiar but somehow different, the buildings, bridges, and bodies of water required a pause, as if I were viewing them through a different lens. Fascinated, I soaked in every detail. Eventually, we reached New Brighton and, finally, Silver Lake Road. As if to welcome me back, the sun peeked over the horizon and painted the eastern sky a pinkish orange.

"Oh, Elle," I said as we turned into the driveway, "the gardens are gorgeous."

All neatly outlined in chocolate-colored mulch, huge trees and bright green shrubs provided the perfect backdrop for blossoms of every color. On the patio, potted begonias thrived in shady spots. Strategically placed hibiscus enjoyed the benefits of sun and breeze. I had entrusted Harry's gardens to Elle, and she had worked magic.

After depositing my luggage inside the entryway, I slowly explored the house. Just like the Minneapolis skyline, each room appeared familiar but somehow different, as if I was viewing each one from a wiser perspective. Not needing to scrutinize, I simply accepted my gut's message that all was okay. Elle and I met in the kitchen to perk coffee and start the teakettle. Standing over the sink, I gasped when I gazed out the window and spotted Harry's greenhouse. The windows gleamed. Through them I could see trays of plants and gardening supplies. Elle, who was retrieving a coffee pod and a tea bag from the cupboard, turned toward me with a look of concern.

"The greenhouse," I said.

Still unable to read my reaction, Elle headed to the back door, opened it, and stepped aside for me to pass through to the backyard. We followed the path that led to the door of the greenhouse and entered. A familiar mix of earthiness and humidity washed over me. "Oh my" was all I could verbalize as I walked from one end of the structure to the other. Every square inch had been cleaned and reclaimed. Finally, I was able to add, "I'm sure Harry is loving how you have resurrected his favorite place."

Spotting my tears, Elle asked, "But what about you, MJ?"

"All's good, Elle. Really. It looks wonderful, just wonderful," I said. "Tell me how you transformed this place."

We walked between the tables as Elle described the cleanup efforts, the contents of each tray of seedlings, and her plans for future landscape projects.

"Did Harry ever tell you about his intentions to build a

retirement home complete with an attached greenhouse?"
I asked.

"No. Were you planning on moving?"

"That was the plan. He spent years drafting the design.
When it was finished, he filed it away until we were ready. I
guess we never were."

"But your home is perfect just the way it is," Elle said.

"And now the gardens and greenhouse are, too," I added
as we turned and headed back to the house.

Before departing for Maui, I had closed the door to my
office, and it appeared Elle had left it that way. Fingering
Harry's wooden plaque on the center of the door, I slowly
turned the knob and walked inside. The familiar space welcomed me home. Not a thing had been touched. On the
side table sat a stack of books. The top one was inverted as
if the reader had casually plopped it down midread. I looked
at the title and was amazed at all that had transpired since
I had read the first 120 pages of a forgotten plot. The dis-
assembled birthday book, its walnut cover, grosgrain ribbon, and remaining pages, sat in pieces on the desk exactly
where I had left them.

"Your coffee's ready," said Elle.

After we enjoyed beverages and conversation on the
patio, Elle left for work and I reentered the empty house.
Tired but keyed up, I unpacked quickly, placing articles of
clothing in separate laundry piles and throwing the first
load into the washing machine. I checked my calendar.
On Saturday, I would be joining the Write Women at Pat's
book launch.

I lugged the carry-ons into my office and began unpacking writing supplies and books. Once the computer was
powered up and connected to the printer, I inserted the
flash drive and located a file. While the final pages of

Rewriting Marguerite quickly stacked one on top of the other in the printer tray, I headed to the basement, opened the cedar chest, and retrieved photo albums and a red leather journal.

Last to be unpacked were the pages of the birthday book that had traveled almost eight thousand miles to Maui and back. A month earlier, instinctively, I had culled out the pages that represented defining moments; left behind had been the ones that covered years of peaceful existence. Together, they documented an ongoing story. Restoring the snapshots of my life to their rightful order, I stopped at the final page. A photo of the Write Women was attached under the heading, "April 30, 2015—Age 80." Picking up a favorite Sharpie, I carefully printed the caption, "Beginning Anew." Then I secured the pages of my eighty-year-old life with decades-old grosgrain ribbon.

Finally, "Marguerite's Birthday Book," the red journal with Nana's stories, the photo albums of Emma, and a three-ring notebook containing a memoir entitled *Rewriting Marguerite* were given a new home, the center shelf of a bookcase handcrafted with love.

With a lightness I had not enjoyed in over a year, I gathered a fresh notebook and a favorite pen, settled into a chair on the patio, and began to write.

Epilogue

"Who do you want in the photos, MJ?" asks Kai as she attempts to herd people out of the air-conditioned store and onto the lanai.

"Everyone," I say as I hang back to encourage the Write Women to break from their browsing and step out for the picture taking. Every person is wearing a fragrant plumeria lei, thanks to Richard.

Kai lines up Ani, Richard, Mike, Elle, and Georgia on the left and Millie, Claire, Ginny, and Pat on the right. Once all are situated, Ken is gently guided by May and Fern onto the lanai and into the front row.

"No photos yet," yells Kai as she disappears for a moment and returns with my birthday gift, a huge framed poster advertising the day's event:

BOOK RELEASE PARTY & BOOK SIGNING

THE MYSTERY OF ICHIRO'S BOX

BY
MJ BURDICK

April 30, 2016
10 a.m.–2 p.m.
at
Captured
Lahaina, Maui

Elle positions the poster in front of the group, while I present the first inscribed copy of my newly released book to my friend Ken, the inspiration for a mystery involving a Nisei soldier from Maui. Cameras appear.

"Everyone, smile!" says Mo, Georgia's life partner, as she deftly aims one cell phone after another at the gathering. Front and center is a smiling Asian gentleman and an author whose eyes are glancing skyward. I capture the moment in a crystalline memory just as Mo snaps the photos. One of them is destined for "Marguerite's Birthday Book" with the caption "Ohana—Family."

Gratitudes

To a teacher from my past, authors I have never met, and friends and family, I offer my appreciation.

Thank you, Mr. Edwin "Bud" Nakasone. Over five decades ago, in a high school history class in White Bear Lake, Minnesota, you presented to students your eyewitness account of the bombing of Pearl Harbor. You left a lasting impression when you described in dramatic fashion how December 7, 1941, changed the world, especially for Japanese Americans. More recently, your book, *The Nisei Soldier: Historical Essays on World War II and the Korean War,* provided valuable background information, which helped to inspire my storyline for the Sato family. Thank you for contributing to my lifetime of education.

Thank you, Julia Cameron, for your book *The Artist's Way: A Spiritual Path to Higher Creativity.* In it, you introduced me to the practice of writing morning pages, a creative tool I shared with my main character, Marguerite, to help her tap her right brain and search for self-understanding. Thank you, Anne Lamott, for your book *Bird by Bird: Some Instructions on Writing and Life*, which offers helpful and entertaining encouragement to all who enjoy writing. I enjoyed boosting Marguerite's creativity and self-assurance with your help.

Similar to Marguerite's supportive writers group, I am fortunate to have an equally supportive book group. I appreciate all of you.

Mary Swanson, thank you for your compassionate support of my story. Your helpful feedback strengthened the book.

Colleen and David Welty, your long-distance support from Maui is so appreciated. David, I am inspired by your design of the beautiful plumeria with an "opening for possibilities," the logo for Ohana Publications. Mahalo.

I could not have completed my novel without the help of two talented and supportive women. Thank you, Judy Gilats, for turning a story printed on paper into a creatively designed book. Shannon Pennefeather, thank you for proofreading with skillful diligence. I enjoyed working with both of you.

I offer a special shout-out to daughter Angie Herron, who, with loving commitment, read the manuscript during numerous stages, offered valuable suggestions, and painstakingly edited.

Similar to Marguerite, I am strengthened by the memories and lessons of love, strength, joy, and resiliency from family, including my parents and grandparents. *Okage sama de*. I feel blessed when three generations of family gather and continue to reinforce these lessons. Thank you, Angie, Becky, Clay, Krista, Nicole, and Steve. Charlie, Makena, Mia, and Zoe, you bring me joy. Tom, I couldn't have written this book without you.

Finally, Minnesota and Maui, together you feed my soul. Yah sure, you betcha! Aloha!

Discussion Questions for Book Groups

1. Although Marguerite did not become a published author until retirement, journaling was a lifelong practice. How was her love of storytelling rooted and nurtured? How did she use writing as a vehicle for self-understanding? What practices have you cultivated as opportunities for self-awareness?

2. Marguerite narrated her story. How did her narrative style illustrate a subtle shift from a logical/analytical approach to a more creative one? How was she able to tap her creative side? Do you feel you are dominantly right brained or left brained? How do you achieve balance?

3. During her memoir writing, Marguerite reflected on the defining moments of a long, full life. How did her life experiences shape her development and outlook? Which of Marguerite's defining moments, if any, resonated with you and how? What have been the critical defining moments of your life, and how have these times influenced you?

4. Marguerite was well loved by her parents and grandparents. Before their deaths, how did Mama, Papa, and Grampa impact Marguerite's understanding of the world? Describe Nana's character and her influence on Marguerite. Which character in the book did you find most relatable and why?

5. Shortly after meeting Harry, Marguerite developed an immediate, strong attraction to him. Which of his characteristics drew her to him and why? How did their personalities differ? Would you describe them as a good match? What characteristics do you seek in a good match?

6. The deaths of Raymond, Grampa, Mama, Papa, Nana, Emma, and Harry figured significantly into Marguerite's life. Compounded grief tested her resilience. How did each loss impact Marguerite? How did she cope with the unexpected tragedy of losing a child? Have loss and grief tested your resilience? If so, how?

7. The Write Women, although physically separated from Marguerite for most of the story, still played valuable roles in Marguerite's life. How would you describe their relationships? Do you have similar friendships? Explain.

8. Although Marguerite did not consider herself religious, through her narrative she provided glimpses into her spirituality. What life events influenced her religious upbringing and her spiritual development? Did you find her uniqueness understandable? Relatable?

9. The Sato family expanded Marguerite's understanding of racism and its lingering effects. What people/events have expanded your understanding of racism? How has racism influenced your life?

10. Marguerite described her unspoken pain as a crusted-over scab that never fully healed at the source. What was the origin of the wound and did you empathize with her initial treatment of it? What was the takeaway from her experience? Discuss the impact of concealed emotions.